KING PENGU

THE GAME

A. S. Byatt was born in 1936 and educated at York and Newnham College, Cambridge, of which she is now an Associate. She has taught at the Central School of Art and Design and since 1972 has been a full-time lecturer in English and American literature at University College, London. She is a regular broadcaster on the B.B.C., and has contributed to *The Times*, *Encounter* and the *New Statesman* as well as many other newspapers and weeklies. She has published two other novels, *Shadow of a Sun* and *The Virgin in the Garden* (Penguin, 1981). She has also written a critical study of Iris Murdoch, *Degrees of Freedom*, a book on Wordsworth and Coleridge, and articles on, amongst others, Tennyson and Wallace Stevens. She has also edited George Eliot's *The Mill on the Floss* for the Penguin English Library.

A. S. BYATT

THE GAME

A KING PENGUIN
PUBLISHED BY PENGUIN BOOKS

Penguin Books Ltd, Harmondsworth, Middlesex, England
Penguin Books, 40 West 23rd Street, New York, New York 10010, U.S.A.
Penguin Books Australia Ltd, Ringwood, Victoria, Australia
Penguin Books Canada Ltd, 2801 John Street, Markham, Ontario, Canada L3R 1B4
Penguin Books (N.Z.) Ltd, 182–190 Wairau Road, Auckland 10, New Zealand

First published by Chatto & Windus 1967
Published in Penguin Books 1983

Filmset, printed and bound in Great Britain by
Hazell Watson & Viney Limited,
Member of the BPCC Group,
Aylesbury, Bucks
Set in VIP Bembo

for John Beer

We wove a web in childhood
A web of sunny air;
We dug a spring in infancy
Of water pure and fair;

We sowed in youth a mustard-seed,
We cut an almond rod;
We are now grown up to riper age –
Are they withered in the sod?

Faded! the web is still of air,
But how its folds are spread,
And from its tints of crimson clear
How deep a glow is shed . . .

The mustard-seed in distant land
Bends down a mighty tree,
The dry unbudding almond-wand
Has touched eternity.

– from *Retrospection*
by Charlotte Brontë (1835)

The principle of the imagination resembles the emblem of the serpent, by which the ancients typified wisdom and the universe, with undulating folds, for ever varying and for ever flowing into itself – circular, and without beginning or end.

S. T. Coleridge

CHAPTER ONE

'Come again *soon,*' Julia said, arresting them again at the top of the stairs, smiling and pleading. 'I mean it, I really mean it. You must come again.' They laughed, drawn together by their departure, their faces pale and round above coat-collars already turned up against the cold. *'Promise,'* said Julia, and they promised, and began to descend the turning staircase. Julia hung over the banister watching their dark heads protectively down three flights, saddened by the receding clatter of their feet. At the bottom they stopped and turned their moon-faces up to her. 'Thank you,' they called, and Julia cried, 'We loved having you.'

She stood a moment twisting her rings on her fingers. She had several rings, all rather boldly designed and clean-cut, silver and bronze, hoops and bosses. Her hands seemed slightly heavy with them. She went back, then, into the flat.

In the attic living-room everything was warm. The wood fire was still alive in the hearth, and the room was hazy with soft smoke. The floor was polished bare boards, spread with long-furred rugs, and there were several low stools on which Julia would sit, her knees drawn up to her chin, close to the fire. There were earthy-brown coffee mugs squat on a low table, two stainless-steel bowls of fruit, a scarlet glass tray with liqueur glasses. Julia sniffed smoke and wine and was aware of worry. Somewhere, plates clashed.

She went through the living-room into the kitchen, where, at a pale blue and grey sink, under a fluorescent light, her husband in shirtsleeves was piling plates shining with water, one after the other, on to a stainless-steel draining-board.

'We don't have to wash up just yet?'

'It doesn't take a minute. I feel better when things are in place.' He cast her a placatory glance. 'You don't have to help.' Julia picked up a tea-towel.

'Thor,' she said, 'it went well, didn't it? They liked it, didn't they? I mean, they were exactly the people to try out that honey sauce on?' She dried some plates. 'They liked me, didn't they? You can tell if people like you. I liked them enormously. The sort of people who can become real *friends* – '

'Yes,' said Thor. He took a deep-blue linen cloth and began to polish carving knives, his cropped blond head very pale under the light. After a moment he offered, 'I think he will ask you to appear on his programme.'

Julia studied her hands. 'I didn't ask him for that.'

'I know. He doesn't think you did. He liked you. He said you were very much alive.'

'Did he?' Julia strode back into the living-room. 'Did he really, Thor? I thought *he* was alive, didn't you? I thought that the moment I met him. He's got such energy. He cares so much about everything. That's rare. And he's so intelligent. Both of them are so intelligent – '

She sat down on a leather stool by the fire.

'I wonder if I talked too much. I always do, I get carried away, I know you think . . . He's a man you could tell anything to. Almost anything. I'm sure he thought I talked too much.'

'Why should he? He was curious.' He thought a moment. 'There are so many people you can tell anything to, Julia.'

Julia was not sure where, in this sentence, the emphasis was; one of the traces of her husband's Norwegian birth was the uniform flatness of his sentences. Thus she did not know whether she was rebuked or not. This was the sort of minor moral indecision he often provoked in her.

'I should hate him to think I was *effusive*.'

'I do not think he thought that.'

'Honestly?'

'Honestly.'

There was a silence. Julia said, 'I wish I didn't always feel so overwhelmed.'

Thor put a large hand across her shoulder, and rubbed her white crêpe dress against her skin.

'Julia – be a little peaceful, sometimes. Don't mind things so much. It isn't good.'

Julia shrugged quickly and then relaxed. 'One *ought* to mind. One ought to care. I love it, meeting people, really – '

'That's not what I mean. You will not simply take what is given. What comes.'

'But that's just what I *do*. That's what I thought you were complaining about. I take and take and take. *Everything's* given. More than I can manage.'

'I do not know what you mean by everything is given,' said Thor, his northern foreignness slightly more pronounced. 'In the nature of things, it cannot be. I agree you will behave as though everything was . . . available. It tires you. Besides you know yourself, you insure against a poverty, Julia.'

'Don't,' said Julia. 'Don't tell me. You know so much, but you don't have to *tell* me.'

He stiffened into silence. Julia leaned her face against his legs. 'You know me, you know me so well. I love you. But don't frighten me. Don't take me up too much.'

'You are easy to frighten,' he said, in the same easy expressionless voice. He knelt down beside her; Julia said quickly, 'And anyway I'm not fussing, it was a good dinner-party, it was a success.'

'It was a good party, yes. And they liked you. I'm glad they liked you.' She leaned towards him, and their mouths met, lightly.

'Thor – ' said Julia.

'I have a lot of work to do,' he said, 'before tomorrow. I don't know why charity – why Christianity – should go with such a lack of sense of hard facts. They have faith, because they have promised grain, it will be forthcoming. They have faith that difficulties with transport and cash can be got round. Well some can, but only with my work. Also, they transfer to me the faith they would do better to reserve for God and then not take into account. I spend my time accomplishing near-miracles: it is different. And today three letters saying we are inefficient and extravagant with the half-crowns they so charitably put into the tin cans – '

Thor was paid administrator of a largish charitable organization run by the Quakers in conjunction with one or two other religious bodies. Often, after parties, he worked into the small hours, making Julia feel guilty, since their visitors were mostly her own professional acquaintances. He seemed indefatigable; but during dinner she had watched his abstracted face once or twice – he did not drink – had thought he was saving himself, and had been exhausted by the tension between keeping the conversation lively, and wondering whether to let it die and the visitors depart, so that he could work. She kissed him. 'Well, mostly, their faith's justified. Their faith in you, that is. You don't promise what you can't perform.'

'No,' he said, standing up. In the doorway he asked casually, 'Will you accept his offer?'

'He hasn't made it. And I haven't thought.'

Thor smiled and closed himself out.

Left alone, slightly let down, Julia walked across the room and back, restlessly. She thought of Ivan, who had just left, and might want her on his television programme. She liked the idea of being promoted from being a woman writer to being – in some sense – an expert on the art of the novel. In her mind her own voice echoed, lively, stimulating. She would meet new people. Hopefully, ready to see it as a new world to be entered, she turned on the television.

The screen flickered. Julia had a momentary, jumping vision of a huge sheet of water in a haze of heat, and then, superimposed on this, the rounded, superlatively normal face of a girl whose cultured voice above her cultured pearls quavered, came into being, and continued. '. . . This is the first in a series of late-night programmes, largely with a scientific emphasis, although there will be plenty of glimpses of the exotic and the dangerous. There is something for everyone: scientists, geographers, animal lovers, arm-chair explorers . . .'

Julia was annoyed; she intended to respect the television and here was this girl addressing her millions of audience with a prepared, gentle condescension – as though they were all very slightly mentally deficient. Also, Julia didn't like travel programmes. She was urban to the depths of her country-bred soul, and couldn't imagine living, or communicating anything to anyone, anywhere outside London. Travellers with travellers' tales were always so jolly, their deserts and jungles so parochial, almost as though they had been built, or at least touched up, in the studio. A lorry-load of sand, a few plastic fronds, a dozen or so Negro extras . . . The young woman tossed her smooth blonde head, was seen deliberately to restrain herself from touching her pearls, announced brightly that there would be a few words from the Reverend William Borran after this programme, and was suddenly swallowed into the jungle. Trees, and then water. Tunnels of water, wastes of water, an aerial view of the great, formless river, broken into innumerable little tributaries, bushy islands, dense clumps of vegetation, yielding again to water which slapped this way and that, sucked in and out of creeks, spread, swelled.

'The Amazon basin,' said the commentator. 'It was first explored in 1500 by Vincent Yañez Pinzon, who referred to it as the Marañon – a name now generally reserved for the Upper Amazon, although geographers differ as to where the Marañon ends and the Amazon begins, or whether both names apply, in fact, to the same river. The Brazilian historian Costancio maintains that *Marañon* is derived from the Spanish word *maraña* – a tangle, a snarl . . .'

The voice was not orotund; there was a hesitance, a kind of suppressed urgency about it, as though these simple facts, maybe, would be misunderstood, or not believed.

'In the rainy season the average depth is a hundred and twenty feet. But it may rise, suddenly, fifty-six feet, and transform the landscape. Nothing is fixed: maps are approximations. What we learn to recognize, or begin to study, one week, may not be there the next. The camera can only give a bare idea of the power, here, of physical flux – weather, as well as growth and decay . . .'

The smooth rapidity of the camera-work was good, Julia thought, as the eye left the water and stared up and out through row after row of huge trees, straining smoothly towards the sky. Only, as the camera made plain, they were not rows, there was no pattern, they were a mass. Julia's eye was bewildered by a series of changes in focus – close-ups of knots of creepers or areas of powdery bark, vistas into the depths of eternally extended, haphazardly cluttered cathedrals, between whose pillars the sun occasionally burst in long, white, hissing stars which rested on the leaves – a phenomenon the camera can hold, as the eye can not. It was alien and enveloping, in no way pretty.

'A great effort of slow growth. Aldous Huxley said once that if Wordsworth had been familiar with tropical forests he would have found Nature less benign and illuminating. There is something here, he said, which is "foreign, appalling, and utterly inimical to intruding life". A German traveller, Burmeister, was distressed by the vegetation here because, he said, "it revealed a spirit of restless selfishness, eager emulation, and craftiness". Well, we take, from what we see, what we bring to it. "In our life alone does Nature live," as Coleridge said. I would hope to approach these forests more neutrally. We are to observe unchecked, unchallenged growth, and the concomitant destruction. I believe we can learn from this; in civilized countries we have suppressed, or rigidly limited, our consciousness of these processes. But they are part of us, however decently we may tuck away, behind curtains, birth and death. We forget what we are . . .'

The voice faded on a possibly querulous note as the camera began suddenly to run over the ground, picking out patterns, breaking them.

'The jungle floor. Dead leaves, reddish, yellowish, pinkish, darkish brown. Decaying, in innumerable layers, back into the soil. Springy to walk on, often treacherous. Patterns picked up by the camera.'

Long lines of dead leaves sagged together, falling into formlessness. Julia could almost smell decaying earth mould. The picture steadied; she was watching a path of ground, raised circles of overlapping leaves, lighter lines of fungus of pale grey mould.

'No shape. Lumps, bumps . . .'

In the centre, on top of the slight mound, something moved and raised itself. The camera caught the momentary black brightness of an eye; triangular, flattened, smooth yet knobby, a shape appeared, a snake's head, staring. A tongue flickered in and out.

'Not a camera pattern, but a life adapted to the jungle floor. This is the bushmaster. *Lachesis muta*. Very venomous. They can grow to twelve feet – this specimen is not so long. The pattern on these coils is in fact a regular pattern designed to melt into the irregular pattern of the leaves, solid dark rhombs on a paler ground, with tubercular ridges, a rough surface. A beautiful creature.'

Julia, who hated snakes, had been trying to neutralize the slight shock this cleverly manoeuvred apparition had given her by telling herself, as she did during unbearable films, those about executions and torture, that the camera-work, the selection, was excellent. Now she was struck, not for the first time, by the phrase. Whatever one ought to think, she told herself, it was not true, snakes were not beautiful creatures; they were mutilated and ugly; their faces were evil. As a man could be ugly and one could so define him and no one would dispute it, so could a beast. We can recognize human beauty, she thought, for reasons. Our traditional horror of the serpent has something behind it. Snakes are dangerous and ugly, we are *meant* to be repelled by them. This thought, of course, led back to the idea that an ugly man must be bad or dangerous, and this, given qualifications for *beauxlaids*, for those whose beautiful thoughts moulded and transfigured their horrid features, Julia was prepared to believe. Things were so much more often than was likely what they seemed. One should not be over-subtle, and to call snakes beautiful was a perversion. Simon – Simon had done that. Simon had –

Julia reached for the *Radio Times*, turned her head back towards the television, and saw him.

He stood a little stiffly beside his snake, holding it down now at the base of the skull with an iron implement that looked as though it had been fetched from some mediaeval torture chamber. He had a long, mournful face, with concave planes spattered with the beginnings of a black beard. His hair was long and sprang away from his head in wiry curls. His expression was both pompous and deprecating, as well as in some way secretive; he had changed, he had changed, but Julia remembered that look. He was long and spindling, and looked at home in bush clothes, peering out from under a kind of floppy sun-hat. Julia remembered that he would fling his arms around himself from time to time as though he had extra joints. His voice was unrecognizable, until he was visible; it had acquired a new clarity and authority, a dry, showmanship. With her he had always muttered huskily, directing his remarks away from her.

The man manoeuvred the snake so that its head was turned with the open mouth exposed to the camera. Against the dark leaves the mouth-tissues were white, bright, clean.

'This whiteness of the mouth is the reason for the name of the cotton-head snake,' he informed them; he went on to expatiate, soberly, technically, on the fangs, the venom, the ducts, the hooking and striking of the creature.

'This snake is a rapid mover; it does not hesitate, or make frenzied manoeuvres for position, as the rattlesnakes do. It strikes on sight . . .'

He paused, looked puzzled. 'It's a much less horrible death than many. I've never understood why people find it so peculiarly distasteful. Compared, for instance, to pig-sticking. Or, for that matter, to being hanged. People get very emotional about snakes. It's a kind of emotion I think we can't afford – in any area of life – to feel. Not many of us feel that motor-cars are evil. But they are equally lethal. And occasionally possessed by murderous rage. I don't know whether people think snakes are evil because they are venomous, or fear the venom – disproportion-ately – because they think the snake is evil. I hope – after a time – to make snakes seem familiar. Familiar. One ought to live neutrally. To see these as a form of life, simply. One *form* of *life*, yes.' He put a weight on the words, almost desperate with unexploded implications; this, too, was a trick Julia remembered; but the public, impersonal intimacy of the television exaggerated it, 'I am a professional herpetologist so we shall be greatly – not exclusively – concerned with snakes.'

The camera left him to settle, suddenly and irrelevantly, on a flock ot white water-birds wading and calling. Then it was over; the Reverend

William Borran smiled fluently, and began to speak of how we have followed too much the devices and desires of our own hearts. Julia stood up and switched him off. Her hands were sweating. The room seemed damp and hot, like a greenhouse. It seemed logical, in retrospect, that he should have come to this; ironing out the knowledge of good and evil in a scientific way, in the jungle. She had never understood what drove him. She had never come to terms with him. She sat for some time, her head in her hands, knotting her red hair with her fingers, looking at the blank screen.

CHAPTER TWO

'We shall do better,' Cassandra wrote, 'to think of chastity as purity, a scrupulous purity and to associate it with innocence, if we are to apprehend at all the moral force either of Lancelot's sin or of Galahad's virtue in the *Morte d'Arthur.* Chastity as the supreme virtue is not an automatically acceptable idea. Most of us would preserve our brother's life before a maiden's maidenhead, or decide, if faced with the alternative of the immediate suicide of not only one but twelve ladies that the preservation of our own virtue in these circumstances is perhaps a little selfish and a little prudish. We shall do better if we think of "that which the maiden would never have again" as an original innocence – and extend the meaning of "intact" to the whole spirit, uninvaded and complete. If we remember that to a true Christian death is not dreadful, we shall face Lionel's death with greater equanimity, even before we discover that it is an illusion of the fiend.'

She laid down her pen and considered these things. About chastity it was difficult to think clearly, if, as she did, one enjoyed it in an occupational and accidental way. It did not appear to her to be either purity or innocence; largely ignorance, perhaps; occasionally the source of a hot, devouring curiosity she had felt as a child and hoped to grow out of. As for death, that seemed increasingly dreadful, and her Christianity made sadly little difference to her imaginings. She looked surreptitiously at her watch. It was ten, not time yet. She had completed her prescribed hours on the Malory edition; she marked these off, in red, in her desk diary, and began a letter.

'Dear Father Rowell, I agree entirely with you about the arrangements for R. S. Thomas's reading. Naturally the Ladies will come. It should also be publicized as far as possible amongst all undergraduates; this must be one of the rare occasions when Church and secular world have a genuine and useful common area of interest. I agree with you also that the Welsh nationalism is an irritant. But clearly the poet is in need of it, if not the poems, many of which I would not be without.'

She stopped again for some time, thinking that she had now made enough conversation but did not know how to open the other topic. She looked at her watch again. She wrote: 'It was kind of you, Father, to write as you did of my nightmare and fears. As you will have guessed, I have regretted intermittently what I told you of this. It was a moment of weakness, but not one for which I can ultimately be sorry since you can write to me with such untroubled understanding.'

She paused again, to reflect that this was not quite true. Father Rowell had expressed only a limited understanding, and what he had said was not entirely untroubled. She should have said nothing: she had lost dignity, exposed herself, forfeited, perhaps, some of his respect. Still, what was done was done. 'I have prayed as you directed,' she continued, 'and I may truly say things are better. We are all afraid of being overwhelmed in one way or another; but I have lived with these fears for many years now and I meet them, to a certain extent, with the ease of familiarity.'

Also not true. Or at least, what familiarity brought was not necessarily ease. She wrote a few carefully relaxed sentences of parish gossip and signed her letter. Then she took up an essay on *Troilus and Criseyde*, written in obvious haste on three sides of paper torn from an exercise book, and clearly largely cribbed from C. S. Lewis.

'If this essay were cleaner,' she wrote, 'it might be possible to read it with closer attention. You seem unaware that the statement of Criseyde's feelings you quote from Lewis, without acknowledgement, on your second page, directly contradicts what you say *in propria persona* on your third. Your work has been consistently of this poor quality. I shall find it almost impossible to report well of it to your Scholarship authorities at the end of the term.'

She looked at this for some moments. She remembered the author of the essay very well; a large, hairy-legged, lumpish girl, the first from her obscure Welsh grammar school to be admitted to the College, and then against Cassandra's advice. She sat almost silent through tutorials, her huge white face staring with carefully black-rimmed eyes out of a Lake-dweller's hut of cross-woven colourless hair, over the shapeless bulk of a dirty white mohair sweater. When Cassandra spoke to her she twisted fat white hands in agitation and pulled at hang-nails. Another don had told Cassandra that she was having an unhappy love affair; last year's work had been markedly better. It happened to all of them, Cassandra thought with distaste, even those apparently *hors de concours* through ugliness. It seemed to reduce them all to the same state of incompetent, inattentive weariness. It was not as though cuddling – or being deprived of cuddling – on a lodging-house sofa made them any more sensitive to the subtleties of Chaucer's portrayal of the protracted decay of affection. It simply made them weary. Whereas her own generation, deprived of such inept experience, had had time to become aware of what was possible, of the subtleties of passion, through the imagination.

And here, she thought, looking again at her watch, I am. Here I am. Imagination and all, God knows. Her mouth was dry; there were fifteen minutes to go. She wrote on the bottom of the essay, 'You had better come and see me about this.' She knew that this, which was in fact a moral concession to the shapeless Miss Wood's problems, would be taken as persecution on her part. She was vaguely aware, too, that she would not be able to resist the temptation to be sarcastic. And that Miss Wood would assume that she did not, herself, 'know'. Well, she did not. But neither did Miss Wood, and money, and Cassandra's time, and Oxford were all being spent on Miss Wood's failure to acquire any relevant knowledge.

She stood up, and went to the window, still tense with fear. She pulled back the curtain and saw, partially, since it was late, Oxford, in winter, at night. The river ran under her window; a few bare trees caught the light from a street lamp; in a patch of light an odd spire stood out, haphazardly suggesting all the rest of the post-card view. Twenty years ago, in the middle of war-time austerity, she had come there – expecting God knew what mediaeval grace of life and significance.

She saw herself, for a moment, coldly from outside – a feeling she disliked, and had invented little rituals to avoid. She dropped the curtain again, now, closing herself in, and looked over her room and her work. She was surrounded by solid things: leather-bound books, a collection of early globes and maps of the heavens, ivory carvings, the crucifix over the desk, some of them rare, acquired, not inherited, and acquired slowly. Velvet curtains, heavy dark furniture, two or three footstools and an immensely high-winged crimson velvet chair – the room had an inhabited thickness. Cassandra looked from object to object and was relieved to see nothing but what was solidly there.

She was thirty-eight and saw herself alternately as much older and much younger; during the nightmares she was younger, but in public she assumed the curt bark and the dogmatism of the old and fixed in their ways; she affected to have been young somewhere at the turn of the century, which was a partial truth since she had had an isolated and traditional country upbringing. Like most mediaevalists she had chosen her subject out of an essentially Romantic preoccupation with the satisfactory remote violence of both the religious and the secular literature of the Middle Ages. She had come to Oxford hungry for the absolutely worked drama of Lancelot and Guenevere, Tristan and Iseult; she had slowly transmuted this into a passion for the symbolic possibilities of the Grail Legend. She combined the mediaevalist's love of the strange with the mediaevalist's passion for precision. The complexities of existence were the interrelations of roots and roses, strange beasts and fruits, in a walled garden, outside which a sea rose in formally dangerous peaks. She had elaborated, and believed, a network of symbols which made the outer world into a dazzling but comprehensible constellation of physical facts whose spiritual interrelations could be grasped and woven by the untiring intellect; suns, moons, stars, roses, cups, lances, lions and serpents, all had their place and also their meaning. This network was overlaid by another network interweaving other roots, footnotes, cross-references, bibliographical data, palaeographical quirks. Somewhere, under the network, the truth shone; Cassandra had come, like many others, looking for final Authority, logically to see it in the Church. This was a symbol, and also real; it was a guarantee. A passion for symbols is in some cases an automatic precursor of a passion for theology. Cassandra had embraced both.

But now and then, in certain moods, Cassandra remembered the root of this passion in the wash of romantic feeling with which she had first seen Oxford, having read indiscriminately in Walter Scott, Tennyson, Morris and Malory, looking for a life as brightly-coloured as books. She had not had then an interest in the conventions of the courtly love of the *Roman de la Rose*; she had cared about the feelings of Lancelot and Guenevere, disturbed in their blood-stained sheets. She had come, not from Ritual to Romance, but in the other direction, from romance to ritual. Her feeling for completeness had betrayed her to a way of life she had not quite chosen; the academic life had become almost accidentally a branch of the contemplative life. She had cultivated her walled-garden skills at the expense of any others she might have had. We become what we are, she told herself, by a series of involuntary half-choices; if this was not what she had meant, she did not know what else she could have done.

She looked at her watch again. She would, at least, go and see. The room might well be empty.

She went out along two corridors, down a flight of stairs into an entrance hall, almost silently, and then along another corridor. She wore, at night, sensibly, she considered, in draughty corridors, a long black woollen evening skirt over which she wore a long-sleeved black jersey with a cowl neck. She affected cuffed and pointed black velvet slippers. These clothes gave her a certain monastic, anachronistic grace; she was thin, and carried herself well although a little rigidly. She was, however, hung about with chains, medallions, crosses, knotting and clinking from neck to waist; she had three rings, all jewelled, the largest a large garnet, clustered round with seed pearls. Her head, covered with a crop of rust-coloured dry curls, she carried stiffly erect. From behind, she looked sexless; from the front formidable, with huge nose and mouth and eyes too deep-set under almost colourless sandy lashes. Her skin was very white and spattered and blotched with freckles. These seemed unexpected, as though freckles should have been outgrown with childhood, they blurred and detracted from the general impression of well-ordered ugliness.

She had decided not to go into the S.C.R. It was there, last week, that she had accidently seen the first programme, but she could not imagine many other dons wanting to watch a travel programme about snakes, and was in any case peculiarly secretive about her own interests. The J.C.R., she had discovered, was usually empty at this time of night, since these girls were not interested in communal living and spent their evenings outside the college until the last possible moment. They showed, too, a commendable lack of interest in the television.

She slipped in, closed the door, and stood with her back against it, breathing rapidly. The room was dark and the television was, in fact, switched on; Cassandra found that she was the back row of an audience – three girls curled on a sofa immediately in front of her, two more squatting at their feet. The room was silent, except for a soft rustle which came from the set itself. Cassandra thought of retreat; but no one looked at her, and then he spoke.

'It is the apparent effortlessness of this movement that makes us feel it is mysterious. And we are naturally afraid of what we do not understand.'

Cassandra found herself watching the progress of a long and apparently heavy snake across a sandy surface. The movement, even in so heavy a body, did seem to be unconnected with any effort; like a creature in a dream landscape it poured forward, stopped suddenly as though it were frozen, head raised, tongue flickering, and then flowed on again, stretched and easy. The ground underneath it seemed still and solid – behind it was a ribbon-like track.

'They are worshipped in association with running water and with lightning. As a symbol – for the life, the life that drives us. Although in our culture, traditionally, we see them as the opposite.'

The snake had come to the edge of a dark pool of water: it bowed its head, swaying the blunted, triangular snout slightly, slid under the surface, was lost, and then the camera held for a moment the raised head and the rippling trail of its body in the water as it swam out and away.

'The people here tell me that during the night the anaconda changes into a dark boat with white sails, and skims over the swamp. They speak of it also as though it were winged. There's an element of fear in what they say – I don't know whether the wings and sails turn the creature into a ship of death, or a more ambiguous symbol of some kind of release from the earth. They believe also, erroneously, that the boas are poisonous.'

There was the recognizable, inconclusive pause for thought; then a tentative 'I suppose as a religious symbol it may well be more paradoxically used than any other – natural phenomenon.' Then, more surely, 'We know, in fact, very little about how snakes move. They have three basic types of progress – lateral, undulatory motion, rectilinear locomotion – which you have just seen – and "sidewinding", usually observed in desert snakes. They are able to travel much faster over rough surfaces than smooth. This snake was in no hurry. If it were, it would progress in a sideways, curving movement, to take advantage of the surface. Contrary to earlier belief, movement is produced, not by the ribs, but by successive contractions of groups of muscles . . .'

A diagram of the muscular contractions of the anaconda was followed somewhat abruptly by the apparition of Simon, who stared anxiously out from under the shade of some canvas hut or shelter where he sat cross-legged like the Buddha, surrounded by his snake-trapping instruments. He expatiated, with nervous fluency, on the muscular structure of the snake, bending with his hands first a closely-knotted metal chain and then a dead snake, twisting them double, turning them, to demonstrate the superior flexibility of the snake. Cassandra watched his hands, hairy, with huge knuckles, and his face, pulled into an intent pout. Her knees shook slightly. He produced a small boa from a canvas bag, looped it about his wrist, and went on to explain how the muscles were used in constriction.

'An economic use of power in a creature which has no exceptional mobility. Most stories of rapid pursuit by snakes are fantasies. There are other fallacies – snakes do not deliberately break bones, nor do they, on the whole, "reshape" their prey – although I have seen snakes tease out a chicken or a monkey into a more easily apprehensible form. Death is due, not as might be imagined, to suffocation, but to constriction of the heart. Constriction of the heart. The constrictors seem to know exactly when death takes place, and will not release any victim before it is dead. Mere unconsciousness does not impress a snake . . .'

Simon's face took on a puzzled, faintly anxious expression which was familiar to Cassandra, who clasped her hands suddenly and defensively in front of her.

'Constriction, like poison when we study it, loses its aura of peculiar terror,' he said. 'Coming close to anything – mortality amongst mortals – changes our attitude to it, changes it, in our minds. Whether we are butchers or doctors or simply scientific observers. Familiarity doesn't make things less mysterious – it does make them less vague. You might say, we learn a *real* fear, instead of a mystical fear. Out here, you might say, one has a chance to begin again – this part of the world has been less documented, either by naturalists, geographers or social scientists, than any other. It's a real Garden of Eden, and we have to find our own bearings – map out for ourselves, not good and evil, but what life and death are really like, since we are not immortal. And what is *really* to be feared. Here, that is not the constrictors. Fire and flood. Certain insects. Bad water. Bathing with a cut finger. Even bad teeth. You have to learn to organize your own survival at first hand. You have to be very close to things that at home you can afford to forget. But, in compensation, they do appear *real*.'

He smiled, a slow, diffident smile, which Cassandra in moods of irritation had been used to call smug. He always believed, she thought now, that he had discovered everything himself, at first hand: the banal, the platitudinous, the startling truth, indiscriminately mixed. This occupation was a logical enough end-product.

'And the scientist with a camera,' he said urgently, 'can, as it were, rediscover innocence. The innocent eye, not ignorant, but trained, detached, seeing everything for itself, for what it is, with no apprehensions and very fluid preconceptions. Once one has one's own feelings in hand – once one's fears are real fears and one's needs are real needs – everything else can be seen with that pure curiosity which is one of the highest human qualities, and I would call it innocence. An achieved, an informed innocence.

'Consider the butterflies,' he said. Cassandra's mouth twisted slightly. The screen was alive with trembling wings, with that irregular vibrating beat of filmed leaves and insects, that seems never apparent when one considers an isolated leaf or insect alone in the open air; it is intense only in the still eye of the camera. The butterflies were settled in dozens on something which was revealed, by the human boot that entered the picture from above and scattered the insects in a beautifully filmed flurry of translucent wings, to be the darkened and raw body of some kind of small pig.

'The colours are delicate and bright,' said Simon. 'Aerial. A hard blue, a brimstone – and many are transparent with a hint of milkiness, or palest blue, or faint red. They live on blood. I have seen them as big as pigeons.'

There was a momentary huge close-up of the trembling head and planted proboscis of the insect, straddling the flesh with its wire-like legs.

'We achieve, with magnification, a new dimension of strangeness. We enter new worlds. Our own becomes less stable. Imagine seeing this butterfly with no preconceptions about its nature. Or imagine knowing about the way it feeds, about the structure of its wing-tissue, in microscopic detail. Our picture of reality is never fixed but can always be elaborated and made more accurate. And this changes us. The weight of the butterfly makes an iron bridge bend – in that it redistributes, ever so slightly, some molecules. Every new piece of knowledge – in the same way – enlarges our world.'

His face appeared, lugubrious, apparently awed by what he had just said; he was, he had always been, Cassandra thought, for a scientist, unduly given to the vague and loaded generalization. She cleared her throat; Simon disappeared again; one of the girls stood up and turned off the set. Another came up to where Cassandra was standing and turned on the light; all the girls blinked. Cassandra looked from face to face, detected, she thought, curiosity, saw one of her better pupils, a terrified, bright, incipient don with protruding rabbit's teeth and gave her an invented message about R. S. Thomas. Another girl, curled up plump and lazy on the corner of the sofa, said:

'What do you think of him, Miss Corbett?'

'Him?'

'Simon Moffitt. This naturalist.'

'I thought it interesting.'

'He's so urgent about it,' said the toothy girl.

'Desperately attractive in a helpless sort of way,' said the plump one. 'I wonder what makes him go out there.'

'Fear,' said Cassandra. 'Curiosity. An unexpected exhibitionism.'

'Unexpected?'

'I knew him once. I should have called it unexpected.'

'You knew him? Was he like this?'

'He kept snakes. In jars and tanks. An *idée fixe*, clearly. No, I shouldn't have said he is much like what he was. Public appearance changes people, I suppose.'

'Was he . . .?'

'Good night,' said Cassandra. She closed the door behind her, trembling; decidedly the S.C.R. might have been better. She felt like a secret drinker whose cache of bottles in the folds of the bedcover was in danger of discovery.

Back in her room, she went round touching the things. She rearranged a group of ivory chessmen on a shelf, laid silk threads of various colours neatly in the pages of the Malory, put all her pens and pencils in a row at the top of the blotter, their bases aligned with precision. She turned on the fire and washed her hands in the bedroom basin. Then she sat down at the desk, unlocked a drawer, brought out a polished box and unlocked that, in turn, with a key that hung on a chain from her person.

The box contained the current volume of the journal she had kept since childhood; she opened this now, selected a pen, and began to write. What she wrote was extensive and apparently unselective; she described, in accurate detail, every event of her day, meals, work, the contraction of the snake's muscles as it moved across the sand. She gave more space to the peculiarly bulbous hairy legs of Miss Wood than to the kind note from Father Rowell. She was occasionally distressed by the extent to which the events and solid objects around her were only remarkable in so far as she 'collected' them for the journal. In moments of solitude she was increasingly obsessed by a sense that her life was weightless and meaningless; she told herself sometimes that she had made of the journal a moral compulsion to treat her life and its details as though they were real. But this was not what it felt like, however the journal gave solidity to round, hot girls in pink dressing-gowns and even noted, carefully, their cracked and dirty toe-nails.

It seemed, lately, that the journal was becoming an increasingly necessary means of distinguishing between what was real and what was imagined. Once she had used it for the opposite purpose, recording moorland rapes and battles alongside vicarage tea-parties with indifferent skill as though the one ran into the other as she had imagined Oxford ran into the past. Daily events had been landmarks, tips of icebergs useful for locating events in the inner drama. Empty rooms had been – were – peopled. Helen Waddell had once seen Peter Abelard peering in through a hospital window. Charlotte Brontë had seen the Duke of Zamorna leaning against a school mantel-shelf and had felt exhilarated and faint. They had played with fear, too; they had deliberately blurred the edges that divided the real from the fantastic. It might be that they too had been hunted, in the long run, and had feared to be absorbed, submerged with no hope of return.

And once the journal had been only raw material for some large imaginative work – something finished and formed, which would, like a magnet, polarize all these unrelated scraps so that they lay in concentric circles or stood and pointed all one way like fur. It was still a guarantee of possible significant communication; it existed and was fluent.

She spent some space on elaborating the physical differences between Simon Moffitt as she saw him now and Simon as she had known him. This was painful, but not without excitement. She ended, 'He has achieved a professional mode of communication, and this has changed him. He is harder; this I expected; but he is also larger. Or so he seems. I find this distressing.'

She thought a moment and then added, '*Notes on the winged snakes*. This is interesting. I should like to know whether you remember my views on this idea, put to you now nearly twenty years ago. I notice that you used some of my quotations last week. The serpent is traditionally, as I told you, a symbol for our horror at finding ourselves necessarily embodied. *It is the brute*. A creature reduced to a mouth and a stomach. On thy belly shalt thou go, etc. In the myth of Psyche, Psyche's curiosity discovers Eros embodied as a serpent. The neo-Platonic interpretation is that this curiosity has transformed spiritual love to bodily lust. The limiting, debasing animal functions. Keats knew this feeling. There is a marginal note in his *Paradise Lost* at the point where Satan informs the brutal sense of the serpent which gives a feeling of distress at physical confinement quite in excess of what Milton meant to convey. He says something like "Whose spirit does not ache at the smothering and confinement – the unwilling stillness – the *'waiting close'*?" *Do we not know this, Simon?* So, of course, we give the creature wings.

> 'The butterfly the ancient Grecians made
> The soul's fair emblem, and its only name –
> But of the soul, escaped the slavish trade
> Of mortal life! For in this earthly frame
> Ours is the reptile's lot, much toil, much blame,
> Manifold motions making little speed,
> And to deform and kill the things whereon we feed.

'Coleridge. Psyche means both butterfly and soul. A nice comment, both on my myth, and on your butterflies, which, as you told us, feed on blood. Just as *your* serpents make greater speed the more manifold the motions. I wish I could tell you, Simon, how much I enjoy the irony of your self-projection as a scientific observer in a topsy-turvy Eden. Well, cherish your illusory neutrality; there is no love – as we both know – that does not deform and kill. We cannot combine butterfly and serpent without corrupting the butterfly. Not that I do not admire, dear Simon, what you are trying to do.

'If, when we were younger, we knew how small were our stores of affection, and how, once they are dispensed, they cannot be retrieved, we should surely be less prodigal?'

She snapped the book shut on this, and locked it away again; she put on a coat and went out into the garden. It was cold there, and the river smelled, a strong smell of fishy slime with a thick, green, fresh overtone. Cassandra sat on a stone bench and stared into some rhododendron bushes. She was becoming more and more insomniac; night after night she paced garden and buildings, arguing with fear. Sometimes it was a vague weight; sometimes it took precise shapes. It could be defeated by changes of position, by concentration on one harmless object. She folded her hands in her lap, experimentally, and waited. Hidden in the river-bank a duck quacked, disturbed.

CHAPTER THREE

Two weeks later Cassandra got out of a train in the early evening, at Newcastle. She carried a suitcase and a brief-case, and looked round momentarily for familiar faces, although she had not thought about whether she would be met. She had not thought very much, and was unprepared for the curiously unreal familiarity of her childhood surroundings, which she now almost never saw; sometimes at Christmas, and not every Christmas. She had stood on these platforms, gaunt and humourless, comparing herself as she waited for the train that would take her south to school, to the yelling cattle packed in trucks in the siding. She still felt a vague need to reassert a private will in some way; to do something here that proved she was her own mistress. Childish, at thirty-eight. She came back as little as possible.

She drifted with the other passengers, up over the footbridge, choking in a sudden cloud of grit and steam, down towards where the crowd was thickening around the ticket-collector's bottleneck. Here, she leaned patiently against a barrier, waiting. She was in no hurry.

'Cassandra!' She turned her head, looking abruptly over the barrier. 'Cassandra! Pass me over your things. And the brief-case. Do you realize, we must have come by the same train? We are complete fools, not to think.'

It was Thor, in a navy-blue duffel coat; he stretched over a long arm and swung away her cases, smiling gently.

'They do not mind, it is not as though we were smuggling. I cannot get over what fools we are. Did you have a good journey?'

'Excellent, thank you,' Cassandra said, somewhat huskily; she had not spoken since she left London. She cleared her throat.

'When they let you out,' he said, 'we are under the clock. We'll wait.'

Cassandra cleared her throat again, and nodded rapidly, once or twice. She wished he had left her the brief-case; without its weight she felt clumsy and at a loss. She thrust her hands into her pockets, and began to advance towards the ticket-collector, moving a dry tongue in a dry mouth. He seemed very friendly. Of course, she hardly knew him. He kept smiling, which was unnerving.

Under the clock were Julia, and a tall, thin early teenager, Julia's daughter, Deborah. Deborah Jane, an over-fashionable name for her generation. Cassandra had not seen Julia for some time – not for three or four Christmasses, since the last time they had coincided. She thought Julia much changed; she had developed a sleekness. She wore a circular scarlet tent of a coat, with sleeves like folded wings, and a huge white fur cone on her head. The sisters looked at each other, and nodded. It was Thor who spoke.

'You see, here is Cassandra. We should have thought, she would have been told too, Oxford to Newcastle is often easier by London. We could have travelled together.'

They looked at each other again, with a certain complicity. They would not, left to themselves, have thought of travelling together.

'Of course, how *silly*,' cried Julia. 'But it has all been so rushed.'

'You look very well, Julia,' Cassandra brought out, and coughed. Then she coughed again; Julia watched her fight it down into a series of chokes, and the silence.

'I shall go and make telephone calls,' said Thor, 'and find out what is best to do. Naturally, with all their trouble, they will not have thought . . .'

Julia watched Cassandra press her lips together over the cough, and felt the minutes run past whilst she tried to think of something nice to say about Cassandra's appearance. Cassandra's eyes were watering a little, with effort. Well, why the hell doesn't she *cough* then? Julia thought. She wore a long – very long – sealskin coat, and a drooping black folded velvet beret, transfixed by a silver dagger with a yellow stone embedded in the hilt. On the corner of her mouth was a faint smear of ink. She wore thick black stockings, elegant enough on her good legs, and a pair of those shoes affected by women dons, cuban-heeled, punched, laced, high in the instep. The sight of these filled Julia with a kind of panic which she could not quite convert into mockery; why does she *have* to, she thought, and looked down momentarily on her own knee-high black boots, with their tassels swinging from the cuff. She was both apprehensive and complacent about her own girlish appearance.

She said, 'Oh, Cass, here is Debbie,' and pushed forward her lanky daughter, who wore a gaberdine raincoat, pulled in very tightly round the waist, a powder-blue woolly hat, and fur boots. Cassandra surveyed this child, whom she did not expect to like, neutrally. They had never spoken much. Each year Cassandra sent her a girls' book for Christmas, but she did not suppose they were read, and chose them on the advice of one of the church ladies. Deborah always sent back accurate, colourless, uninformative thank-you letters.

She was freckled, had a large nose, and looked tired.

'How do you do?' said Cassandra, in a don's bark.

'Hullo,' said Deborah, on a vanishing note. Her teeth were chattering. 'It's cold,' she said apologetically.

'It's going to get worse,' said Cassandra.

Deborah, apparently finding no answer to the tone of voice in which this was said, looked at her feet, and settled her features, a little ostentatiously, into a grim patience. Julia shrugged her shoulders and wriggled her toes. Cassandra took two steps to the right, leaned down, and defensively repossessed herself of her brief-case, which contained her journal; when she looked up again, Julia was watching her. Julia grinned. Thor came back from the Booking Hall.

'Apparently Mr Merton is waiting for us,' Thor said. 'He has had business in Newcastle, and is driving back. They cannot think how they neglected to tell us.'

When he mentioned the Vicar, Cassandra and Julia looked at each other, and for the first time their mouths lifted together with a smile. They knew they were remembering the same things, and the smile flickered with embarrassment.

Thor raised his head and cried, 'Porter!' Two porters immediately came; Cassandra, who had never had a man to look after her, and who was, despite her firm manner, always confused and ignored on stations, looked at Julia to see how she took this. Julia inclined her head, and smiled benignly. Maybe, Cassandra thought, with unexpected surprise, Julia is happy.

The Reverend Edwin Merton was waiting under the heavy portico beside his cream-coloured Rover; he opened doors, ushered them in, and slammed doors with a great deal of brisk and graceful bending of the body. Julia sat beside him; Cassandra, immediately behind the Vicar, noticed that his neck, above his collar, had grown thicker and redder, and that he had a real bald patch amongst the iron-grey curls. This was normally not noticeable, because of his great height; he was still a very handsome man. When he had turned the car out into the main streets, with a great deal of swelling shoulder-muscles and creaking of seats, he said, 'I'm glad you were able to come. I think it was necessary. This was all completely unexpected, I understand, and a great shock to your mother.'

Julia looked out at grey Newcastle, trolley wires and blackened churches. Carrick's café, where her first packet of cigarettes and ice-cream in one of those grained silver goblets had been symbols, more or less fantastic, for the real, sophisticated city life she was going to lead. The Theatre Royal, all pillars and round lamps on iron chains, where coming out from a pantomime in a cinnamon velvet dress with a lace collar, and a silver purse dangling on a ring from one finger, she had imagined herself one of a furred and scented London crowd about to go on to dance in some night club, vaguely wicked, vaguely risky. She still didn't know very much about night clubs, but was able whole-heartedly to enjoy being part of a crowd outside a London theatre in the dark simply by remembering her own feelings at ten, eleven, or twelve in the cinnamon dress. I was hungry for life, she thought, wherever I look in these streets I remember wanting something; they were images of London. She looked sideways at Cassandra, who had certainly shared this dream, and wondered what she was thinking.

Thor said, 'Can you tell us, Mr Merton, what we must expect? I think we should know what to expect. We were told nothing definite.'

Cassandra thought, he finds it easier to be a son-in-law – more natural – than I do to be a daughter.

'Well –' said the Vicar, turning a corner.

'Yes, *please*, we need to know,' said Julia, warmly.

'Well –' said the Vicar, 'it was a bad stroke. It would be wrong of me to tell you that he is certainly dying. But Dr Moore told me that – as things seem, as things seem – it is unlikely he will recover. Or, if he *does* recover – he will not be strong again. You know that he is paralysed completely, and can't speak? That may, of course, improve to a certain extent. But I don't think you should hope too much.'

'I see,' said Thor. 'Thank you. And my mother?'

'Bearing up splendidly,' said the Vicar. 'Splendidly. Very calm. I think it's telling on her. But she is splendid . . .'

'She would have to be,' said Julia. 'She wouldn't know what else to be.'

'I think,' he said carefully, 'that she expects perhaps too much of herself.'

He likes summing people up, Cassandra thought. He always has. He liked to have authority to understand and judge other people. Nevertheless, he did it quite well. Her mother's life was largely a faithful attempt to draw on strength not apparently available, in the hope that the expectation would create it. She was a woman who would take on any duty, and accept any misfortune, on this basis, and then through sheer effort of will preserve a climate of calm around an increasing struggle. So she had survived war, and refugees, and her husband's imprisonment, and Cassandra's own defection, simply by assuming that nothing else was possible. Well, Cassandra thought, if strength had not been given, something else had. A kind of toughness in defeat. She thought of her mother's square, thick body, her square corsets, her horn-rimmed glasses on their long chain, her sensible hands and sensible shoes. Her strength was a shell's strength, that was the trouble; it provided a shell's simple invulnerability. A layer of hardened scales. And slowed her movements. Cassandra, angry with herself for thinking in this way at this time, shrugged her shoulders silently and looked out of the window.

Thor said, 'We can at least relieve her of much of the burden, now.'

Something in his tone brought home to both sisters that they had been expecting to assist at a ceremonial, in so far as they had been expecting anything at all: his voice made them aware that death was a matter of holding basins, washing sheets, sweat, incontinence, swabs, sedatives. Cassandra turned her head uneasily, allowing herself to think of death, her stomach contracting with real fear. She was aware of the movement of Deborah, beside her, sliding one hand into Thor's large one, across his knee. Why did Julia bring that child? she asked herself angrily. She can't bear it. She did not ask herself how she had come by this knowledge.

There was a silence; then the Vicar said, 'I remember driving the two of you along this road, in different circumstances. When we were all younger, yes. I still feel a certain proprietary interest in you. I read your novels with – great interest, Julia, if I may say so. Very evocative. They provide me with an insight into the modern generation I shouldn't otherwise have. You speak for a generation, or so the girls in the village tell me . . .'

Julia smiled, and said thank you, once or twice; she felt inhibited from any discussion by the presence of Thor and Cassandra.

'Opinions of friends, I find,' she said with enthusiasm, 'are all one *really* cares about, after a bit. If people one really *cares* for know what one is trying to do . . . this is what matters.'

'Oh, I tell them I knew you as a little girl,' said the Vicar, smiling his sad, handsome smile, as though he was really thinking about something quite different, as though his friendliness was a result of pure generosity.

Cassandra caught sight of it as he turned to Julia; it was a look which, for several reasons, she associated with Simon. She leaned her own head slightly against the window, away from them all; they were coming out of the suburbs now, along the long dull road up into Northumberland. Fine February snow was beginning to fall. She was beginning to feel constricted already.

'I remember you running away from home,' said the Vicar. 'Both of you. Quite regularly. I've fetched you both back from all sorts of places in that little old Austin, do you remember?'

Julia laughed.

'You were always the extravagant one. I remember a time when you ran away in nothing but a nightdress. Cassandra' – he hesitated over the Christian name as though it was no longer appropriate – 'Cassandra was always – better prepared.'

With suitcase, and savings, Cassandra thought. I meant to go. I must have meant to go. It may have been a failure, but it was not simply a gesture – it was an instinct of flight, powerful and unquestioned, bred of no particular complaint. She remembered the summer night when she had walked out of the front door and headed south, mile after mile down country lanes towards a carefully selected country station. After some time, she had become afraid, too afraid to look round, or do anything but walk more rapidly. Blood beat behind her eyes. There was something crawling in the hedgerow, breathing heavily in the next field. Her hands were wet with fear.

Julia came up with her in the main street of a village, her face flaming with exertion, judging that by now she had achieved a *fait accompli*; they were far enough from home for her to be able to give up running and hiding, and approach openly.

'Let me come too, Cassandra, let me come too, it isn't *fair*.'

Cassandra had waited until she was there, and had then attacked, desperately, using the suitcase, nails, teeth, shoes, silently intent on real damage, grunting like an animal with effort. And Julia laughing hysterically, her coat falling open to display the sprigged winceyette nightdress, had warded off the blows patiently keeping up a shrill stream of cries. 'You always leave me out. You won't let me have *anything, ever*. It isn't fair, it isn't fair, it isn't *fair*.'

People had come out of houses, and had torn Cassandra away – it had taken this – had applied lint to Julia's cuts and scratches, and had asked her various questions, and then telephoned. And the Vicar – since, as so often, Father was away – had come. And they had gone home.

'All children feel the need to run away from time to time,' Julia said wisely to the Vicar. 'From the happiest homes particularly. It's just an assertion of premature independence. Desire for the unknown.'

Cassandra remembered the Vicar, left alone with her in his sitting-room whilst Julia was questioned elsewhere, asking:

'Well, why, Cassandra?'

'I don't know. I don't know. I want to lose myself. I can't bear to be as I am.'

'Does anything particular worry you?'

'No, no, *everything*.'

'That's fairly common. There are remedies. Try running to me, next time, will you? You can tell me as much as you like and no more.' With the same abstract good-will, not personal, and therefore partly daunting, partly reassuring. It would have been nice if he cared, she had thought then; but there was something very safe about his god-like calm. Still, she had not run to him for another eight years, or so.

'Fear of the unknown,' she said, with unexpected harshness. 'Or fear of the familiar. Maybe the same.'

'Like suicide,' said Thor. 'A bid for attention, a reproach to those who have noticed nothing, usually intended not to succeed.'

During the uneasy silence which followed Thor's remark, the Vicar thought about Cassandra Corbett. She had made his life difficult at one stage – although this was an improper way to see it; the Corbetts were an old Quaker family and Cassandra's violent conversion to Anglo-Catholicism at the age of eighteen had created the maximum discomfort for himself and his friends, her parents, who, however tolerant they were, felt her mood as a rejection of themselves. And in this they were right, he was sure, though he had never been able to understand precisely what Cassandra was rejecting. He reflected on the curious prevalence of women in the Anglican Church, and grimaced – all those years ago, when he had decided to become ordained, one of his less noble motives had been the glamour of a legitimately bachelor existence, no domestic details, no women, no claims. Well, he thought, we learn virtue by putting ourselves in a position where we cannot refuse to exercise it, for shame. There are always the faithful who knit and embroider and arrange flowers. But, in his experience, those who made intense religious demands were the young girls, wracked in the abstract by physiological changes he knew nothing about and was too nice to mention – or closed-in women, a little older than Cassandra was now. In his thirties he had sat, embarrassed, whilst she sat in his study, night after night, alternately weeping and making him passionate intellectual speeches about the nature of despair; he had read her letters and dutifully written replies a quarter of their length. He remembered, too, discussing St Augustine with her and Simon Moffitt; the girl in a square, military-cut navy-blue suit, an expression of acute, elated anxiety on her clever face, doing most of the talking; and Simon's eyes meeting his own across her, with amusement, embarrassment, a flicker of male complicity? He had never, in fact, made any direct effort to ascertain Simon's feelings, and had never done so. Indeed, the regularity with which Cassandra had made a third at their meetings had made this unnecessary; her presence had created an automatic and easy silent bond between them and had inhibited this from becoming anything else. We learn virtue by putting ourselves in a position where we cannot refuse to exercise it. The Vicar tapped his fingers on the wheel, and smiled to himself. He was sorry he had lost Simon; that something had prevented Simon from going into the Church. He would have thought it would have been the girl who was suffering from the temporary hysterical religiosity of late adolescence. But Cassandra, in his fifties, was still with him; authoritatively Anglican, dryly knowledgeable, certainly devout, only slightly addicted to cliqueish jokes about vestments or Jesuits. And he, used to women now, enjoyed her company more than he might have imagined possible, and was a little afraid of her. She struck him, now as when she was eighteen, as a spiritual desperado, and one whose capacity for violence was by no means spent. I wonder what she lives *for*, he thought, and said aloud:

'And you, Cassandra, how are your studies progressing?'

But she was not disposed to talk, had to be asked twice, and then merely said, 'Very well.'

By the time they had passed through Alnwick, conversation had fluttered to a stop – only Julia asked spasmodic questions about old acquaintances, brightly. The snow was thickening, and the air in the car, fanned round by the heater, was soporific and heavy. Deborah still held Thor's hand. Cassandra, turned away to the outside, was aware in spite of herself of the tightness of the grip.

At last they reached Benstone village. Here, in summer, little gardens of purple and white flowers grew in the road without fences; tough, shrubby flowers, blown by a sea-wind. To the north and east were the long beaches Swinburne had chanted about. The village was built on a steep hill. At the bottom were the church and the vicarage, the village stores and the post office; at the top was the Old House, last in a line of increasingly large grey stone houses fronting the street directly. Here the Corbetts had lived for three generations: they were one of the oldest Quaker families, solid, unpretentious, civilized *bourgeoisie*.

Numbed by the long drive and the car heater they all crowded into the hall – a large, low room with a wood fire burning in a stone fireplace, into which they came straight from the street. The roof was beamed, and the floor was bare wood, with various large rugs, comfortable rather than elegant, spread about between leather arm-chairs. The main staircase, uncarpeted and wooden, came straight down into the room from a narrow landing like a kind of minstrel's gallery. Underneath it, rather dimly lit, was a huge Burne-Jones painting of knights, ladies, hounds and horses plunging through a tangled wood drawn in meticulous detail. It had happened that some of the more worthy of the worthy Friends would complain to the liberal elder Corbetts that the painting represented blood-sports, and was unsuitable; but it had been bought by a Corbett who had been acquainted with Christina Rossetti, and thus had a certain degree of virtue attached to it. Cassandra stared absently at this painting, whilst Julia looked rapidly from object to object – piano, books, terracotta groups they had done themselves, years ago, feeling suddenly the habitual pleasure of coming home.

It was Thor who crossed to the foot of the staircase to meet Mrs Corbett as she came down, and it was to him she cried, 'Oh, at last –' in her booming, committee-woman's voice. He took her firmly in his long arms, cracking against him the glasses which hung against her bosom.

'How is he?' said Thor.

'Much the same. I don't know. He can't speak.'

'Does he – seem to want to speak?'

'I don't know. He seems – frightened. That's what I can't bear, I can't do anything to make that better, he just seems frightened.'

There was, Cassandra thought, a basic absurdity about this fear, spoken in this brisk, summing-up voice.

'It may be your own fright,' said Thor, directly. 'You can't know. Now, sit down. We're all here; you must rest a little. Keep your strength.'

He assisted her into a chair: Thor was the only person who unfailingly assisted Elizabeth Corbett. Julia pulled off her coat, dropped it over a chair, and ran forward to sit at her mother's feet.

'I *wish* we had been here to – to be with you,' she said. Elizabeth

Corbett looked down on her with a face momentarily creased towards tears.

'I'm sorry to fetch you all this way, Julia. There may have been no – no need. But –'

'I know, I know, darling,' Julia said. She took her mother's hand and held it against her face. 'We'll do all we can.'

'Let me take your coat,' said Cassandra to Deborah. Deborah nodded, speechless, and struggled out. She was wearing a smart navy-blue knitted suit, with a red and white collar. She pulled off the blue woolly hat, revealing a head with her father's bulging brow topped by a springing mass of gingery, wiry curls. Cassandra, taken aback, stared at her, and Deborah, somewhat consciously, cast down her eyes. She followed Cassandra through into the little cloakroom in the corridor leading to the back of the house, where Cassandra hung up everything except her own velvet hat. Then she said, loudly:

'Please, what are we supposed to do?'

'I don't know. Keep quiet. Lend moral support. Your father seems to know.'

'It's his job. Lending moral support's his job. I – I'm scared of – of people dying. I'm sorry.'

It was a long time since anyone had made any kind of a personal appeal to Cassandra. She thought again, crossly, Julia should not have brought this girl.

'It is one of the things we all have to accept,' she said.

'Oh, that's what we *say*.'

'That's what's true.'

'Yes,' said Deborah. 'But – but it's still often something we just say.'

'There are ways and ways of accepting.'

'Yes. And one is always afraid one might not manage it. Don't you think?'

'I don't know,' said Cassandra slowly. She looked again at Deborah's hair and freckled nose; it was uncanny that she had not noticed this at their earlier meetings. She said, 'One has to learn to cultivate detachment. Are you fond of reading? Let me find you a book.'

Deborah gave her, on this, an odd grin that could only have been called conspiratorial; the thought of this recurred uneasily to Cassandra at several moments during that long evening.

CHAPTER FOUR

During the next week and a half, only one thing changed; the snow fell steadily, and blew and piled around the house, and out on the hills behind the house. It was one of those late, freak winters, and the family, held there initially by Jonathan Corbett's unchanging condition, found that when it still did not change any decision to return south was postponed because the roads were impassable.

Before the snow fell, a nurse had arrived, who took over Inge's room; Inge had come in her teens to look after Cassandra and Julia when they were children, and told them Scandinavian legends of long dark nights and ice mountains, and had gone home to marry, in her late thirties, a childhood friend who had suddenly made a fortune from hand-turned wooden furniture and bowls. It was through Inge, and the proximity of the shipping line to Oslo and Bergen that the Old House had become a centre for visiting Scandinavian Quakers, including Thor. Inge had left, but there was still Elsie, the maid, who had been there as long as Julia could remember and was part of the family; Elsie cooked, and cleaned, and carried things for Jonathan Corbett up and down the stairs. Julia spent some time chatting to Elsie in the kitchen, reminiscing. She remembered Inge and Elsie as the stable part of her childhood; her parents had been often away, and always busy; the house had been often enough full of visiting deputations and then, in the war, had been a depot for milling refugee children. Inge and Elsie had been constant; they had done the scolding and loving.

Thor and Julia slept in what had been her parents' bedroom before they moved out into separate rooms. This always gave Julia a feeling that an adult, married state had been thrust upon her such as she had imagined it in childhood, and not as she had in fact experienced it in the warm muddle of her Great Ormond Street flat. Thor, naturally enough, was quite unawed by this. He was very busy, and organized everything, ordered meals, ordered people to put on gumboots and go down into the village to buy food. On Sunday, when the nurse had her day off, he took his wife, his mother-in-law, and Deborah to the Quaker Meeting-house, whilst Cassandra, who had got up very early to go to the Vicar's communion service, took her turn at sitting beside the long, slightly bubbling body of her father.

There were only about six people at Meeting, besides the family. Julia, who, in spite of having married an active Friend, rarely went to Meeting now, found the Meeting-house, for all its scrubbed wooden bareness of benches and tables, distressing. She did not, as she imagined Cassandra did, find the house itself, or the daily routine, oppressive, but the Meeting-house, stripped for deep thought, was both the place where she had time to examine her own moments of distress, and the place where, over the years, her family had burst out from time to time in embarrassing speech. All this formulation of thought, she said to herself, here without any framework of ritual as Cassandra has it, seems so far from the sort of thing most of us are really prooccupied with most of the time.

She remembered her father, labouring at length, so scrupulously, blowing out his long moustache, to define the precise moral position of those who were not pacifists and believed killing was justified, then repudiating this position, equally scrupulously, absolutely finally, and, still not finished, exhorting Friends to tolerate those who killed, and ending with a flourish 'Father forgive them, they know not what they do.' She had looked across at Cassandra, on this, who had closed her eyes and tightened her mouth in pain. Both the girls had intensely disliked the way in which Friends familiarized the terrible and made it a comfortable possession. She supposed that this might be inevitably true of all Christians. Cassandra, herself, might now be less intolerant; she had always had a proprietary interest in the terrible which might, in terms of the Church, music, painting, litany, have become in its turn another kind of domestication. As for herself, she was not sure how much good it did to expend a lot of thought on death and suffering at a distance. It could so easily lead to an ignoring of the little daily agonies which were all that deeply affected the fabric of her own life. She felt both determined and vaguely guilty about her shelving of the whole problem.

She remembered Cassandra's last appearance in the Meeting-house. By then, they were not speaking to each other, and she had been largely unaware of what Cassandra was thinking. Indeed, when she had risen pale and shivering to her feet, Julia had had a moment of fear that she was about to utter an indictment of her own duplicity with regard to Simon. But Cassandra, with what the Quakers agreed tolerantly later to have been excusably unhelpful bad taste, had lectured them with abstract passion on her reasons for leaving the Society of Friends. They had, she had told them, too simple and idealistic a view of human nature. She had been twenty at the time, with a curious maturity of phraseology and an unformed, over-expressive girl's face. After speaking for five minutes or so she had begun to weep, pushing the tears away clumsily with the sides of her hands and still pouring out the same long, formed, urgent sentences. Julia, who agreed with her, whose views had in this area been formed by Cassandra, had been horribly embarrassed.

'You never question that it is possible for us to become good,' Cassandra cried. 'You believe that if we try to be good we shall affect things, make other people good. You appropriate the story of the Roman senators who sat so still that the Goths and Vandals dared not touch them as a pacifist triumph. I've heard it told so in Meeting. But this was no triumph of anything but empty dignity, the Goths beat out the brains of those senators on the marble pavement. You always talk as though passive resistance could convert violence to love. But it can't, and it doesn't, and we ought to admit it. There *will always be* people who will slash open the other cheek when it is turned to them. In this life love *will not* overcome, it *will not*, it will go to waste and it is no good to preach anything else. We need God because we are desperate and wicked and we can find Him only through Himself. The Inner Light doesn't necessarily shine, and doesn't illuminate much. You will find no *meaning* by simply examining your consciences, maybe, ever. What I am saying is, we have got to find a way of *living in* a world that eats and destroys and pays nothing back . . .'

Julia had had the illusion that no one was listening but herself because they were all too embarrassed by her sister's tears. Cassandra had brought public humiliation on them yet again. And her wild words, like most statements of faith, overstated her case horribly and alienated sympathy. She could have done it better herself, and made the Quakers much more uncomfortable by producing partially sympathetic examples of their state of mind. When she heard Cassandra speak of God intimately, as Him, Himself, she knew she did not believe in it. Not, at least, in any way that would ever be practically meaningful in her life. When Cassandra sat down she had felt a mixture of relief, and pity, and anger, at the Quakers because she was sure that simple pity was what they would feel, at Cassandra because she couldn't be subtle enough to avoid this. Cassandra had no understanding of people's reactions. She had felt, also, release; Cassandra would never talk to her about these things again, and this was humiliating, and left her lonely – but at least she had a view of her own, and could live from it. After a bit, stooping, her face in her hands, Cassandra had got up and left the Meeting-house. Everyone had agreed that this was unnecessary.

Here, too, Julia had first seen Thor, who had come to speak to Friends at Benstone in 1947 about Quaker witness to peace in occupied countries. She had felt, with him as with Cassandra, for opposite reasons, that the force of what he had said was dissipated by his incapacity to present it persuasively. He had told, in a slightly choked voice, faltering occasionally and repeating himself, a string of the sad little Quaker stories of the moral victories gained by passive resistance that she was used to; the soldier who threw down his arms when ordered to slaughter the schoolmaster and his patiently waiting family; the men of faith who had survived the concentration camps without hatred. He had told them in rather a hurry, as though they were simply additional evidence to prove a main point; it was only at the end of his talk that Julia herself made the imaginative effort to see that the choking was real emotion, that the stories were told flatly because they were facts and he was the witness, and he believed passionately that facts should speak for themselves. She had looked at him and wanted to shake him for deliberately draining his stories of their urgency, for not stressing his own personal reactions, for making his people into examples, not individuals. In those days – he must have been twenty-four – he was gaunt, so that his cheek-bones, which were very pronounced, almost shone through his skin, and his pale eyes slanted deeply back above them as though the whole surface of his head was being forcibly tugged towards his crown. This had given him a slightly staring look, almost unbalanced. Julia, remembering this, and how she had approached him after the talk so gingerly, stole a glance at his solid, clean-cut face beside her. He had rounded out, he had a heavy look now, a supremely sane look. She had not the slightest idea what he was thinking.

The faces in the Meeting-house were mostly familiar, still; she looked from one to the other, and then up at the single high window, with its dangling cord in the gable; outside was a smoky sky pocked by falling white snow. In here an attempt had been made to reduce life to its elements, an attempt increasingly compromised, over the centuries. Well, she had never spoken here, she had only watched, and now she came back out of politeness and nostalgia. She didn't want life reduced to its elements. She didn't want simplicity. She wanted the complicated, irreducible social world outside, where it was possible to believe in people who really cared more for their motor-cars than for anything else, people who spent *most of their time* thinking about who had snubbed whom at whose party in what dress, people the Quakers would have reduced to a formula and simply judged, or would perhaps have defended on the grounds that they were not as they appeared. Well, they existed outrageously, and, as far as Julia could see, they were as they appeared, and that was enough for her. She needed them, she wanted them, she wrote about them, she fed off them. She expected nothing, and this seemed to her the only possible form of moral activity. She leaned back against her bench with a certain defiance, on this thought, as the first Friend stood up to pay his tribute to her father. 'Our prayers go with him in his suffering,' he said. Julia thought there was a short story somewhere in a Quaker meeting, but wasn't sure that she was detached enough to write it.

Cassandra sat still beside her father, trying very hard to take her own advice to Deborah, to detach herself, not to think. She had a book open on her knee, but was not looking at it. Above all, she thought, she must not sum up in her mind her father, who was not dead, and might not be dying. His skin was yellowish and opaque, like cheese, and the white moustache was draggled by sweat. His eyes were open and motionless. Cassandra had no idea what he knew, or felt, whether he wanted to communicate, whether he was aware of her presence.

Cassandra had loved him, at first passionately, and then with hopeless devotion. He had loved her, too, certainly. One of her mother's favourite sayings had been 'Our children cannot doubt that they are loved', and they never had doubted, they had never, Cassandra thought, surprised at the image her mind naturally produced, had a foothold for doubt. It was only that she had had to share his love with so much else: prisoners, a model village, refugees, lepers, delinquents, prostitutes . . .

He was, Cassandra thought sadly, an infinitely tolerant man, and took everything as it came. Because of this, unfairly, she never quite trusted him – she found herself striving to shake this inevitable love into admiration. She felt that he affectionately tolerated her chosen pursuits – Oxford, Malory, the Church – with a simple refusal to judge her which blunted any attempt she might make intellectually to shake him, or emotionally to touch him. She could not tell him her life was not arid because he had never allowed himself to form the opinion that it was. She suspected him of finding more human value in Julia's domestic novels than in her own work, and resented this vaguely, without ever tackling him about it. She was aware that he tolerated Julia, too – she had watched him amusedly 'loving' one of Julia's intense enthusiasms for new friends.

She was angry with herself for letting her thoughts stray that way, and wished there was something she could do, practically, for him. She dared not touch his pillows. She was no good at this kind of thing. She would have liked to take his hand, too, but dared not, and when she looked into his faded eyes she felt that he must feel, if he felt anything, that she was peering at him with indecent curiosity.

She wondered what he felt passionately about; his most apparently passionate acts had been gestures of self-denial, long imprisonments for pacifism, and, lately, lying down outside military installations, all six-feet-two of him in a speckled tweed suit, absurd and dignified. He had fought injustice and unreason violently, as though it was possible to win.

And as far as bringing up children went, he had been a negative idealist, a passive idealist. He had laid down no laws, exerted no pressure, expected nothing, left them to make their own choices. From very early he had offered to his children, by way of precept, nothing more than a reasoned *exposé* of alternative courses of action: the decision must be theirs. He did not drink, but they must choose for themselves; they were left to choose their school, their future, their companions, their religions. Both of them had at different times felt it as an affront that he could apparently feel so little involuntary emotion about them as to pursue this course so successfully. We were not – especially I was not – ever *sure* of him, Cassandra said to herself. And out of all this liberalism, extremism grows. What was in fact given to us was space to discover violence. It was too hard for us, all this choosing, we lacked the enclosing warmth of anything either to rebel against or to welcome in weak moments as absolute restriction. One tends to think that those who are brought up libertine will compensate by growing strict, and those who are marshalled and punished will turn Bohemian. But with us, make your own decisions, anything reasonable is permitted, shifts so easily to everything is permitted, any decision is possible. The Inner Light can indicate the edges of a limitless darkness. Better to grow up believing that it is, *de fide*, not so.

Her father's hand twitched beside her; he gave a flurry and a gulp; something ran out of the corner of his mouth; and then he slackened. The heavy, bubbling breathing was no longer evident. Cassandra leaned over him cautiously; the tired eyes looked expressionlessly back at her; she touched his cheek and his hand with a trembling finger. She was horrified that she did not know whether he was alive or not. One did not expect not to know. Her knees began to tremble. For a moment she kept very still, thinking of literary acts, looking glass, feather, closing those eyes. She began to shake all over, stumbled to her feet, and hurried out into the corridor calling, in a crackled voice, 'Nurse, nurse.'

If Nurse could have gone out on her day off, she would, but the snow prevented it, so she was writing letters when Cassandra burst in. This wild irruption was something Nurse would describe to cronies for years; one of the moments of ultimate drama that made tolerable long periods spent by querulous sick-beds and hopeless death-beds. At least you saw life, Nurse would say. Miss Corbett had been a horrible sight; all necklaces flying, and open-mouthed and gasping, and *staring* eyes. One never knew how death would take people. Shaking like a leaf. And the poor old gentleman lying there, not even certainly dead. Though he had been dead all right, at least when *she* got there, and had probably known nothing.

Cassandra watched Nurse trot away down the corridor and then went to be sick in the bathroom. There she sat on the floor, legs outstretched, mopping her nostrils with a handkerchief. Death was such a fact. She ought to go back in there. She ought to go and help Nurse. Her stomach heaved again. Even this, I can't do with any dignity. And the father I was thinking about, all that network of love and responsibility, nothing left. The thought and the physical unpleasantness of the fact were somehow unconnected. I could manage one or the other.

After a time she stood up, and went out into the garden, which sloped up behind the house into the hills. She sat on the low wall that marked off garden from hill grass – today, all was indistinguishable thick snow – and clenched her fists on her knees. She thought she ought to pray. She felt trapped – as though her past was fixed now, and could not be remodelled, and her own behaviour had finished it with the largest amount of mess, and lack of warmth possible. I should have spoken to him, she thought, he might have heard. She began to weep, angry and choking, fighting back each sob; she sat there in the cold, until her face was purple and crimson and blotched.

When the others came back from Meeting they were met by Nurse, who had done what was necessary. Miss Corbett, she said, had been present at the end, but had gone out somewhere. Elizabeth Corbett went up with Nurse to look at the body; she stood a long time, in a decent silence, and went to bed, after Nurse had telephoned the doctor, where she wept for some time, and fell into a heavy sleep.

Deborah became hysterical. She was carried off, rigid and choking, by Thor, and put to bed. Julia said, 'But after all you hardly *knew* him, darling,' and Thor said, 'Julia, please don't be silly, be quiet,' and appeared downstairs again only briefly, to tell Elsie to bring his supper and Deborah's upstairs.

Julia found herself suddenly alone. She sat down in the hall by the fire and thought about her father. She had always been the one who could make him laugh: he didn't mind what she said to him, they shared a whole world of private jokes. They had gone for walks by the river together, and she had amused him with stories, this side of malicious, about girls from school, and, later, not quite *risqué* stories about worthy Friends. He liked this, because most people he met respected him too much and thought him too good to be amused in this way, and he did not want to feel isolated, or rarefied. Later, she had brought him all her novels and begged him to tell her what he thought of them, partly because she wanted to be assured of his approval, but partly because he was one of the few people she knew who found no difficulty in assuming that fiction was fiction. Other people tended, if they knew her at all well, to be a little embarrassed in her presence, as though she was given to constant indiscretion. Oh, she would miss him.

She became aware that she was admiring herself for her plucky reaction, and constructing a chain of near-sentimental thoughts about her father as though he was a character in a novel. Well, she told herself, either self-indulgently or practically, that's natural enough, there'll come a moment when I really take it in, I can't expect to realize what's happened, all at once. He wouldn't expect me to . . .

She was suddenly completely oppressed by the sense that there was no figure now between herself and the end. She was herself the adult generation – a woman with a great daughter, in the last stretch of life. She wasn't ready for that. She lived so much on the assumption that she was 'still young'.

Perhaps she should go and see him. When she thought this, her scalp pricked; she could imagine the body only through Nurse's restrained hints at Cassandra's extreme reaction to it. Something vaguely hideous, something nasty . . . not her father, who had laughed. When she thought of Cassandra, running away, locked in the bathroom, she had a sudden sense of a real and monstrous event, and felt herself lonely and afraid. They had left her alone here, and this she could not bear.

Cassandra would be in the garden. She put on her red cape, and went out through the back door, following the blurred footprints through the snow. Once she saw how Cassandra was taking it, she would know what had happened.

She sat down on the wall, next to her rigid sister.

'Aren't you cold, Cass?' Cassandra's bony hands were blue.

'No,' said Cassandra. Then, 'It's still snowing.' Snow was blowing in little clouds on the hill.

'Cass,' said Julia, 'you ought to come in. Do come in.'

Cassandra shrugged her shoulders.

'I'm sorry,' said Julia desperately. 'I need company, Cassandra.' It had always been like this. Always asking, for something she should long ago have known better than to expect. Cassandra looked at her, silently; the muscles of her face were stiff, and Julia could see the swelling round her eyes. She was nobody you could comfort.

'I know you don't want – to talk.'

'There's nothing to say.'

Well, *some* sisters might bloody well talk to each other, Julia's mind snapped, crossly. For company.

'Mother's gone to sleep. Out of exhaustion. Thor's with Debbie. Debbie's gone all hysterical. Probably I shouldn't have brought her. But there didn't seem much else . . . *He* said better to bring her . . .'

'He seems to know what's best,' Cassandra said, entering the conversation with an effort. She added, flatly, 'He seems good.'

'I don't know. He's *too* good, do you know?'

Cassandra shivered.

'Like Father was too good,' Julia went on. 'He will give and give and think he can change everything.'

'It might be best at least to live like that,' Cassandra said, with a touch of her old authoritative tone. Julia wanted her to go on talking, to make their father real, by talking. But Cassandra said, more faintly. 'I'm sorry about Deborah. She seems highly strung.' A teacher's assessment, Julia said with a rush. 'She reminds me of *you*, Cass. All nerves and sharp edges and will-power. She's clever, too, school-clever. I wish you'd *talk* to her. She needs . . . I wish . . .'

Cassandra's hands plucked at her skirt. She fills me with embarrassment and a kind of respect, Julia thought. Why do I always lie? I don't want her to talk to Debbie at all. I said that because I always think I need to make contact, somehow; anyhow, make her see I exist, make her *care*. I want her to take me into account. I want to be nice to her. Foolish. Useless.

'Cassandra, nobody's left us anything to do. Come in now, *please*. We could play cards, or something. Like we used to do, remember?'

'If you like,' said Cassandra, who was now beginning to feel the cold.

So, all afternoon, whilst Thor made telephone calls, and held his daughter's hand, the sisters sat in front of the fire in the hall and played games. They played snakes and ladders, chequers, bezique and piquet. Then they played chess. Julia had changed into tight black velvet trousers and a Swedish rough woollen overshirt, square, high-necked, patterned in purple and scarlet. Round her neck she wore a hammered lump of silver on a chain, from a Knightsbridge crafts shop. Leaning across the chess board, moving the pieces with ringed fingers, they looked surprisingly in keeping with each other, as though Burne-Jones or Rossetti could have used them for models for a painting of a mediaeval lady and her page; Julia's hair dropped forward in a long, pointed curve along her jaw. She was winning; both of them were accurate players, but Julia was more courageous. They played almost silently.

At supper-time Julia went to see if she was needed and found that she was not; she came back to Cassandra with a plate of ham and tomatoes, and announced this to her.

'It seems funny we're not needed, Cass.'

'Tomorrow, maybe . . .'

'Have some bread. Cass . . . do you think they've kept the Game?'

'It was in my room. It must still be there. I haven't looked.'

'Would you look? Do you think we could get it out? We've played everything else, it would be exciting to see if we could remember . . .'

'If you like,' said Cassandra.

'I'll come up with you.'

When they were children, there were rules which governed Julia's going into Cassandra's room – passwords, which changed with bewildering frequency, and all sorts of locked drawers, and locked boxes. She had expended some ingenuity on getting into these; she considered

Cassandra laid herself open to espionage. For years she had kept secret the fact that the drawer which held Cassandra's journal could be worked open with the key of her mother's sewing-machine. Indeed, she did not know now whether Cassandra had known this.

She had still a slight feeling of sacrilege on going into Cassandra's tiny dark room.

'It was in the window-seat,' said Cassandra. 'As I remember.' She knelt down in the bay of the window and turned back the lid. There were armfuls of the Game; an enormous roll of oilskin, several shoe boxes of clay figures, more boxes of little cards, which were written over with rules and forfeits laid out like laws, long, heavy ledgers written up alternately by Cassandra and Julia; move by move chronicles, increasing in length and complexity over the years. It had all begun when they were seven and nine, with the personification of a pack of cards which they had divided into four armies – the red were Julia's, the black Cassandra's. From day to day they had expanded the account of their battles, rounding out characters and creating rules for movement – the oilskin map had come next with a whole countryside laid out on it, castles, rivers, cottages, chapels, glued and varnished largely by Cassandra who was capable of producing fine and delicate lines with a paint brush and pen. This oilskin map covered a good half of their hall area, when unrolled now; they had wanted to make it three-dimensional, but had run into storage problems.

The clay figures had been a later development, when the armies had expanded beyond their original thirteen men, and when Cassandra had discovered Morris, Tennyson and the *Morte d'Arthur* indiscriminately together. In the early days, they had worked entirely together, and the plots they created had consisted largely of the machinations of organized military antagonism. Later, the emphasis shifted from the moves on the board to the chronicling of intrigue, misguided love and eternal hatred: Cassandra wrote long poems in ballad metre about the affairs of Queen Morgan, and Julia chronicled every stage of the hopeless passion of Elaine of Astolat. Both sisters at this stage were aware that the other's imagination was also vigorously working in private on what was discussed less hotly in public, over the map. Julia had what she read of Cassandra's journal to prove it. But it had been completely absorbing, Julia thought now, it had taken up almost all her attention between the ages of seven and seventeen: they had worked out already attitudes to all sorts of adult problems which she for one had found alternately percipient and fantastically thwarting – how did one ever rid oneself of a longing for a devouring love which one saw, wisely, to be impossible, but had enjoyed in such verisimilitude and detail when nothing else was happening to one at all? She looked at Cassandra, who was silently, with pursed lips, deploying her black forces across the map. The things *she* had imagined had frightened Julia, who as a child had had nightmares, and woken screaming and sweating to be comforted by Inge on account of things she had lived through with Cassandra earlier in the day. Cassandra had always seen the nightmares as a simple manoeuvre to gain credit for herself and put Cassandra in the wrong; but for days together Julia had walked up and down the village streets pursued by vague fears and a sense of doom. Her attempts to palliate Cassandra's dramas with happy endings, or innocent affections, had been no use – Cassandra paid little attention, and when she did twisted Julia's stories towards her own grim conclusions.

Well, she had shaken it off, slowly, and felt impoverished for it. She had shaken off, that was, almost everything but the nightmares, which persisted; her own countryside peopled by Cassandra's characters and events. It was easy enough to see what Cassandra had made of it all – an object for detailed examination, sterilized with footnotes and things.

She could guess, she thought, what Cassandra dreamed – and not only at night. As for herself, it could have been clear enough to Cassandra what use she had made of their stories. 'In Miss Julia Corbett's first two novels an element of romantic fantasy was uneasily blended with a warm, human understanding of very real daily problems. In her later work she has consolidated her achievement in the second field – she is probably the best of that increasing number of women writers who explore in loving detail the lives of those trapped in comfort by washing-machines and small children – but with the fantastic romantic overtones some of the vigour has been lost. In the earlier books, clumsily conveyed, was a sense of possibilities and concerns outside domestic claustrophobia. I sometimes wish Miss Corbett could see her way to reopening, reinvigorating her fantastic vein; she might then have it in her to be a very good writer.' This was from the *Guardian*, Julia had it by heart; it had both irked and vaguely encouraged her. She wondered whether Cassandra had ever read her novels, and whether Cassandra had written anything herself. She thought: she is not creative. She is critical. But it wasn't the whole truth. It was strange how even now what she saw to be the childish clumsiness of the little figures seemed so much alive.

They began to play, very self-consciously, going back to the very early days of their partnership when the game had depended on the organization of the moves rather than on sustained imaginative effort. In the later days, they had sat and narrated the feelings of their characters in high romantic prose, with a certain formality. Julia was aware that they were both pretending to forget things; she herself 'lost' several characters in the Forêt Sauvage and could not remember how they could be extricated; Cassandra had to ask whether the Abbey grounds, as well as the Abbey, were sanctuary. Cassandra was smiling slightly – Julia, losing a slice of land and several soldiers cried, 'Do you remember when we decided they were all immortal the day I cried too much to go on? Oh, I *was* a bad loser.'

Cassandra laughed, and settled the red knights in her dungeon.

'At least they are immortal,' said Julia, feeling a sudden rush of warmth towards Cassandra, the Game, her childhood and herself, as a child, mourning and reviving the dead knights.

'Immortal?' said Thor from the gallery. 'Who is immortal?'

He leaned over the banister, a pale figure in a thick white fisherman's sweater, his blond hair gleaming. Julia stared up at him.

'Characters,' she said. 'You wouldn't understand.'

'No,' he said, 'I wouldn't. They have gone to sleep. I am going to bed.'

'It's a bit early. I'll come. I'll come in a moment.'

'As you will,' said Thor, vanishing.

When he had gone, Julia said, 'Oh, dear. Oh damn. He makes me feel I behave so badly. At least, I just let him do all the things I ought to be doing. Oh God, Cassandra, I hate myself.'

'Do you?' said Cassandra. She added, 'We all need to protect ourselves from thinking too much. We all have different ways. I should think he might understand that. He's intelligent.'

'You know it's not only self-protection. It's a kind of self-indulgence.' Julia looked almost pleadingly at Cassandra.

'Well –' said Cassandra. Then, 'In any case, what does he know? If he does know, he's likely to forgive. He seems forgiving.'

'*Forgiving?*' said Julia.

'Not that I'm in a position to judge,' said Cassandra, balancing the black Queen on the palm of her hand. The Queen's face, by some lucky accident, had a real severity of expression, whilst her skirts were sculpted into real movement. Cassandra closed her hand over her; she was an object still so familiar that she was difficult to see clearly. Julia thought; that was almost a conversation with Cassandra. She bent her head over the network of paths and rivers on the carpet, traced one with her finger, and plunged.

'Have you been watching the telly, lately, Cass?'

'Yes.'

'Would you – would you mind watching?'

'If you like,' said Cassandra. Julia could not tell whether the suggestion had pleased or displeased her; nor was she quite sure what feeling had driven her to make it. Cassandra had behaved abominably over the whole thing with Simon; and to watch him, together, at that distance beside their own fire, might neutralize some of the bad feeling; clean something up. Though anything that had had to wait so many years to be cleared up might well take more than one television rite. She stood up and switched on the set, and put out the lights.

The picture jiggled into shape.

'Don't you hate that girl?' said Julia. 'All coy and routine. Having to do all that smiling. Awful job. Ugh, I *hate* her. Do you know, Cass, I'm going to be on the telly myself, on a rather highbrow sort of quiz programme thing, called *The Lively Arts*. Run by a *lovely* man called Ivan Rostrevor, who has all sorts of super ideas and loves *me*, which is always nice, isn't it? We're going to be a sort of panel, of all different kinds of artists, and study our different reactions to different sorts of things – Ivan wants to show how daily life affects the artists, and how the artists' daily lives are affected by *being* artists. I mean, he might show us a film of a road accident. Or a rocket. Or children at nursery school. Or a revivalist talking about C.N.D. He's got all sorts of ideas. He says the artist's both different from and the same as the common man . . . some weeks we're going to examine our own daily lives . . .'

Nervousness, Julia thought, is making me talk to her as I talk to people in the studio, or something. The cultured girl bent the bow of her smile for the last time on the details of the new series of broadcasts of genuine religious services.

'I suppose they pay well,' Cassandra said. Julia twisted her rings.

Simon appeared at a distance, pushing a hollowed log canoe down a slight slope, into water that rippled and splashed. For some time he paddled silently across the screen; first across a pool of open water, then into a dark tunnel of arching creepers. Then they watched a caiman, on its bandy legs, hoist itself out of the water on to a narrow beach, where it lay, staring. Simon explained, precisely, how it breathed – 'the air enters the raised nostrils at the end of the snout and passes over the palate into the throat, which can be closed by a flap of mucosa. Thus, when it opens its mouth under water to seize its prey, this does not interfere with its breathing.' He expatiated upon its teeth, which, before he had explained how one tooth slotted into the other jaw, had seemed to sprout haphazardly, stump-like all along it. 'This is a smooth-fronted caiman: it and the dwarf caiman – the smallest alligators – appear to violate the rule that two very similar species are not found closely associated in nature. Normally, we find that some kind of "competition" for survival does appear to operate: exact studies of apparently similar species which do coexist seem to suggest that they are in some ways importantly separated – one may live in the trees, the other on the ground, one may – must – eat food entirely different from the other. And so on. In other words – except in the case of the smooth-fronted and the dwarf caimans, you will find that crocodilians in the same area are either of the same species, or so dissimilar that there is no clash of interest between them.

'A naturalist,' Simon said, as the camera held him and his caiman together in one picture, 'has to be making constant distinctions between the individual and the species, between form and the apparent breaking of that form. Between general laws – like the one about competition – which explains certain facts, and the particular exception which may teach one something about both the law, and the species which does not conform. I am making a detailed study of the habits of these two species of caiman. But the individual caiman is of interest in himself, and because of what he adds to our knowledge of his species. This one, for instance, will have stomach contents not *precisely* the same as any other. We are delighted both by the inevitable recurrence of patterning – the veining of a leaf – and the fact that no two leaves, no two faces, no two alligators are ever the same. In the case of faces, we are trained to observed differences – though we are less skilled in the case of people not of our own race. But what I have to teach myself is to attend so sharply to these creatures as to pick up differences even in their scale formation.'

The caiman was raising itself to its feet. It lifted a slow, clawed foot, amongst folds of skin, and then rested, in mid-motion: the camera insisted, for a moment, on the ticking pulse of life in the soft skin of its throat, under its immobile state. Then, heavy and slow, it began to walk away, raised, almost strutting, on its disproportionately thin legs, its huge tail stretched out like a weight behind it. Simon explained that it was an illusion to think that they dragged themselves; they walked, as the crocodilians had walked in the early days of the earth, though some of those had leaped on two legs. 'Living fossils,' said Simon. 'A form of life that really flourished in another climate, and on the whole couldn't adapt. But again, the individual fate – the fate of the species, or of the individual creature – is different from what may seem laid down by general laws of change or fate. We don't know why almost all reptiles died. Nor do we know why these did not.'

The camera rested for a moment on a whole floating group of the animals, thick bodies floating indistinguishably together.

'Reptiles are fairly well classified,' said Simon. 'I spend time studying the water, too.'

He was shown, dipping jars, measuring, paddling a little farther along the creek, dipping, measuring. They saw his face, peering mournfully at them over the side of the boat, shadowed by beard-stubble, with the ungainly shoulders hunched behind it. He gave a snort of discomfort. Cassandra tied a knot in a gold chain. Julia said:

'Cassandra, who takes the photographs?'

'I have asked myself that.'

'I mean, it must be somebody bloody good with a camera. They don't seem to mention whoever it is. It's funny, now it's all presented as though there aren't any other *people* there, isn't it? I mean, most of these explorer bods have whole *teams* of bearded workers, don't they? And Indians, and chaps with bales on their heads.'

'Hudson,' said Cassandra. 'No camera. Whoever it is, it's good, I agree. So good – so fluid – it all seems unreal, somehow. I mean, unreal, because so much an image for man observing – his origins? His animal nature? The roots of life? I don't know what he thinks he's doing.'

'No, but it is all a bit self-conscious, Cass, you've hit it exactly. A bit *produced*. I mean, he's pretending to be a naked hermit, but we can all *see* it's been put together with fantastic skill for the telly – all those magnifications and things . . . I mean, it makes all the appeal he has somehow dishonest . . .'

'Has he appeal?' said Cassandra.

'Oh, *enormous*. He's a sort of popular symbol of what's got crowded out of our urban lives. In certain circles. A nature image in their very own drawing-rooms. He doen't go in much for fertility, unfortunately. He's got a vogue. Women think he wants cuddling and domesticating . . .'

'My undergraduates like him.'

'*Simon*,' said Julia, and laughed.

'I know.'

'That means – there is someone out there – to whom he talks . . . Someone whose idea all this is, perhaps. What does he do when the camera's off him?'

'Charm snakes,' said Cassandra. 'We shan't ever know.'

Simon said, 'Here is a magnification of the things in the kind of water I just bottled. The kind of activity outside our normal consciousness. Outside our sense of proportion. Like the speed of grass growing. Or the spread of cancer. Things we have to make an effort to be aware of.'

He peered at them for a moment almost crossly, as though troubled by his own natural inadequacy. A shot of the normal cloudiness of the glass beaker of water was followed by a microscopic expansion of it, a bursting open of vague specks into things alive, transparent, reticulated, shapeless, with waving tentacles and gaping mouths, which jumped and squirmed and floated and writhed across the scene. Something like a parasol, ribbed and frilled, ballooned gently down from the top right-hand corner to the opposite lower corner. Somewhere else a strange string of long beads broke apart and reformed. A flabby blob of jelly made itself a long mouth, ingested a black speck and closed over it, swelling slightly, whilst the scar of the mouth opening slowly disappeared. For a moment Simon lectured them on the alien movements of this unfamiliar life; what was known about the pattern of it, what was not. He told them some names, and pointed out with elation nameless scraps of life. 'No wonder we lose our sense of our own place,' he said, reappearing, and fading. 'We shall never know very much about all this: this is what draws us. As it should.'

A large white bird strode through the water, peering elegantly this way and that, leaving behind it a trail of wavering liquid arrows, that lost their directness in the weeds at the water's edge. Cassandra could almost feel the packed, silky texture of the feathers.

Julia said, 'Shall I turn it off?'

'Yes.'

'I can't *bear* the clergymen. Sorry, Cass – but I just can't.'

'You don't have to.'

'No. It's been a – a funny day. Do you think it was a good thing for us – playing – and so on?'

'We do the best we can,' said Cassandra, dubiously.

'Do we?'

'Apparently. I don't know what else we could have done.'

'I'm glad we –' Julia had been going to say 'talked' but they hadn't really. 'I enjoyed the Game. I hope . . . We can have a long talk tomorrow?'

'If you like. He must be waiting. Go to bed, Julia. I'll lock up.'

Julia thought of putting her hand out to Cassandra, but they had never touched each other. She said, 'Sleep well, Cass,' with warmth, and ran up the stairs. When she had gone, Cassandra rolled up the oilskin and packed away the pieces; when she had done this, she walked round the house, putting out lights, closing doors. In each dark corridor or room she listened for sounds, doing what she had to do with clumsy fingers. When finally she closed her own door, latch and bolt, she undressed without washing, slid into bed like a scared child, and held herself in a rigid ball, bony knees to chin, fists clenched. She was pleased with the effort she had made to walk about so calmly in the dark, but now she was paying. It was a long time before she went to sleep.

CHAPTER FIVE

Elizabeth Corbett would have chosen cremation, but this was out of the question since the snow was still deepening and the roads to the towns were blocked. Burial was delayed for some days by the hardness of the ground in the little orchard behind the Meeting-house, but Thor organized, shovelled, went down to the village, and finally something was done with a road-drill and picks. The post was erratic; distant members of the family could not gather; but in the end they found themselves following the coffin through elbow-high tunnels of scooped-out snow. No one particularly wore black. Cassandra was naturally sombre. Julia wore her scarlet and white, and looked, she thought, incongruously like Father Christmas where the snow had brushed against her. Mrs Corbett's square body was bundled into her usual square grey tweed coat. She was pinched round the mouth and had aged perceptibly, but seemed, like the rest of them, numbed, responding only to the cold. Deborah screwed graceless knuckles into red eyes. Thor said a few words, in a clear, hard voice, about the continuation of consciousness. 'He will live on, not only in the awareness of all of us – and countless others – which has been profoundly altered by our love for him, but in that larger consciousness which contains and transcends our individual love and knowledge. What was separate is restored to what is eternal, what was finite to what is infinite . . .' Julia thought, that has no meaning for me. But these generalities mean something to Thor; he experiences them, he finds his way round them. I only notice at times like this – death, meeting for worship – where his mind is.

She remembered her wedding in this Meeting-house; she and her father had stopped, on their way in, in the spring sun, under a cherry tree. She was twenty, and had wanted to be married in a long, white, sophisticated dress with yards of floating veil and an armful of flowers. Her mother had overruled her. 'I know these things are done, dear, but I always feel they are a little out of place in the simplicity of a Meeting-house, doesn't thou agree?' She had worn short white muslin with a sash, a round collar and a row of pearl buttons, a white hat like a Quaker bonnet and a posy of rosebuds and forget-me-nots. She looked more like a first communicant than a bride, which irked her, for she had meant Cassandra, a reluctant bridesmaid stumping along behind in grey poplin and a kind of glorified boater, to see that she had achieved womanhood first. Her father had said, 'He has a special love for thee, Julia. And we love him. Thou has known him only two months, and thou art very young. But he is a good man.' 'Yes,' she had said, 'I know. There are some things, if you don't find out in two months, you never find out. If you're willing to find them out.' Well, it had been something to say. He had kissed her, and reiterated his assurance that Thor loved her, and they had gone in.

Now, here was Thor, speaking at his funeral. His love for Thor had been deliberately given but at least he had never been given occasion to decide not to retract it. Thor had been all that a son should be. He had been moved by the spirit to claim his wife abruptly and dramatically. 'In the fear of the Lord and in the presence of this assembly, I take this my friend, Julia Corbett, to be my wife . . .' He had startled her; she had thrust her flowers at Cassandra, who had fumbled with them. She had caught Cassandra's hard grey eye. And thought, because she was willing herself not to, of Simon, sitting on the edge of his bed in that bare boy's bedroom he had with a crucifix over the bed, a marble madonna smirking on the mantelpiece, the occasional dry slither and rustle of a snake in a cardboard box under the bed.

We ought to do things properly. She wished Deborah would stop sniffing. It was too cold to cry. It was too cold to feel; she was glad when they all trooped home again, together with one or two worthy Friends who had struggled through the snow to be present. They ate tomato soup, roast lamb with mint sauce, apple pie. Elsie had been moved to prepare Jonathan Corbett's favourite meal; this, at last, Julia found concrete and distressing.

The next day the letters came through. There was a large sheaf of condolences from friends and relations for Mrs Corbett, two or three for Julia, one for Cassandra, and several business-like long envelopes for Thor. Julia had one from Ivan; the cramped, square handwriting stirred her to sudden excitement.

'Darling Julia, yours was a lovely letter, if a bit gloomy, tho' of course that's understandable. I'm sorry about your Dad, love; he was an admirable man, from all I've heard.

'As for the rest of your letter, you do let things get you down, don't you? And make an awful fuss about personal relations and such like which it's much better to take with a bit of gay abandon as they come. All this about this sister you never see, and all these ominous murmurings about guilt. As anyone can see from your lovely books, my dearest girl, you're a brooder, but you will positively *wear yourself out* if you take everything with this personal intensity, *really*. Try a bit of deliberate and *conscious* selfishness for a change. You're an artist of sorts after all and artists have got to be detached and ruthless. And better if they admit it sincerely? When I get you on The Programme you are going to be splendidly sincere with your disturbing, diffident, bloody-minded straight-look-in-the-eye about *just what ruthlessness* is required to turn your life into a commodity so saleable and comforting. So be warned. And don't try to be a sensitive plant. You've got a tough hide, sweetie, cultivate it, it's an asset and there's nothing wrong with it.

'I don't understand your obscure references to Simon Moffitt. Apparently teenage girls keep sending him understanding letters. I've not met him, but he seems a bit broody too, and not madly your sort of thing, love? though there's no accounting for tastes. A bit obvious, S. Moffitt. But then, so are you, and it has its attractions.

'You had better come home as soon as maybe and enjoy yourself a bit. Take care of yourself. I've got lots to tell you, as you may imagine . . .'

Cassandra's letter was from Gerald Rowell.

'My dear Cassandra, I was very touched that you should write to me so unexpectedly, and I was naturally distressed to hear of the death of your father. His work will be always remembered, and he himself will be remembered as a truly good man, and, in the deepest sense, a true Christian. I cannot believe that he did not die in peace, and better prepared to meet his Maker than most of us.

'I am distressed that you should reproach yourself for your feelings. As I have had occasion to suggest to you before, you are too scrupulous and expect too much of yourself. You loved your father, and you love him now. A momentary revulsion is of little account beside a lifetime of love. A horror of dissolution, please believe me, is more commonplace than you suppose, and not usually of long endurance. You must offer your weakness to God, who is Infinite Charity, and rest in Him. You have also a duty to your mother, who will be in need of your comfort and support. As I have also said before, you must make your peace with yourself. I am sure you will find your way to it.

'You are missed here; many of the ladies have asked me to convey their sympathy; also the Dean. I have prayed for you and for your family. Yours ever, Gerald Rowell.'

Julia thought: I asked for sympathy and what I get is flirtatious malice. But she smiled to herself, and felt lightened at the thought of being back with people like Ivan, who took life with a bit of irony, liked people vulgar, self-centred and malicious, didn't expect, or want, anyone to be perfect. Unlike the Quakers and Cassandra. The Quakers, if not Cassandra, would have denied indignantly that they expected people to be perfect. But they simply tolerated things that Ivan positively admired. Whereas Cassandra tolerated nothing and admired very little. Ivan had not understood her claustrophobia; she would have to explain it again. She was amused but worried by his description of her probable TV personality; she was uncomfortably sure that she could achieve what he wanted. She began to read the letter again.

Cassandra regarded her letter with slight distaste. It was a distaste already familiar, from moments of communication with Edwin Merton or with Simon himself. It seemed to her that she was capable of only two kinds of approach to men: a constrained dignity, and an overwrought and vague appeal for help of some kind. And her undignified outbursts produced, invariably, from those to whom she exposed herself a defensive professional reaction. I am not a woman, she thought sharply, her intelligence restored by a renewed sense of her own isolation, to be comforted in that tone of voice. But I am afraid I may write letters that ask for replies in that tone of voice. I certainly did to Simon.

She did not like Gerald Rowell's facile assumptions that she 'loved' her father and was in a position to 'comfort and support' her mother. She had embarrassed him, of course, and he had retreated into the conventions. However silly her letter, she was right to feel disappointed. He could, and should, have written more warmly. He should have preserved her from the consequences of her own unbalance. When Cassandra was troubled she retreated into a series of remote judgements as though she herself was completely uninvolved. Father Rowell had been a hope; he had proved to be of no significance. It was safer that way, she thought grimly.

Thor said, 'They write to ask me to go to the Congo, to run a relief centre near Elizabethville.'

Cassandra folded her letter back into its envelope and observed him with an abstract interest. He looked alert; his voice was carefully casual. He waited. Cassandra looked at Julia, who looked at her plate.

'When?' said Deborah. Cassandra, observing her in her turn, remarked a certain eagerness.

'What do they want with thee, dear?' said Elizabeth Corbett, stirring from the ruined silence in which she was now usually sunk.

'They want the impossible, of course.' He was smiling slightly. 'Management of funds. Administration. Transport, food, drugs. Liaison work. Keeping the peace between charitable bodies. Everything.'

'When?' said Deborah again. She, and Cassandra, looked at Julia, who said, with apparent reluctance, 'How long do they want you for?'

'Indefinitely. As far as these things are certain, indefinitely. It has to be long-term, they need continuity. It means living there.'

'We could all go,' said Deborah. Julia said hastily, 'Don't be silly, Deb, it's out of the question. What about your education? Or mother, now?'

'Thou need not bother about me, dear. I don't mean to be idle.'

Cassandra thought Julia could well have done without this unconsidered piece of support. It was clear what Julia felt; what he, Thor, felt was less certain. There was silence. Deborah spoke.

'It wouldn't be that bad for my education. It'd be a new experience. A different kind of life.'

'I wish you wouldn't talk about things you don't understand. You don't know what's going on out there. Rape and murder and all sorts of violence. They've been evacuating women and children. I can't see what Friends are thinking of to offer a thing like that to a man with Thor's responsibilities. It's absurd. They can't have spent any time . . .'

'They spend some,' said Thor. He folded and unfolded his letter, with an expression Cassandra recognized as one familiar in her own research students, when presented with a piece of evidence that seriously damaged an argument they were nevertheless not prepared to abandon.

Deborah said, '*Some* people go, all the same. Some missionaries, that sort of person. Somebody's got to. It'd be good for you, Julia, you could write completely different books.'

'Don't be stupid. Nobody wants any more unsubtle books about race-relations. Or spiritual allegories about jungle warfare. Golding and Bellow worked those out. And anyway I couldn't do them. I've got to have civilization and social nuances. It'd be the death of me.'

Like most serious statements disguised as flippancy this simply produced tension. Deborah shrugged her shoulders. She knows when to stop, Cassandra thought, herself an expert at provoking Julia. Although perhaps Deborah, like herself, always lost in the end; Julia was easily embarrassed but very determined. Cassandra looked severely at her niece, who disconcertingly winked.

'Thor,' Julia cried, 'it is silly of them, isn't it, just to spring this on a man in your position? I mean, they could have discussed it with you, at least. They could have –'

'They did discuss it with me,' he said, slowly. 'There is real need. Real need. Someone must go. Something must be done. And there are things that can be done –'

'But not by you. Not by a man in your position. They can't expect it.'

He stood up. 'Apparently not.' He repeated coldly. 'Not by a man in my position, clearly.'

'Thor – if you really *want* . . . If you've really told Friends . . .'

'There is no point in discussing it,' he said, and walked out. Julia looked from one to the other of the three women. She was the only one wearing make-up; her face seemed too bright, exaggerated, against Cassandra's pale skull-face with its dry lips, her mother's grey, slightly puffy skin, and Deborah's chalk and freckles. She was grieved and belligerent.

'All the same, I'm right,' she said. 'I can't see why everyone has to get at me just because I say something's impossible that clearly isn't anything *but* impossible. Well, is it? None of you ever face facts.'

Nobody answered.

'I suppose you all think I ought just to pack up and follow him to the Congo?'

'Well, dear . . .' her mother began.

'You think I ought to let him do what he wants? Well, if everyone would leave me alone, and he was sure what he *did* want, I'd be happy too.'

'As long as he wanted the right thing,' said Deborah.

'Shut up, you,' Julia cried. 'You're just meddling. Oh what's the use, what's the use? You all just side against me. You think my work's completely worthless.' She glared at Cassandra. 'All your feelings are so refined.'

'He feels guilty, Julia,' her mother offered. 'He wants to be able to help.'

'And what do you think he makes *me* feel? He won't let me help with anything. It's not so easy, living with someone perfect.'

'Well, he won't go, because you don't want him to, and you *know* that,' said Deborah, 'so let's stop this discussion.'

Julia burst into tears and ran out of the room.

'That,' said Deborah, 'will be a hundred guineas from the New Yorker when it's written up. She always writes up rows.'

'Deborah!' said Cassandra.

'That was not a row, dear,' said Mrs Corbett, reprovingly. Cassandra thought, she always slides away from any mention of real antagonism; she always did. She asked Deborah, 'Would you like to go to the Congo, then?'

'No. I should loathe it. But someone ought to see how much he wants . . . how much he needs . . .' She stared at Cassandra with an undisguised appeal. 'I do see things,' she said meaningfully.

'I'm sure you do,' said Cassandra, and met her look squarely and without smiling.

Julia went up to their bedroom. Thor was not there. She walked up and down, looking into the mirror and out of the window at the snow. She wondered if she ought to go after him; but she was, in a way, afraid to. Since they had been closed up all day together, always falling over each other, she had begun to notice several things. He showed what she considered a disturbing tendency to humour her, take burdens for her, treat her as though she was not quite responsible. As though, she thought, he had some time ago decided, without her noticing it, to stop taking her seriously.

When they had married it had been understood that Thor was waiting for her to grow up, forget and settle. He had, in a sense, 'taken her on' as a problem; it was a relationship that suited them both peculiarly well. He had been staying in the house in the hot summer of 1947, breaking a pilgrimage across the north of England to Pendle Hill, where George Fox, that irate and driven man, had had his vision. But he had never got there, on that occasion. He had taken Julia for walks, and she had told him, in a confidential outburst, all the trouble with Simon and Cassandra. She was hysterical; she had been needing someone to tell for nearly a year, and had rehearsed to herself explanations of her own conduct until she was silly. She had told two young farmers and a journalist on the local paper for which she worked but none of these had treated the problem with the proper gravity. Julia always told everyone everything, holding nothing back on the principle that however much one tells there will always remain some ultimate mystery that cannot be imparted anyway, and thus privacy cannot finally be betrayed.

'I know *you* will understand,' she had cried, undaunted and hopeful, to the serious Scandinavian; many people would not have risked it. She knew whilst she told him that he was not a man in whom people naturally confided, and that he wanted desperately to be. He was both too formidable and too apparently simple, like most men professionally concerned with goodness. He was flattered and moved that she should speak to him with such intimacy, without premeditation. And she was flattered and moved that he should allow her to impinge on his withdrawn austerity, to shake his dignity. He was a man with real purposes, about which he was reticent, an adult; he had none of her own confessional sloppiness as Simon, disconcertingly, had. But she suspected him, at first, of a respectable innocence, born of ignorance; she did not decide to marry him until the night he appeared, silent and unexpected, in her bedroom, his face desperate, green and white striped pyjamas hanging in folds about his body, long, pale, bare feet protruding under them.

This episode had seemed to her a guarantee that he was neither simply respectable, nor innocent; it was an explosion of secret violence within the peaceful order of her parents' house; the silly, respectable look of the pyjamas, the familiarity of her own room, wooden floor, circular pegged rug, tall wooden bed, only emphasized what she found decisively romantic about it.

And so she had come to be married, and wondered sometimes, vaguely, whether she had been silly to rush into it so young and ignorant. Deborah had been born unexpectedly just under a year later; suddenly, with no breathing-space, there had been too much responsibility, too little sleep, no privacy, no time to talk. Both of them tried; Thor worked hard with the baby, Julia complained as little as possible. But she had had what amounted to a nervous breakdown, a year later. Deborah had come to the Old House, Julia had written her first novel during convalescence; surprisingly, it was accepted. Julia was insanely happy, Deborah came home; they juggled with charity, writing, pot-training, telephone calls, teeth, tight schedules, occasional conversation. It was still *mutatis mutandis*, like that.

Julia did not really think she could have done much better; she was sane, and productive; she owed this to Thor. She was anxious to do things for him – she wanted to believe she would do everything for him – everything, that was, that she could rely on herself realistically to carry out. We must know our own limitations: this was a theme she often wrote on. Julia was very well acquainted with her own limitations. She wished, now, she dared go and look for him – but what was there, on this topic, to say to him? She took out Ivan's letter and re-read it. Then she re-read it again.

At this point Thor came into the room carrying a sheaf of letters and a typewriter. He intended, clearly, to deal with her mother's correspondence; she might have done that herself. If he had not been there first to do it.

'What are you doing, Julia?'

'Reading a letter. From Ivan.' Julia always told him the truth; this was a point of honour.

'You write a great many letters.'

'I know, it's a nuisance. If we could only get out of this place . . .'

'I don't think we should speak like that.'

'No, I'm sorry.' She paused. 'I get a bit worried about the programme.'

'When that was first suggested, I remember you did not want to take part.'

'Yes,' said Julia, not sure what the issue was. 'Yes, I know. But when I do take anything on, I like to do it thoroughly. It's my conscience.' She smiled, faintly.

'Conscience!' cried Thor. He struck the desk violently with a heavy fist, rattling the typewriter keys. 'Conscience! Oh, for Christ's sake, Julia . . .'

He swore very rarely. Julia jumped at the noise and trembled. Then he was silent: one of the things about him for which Julia had initially been grateful and which she now found unnerving was his capacity to swallow abruptly any momentary anger.

'Thor,' she said, 'I'm sorry I was stupid. I mean, I didn't realize, I just didn't realize how seriously you . . . Look, darling, if you really want to go, that makes it different. If it's something *you* really *want*, then I – I really don't mean to stand in your way. I didn't know you'd talked to Friends . . .' She swallowed nervously, believing herself partially. His face tightened.

'What I want? You see it as a question of what I want? You are probably right.'

'I want you to be happy.'

'Oh,' he said, 'happy.' He sat down on the bed. 'Julia, I need help. I should have talked to you earlier. I keep things too much to myself. I know it's a fault. I – I feel a need, and a duty, I don't know – to use myself. To do something fully. Can you understand? To expend all my – my power. Julia? The world is so full of – of heavy tasks to which one man's energy would make some difference. And we leave them undone. I feel often I have failed. Sometimes I feel I shall go mad. I – I have always seen – heroism – as something the situation – a situation – called up. Seeking it out can be wrong. I've thought of that. It could come from a childish desire to assert oneself. Or a need for glamour. Or a childish need to shake off restrictions. Morality – means recognizing restrictions. One must live within the duties one acquires, I know. I know I have responsibilities which make violent action impossible. It may be that God does not intend me to live violently. I have to see that I am not called. I do see that I am not called. But, Julia, it beats in my head. It is not admirable. But –'

He stared out of the window with an expression Julia found unnerving. She thought: how the religious man is separated for ever from the irreligious because there is a whole set of moral problems created for him by the assumption that there is a God whose meaningful intention placed him where he is.

'It frightens me that you feel me and Deborah as a restriction. I didn't know you felt that.'

'You feel me and Deborah as a restriction. You write it.'

'Oh, darling, yes. But I'm a woman, and women are restricted. Men have so many choices. Almost any – except this dangerous kind. And my books do try to say we must accept things, I hope, they do come down to acceptance. Love is a prison, it's unrealistic to suppose it's not. Everybody's possibilities solidify round them and become limitations. It's common.'

'Acceptance? Sometimes I think we pride ourselves too much on that. Psychologists have taught it to us. With their "normals" and so on. Their "adjustment". Oh, never mind. Never mind.'

'Thor, if you really want to go out there . . .'

'No, I shan't go. You know I won't go. What would Deborah do?' Suddenly, without warning, his anger flared. 'How could I leave Deborah to you?'

'Thor!'

'I'm sorry. You should learn to be honest. You cannot tell me you will come if I want it and then tell me I have all sorts of choices but this. It has not entered your head to come. Probably it should not. It doesn't matter. Let it go.'

'Oh, God, I feel wicked.'

'You must not feel wicked. Because you are right. So there is no need.'

Momentarily, he buried his face in his hands. Julia was ashamed to have been caught out manipulating the argument, and was keenly aware of the disproportion between the relief of the starving and a television parlour-game. But there was nothing to do, and she wished miserably that he would go away. After a few moments' silence he stood up and went to the door.

'You know, you can be just as much use, over here,' she said timidly; on this he got out, silently and fast, pulling the door sharply behind him.

Oh, Christ, Julia thought, how horrible I am. She was always capable, after the event, of seeing what she had done with some clarity and not too much evasion. She admired herself for this, and felt her lack of self-deceit as a strength in reserve.

On this occasion she was disturbed and pleased to note that she felt strongly that at all costs she must not go away from Ivan. Her life consisted of a series of passionate encounters with, and evasions of, a series of potential perfect friends. She had only once been unfaithful to Thor, some years earlier, because the situation as she saw it seemed absolutely to demand it, and Julia always submitted unquestioningly to the beauty of a situation. It was true that she had taken care, in an elaborately unconscious way, that the situation should not be repeated. But she alternated, normally, between an over-excited readiness to fall slightly in love and a weary scrambling out of the complications resulting from that last love into which she had fallen. She thought fleetingly of Simon, who was different, and began a letter.

'Dearest Ivan, it is getting intolerable to be snowed up here for so long. You can't possibly believe how primitive things get in a place where supplies of coal and milk, even, things one thinks one has a right to, become blocked. You know, this house has always been a bit like that. A great air of normality, but it doesn't quite run. Supplies of things I think are essential are blocked, and one has to exist on resources one finds one hasn't after all got. My sister Cassandra lives naturally at that level – she's appallingly self-contained, she's a genuine brooder, unlike me, I hope, whatever you say. At the moment I die for a good joke, a real bawdy companionable joke. Even after a funeral. Thor thinks I take to jokes as other people take to drugs, but I can't be any different, I need a good belly-laugh to remind me I'm human. I miss nice fallible human beings like you, dreadfully. Oh, why are you not here?'

She stopped, and crossed out that sentence. She began again 'Rather a row has arisen, which it may amuse you to read about, since I have, as usual, Behaved Badly . . .'

CHAPTER SIX

Cassandra climbed up to her bedroom; as she went past Julia's door she heard raised voices. She closed herself in and turned up the window-seat. She was reading, in the spare hours, with a kind of illicit excitement, all the past volumes of her journal, and the other manuscripts – exercise books of blank verse and heroic dialogue, notes for an unwritten epic. There were wads of it, limp and compressed now, so prodigal of energy then. We were fearfully articulate, she thought. When she started reading, she noticed with detachment the rawness of the feeling; after half an hour she was invariably absorbed.

Someone knocked. Cassandra jumped as though caught out in an indecency, pushed the papers together and called, 'Come in.'

Deborah closed herself in almost conspiratorially, and looked down on her aunt. Cassandra stood up. 'Yes?' she said.

Deborah walked over, closed the window-seat, climbed up on it and looked out. This air of taking possession irritated Cassandra, who was reminded of the times when she had found Julia seated there, reading her books with apparent composure, flushing and laughing when told to get out.

'What do you want?' she said crossly, somewhere between her angry adolescent self and the minatory don she had become.

'I wanted to talk to you. But not if you're busy.'

'What did you want to talk about?'

'Oh, as for that . . . I hoped it might develop . . . I don't like Julia crying.'

'She always has,' said Cassandra, before she could stop herself. 'Do you always call your mother by her Christian name?'

'She says the thought of being called Mummy made her feel sick.' She looked out of the window. She wore a mustard coloured polo-necked sweater, a pleated navy skirt, and thick tartan stockings which Cassandra thought ugly. She said, 'Have a cigarette?'

Deborah slewed round. 'Thanks. I don't – I don't smoke. But I'd like one.'

Cassandra tossed her the cigarette packet and the matchbox; Deborah clumsily lit and sucked.

'I've always had a sort of picture of you as the person I could talk to.'

Cassandra thought. 'I see that. But I think you're probably wrong.'

Deborah sighed. 'I can't cope with this family.' She tapped non-existent ash off the end of her cigarette. 'I certainly can't cope with Julia crying.'

'Do you have to cope?'

'She likes moral support. I always end up comforting her. That's the funny thing. Once I was invited to stay with a girl from school – something that doesn't happen to *me* often, I may say, and she rang up the second day and said would I come back, we didn't see enough of each other, she said she thought we ought to be together. That was the time they said *The Silver Swan* sounded one plaintive note of self-pity all the time. So I went home and told her that there comes a time in every writer's life when the critics think they're important enough to slate –' She looked at the floor and twisted her hands. 'But she doesn't *like* me,' she said.

'No, she specially doesn't. It's partly this thing – why she's crying now. I – I wish she didn't always write books about how we – Father and I – how we diminish her, stop her living . . . I don't want to stop her living. I want to live myself. But she – but she – You know what she's like, you might understand.'

'We all diminish each other. We all impinge on each other. It's natural.'

'And I remind her of you,' said Deborah. 'I can't help that. She's always telling him – writing letters to people – She doesn't let me exist. I thought – *you* might see I existed. I've been thinking, if I met you, properly –'

It was all clearly so well thought out. Cassandra shivered slightly. She said, 'You don't know me. One should never exercise one's imagination on people one doesn't know. It's a kind of theft. Savages believe photographs are a theft. So are expectations. What can I do?'

This puzzled Deborah, who wrinkled her face, and returned to the attack.

'She steals, too. She says I never tell her anything, and when I do, she puts it in books. And gives me copies. So that my thoughts aren't mine. Look – Once – once I told . . . Once one of the mistresses at school wrote her a letter saying she ought to respect my confidences. That I was an unduly secretive child.' She laughed. 'So Julia showed me the letter, and burst into tears, and I had to comfort her about that. I had to tell her it was all silly and I knew a book was a book, and life was life . . . and I didn't mind . . .'

'What do you want me to say? Of course your confidences should be respected.'

'Of course.' Deborah's assurance was suddenly shaken. She said uncertainly, 'Of course they're very good books. I know they're very good books. I know Julia's a creative writer. A person has to write what they know . . .'

'I think that no one has any necessary right to publish what they know – however good it may be for them to write it. Or even if what they have written is very good. That a piece of writing is good doesn't override other considerations – moral considerations – when it comes to damaging others. That's an absurd overvaluation of the printed word.

'And as a Christian I mistrust your use of the word "creative". Only God creates. Our works are imaginative, at the highest. If we *imagine* our experience we transmute it – rearrange it, meditate on it, light it differently, change it, relate it to the rest of the world. Stories in themselves have no necessary imaginative value. They may be simply therapeutic for the author. They may be positively dangerous – not a lighting up of facts but a refusal to face facts, a distortion. This always happens, not usually to a harmful degree. But the imagination can be violently dangerous. Not enough – mere recording – is valueless. Too much is an evasion of truth. I know this.'

Deborah appeared very puzzled by this speech, which was delivered in a harsh, lecturing voice. Cassandra turned the garnet on her finger. 'Even in my work – the discovery of facts isn't enough. One has to imagine them – think about them, light them up – and one inevitably intrudes one's own personality. Ideally, one should not. Facts should speak for themselves. But they never do.'

'I like your work. I want to do that sort of thing. Something objective and private. I want to be a historian. To go to Oxford.' She looked at her aunt. 'I was going to write to you about it. For advice.' She bowed her head. Cassandra was touched, but cautious. She thought Deborah had her own infinite capacity for bearing grudges, and that likeness of temperament was no necessary basis for close relationships; at the same time she was able to recognize the appeal here.

'Anything I can do to help, I will.'

'If I could just write, now and then.'

'Naturally.'

They were silent. Deborah went on looking out of the window.

'That you can just see out there – that's Simon Moffitt's house, isn't it?'

'He's in South America.'

'Yes, but that's his *house*, isn't it? I know a lot about him. Julia talks a lot about him, to Father . . . She . . .'

Cassandra winced. 'You'll do no good by asking too many questions.'

'Oh, in our house, you get told,' Deborah slid off the window-seat. 'Like a myth, your childhood. I've envied you, you seem to have had so much –' She said, 'Look, you don't seem to see, I can't tell you – I feel I know you, and that you're the one who *knows* –'

'What about your father?'

'Oh, he cares . . . All this is bad for him. Don't you think? I'd be worried for him if it wasn't an insult. But he's not quite there. What he wants, what he really wants, is to give out bowls of milk and penicillin.'

And that, too, I know about, Cassandra thought. She felt Deborah's interest as a temptation; she had already made one uncharacteristic gesture towards her, in offering the cigarette. Here was someone to whom what she knew was relevant and useful. Someone who could learn from her. They looked at each other with a similar wariness; Deborah grinned.

'I only want someone to talk to.'

'Well,' said Cassandra, 'there's no harm in talk. If you find it necessary.'

'I wouldn't persecute you.'

Cassandra smiled. Deborah made her feel, briefly, human; an object neither of fear, nor patronage. Though this was not without its frightening side. And Julia's daughter was the last child to whom she could play imaginary mother.

'And now, if you've nothing else to say, perhaps I could get on . . . Come back, when you like.'

Deborah left immediately, with a cool, leisurely, and slightly mocking look over what Cassandra was 'getting on' with.

Cassandra went on leafing through the papers, then she climbed into the window-seat and stared, not for the first time, across the snowy hills at the chimneys of the Moffitts' house: the Castle, the Joyous Garde. Deborah's speculation seemed to solidify, in time, events she thought were significant now only in her own head. This question of theft. And the related question of Simon Moffitt.

She remembered Julia's first published work. She had been eighteen, going up to Oxford; Julia had been sixteen. She had come running from the post, like a character, Cassandra thought, from *Little Women*, crying, 'Look, look what I've done.' They had all looked. It was a serious children's magazine, printed on utility paper, and Julia had it open where it said 'Winner of our 1943 Short Story competition. *Vigil in the Forest*, by Julia Corbett, of Benstone, Northumberland.' Julia had her mouth closed on an uncontrollable smile. Their father gave her one of his rare, smacking kisses, and Cassandra knew immediately what had happened. She thought she had always known it would happen, and had pushed it out of her mind.

She had in the window-seat several versions of the same story. It had been a central episode in the myth from the early days; it concerned Sir Lancelot, benighted in the forest, and bludgeoned into temptation by four queens. 'For hit behovyth the now to chose one of us four, for I am quene Morgan le Fay, quene of the londe of Gore, and here is the quene of North Galys, and the quene of Estlonde, and the quene of the Oute Iles. Now chose one of us, whyche that thow wolte have to thy peramour, other ellys to dye in this preson.' 'This is a harde case,' seyde Sir Lancelot, 'that other I muste dye, other to chose one of you . . . Yea, on my lyff,' seyde Sir Lancelot, 'refused ye bene of me.'

This episode had been cast, and re-cast; the issue had been in doubt more ways than one. Besides Cassandra's highly complicated and privately violent version of it, which she had not written down, there were several public chronicles of paths taken and escapes made and an adaptation she had made at fifteen, for a school exercise entitled 'A Walk in the Woods'. On this the English mistress had written, 'This is not quite what I intended. Although your vocabulary is good and you express yourself well you must learn to curb the more lurid flights of your imagination and write with more discipline to be really effective.' From this version, a study in benighted fear, the predatory queens excised, had grown Cassandra's own tentative attempt at a public story. And it was an adaptation of this which Julia had successfully submitted to the competition.

Cassandra had felt outrage. She could not accuse Julia of simple theft – the story was, or had been, common property. And Julia's story, although it abounded in similarities of phrasing and passages of description, was in many ways better than her own lumpy version: it was more controlled, and had an element of amused irony that was intensified by the drawings – rather *art nouveau* – which accompanied it.

But she felt that the imagined world had been violated; that exposure had rendered it lifeless. The long partnership came to an end; there was no more Game; and Cassandra herself was for many months unable to write. The essence of the Game was privacy; privacy could only be preserved by absolute silence. But more deeply, she was in some way prohibited – outside the Journal – from putting pen to paper.

She punished Julia by silence. Cassandra was, and always had been, an artist in not being on speaking terms; and Julia was an ideal victim. Over the years Cassandra the tyrant had laid down rules about this as about everything else. In childhood they had gone out to play, apparently together, separated at the gate and not met until lunch-time. Julia was trained to recognize which remarks, addressed to her over meals, were simple face-savers, before family, and which were genuine overtures. She was always wounded; she never learned; she would always, this time as every other approach hopefully and far too early, be snubbed, and not only be snubbed, but mind. This time she tried independence and wrote another story, which was rejected by the magazine; she could not keep up the Game alone, and had little else to do; she suffered a wild and aimless despair.

Cassandra too, despaired: for the second time in her life she experienced paralysing, irrational, overwhelming fear. The first time this had happened had been when she was sent away to school, a colourless eleven years old in liberty bodice, wrinkled lisle stockings, and a tunic bought prudently one size too large. The other girls were enemies, the building menacing, objects threatening: the notice-board with dangerous pins, the gallows-like wooden swing, the horn spoons with which they ate their Sunday eggs. She wept all night, and then the weeping spilled over into the day; she sat on benches, immobile, with a wet face, and grew thinner. The terror wore off gradually; when Julia arrived, the next year, the two of them pursued their private life in breaks and in the evening. Cassandra's work improved, and she showed to other girls, at last, the same condescending helpfulness with prep that she gave to Julia.

In the autumn of 1943, when she went to Oxford, the terror returned. For the whole summer she had not spoken to Julia. In Oxford, she approached people with mistrust, expected to be disliked, and burst out occasionally with authoritative and grating literary pronouncements. She ate alone, went to lectures alone, observed with fear the cracks in her window, the scratching of other people's pens in lectures. She attended lectures obsessively; attempting to find out about Malory, she found herself being enlightened about the Cloud of Unknowing, the Ancrene Riwle, and Dame Julian. Unknowing was what she craved, and religion seemed harder, more inevitable and more reliable than the Game. She attended evensong in Magdalen Chapel, lost herself in the smell of candles and the boys' voices, went back to Benstone at Christmas drunk with despair and carols, and invaded the study of her parents' friend Edwin Merton with a desperate and lengthy confession of abstract fear and sense of meaninglessness. Merton did his embarrassed best. He also introduced Cassandra to Simon Moffitt. Simon was desperate too; he and Cassandra met, and talked, several times, at first unintentionally and then deliberately. Simon had more concrete cause for despair, and had made, apparently, more spiritual progress. He was intending to be ordained.

Simon had already some of the glamour of the imaginary world; indeed, she had incorporated into it some of his violent family history.

He belonged to an old Northumberland family, remarkable for persistent Catholicism under persecution and for little else – there had been a Robert Moffitt whose two-volume *Flora and Fauna of Northumberland* had been illustrated by Bewick, and now Simon. The Moffitts kept themselves to themselves. A year earlier, Simon's father, who had fought in the First World War, and worked for the Government in this, had come home on leave and shot himself. Simon's mother had married an army officer, considerably younger than herself, immediately. This was all Cassandra knew – she did not attract village gossip herself, and remained largely unaware of it.

The lanky, lugubrious boy, with his distant courtesy, and his clear first-hand knowledge of her misery proved a better confidant than the weary vicar. She had been ready either to fall in love, or to undergo a religious upheaval, and for some months she juggled with the two fairly successfully. The relationship depended upon her producing and discussing despair of one kind; loving Simon produced despair of another, which in turn made the religious refuge necessary. She never knew whether Simon liked her or not; she suspected that their walks and picnics were due to a mixture of a need for an audience and an unflattering desire, on his part, to exercise a newly-discovered and indifferent Christian charity. She was his first clumsy experiment in pastoral care. She was content to be so – she needed a great deal of time to change herself before she was capable of anything else. She was shrewd enough to see that he, too, was not at ease in the world of ascesis and self-denial they spent their time talking about; his self-effacement was a little strained, his security too hardly achieved. She offered him, however, respect on trust, and argued passionately every inch of the way; at no point on her long journey into the Church was she more apparently, even angrily, agnostic. What she dreamed of was her business. She was skilled with dreams. She wrote to him throughout the term, and at Easter they met again.

Cassandra's Journal. Easter 1944.

Today he showed me the snakes. I hoped he might, as I imagine he would not show them to most people. He says he has 'for some reason' always kept them a secret. So I was very flattered, but could not comment as intelligently or enthusiastically as I would have liked to. I hoped to feel we were sharing something, but he was a bit schoolmasterish – more letting me be there than wanting me. I refine too much on what he says. I said, 'Is there anything I can do?' He said, 'Just sit there and keep me company.' I was absurdly pleased by this. (Must watch myself, no lies, no lies.) One must never ask for more than is offered – not out of virtue, but because if one does one loses what one has.

Snakes are strange things. Not evil-looking, as I had supposed, not anything much, just little heaps like coils of rope or something one might have dropped. He keeps them hidden in this cave. In glass tanks. He has earth on the bottom, and odd stones, and dishes of water for them to swim in. None were swimming. I would make it all look much better, but he clearly doesn't care how it looks. There is water running down the back wall; the stone is stained, silver and gold and olive; there are minute ferns growing in crevices. One could perhaps grow ferns all round, put in a few shelves.

It is strange to me to think anyone could love those snakes – stranger than before I saw them – but in some way he clearly does. He has ten grass-snakes, three smooth-snakes and two adders he caught in the heather. He has a collection of skins, wrapped in oilskin, in a metal box, and a book full of observations. There are no thoughts, only notes on how they excrete, how and when they cast their skins, how they swallow, how long they go without food, what they will and won't eat. They have no names, although he knows them all apart. He told me they were beautiful, which I suppose is a kind of thought. I expected to find them beautiful myself – I am the sort of person you would think would – but I didn't. There was a dryness and nothingness about them. I was somehow surprised they were alive. They were *nothing*, really, just accidental tubular shapes of things. He says spring is late so they are torpid; they are inert, as though the step from life to death was insignificant to them. Snakes have no lids to their eyes, and so look plainly out at you; this makes them seem not so much fascinating as stupid.

I like watching him watch them. One of the things about knowing him is the excitement of mapping out all the directions in which there are things to learn I shall never know more of than that they are there. (Prose!!) I really don't want to know more than he voluntarily tells me, partly because I am shy. I stand around in a waiting silence much of the time but he doesn't seem to mind too much. I hope my waiting doesn't oppress him. God knows I don't mean it to. He said last week I was censorious, but oh, Simon, not with you, ever.

We had for lunch spam, tomatoes from his greenhouse, half a hard-boiled egg each and an apple.

We had another argument about the Incarnation. I was trying to say I didn't see it was *necessary* for Christ to have been God or to have died. It seems to have made, proportionately to what is claimed for it, so little difference – historically, that is – it hasn't changed war or murder or cruelty, *most people* still know nothing about it. I said I didn't want God to have been made flesh, as far as I was concerned if there was any point in the idea of God it was precisely that He was *not* flesh, He was something else, something other. He said might we not then feel God was inaccessible, and I said that individually, for myself, that was how I did feel. I see the flaw in my argument here.

He said, surely I saw something was wrong with the world – 'Something horribly twisted' was how he put it. He said some twisting back on a really grand scale was needed, some 're-wrenching', not done by us, to counteract this.

I said, something was certainly horribly wrong, but it seemed to me like that it had *always been* wrong and had not at one point in time 'gone wrong'. I said we have no right to think this re-wrenching actually took place just because we think it ought to have. He said the point about the Crucifixion was that it was the moment when the eternal was involved in history thus its effects were eternal (we are now for ever able to be saved) and historical (it has to be worked out). I said this was too metaphorical. I was angry because he didn't see that if the 'going wrong' wasn't historical, the atonement needn't be. He was angry with me; he wants me to believe.

I told him that what I found saving was the order and structure one could see in things, smooth-running, meaningful. The growth of plants, the circulation of the blood, networks of working muscles, veins on leaves, movements of planets and shoals of fish. A harmony one could see. This is what we are for, to pay attention to this beautiful network of designed movement that we and our tragedies are held in. He said that suffering and sin were rents in this network, and that Christ was a guarantee that they could be mended, the fabric could be restored. I said I thought the need for Christ was a need to simplify, to reduce to terms of human suffering something that is neutral, not loving, inhuman, not human.

We were angry with each other. I wish I didn't have to win arguments, especially with him. It doesn't do me much good. Moreover, about concrete suffering at least, he knows more than I do. Mine is all in the head. But he knows. I feel he is always on edge and menaced. I don't know why. I speculate about how he lives in that house; going into it is unthinkable. He must do normal things, brush his hair and teeth, sit by the fire . . . He doesn't talk about his family. I don't ask.

In the afternoon, he fed one of the snakes.

Cassandra's Journal. February 1963

We are still all in Benstone; I had hoped to be able to leave before now. The protracted stay frets everyone's temper. J. displays her usual partial and superficial awareness of other people's feelings; this can cause more damage than a complete lack of concern with them. Moreover, she obtrudes her own feelings. When I was younger I used to feel that emotional self-indulgence must later be paid for. It occurs to me in middle age that those who learn to take in childhood equip themselves to take as adults, and so it continues. A hard thought. There is an aesthetic pleasure in the recognition of hard facts which is intense and brilliant and pales very quickly as one realizes that knowing a fact changes it little, or not at all. (Here is the fallacy behind the more vulgar hopes of psycho-analysis: we cannot think away poverty, ugliness, fear.)

He understood and understands this supremacy of facts. The pleasure in knowing that what is thwarting exists and is thwarting. But he does not pay sufficient attention to the human need to imagine. We cannot, in fact, recognize a simple fact, and we must have more than facts to live by. So much of what most deeply affects us is at best dubiously factual.

I have been reading – with pain – some early parts of this journal. He and I have – like dancers – changed position over the years. Then we were both more concerned with the historical truth of Christianity. Now I have come to see that the death of Christ is *imaginatively* necessary to us. It is the supreme event of both factual and imaginative worlds, it relates the factual world of meaningless suffering to the imagined world of where action is meaningful, love is purposeful. We are *in need* of this relationship. Whatever we can imagine a man should be, He is, and whatever we factually suffer, He suffered – since each man's death is, for him, the extreme of suffering. So here our worlds are welded.

Whereas Simon seems to have abdicated the attempt to reconcile love and suffering; he regards the order of facts as the only available truth, and uses the imagination primarily as an instrument for scientific comparison. He perceives similarities in dissimilarities and produces, not metaphysical metaphors, but tentative scientific laws. We have both hardened, we are both more limited.

I think also, although this may be fanciful (God knows I have had long enough to work on it, and no distractions) that our present attitudes were implicit in the way we watched the snake feed, that afternoon. It was I, not he, who found the raw fact intolerable. I think his religion was more robust, a simpler need for immediate consolation. That – coupled with the usual adolescent rebelliousness – was why he left the Roman Church. He had no need for assent, but a need (apparently still unfulfilled and now abandoned) for human assurance. Oh, Simon, how we change. I should relinquish the possibility of knowing you with more ease and more grace if what there was had simply worn itself away.

He had given the snake – one of the larger grass-snakes – a live frog, from a tank full of the creatures which he kept for this purpose.

He explained to Cassandra what was happening, as though, she felt, the knowing accuracy of his description was a defence against the fact of the frog's being swallowed.

'They like,' he said, proffering the frog, gathering its legs gently in his hand, cupping its body, 'something bigger than their own heads, to get a grip on.' The frog jerked. 'Come on,' said Simon to the snake, pushing it a little. 'This one is used to being hand-fed.'

The snake suddenly stretched out and sank its teeth into the frog. 'The teeth are very well designed. If we are talking about design. The backward slope gives it a good grip.' Cassandra said nothing. He looked sideways at her, one of his flickering looks that rested on her face and ended over her shoulder. 'I can't get this one to take dead food yet.'

The snake began to walk its head, stretched and ungainly, over the frog. The frog wriggled a little and the teeth sank deeper.

'Each half of each jaw can be moved independently. Like pulling a bag over something in separate tugs. When it gets to a wide bit, it can separate the lower jaw halves completely and push them right down. Then it pushes sideways with its throat muscles. It will take a longish time to swallow this big frog. All that saliva helps it down. You may have read somewhere' – Cassandra had not – 'that they cover their prey with saliva first, to soften it. People get that idea because if you frighten a snake that's just fed, it will throw up whatever it's swallowed . . .'

The snake's four jaw parts and its stuffed and choked mouth were still progressing.

'It can digest one end of the frog whilst it's still swallowing the other. For instance, it may digest the feet before the frog is dead. Frogs are very resistant to death.'

Cassandra sat still, and neither protested nor wriggled. She felt Simon was forbidding. Since then she had watched an anaconda swallow a small pig, on the television, under his surveillance, but both his commentary and her observation had become more remote, she thought, cooler. In the jungle he, perhaps, had sweated something off. Whereas the screen made him and his snake, for her, unreal somehow; her watching was pitiless. A loss? One cannot suffer with all frogs and pigs. One cannot. There had been on the stretched faces of both grass-snake and anaconda a kind of rigid, anonymous grin.

CHAPTER SEVEN

'As for what you call my obscure references to Simon Moffitt,' Julia wrote, 'they are obscure because my feelings are obscure. I suppose you might say he was my first love. (Are you interested in that, Ivan? Well, if not, you can always skip through this letter – you don't even have to *look* as though you're politely listening.) In those days I saw him as a sort of cross between Heathcliff and Sebastian Flyte. He had a romantic Bridesheady sort of charm – a rather sordid family history that was the object of much village speculation – and the sort of glamour that comes of having thrown over the Family Tradition – although only far enough to be flirting with the C. of E. in the person of our local vicar (also a charmer). You get the picture. Things were complicated because of my sister – whom I loved and was terrified of – having violent feelings – again obscure – about him, let alone me. It all got a bit like a cheap novelette. That upset her too, she hates even a hint of vulgarity. And whereas my life *is* like a novelette, I do like it to be the muted, not the melodramatic kind, lowest common denominator not highest common multiple of emotion, if I've got my terminology right, love?

'Simon doesn't look as though he's a straightforward man; he was certainly anything *but* a straightforward boy. A sexual twister, and an (unconscious?) cajoler . . . The sort of man who makes women feel, erroneously, that they can do things to bring him out or straighten him up. Hence your teenagers, which I find absolutely understandable . . .'

They met outside the post office. Julia pushed her pennies into the stamp machine and watched the stamps uncoil through the slit. She stuck them on, and took the letter out of the envelope to read through, partly in case she had said something embarrassing, partly out of a giddy pleasure in her own eloquence.

'You wouldn't have a penny, would you? I mean, could you change a threepenny piece?'

'I think I could *give* you a penny.' Julia turned out her pockets, clutching handkerchief, key, residual biscuit-crumbs. Her letter fell on the pavement. They bent down, together, both clumsily.

'Coincidence,' he said, holding out to her, one in each hand, her envelope and the one he had come to post. Both were addressed to Miss Cassandra Corbett, in Oxford. His was clean and flat, as though it contained only one folded slip of paper. She held out her own wad of school-book scribble.

'How funny,' she said. 'She almost never answers mine . . .'

'I'm a shocking correspondent myself. I hate writing letters; I don't, often . . .'

Julia handed him the penny. He stamped his letter and tossed it into the mouth of the box.

'Aren't you going to post yours? It looks much more exciting than mine.' He laughed, rather disagreeably, Julia thought.

'I don't suppose *she'll* think so. I write them for my own benefit really. One can't talk to oneself.'

'Well, go on, post it.'

'But I'm always afraid she'll laugh.'

'Laugh?'

Julia gummed up the envelope and pushed it into the box. 'Good for you,' he said. Empty-handed now, they looked at each other.

He was much younger than she had expected, she thought immediately. His face, with the full, pouting mouth, had an unformed look, reinforced by a few pale purple scars where pimples had presumably been, and odd patches of hair sprouting at the mouth corners, along the jaw-line, silky, not bristling, as though this was all the hair he grew and he believed he need not shave often. A tangle of curls flopped on his forehead. His lack of assured physical presence encouraged Julia. At the same time, it disappointed her; she had expected him formidable.

'I can't imagine Cassandra *laughing* at anyone,' he said. 'Such a serious girl.'

'Well, she probably wouldn't laugh at you.' Julia swallowed her words. She had imagined this meeting so many times and was now at a loss about what to make of it or how to prolong it. He gave a deprecating shrug and said nothing to this; Julia began to walk away, rapidly, without having said good-bye. He came with her, falling over his feet, and then, catching her up, he took a swinging step that was too long and brought them into collision.

'Damn,' he said. 'Sorry, damn.'

Julia brushed her skirt and laughed. He blushed.

'Does she like Oxford then, Cassandra?'

'I don't really know. She'd be far more likely to tell you what she really thought than me, anyway.'

'W-wait,' he said. 'W-we don't know each other, do we?'

'I know who you are. I'm Julia.' He waited. 'Julia Corbett.'

'Oh – Cassandra's *sister*. I remember, she said she . . . Why haven't I met you?'

'I've been away at school.'

'But you know who I am?'

'Oh, yes. I know an awful lot about you.' She did not explain that what she knew had been gleaned from Cassandra's diary. 'All sorts of things.'

'What sort of things?'

'Nothing that's not nice. How very clever you are. And understanding and wise. That sort of thing.'

She said this with a slight touch of mockery and he looked at her suspiciously. 'I don't know about that,' he said, rapidly, frowning. Julia felt suddenly powerful. 'It's a funny name, Cassandra.'

'I suppose so. We've had one in the family since the beginning of the eighteenth century. Every other generation. My name's a family name, too. I used to call her Antimacassar. And Cassowary.'

Simon laughed.

'Children are awfully mean,' said Julia. He said nothing; Julia was afraid she had lost him; he stared moodily at the pavement, troubling over something; she walked calmly beside him, smiling slightly.

'I say,' he said, suddenly. 'You wouldn't like a cup of tea, would you? It's a bit of a walk, I suppose. Not a bad walk.'

'I'd love one,' said Julia. 'I'd love one.'

'It'd be something to tell Cassandra.'

'Yes,' said Julia, meekly.

'You both go in for long letters,' he said. 'I don't know where you find so much to say . . .'

Julia expatiated.

After that, he came to tea in the Old House, several times. They talked about Cassandra, and then about Life; Simon revealed a gossipy side that she would not, from what she had read of him, have suspected in him. Julia took care not to dress with care for him. On the last of these occasions, when they were sitting alone by the fire in the living-room, she said, 'Cassandra comes back, next week.'

'Good.'

'Did you – mention these tea-parties?'

'No, actually,' he said. 'Should I have?' His long-legged body was laid diagonally across the arm-chair, so that parts of it sagged loosely into the cushion and parts were rigid. He did not look comfortable. 'We don't write that sort of letter, actually.'

He pushed at his mouth with one finger so that his lips bulged in an ugly scowl, and then released it again. Julia thought he was unattractive. She remembered, on later occasions, that this was what she had thought. He was also, she considered, neither direct nor honest.

'Did you?' he said.

'Did I what?'

'Tell Cassandra. I should have thought you might have, the letters you write.'

'I didn't think there was much to tell.'

'No,' he agreed.

'But don't you think we ought? I mean, it isn't a secret. It oughtn't to look like one.'

'Well, if it isn't, I'd just let it be, if I were you.'

'But she won't *like* it, Si.'

Simon folded up various limbs, and sat up, more or less normally.

'Why not?'

'Well, because . . . Because she cares so much about you. About talking to you. You mean something to her.' She had noticed that to tell him this always irritated him: nevertheless, it was surely necessary.

'Well, what's that got to say to it?'

'Oh, Si, don't be stupid. She doesn't like *me*, that's what I'm trying to say. She never has, for as long as I can remember. She – she doesn't like sharing things. She won't want me – sharing her particular friends.'

'Why doesn't she like you?'

'Oh – because I – I don't know. I – I used to worship her. I – I suppose I was always after her. Finding out what she was doing and trying to do it too. I can see it might have been maddening. She ignores me a lot. Tries to pretend I'm not there. Though at school – we didn't really know anyone except each other. She – she isn't easy to get on with. She despises people. Sometimes I think, if she were less prickly and proud, I might've made more friends and then I wouldn't need her so . . . It was all a bit awful, really. She hasn't had much. I don't want to – look as though I'm trying to – take anything.'

'That's my business,' said Simon, with youthful judiciousness. 'Why are you so frightened of her?'

'Well, she's so clever. So uncompromising. She sets impossible standards.' Also, she conducts the Game.

'Yes, but I shouldn't have thought you need mind her. You've got all sorts of advantages she hasn't. I can see she might be jealous of you, that makes sense. You engage with life, if I may put it that way. Cassandra – for all her cleverness – Cassandra's a bit silly. The thing about Cassandra is, you never feel she's all there, do you? Sorry, I didn't mean that vulgarly. But she just doesn't quite exist.'

Julia felt this was heresy, delicious and terrible. And Simon saw her, he saw she was someone. Simon wriggled, and flopped again in the chair. He gave her a sudden warm, questioning smile; tentatively, she smiled back.

'I can't see any use in making a point of telling her if you think it'll annoy her. We'll sort it all out.'

Since Julia had no precise desire to tell Cassandra anything she dropped the question.

The day before Cassandra came home he called and took her out, for the day, to Craster. At the Old House he talked for some time to Jonathan Corbett, vaguely, about the weather and the war. One of the things that was worrying Julia was the way in which her parents – and Inge, and Elsie – so clearly and tactfully saw Simon as Julia's first boy-friend. They were glad for her; Cassandra had Oxford; she had worryingly insisted on leaving school to make tea for the local newspapermen. Inge brought out a packet of sandwiches and a Thermos flask of sweet tea. These they consumed on the beach, having walked northwards towards Bamburgh over stones and rocks slippery with seaweed.

'I like your father, Julia. He thinks life's worth making an effort with. I like that. I envy him that.'

'I love him,' said Julia. 'He's a good man. He does so much. Cass gets furious that he's not with us more – she says he's got no right to keep being imprisoned at the State's expense, not in *this* war – and anyway, she just gets furious. But I like to see anyone care so much for anything. I really admire him.'

'You know my father shot himself?'

'Yes,' said Julia. She added hastily, 'That's all I do know. Someone told me. In the post office.'

'People do tell you things.'

'Why did he, Si?'

'Oh, all sorts of reasons. He wasn't like your father. He was gassed in the trenches in the last war, you know – he still had nightmares, absolutely regularly, about that. He used to go on and on about the trenches. Terrible detailed stories. You can imagine. No, you probably can't. I don't think anything was real to him that happened since. This war was a fearful blow. He – oh, in some way, he saw it as the end of the civilized world, all right. So it was bad enough for him, without my mother. Did they tell you in the post office about my mother?'

'No,' said Julia, mendaciously.

'My mother is a very silly woman. Beautiful, in a girlish way. Very promiscuous.'

'I see.'

'We lived in London, a lot of the time, that's why I've never met you. My mother – used to confide in me. As though,' Simon shrugged and smiled, 'I was a sort of girl-friend. She kept saying society is disintegrating and people are desperate and have a sort of wild freedom. I did things like hide letters for her. She's careless. She thought I thought it was romantic. I thought it was all rather disgusting, really –'

'It didn't,' Julia cried out of her own grievance, 'give you much of a chance to grow up normally, did it? To have things children do have – ought to have?'

'Exactly. That's exactly what I –'

'So you felt for your father.'

'He didn't make that easy. We were both – Mama and I – scared of him. He was a foul-tempered man. Disappointed. Not only with Mama – he wanted to be a serious politician, and never got on. Too reactionary. He didn't like me. He didn't know he didn't, but I knew.

'When I – when I decided to go into the Church, I did try, with him. He hated the idea of my going into the Church, he said it was for half-men. I hated him shouting. The more afraid I . . . the more angry he . . . Sometimes he drove me to tears, that maddened him.'

'I suppose I partly think that about the Church. Because of this thing I have about coming to grips with normal life – not cutting yourself off, at all costs. The Church does cut you off. I'm sorry, Si—'

'No.' He paused. Then he glanced at her quickly and said, 'Religion's a funny thing. There are times when one needs it desperately, it's all there is. When one needs a structure – some rules, some idea of what's best to do, an end for one's actions. And then, one morning one wakes up and finds the whole thing's completely meaningless. Completely. One is just not the same person. It all seems absurd and forced and obscene. Above all, forced.'

'I know,' said Julia, who had never experienced more than a momentary religious twinge herself, and supposed serenely that the revelation of meaninglessness awaited every religious person sooner or later, in death if not in life. 'I know.' They shared a silence. Julia thought, poor Cassandra. She said, 'So what happened then about your father?' Her curiosity invigorated him; he said, eagerly, 'Well, my mother got into a real mess. A classic mess. Father and I – we walked in – and caught her out in – *in flagrante delicto*,' he finished up, with a pompous intonation that caused Julia to suppress an involuntary snort of laughter.

'Evidence meant he had to do something, you see. So he brought me home, and we sat in gloom for a week. He wrote letters, and in the night he shouted, and I kept getting up, and . . .

'Then he took me and the dog into the conservatory one day. Things were pretty bad by then. He said to the dog, "Come here, you," and he – dragged her a bit – she didn't want – and then he, he shot the dog. So then he, he said to me, "Come here," so I – I hid behind the water-butt, and he stood – looking stupid – for a bit, and then he gave a sort of snort and said, "Oh, well, never mind," in a sort of puzzled voice and he – he shot himself. And then panes of glass fell in, and potted plants dropped off the edges of shelves. One hit me. On the shoulder.'

Julia spread one hand across her face to choke another involuntary burst of laughter.

'Oh, poor Simon. How mean. In front of you – how beastly mean.'

'Yes, that's what I thought. Not only that, but –' He bent to gather up two stones and flung them with wild inaccuracy at the surface of the sea beyond the foam-line; neither of them bounced, but spurted and sank. 'Why did I tell you all that? You're the sort of person people do tell things to, aren't you? You accept what people tell you.'

His story seemed to Julia unreal, like one of Cassandra's more Byronic inventions. For a moment she visualized Cassandra, listening dourly and with a tense respect to the same story and suffering every shot.

'Nothing shocks you, that's part of it.'

'Well, one can't afford to be shocked. I think you ought to think it was mean, and be angry. You've got your own life to live, you can't give his back.'

He gave these clichés the same patient, slightly abstracted attention he gave everything she said. Then, stammering slightly, he told her, 'You're quite right about this need to be normal. I should have thought you *were*, on the whole. It's one of the attractive things about you.'

'But normal with such an effort,' Julia said eagerly. 'Quakers are so self-consciously normal, there are no laws, only a sort of *laissez-faire* puritanism that means you're always making scrupulous decisions about things other people take for granted. It's a strain. And our house is so unsettled – we've always got refugees, and out-of-work miners, and prisoners on parole and unmarried mothers – and we're all so reasonable and it makes so much tension. We just *behave* like a normal family. We know a – a hell of a lot about it, but we've no time left to spend *being* it. And living with Cassandra can't be called normal.'

Much of this speech was something Cassandra had once said to her in anger. It was also her own considered opinion.

'You are tremendously aware of what goes on,' Simon said, changing back from the wildly confidential boy to the judicious student of character. 'I like talking to you.'

He took her hand, clumsily, intertwining their fingers. His hand was slightly clammy; along the back of his fingers black hair grew thickly, in oblong patches, prickling slightly. She felt this was a dramatic moment – something had changed – and that she would much rather he did not touch her. She returned the handclasp warmly, caressed him briefly, stood up, and ran to the sea's edge. It was a clear day, with bright December sunshine, and no wind. The sound of the long breakers and the smell of the sea made Julia feel as she supposed being drunk must feel. She had never, coming from this family, tasted drink.

She turned over flotsam with a piece of driftwood. 'Sometimes we find lovely stones here,' she said, throwing aside a clump of bladderwrack with a spatter of sand, uncovering, under its tangled meshes, a pile of damp and broken feathers and half a cod, whose eyeless head gaped, whose needle-fine teeth curved back from the plated oval jaw, whose insides spilled on the sand. Small creatures hopped and scuttled over feathers and scales. There was a smell; not a warm decaying smell, but a cold, salt stench.

'Oh, God,' said Julia, 'what a mess.' She moved briskly along the black line of shells and seaweed. 'What one *finds*.' She gathered two flat stones and sent them skipping across the water. Behind her, Simon slowly turned over the fish, squatting on the sand, knees and shoulders pushed together. His confidences increased Julia. She ran along the beach, and hummed, and sang feeling powerful.

She would do anything for him. He needed her. She looked at him with love.

Some, not all, of this Julia wrote into her letter. She finished 'But all the same, Ivan, how could I ever know what I felt? I felt so pushed about, by what he wanted, by what she wanted, I didn't stand a chance. It wasn't only her that wasn't quite real – he wasn't, either, he never knew how much I just simply didn't understand. Of course I was excited by him telling me things – I'd started out by thinking of him as taboo – and even at the end, long after it all came out, I got this funny sacrilegious pleasure from it. I think I did love him. I think I could have loved him, if we'd met naked, as it were. But with Cassandra *watching* – I've always been scared stiff of waking up and finding out I was nothing but a thought in Cassandra's mind.

'We used to sit about saying, "Why don't you stop talking about Cassandra?" to each other. He said that more. So I supposed I talked more.

'You'd better read this as the first instalment of an unwritten novel. The bare, the thread-bare soul of Julia Corbett. Christ, if I didn't have to be shut up in this house I wouldn't think about it, I assure you. Do you know, we even sat together watching him on the telly. All her feelings are unreal, they are attached to unrealities, but they still affect other people's lives . . .'

CHAPTER EIGHT

Cassandra turned on the television. Julia was not there. It was snowing again and the reception was bad. Metal flashes cracked across the pretty girl's silly face. Simon, when he appeared, pottered about unconcernedly in his still, damp jungle, behind jagged thickets of lightning and growls of thunder, his voice rising only fitfully above the elemental pother. Cassandra put another log on the fire and turned up the sound.

'We bring death to these people in the form of firearms and whisky,' he said, suddenly clear. He could be seen, now, standing in the centre of a semicircle of women, most of them naked, some pregnant, some carrying nursing children, few of them taller than his elbow, all with the same flat noses and dark, incomprehensible stare. 'We kill them off with V.D. and flu.' He looked at his own feet with a faint, defiant embarrassment Cassandra remembered accurately. 'We make use of them. We come and take photographs. They see this as the theft of the personality. These, however' – he gestured to his companions – 'have been regularly paid with beads, they come out and clamour to be photographed.' He smiled.

'We classify their sexual and religious behaviour and interpret our own by them.' He looked up anxiously. 'We destroy the rhythms of their lives and do them no commensurate good. Oh, we *could* do good, but not to them as they are now, only by so much changing that some would be lost in the process. At the moment we just make them self-conscious – conscious of themselves in our terms – and erode their basic dignity, their sense of themselves in *their* lives. I'm not being sentimental. We ignore differences – radical differences.' He said desperately, 'The brotherhood of man is so much more a myth than the opposite. I shall never know these people. In important ways – important ways – I am *not* like them.'

The flat faces wavered and a black hole appeared and spread in the centre of Simon's face. Little silver lines, spearheads, threads of water, moved against and dissected his limbs. A low buzzing hum appeared and increased in pitch. Simon mouthed at them – presumably about the limits of human communication – from a horribly distorted head; the hole spread to include his mouth and his body swelled and jiggled uncontrollably. Cassandra continued to stare at him, unmoving.

Thor, who had come unremarked down the stairs, sat in the armchair next to her.

'You persist in contemplating even broken images.' He smiled briefly. 'Or may I turn him off?'

Cassandra stood up and turned the switch, diminishing Simon to a line and then nothing.

'I am at a loss to understand his fascination. He produces all our current clichés. Exaggerated respect for what is primitive and animal. Coupled with the current fashionable hopelessness. We find our roots and they are violent and savage, but we respect them. And so give up. World wars and serpents will always be too much for intelligence and charity. He is simple-minded.'

'Simple-minded may also be right-minded,' Cassandra said slowly. 'As far as it goes.'

'I am at a loss to understand his fascination,' her brother-in-law repeated doggedly, as though he liked the phrase.

'I should have thought you had just excellently described his fascination,' Cassandra said. 'Simon Moffitt was never an original thinker. It's what he *is* – it's the fact that these things so patently affect him. I wouldn't have thought he would have gone in for – this kind of popular dissemination of – of spiritual musings on physical facts. But now he has, I see of course that he always had it in him.' She warmed to her subject. 'You see, he panders to a need that's slowly reached the surface of our consciousness in our time. A need to relate the mind and the body. To see ourselves connected to, in terms of, the primitive animals, blood and food, the eternal rhythms, inevitable destruction – we do feel, don't we, fatally out of touch?' She shivered. 'And just as society as a whole – oh, through things like all this jungle music I understand they listen to – has become generally aware of this need, here is a man who can be seen living it. I think he does it quite well.'

'Oh, yes,' said Thor. 'He is a *personality*. He bares his soul for other people. As those savages bare their bodies for his camera and he despises them. Albert Schweitzer – that I can understand and admire. But this is conceit.'

'No, I don't think conceit,' Cassandra began judiciously. Her love for Simon had always included a certain contempt for his simplicities. In the early days, when she had needed to worship, this contempt had been a private and unconsidered pleasure. Later she had needed it to comfort herself and had elaborated and explored it. 'Not conceit. I think he's probably not fully aware of the public nature of what he's doing. He's a natural because he's not deliberately appealing to an audience. Which is not to say he doesn't appeal . . .'

Thor cut across this with a remark which, Cassandra decided later, he had come downstairs prepared to deliver.

'But what good is there in this for you and Julia? Don't you think you had better let it lie?'

Cassandra's skin prickled. She looked sharply across at him and surprised on his polished, slightly flushed face a look of determined helpfulness, a deliberate, clerical kindness.

'I don't know what Julia thinks. That is her business.'

'I think you should make it your business.'

'We rarely see each other.'

'Don't you think you've done enough damage?' Cassandra closed her mouth, tightly, and sat, exploring the implications of this. Thor said, in a rough, judging tone, 'Why don't you let go? Julia is afraid of you. Let him go, let Julia go. Make – some gesture – to Julia. You could free yourself, as well as Julia. This Simon has really nothing to do with it. Forgive me speaking so openly, someone must. You know yourself I am not making something out of nothing.'

Cassandra stood up. 'I see you and Julia have been talking me over. I should have expected that. But I dislike thinking about it.' She paused. 'I sympathize with you to a certain extent. Being told things, over and over, by Julia, can be very exhausting. But it should make you careful what you say to other people.'

She walked over to the stairs and then looked back.

'You will neither of you face facts,' he said, making no effort to detain her. In the firelight his face had the same look of petulance and indignant judgement it had had over Julia's refusal to go to the Congo. Trembling slightly, Cassandra went silently up the stairs and into her room.

She drew the curtains, lit the gas-fire, sat for a moment or two, her hands crossed and working on her knees, and then lit a cigarette and began to pace, round the end of the bed, turning with military precision on her heel.

'Haven't you done enough damage?'

What did he mean, damage? She had protected herself, simply, and she had left Julia a clear field to act. It must be galling for him, she thought with distant malice, to be so anxious to go to the African jungle to do good and have his wife hanging nervously on every word of some charlatan in the American jungle, out for money and exhibitionism. She wondered what he had been told, and was seized by the sharp, futile pain of remembering past embarrassments, so that she shook her head, and gasped, and said aloud, 'No,' once or twice. This was a pain she had supposed, wrongly, she would grow out of. As she had supposed that she would grow out of Simon, and her humiliation over Simon. Since the television appearances, which gave his pronouncements the illusory appearance of privacy and intimacy, Simon had become again accessible to the imagination, to dispute, to thought, to dreams. It had created a clearing in which thinking about him was not intolerable. But the house, Deborah, and Thor, made her realize that she was just as much as ever an object of Julia's speculation, Julia's tale-telling. She had tried, God knew, to avoid that. At all costs. She wheeled and shook unnecessary ash from the glowing cigarette into the waste-paper basket.

'Cass, being friends with you is more important in the long run than anything Simon can ever mean to me.'

That was not true for her. But it had had to be. Slowly her own sentences came back at her out of the past, in other contexts. 'Being told things by Julia can be very exhausting.' 'You and Julia have been talking about me; I find that intolerable.' 'More important than anything Simon can ever . . .' Oh, no.

On the day of her return from Oxford she and Julia had tea in the kitchen. The house was otherwise empty: Inge, Nelly and a flock of refugee children were at the W.I. Christmas Bazaar. Cassandra came in, made certain all her papers were reassuringly cold and dusty, locked her journal into her desk, gathered, in the hall, a letter from Simon and thrust it into her pocket to read later. Cassandra never seized the moment.

Julia was putting the kettle on the Aga. She looked very young, and was wearing a yellow polo-neck sweater and Black Watch tartan skirt. She did not look round as Cassandra came in, which irritated Cassandra vaguely; for once, fairly sure of who she was, Cassandra was simply glad to see her. She offered to help; Julia with downcast eyes said no, it was all nearly ready; Cassandra sat at the kitchen table and told Julia about Oxford, Sir Gawaine and the Grene Knight, mediaeval pronunciation, rivers, bells, college customs, rationing. Their relationship was always easiest when Cassandra was offering information; she became almost animated. Julia sliced bread, laid it on the round grid of the Aga toaster, saying, in a muted voice, 'Gosh' and 'Oh, Cass,' from time to time. When Cassandra ran to a stop, she said:

'There's something I've got to tell you.'

'Well?'

'I – I've been seeing quite a lot of Simon.'

'Well?' more sharply.

'He asked me to tea. Once or twice. And came here.'

Cassandra said nothing.

'I'm sorry, Cass.'

'You'll burn that toast, for God's sake be careful.'

'It was funny really, we met because we were both posting letters to you.'

Cassandra closed her eyes, like a child which gives itself, through closing out its surroundings, the illusion that it is not there. When she opened them Julia was looking at her with gentle concern.

'He only came because he likes to talk about you. Because he knew you.'

'I don't like being talked about. I don't like being thought about. I know it is not a human right, not to be talked about.' Cassandra stood up and set out for her room.

'Cass – no, wait – Cass, listen – he asked me to ask you, will we both go to tea there tomorrow. He wants to see you.'

She gathered herself. 'Well, then, we must go.' She got out of the kitchen, somehow. Behind her, to seal, she thought, the real importance of the occasion, Julia burst into tears.

Simon's letter thanked her for her two last, apologized for his dilatory reply, made a good point about the essentially predatory nature of little boys being a clear evidence of original sin, and ended, 'I have asked Julia, too. Love, Simon.'

At Oxford she had a recurrent nightmare all term. She still had it. It combined bright colour with black and white. Only the carpet was coloured – grass-green, expansive, bedizened with pink and silver roses and trellis-work it extended across a room round whose remote edge, in black and white, on sofas, on arm-chairs, with tea-trollies at their elbows and nests of tables opened out and scattered, her family sat, still as photographs. The door would open slowly, and Simon would come in, awkward, graceful. At this point she always struggled close enough to consciousness to express to herself surprise that she should have called him up with such solid authority; as though he should have been vaguer or more oblique. He would smile at them with impartial friendliness, take their hands, kiss Julia, her mother, Inge, and turn to her. She would disgrace herself by crawling away on hands and knees over the vivid carpet to lie, panting and hunted, face down behind the sofa. She heard sounds: a disconnected hum of conversation, the twang of the springs on the sofa, jaws moving, masticating sandwiches, the quick gulping of tea. She supposed now that this horror derived from some childhood tantrum that her conscious mind had suppressed. At some stage in the dream she always saw Simon, full face, eating and smiling politely, his Adam's apple rising and falling.

Cassandra did not, even at their best, like tea-parties. About Simon's tea-party she thought, now, as little as possible: she had gone there only in order not to be asked why she had not gone; to make certain that she should never be asked questions of that kind in the future. They had walked there in their Sunday dresses, Julia, two steps behind, stopping occasionally to expostulate. Cassandra felt the constant adjustment of pace as a bursting in the diaphragm.

'Honestly, Cass, I don't want to come if you don't want me to. Don't think I shouldn't understand, if you wanted to talk to him on your own or anything. Cass, you do know I'd do anything rather than upset you.'

'He asked you,' said Cassandra. 'Didn't he?'

Tea-parties represented a normality of behaviour she had feared and avoided. Simon, normal and diminished, let them into the elegant, bleak house she had vaguely expected never to enter. Julia displayed a brisk familiarity with where to hang coats and the whereabouts of bread-knife and tea-pot stand. They had tea in a room which, Julia told Cassandra, had been Simon's father's study – book-lined, gloomy, with red leather arm-chairs and a mahogany desk with brass drawer-handles on which Simon stacked his uneven slices of utility bread and a dish of home-made jam. Over the hearth hung a huge Martyrdom of St Sebastian; the saint's limbs were elongated and female, his mouth somewhere between pouting and secretively smiling, his flesh precisely punctured by the arrows so that the wounds recalled the raised red mouths of rubber suckers. The enjoyment of pain with the pain taken out, she had thought. She made no attempt to communicate the thought.

She could remember very little of the conversation, although it flowed easily enough; she had not gone there with any intention of conversing. Both the others eagerly directed their remarks to her, deferring to her opinions; she gave them brief, undeveloped answers, sat stiff, and looked remotely out of the window.

She wondered, now, what Simon had made or intended of that tea-party. He had smiled steadily through it, sitting easy and animated, talking with more apparent openness in the company of both of them than he did, at least, alone with her. He had seemed to find the situation he had brought about both comfortable and satisfactory. There had been a time when she had hoped that after a long and cautiously developed acquaintance – when both of them had changed – she would have been able at last to share normal things with him, and then tea-parties would have had the drama, the inevitability, the beauty, the freedom, of her other world. But meeting him in this way precluded for ever meeting him in any other. She watched him laugh with Julia, and thought she would not know him, and had not known him. A fine observation, however scrupulous, however impassioned, was no substitute for the desire on his part to communicate. Detaching herself, she allowed her contempt to flourish at last, remembering things she had ignored: awkwardnesses, inaccuracies, small unkindnesses, unnecessary fulsomeness with the Vicar. She held to that. She was prematurely resigned, indeed, almost indecently anxious, never to see him again. Her abdication was grim and complete.

Since that afternoon she had never spoken more than was in politeness required of her, either to Simon, or to her sister. She had evaded, with polite and apparent fictions, any further invitations, she had avoided Simon when, inevitably, he came to the house. She had left unanswered a letter he wrote her about Plato. The tea-party had been a concession to dignity. It was all she could do. Once, a few weeks later, she had opened the door to him by mistake.

'Ah,' he said, 'Cassandra. Come up and see the snakes?'

'I have to work.'

'Don't say that. You cut yourself off. It isn't good for you.' There was no answer to this; his kindness, since he had talked of her to Julia, was an insult. It always had been; she had chosen not to notice. At least he was incapable of a direct question.

'You shouldn't cut yourself off. You must make some contact with people.'

'I do, in my own way. I know what I'm doing.'

'I doubt that. Neither you nor I know that.'

She looked at him with a flicker of interest.

'We don't think it matters what we do. But it does. Now Julia –' he said. 'Julia –'

'Julia is in the garden.'

'No, wait, Cassandra –'

She did not see why he should preserve his good opinion of himself at her expense. It was refusing these small encounters that exhausted her; that, and fending off Julia's attempts to confess, discuss, or clear the air. She walked away from him. She did not think he had expected this precisely; but all that was left, as she saw it, to do, was to uncreate him in her mind. If she could have worked through the relationship, unhindered, if she could have cast him off, and held him as an interesting memory when they had nothing more to say to each other, she would not now feel so stunted, so trapped in his view of her then, which he had shared, and modified, with Julia. There was nothing to do but behave as though he had never been.

Julia, on the other hand, was real and dangerous. In the beginning she had been merely inquisitive eyes, scuffling, proprietary curiosity the other side of the locked door. But lately she had come to see her as an almost impersonal menace, something which would infallibly take what she, Cassandra, wanted because its only function was to want precisely that. She had the story. Which could be abandoned. She had Simon. Who could be forgotten. It was important to keep secret what she herself now wanted – whatever that was. At the time, the remorseless logic of this as a guide to behaviour had pleased her. She went back to Oxford ignorant of what the two, in each other's company, were doing.

After another term and another vacation Julia trapped her at the end of the garden, where she was reaching up with the secateurs into the lilac, gathering branches for Easter vases on altar and Meeting-house table. Julia appeared purposefully at the end of the path. She had lately become a proper reporter and was rarely at home. Her face and pale eyes seemed more colourless than usual; as she came up Cassandra saw that her expression had a harshness quite different from her usual placatory grin. She had been very patient with Cassandra, had risked innumerable rebuffs, had persistently and gently reopened conversations, and allowed herself to be humiliated by silence. Cassandra thrust her head into the bush so that her vision was criss-crossed with twigs and close white flowers.

'I want to talk to you. There is only you.' Cassandra snipped two sprigs and inclined her head.

'You knew Simon had gone?' Julia informed her abruptly. Cassandra swallowed and did not answer. 'He went to London a week ago. Now he writes and says he's off to Malaya with a zoological team. He must have known he was going for weeks – for months. Secretly fixing. He wrote me a sort of apologetic letter. A final letter. Just cutting off contact.' She said, 'You know, Cass, he's an awful emotional dabbler.'

'He's afraid of committing himself. And afraid of feeling,' Cassandra said. 'He explores other people's emotions partly to see if he's got any himself – he fears he may not have – and partly just to keep other people off him. To distance them.'

The contempt was coming out finely. This was the first thing Cassandra had said to Julia about Simon: Julia clearly found it encouraging.

'Oh, yes,' she cried, 'that's exactly what I feel.' She added, unfortunately, 'I'm so glad you know. I thought you didn't know.'

Cassandra plunged back into the bush and made several well-directed slashes with the secateurs; lilac stems fell and tangled round her feet.

'I've had an awful time, Cass. I haven't the slightest idea – really I haven't – what I really feel about him. He's so very odd. I don't understand what he's saying half the time. Or why he – Sometimes so desperate and insistent. Sometimes just standoffish and kind. I've never felt so uncertain in my life. And begging, and begging . . . And then, just when you give in, just *going off* –'

Her voice rose. 'Cass, you've got to listen, you're the only person I know, you're the only one who'd understand.'

'Clearly I wouldn't understand. That seems to me all that's certain.'

'No, you must let me talk, this time. We've got to clear this up. We've got to go on knowing each other all our lives. Cass, being friends with you is more important in the long run than anything Simon can ever mean to me.'

'There is no good to be done by talking.'

'Oh, there is, there is. Cassandra, I know – with Simon – you think I – only because you –'

'Yes,' said Cassandra. She stood with secateurs dangling and held her face together.

'But you know that's unjust. What about *him*, then? What about him? Isn't he someone, doesn't he want things and do things, didn't he start it? I told him I couldn't because of you. If only you hadn't – But he does exist, I can't just not *notice* him.'

Cassandra winced.

'Why must everything always be my fault?' Because it was, Cassandra had thought. She had thought, too, that Julia needed to tell her the details because whatever they had done was not real or finished until she had been made to be the audience, fully informed. As though they were only acting out her fate, her story; their love, or whatever it was, was simply a function of her own fear. Well, it should stay that way; she would not lose what power she had by becoming involved as an actor, or suffering with Julia. That would be the final constriction, the final limitation. She would keep what freedom detachment, or ignorance, provided.

'You must let me tell you.'

'When you've learned you can't have things both ways,' said Cassandra, 'you'll begin to grow up. I don't want to know.'

She walked round her sister, head up, her arms full of branches and flowers. Behind her she heard Julia running, stumbling, in the other direction. She thought that Julia knew where she was vulnerable but could never really believe it, and so was compelled to go on probing. This was only partly Julia's fault. She felt – as she often felt when she had just parted from Julia – a kind of useless, accepting affection; an inactive understanding.

And then she had been hurt by the phrase 'just when you give in'. She had, perhaps, after all, allowed herself to be told too much.

After she had walked for some time Cassandra lay down on her bed, her hands folded under her face, her nose pressing her knuckles. She had done this since childhood. It was not relaxation; she put effort into it; but after a time she could usually reduce herself to being conscious of nothing but black space in the head and peripheral, defining discomfort, coldness, or pains in the ankles. In the dark behind the closed lids aquamarine plants grew, and shattered into splinters of light; crimson fluid welled up and held momentary globular shapes; in a dancing network of green glass threads apparitions like Simon's caerulean butterflies spread and were disembodied. Cassandra pressed her body against the bed. If she released the pressure of the knuckles, the patterns of light became gentler, and then still.

Julia had assumed that they must be more real to each other, more durable, than anything else. Well, there was a partial truth to that. At best, or at worst, they had been too real to each other, sharing the same thoughts. Not defined, setting up, therefore, a struggle to separate. In an ideal state they should be no more and no less real to each other than anyone else. Thor, for instance. Or Simon.

What I do, what means most to me, she thought, in a moment of panic, is patterns created by the pressure of my own hands on my eyes. She had been allowing herself to forget how Julia's touch had made Simon seem for ever inaccessible. The television screen was like the Looking Glass, beyond which was a different space, where certain laws did not obtain. She had entered this world, she had hacked creepers and trodden trails, she had analysed the hum of insects and the screech of macaws, she had suffered flies and heat and scoured pots on stones by the river. In the literature she studied, the dream was a mode of knowledge. Beyond Simon were the remote knights, in their thickets, and the lover, in the knee-high, delicate, grass-green forest, set within its sheltering walls, reaching out at last, with his serious, anxious expression, to pluck the rose.

It is no accident, Cassandra told herself, that I chose a field of study where the great images are those of unsatisfied desire, formalized, made into a mode of apprehension.

She shifted her body, and the lights all ran together inside her head, white.

CHAPTER NINE

Then, suddenly, the thaw came. All night sections of the roof-load of snow cracked away, gathered momentum, buckled at the gutter, and splatted into paths and garden. Snow in the flowerbeds filmed over with deepening water, and in the morning lawns were spattered with black dots across the white – like fruit cake under icing. Elizabeth Corbett said they must all leave before floods in their turn detained them. Thor concurred and rang the station. That evening, they packed.

Cassandra was packing when Julia found her. Her bed was strewn with apparently identical black garments rolled into long tubes. On the dressing-table was a pile of jewels, ready to be put in tissue paper and chamois: chains, brooches, rings, lumps of unset stone. There was a strong smell of leather and old books; Julia thought she must be imagining the hint of incense. She herself, in hooded and fringed Scandinavian jersey, purple clocked with black and olive, over purple tights and pointed purple suède boots, fitted the picture indifferently well. She thought: it's ironic that what Thor gives me can so easily be worn to suit Cassandra. She closed the door behind her.

'May I come in?'

'As usual, you ask for what you have accomplished. Clear yourself a chair, sit down.'

Julia moved from Cassandra's round, carved wood and plum velvet chair what looked like a spencer and a pair of knee-length knitted woollen knickers, the elastic broken and knotted in two places. She sat down, and said, folding these garments, 'It must be draughty in your college.'

'It is.'

Cassandra began to roll the jewels into little balls of tissue paper.

'But you'll be glad to get back?'

'One comes to need one's own routine.'

'If Thor had his way we'd be breaking right out of ours. Into a new life. Cass, you don't think I was wrong about that, do you?'

Cassandra hesitated perceptibly. She said, 'No,' and then, 'does he?'

'I don't honestly know what he thinks. Sometimes I even think he only brought it up at all to call my bluff.'

She watched Cassandra's mouth compress, and the thought on Cassandra's face: Julia in a confessional mood. However Cassandra said, surprisingly, 'What bluff?'

'Well – I write these books. About people confined in a domestic pressure-chamber. Needing an outburst, a whole-hearted gesture, some sort of extravagance or violence . . .'

Cassandra did not say whether she read the books.

'And you think he wants you to know you're not the only one.'

'Well, it might be that.'

'Or it might be genuine concern with non-domestic problems.'

Cassandra lugged out a suitcase from under the bed and began to push rolled-up stockings and handkerchiefs into her shoes, as she had done when they left for school.

'He's been funny since we got here. I don't know if you've noticed. He's cold. He *resents* all sorts of things about me lately. But he ought to have known what I – was like.'

'Perhaps he thought you might change.'

Julia took this. 'Oh yes, he did. So did I. But it's him that's changed. He – I –'

'Changed?'

'Well, when I married him he seemed safe. And concerned with real things. After living here. I wanted a real life of my own. He seemed so *normal*.'

'He's a little like Father,' said Cassandra. 'Of course, nobody is as much like anyone else as one initially thinks they may be.'

'That's clever of you. Yes, he wants to understand, and he's limited by his own goodness. He can't really think ill of you, or get impatient, or understand meanness intuitively. I used to think that was marvellous. Real wisdom I'd live up to, in time.'

'And now?'

'Now he frightens me. And I understand better. He is – sexually rather constrained, you know, and makes it – made it, when he was younger – worse, by keeping his distance. He never knew enough to take it easy. So when we met – and I know I do rather throw myself at people, though I try not to because it always causes trouble' – Julia hurried on – 'he – he felt violently attracted, and took this as a sign from God that he was in love. No, don't grin, he did think that, he told me so. Damn it,' said Julia, 'he always *looks* as though he knows what he's doing.'

Cassandra, slightly unnerved by these near-revelations of what went on in the marriage bed, both pruriently curious and instinctively afraid of learning more, made a non-committal noise and busied herself with a jar of cold cream and a bottle of lavender water.

'I wasn't up to it. For all sorts of reasons I wasn't up to it. I – I cheated him. I wasn't what he expected. I'm not – like that. I – didn't know I wasn't, either. Now he goes about behaving like a frustrated saint. Well, he may be, but it's not only the saint . . . In any case, he seems to think everything's my fault.'

Cassandra came sideways round the bed-foot and gathered up an armful of what looked like bandages.

'He blames some of it on me,' Cassandra said. 'He told me so. Over the television.'

'But I never see you or think about you,' said Julia with automatic and patent untruth.

'He asked me if I hadn't done enough damage.' They thought this over, in silence, and then looked at each other with curious complicity; Cassandra finished, smoothly, 'I didn't know precisely what he meant.'

'Coming back here does bring things up. Old fears. I feel everyone's against me. I feel everyone thinks I'm a fool. Everything matters too much. It's suffocating.'

'That's natural.'

'Oh, do you think so? I think *he* thinks we're unnatural, that there's something really wrong with us. That we're abnormal. Trapped.'

'You always worried obsessively about what was natural, or normal. You may well be normal. I don't suppose many people would describe me so. I can't say it worries me.'

'There you go, dismissing me again.'

'I'm not dismissing you.'

'You always have. I – I meant to stop that. I meant to shock you, to make you see I could . . .' She took off several rings, dropped one on the carpet, and got down. From under the chair her voice went on, 'That isn't to say that's what I still want, but the idea crops up from time to time. All my childhood!' – accusing, offering, struggling to her knees – 'I meant simply to catch up and do something that would stagger you, that would make you admire me. And then we could have been friends. Well, we made a nice mess of it. Between us and Simon.'

Cassandra went over to the window-seat. She began to roll up the oilskin and tie up papers in taped bundles.

'What are you doing with that?'

'Putting it away.' She grinned, briefly. 'It's done enough damage.'

'Damage to you?'

'Not exactly. I wasn't thinking of that. I've made a life out of it, in a way.'

'No, but, Cass, is that what you *wanted*? Is that all you wanted?'

'Not all, no.'

'You should have written,' Julia cried, with love, with pity, with the old admiration, with a furious sense of the openness to mockery of the spencer and the knitted knickers. Cassandra, hurt by the unquestioning past tense, leaned over the window-seat and snapped an elastic band round the shoe box of plaster figures.

'Oh, what did it come to, all the life we had then, Cassandra? Aren't you appalled that nothing we can do now can possibly measure up to the – the sheer urgency, and beauty and importance of all – all we imagined? I didn't mean to write the sort of stuff I write. And I don't suppose you meant – Don't you feel you've been shut out of something? Don't you hanker? I hanker. A lot of the time.'

The question was disingenuous. Julia knew that Cassandra, in her draughty college, felt like Charlotte Brontë, cut off from Branwell and Zamorna, like Emily, silently pining for another world. She knew, too, that Cassandra, like herself, had been reliving large parts of the past. She was still surprised when Cassandra spoke.

'Shut out of Eden with the flaming sword across the gate? Oh, yes, I hanker. As you put it. But I think we should not.' Her voice was dry and pedantic; they were back where they had begun and Cassandra was lecturing. 'Don't you think we were illegitimately appropriating to ourselves experience of a kind and intensity we had no right to? I think this was partly because of our background. The whole Quaker tradition emphasizes the practical at the expense of the imaginative – unless, of course, you include the experience of the Inner Light as an imaginative experience. It could be, but it isn't; that light which lights up and transfigures the real world. But Quakers – historically – solidified into a preoccupation with the real world, with action, with altering things. Father was the tailend of that tradition. We belong to the decadence. What with the literary emphasis of liberal education as it now is, and servants' gossip, and Inge's stories, and the constant flooding outwards and dissipation of the concept of tolerance – oh, we were far enough away from the days when music and painting were wicked, and romances were lies.

'So you and I created a world, we explored, in the imagination, things that were deficient in our experience. A normal procedure, I assume, only we carried it beyond the point where it was normal. There was a gulf between the life we created and the life we lived. I had hoped to be able to bridge it, in time.' She paused. 'You were right to want to be normal. You should never have let me mock you. It ought to be possible for you now, to find your daily life real, and full enough?'

'All I do is turn my daily life into imaginary books.'

'You know, Julia,' said Cassandra, 'I think perhaps one should make a real moral effort to forgo one's need for a sense of glory.'

She talks a kind of mad shorthand, Julia thought, which I understand because I share it.

'We ought to see things duller, flatter, more on the surface.'

'What things? No, Cass, life ought surely *not* to be on the surface.'

'I think I meant we ought to see each other so. I was thinking of what your husband said.'

Julia could not find an opening to mention Simon. She said, 'You mean, it would be better for us to be ordinary friends.'

'I'm not blessed with your capacity for friendship. But yes, something like that.'

They were silent. Julia was surprised, and moved, that Cassandra had made such an effort to communicate: Thor must have had more effect on her than she bargained for. She thought that Cassandra was much worse off than she was; attachment to the Game had betrayed Cassandra into a bleak enough solitude. All the same, she felt a little flicker of irrational envy; Cassandra had appropriated their world, taken it over, turned in on herself. She could afford to be kind to Julia because she had at last efficiently shut her out. Cassandra, frowning, packed the papers together with dusty hands. Then she brushed these against each other, closed the window-seat and sat down on it.

'Well?' she said.

'We ought to see more of each other. We ought – we ought to get used to each other, oh, I do agree. Neither of us is a monster. It's all been rather silly. And it's still true I can talk better to you than to anyone – this is a real talk we've just had, the first I've had for ages. We ought to have grown out of – all that other.'

'Yes.' Cassandra felt tired; she recognized in herself a feeling, familiar enough, that Julia, present, was not formidable, was even likeable.

'Why don't I come and look you up in Oxford? We could do some sight-seeing together. And have nice normal cups of tea.'

Julia felt splendidly that she was at last knitting up a rent that ran across the whole web of her life. And Cassandra smiled, briefly. 'If you can find the time, I'd like that,' she said. She looked round her room. 'Have a cigarette,' she said, repeating, belatedly, her gesture to Deborah. Julia accepted, smiling; they could pick up where they had left off at school. They could face each other and grow. They would diminish, in each other's mind, to manageable proportions.

Cassandra went to bed congratulating herself on having at least made some effort to pay the debt she owed to the pale Scandinavian. She had tried, because of what he had said, to face a fact, and found it now rather exhausting. Like Julia, she had felt unable to mention Simon, who had been, she thought, in many ways just another piece in the Looking-Glass chess game whose moves and maps had been laid out long before his arrival. He had a real existence of his own, but it did not, whatever she had hoped or wanted, concern her. He was far enough away, now. Whereas Julia was at hand. One should live in the real world, she told herself, getting into bed.

That night she had again one of the recurrent nightmares that had begun shortly after Simon's departure, when he might have been supposed to have left the country, and had continued with varying frequency. From these dreams she always woke changed – relieved, informed, moved, afraid, not the same woman who had put her head on the pillow. Considerable moral and emotional effort went into undoing them, into persuading herself that nothing had happened or would happen. They were so vivid and bright.

They always began with herself walking through some foreign landscape, in brilliant sunlight, in an impossible clarity – over prairie grass, over desert, through jungle creepers, along tropical beaches. They had that obsessive visual detail that was part of Cassandra. Over the months, over the years, she had studied a whole flora and fauna. She held tiny birds and remembered the cold, twig-like texture of their pink legs, the clutch of tiny claws, the area of blue, fragile skin around golden eyes, and needle-fine black beaks. One night she walked over a sandy wood floor beneath a whole flock of roosting birds the size of terriers, whose purple and gold plumage dangled from bulky pillow-case-like bodies, and, swaying between branches, brushed her hair. Another night a whole file of grass was alive with elongated, hurrying creatures, a cross between rats and lizards, with black snouts and tiny blood-red hands.

In the early stages, she had a sense of largeness. Landscape, forms of life, were capable of infinite extension. Warmth and light invaded her, like the aura of a migraine.

Simon would appear, walking unhurried. He would be glad to see her and would hold out his hands, which she never took: she knew that the impossible embrace would take place, with certainty, but that they had all the time in the world. They talked: she could usually remember what he had said. They climbed mountain paths and peered down rabbit-holes. Simon turned aside leaves and showed her, maybe, a nest of oval and circular insects, with iridescent turquoise backs, and fringes of flickering jetty legs. He had the authoritative physical presence he had in the drawing-room dream, and moved rapidly, laughing; she had to strive to keep up. Occasionally he was bizarrely dressed. Once he appeared in crimson tights, sword and frilled jabot. More usually, he wore his dirty grey flannels and swinging sports-coat. She could have counted the wrinkles in his socks. Lately, he wore bush-clothes, and there was beard-stubble on his face.

After the walking, and the shared certainty of expectation, everything gained speed, like a film taken at the wrong pace. Leaves and bushes would begin to flutter wildly. Creatures multiplied. She would notice a tree-trunk alive with scuttering mice or a section of a path boiling with innumerable insects, crawling over each other, hurrying, falling. Simon's warm presence would vanish whilst her attention was elsewhere. She would see things she recognized; a pile of those clammy, featherless baby birds, blind reptiles with gaunt triangular heads, that fall from trees. A dead mouse, with maggots lumping themselves shapelessly across the browning flesh. A flattened hedgehog, like a blood-fringed doormat. The cat, using its teeth sideways, crackling shears, on the rib-cage of a rabbit, shaking its head to free a caught tooth, making, in its throat, a low rasping sound.

CHAPTER TEN

Cassandra was glad to be back in Oxford, which was grey and muddy. She was glad to close her own door on herself, and pleased and surprised to find how many people she was, after all, connected to, by little threads of common surface conversation. The Old House always gave her an exaggerated sense that she was socially entirely isolated. But she returned energetic, made small efforts herself, and was generally thought to have mellowed. After a week she went out and hired a television set, explaining that she had a sister who was about to appear on it. On top of the box she stood the small plaster figure of Morgan, whom she had brought back from Northumberland. Both these new objects seemed slightly out of place.

She was more lively, but she was also restless, and went for long afternoon walks in the Botanical Gardens, where the river was in flood; the lawns were lakes of frozen, muddy water, ice-flakes cracking on the grass at the edges. Cassandra, coming daily, watched the water slide up strange shrubs and bushes from all parts of the world, and then slide down again, leaving the lower branches strung with roots and trails of dead grass. Leafless, they were all similar. Cassandra purchased Wellington boots and splashed around reading, with her collector's zeal for catalogued information, the little metal tags which labelled and separated them. These expeditions invigorated her: she came back to college smiling.

Immediate contact with her family was small. Deborah wrote several times – long, carefully reasoned, amusing letters, largely about literature. There was no sign of the hysteria or malice Cassandra had suspected, and she answered scrupulously and with some pleasure. This sustained, impersonal contact pleased her, too.

Deborah said nothing about Julia. Cassandra watched the first issue of *The Lively Arts*. It was called 'All in a day's work' and combined snippets of film from studio and concert hall with interviews with the artists explaining themselves and their methods. Cassandra watched Julia, curled on a Swedish daybed, with Deborah standing silent at her elbow, explain that she found it impossible to put an object in a book that wasn't a real object, somewhere. 'I need to be in touch with what's concrete.' Cassandra had never been in Julia's flat; like Simon's dark hut, it was a visible corner of a world whose dimensions were there, behind it, to be guessed, or imagined.

Three days after this, she had a letter from Julia.

Dearest Cass,

I am absolutely exhausted, and in a very funny frame of mind, and could do with a day off. I wonder if I could come for that visit we were talking about? Or didn't we mean it? I should like to think we did. Would you invite me over for the week-end or something and see how we make out? Oxford must be rather nicely mournful at this time of year I should think. I'd love to do some serious looking at buildings, that's the sort of thing I need.

That telly programme was *ghastly*, Cass, I don't expect you saw it. When it comes to it I have a horror of saying what I think, I really can't bear being pinned down. I probably just don't think *enough*, that's why it seems woolly. Still, I seem to have gone down quite well, people keep writing and asking for bits of my hair and more unmentionable things, imagine. But I feel a bit reduced and humiliated, I don't know quite why, you might know.

I see you've been writing to Debbie. Good for you. She doesn't have much to say to me, but that's supposed to be normal with mothers of adolescent girls. But you don't know much about me in that capacity do you?

Thor is well. He entertains a lot of churchy ladies, and works an eighteen-hour day at least, which is exhausting to live with.

I'm completely bogged in my next book. I seem to have just come to a stop, I don't know why. I feel I've got to change everything – my whole way of writing, my subject-matter, everything. I've got to dig deeper and spread wider. I want to write something with a few symbols and a Message. The telly makes one awfully conscious of one's lack of Message. I've got such a slithery, shapeless personality to project, no *grip*. You would have. I do want to talk to you. Look, do answer this, Cass, I need you to.

Love, J.

Cassandra read this letter several times. She found it curiously menacing in tone. She did not know whether it was a calculated appeal to her own vestigial, but occasionally powerful, protective feeling towards Julia. She decided that it might not be calculated, but that she would write back, pleasantly, and say that she was very busy. Then she read the letter again, and decided that what was threatening in it was her own contribution to it, and that the only dignified course was to ignore these feelings. She therefore booked the college's principal guest-room, wrote to invite Julia from Friday to Sunday two weeks later, and even arranged a dinner-party for the Saturday night. She was asked to comparatively few dinner-parties, and found this occasion useful for gathering together the small number of people to whom she owed invitations.

When the time came she went to meet Julia on the station, and noticed that she was gritting her teeth with apprehension. Julia stepped down from a punctual train, looking like an undergraduate, in a black soft leather coat with a fur-edged hood that gripped her face, and a black corduroy tunic over purple sleeves and purple stockings. Cassandra's huge fear settled into the recognition of a small, self-contained human being. Velvet hat nodding under its topaz pin she advanced. Julia gave a welcoming cry, and after a brief hesitation they took each other's hand. It was the first time they had met, or arranged to meet, simply to see each other.

Julia began talking very fast. 'This is wonderful. *Oxford*. I want you to take me on a real tourist's guided tour. I want to see everything, absolutely everything . . .'

Cassandra took Julia's case in her little, black-gloved hand, and they found a taxi.

'I thought you might find it interesting to dine in Hall tonight. But you might prefer a restaurant? The food in Hall is said to be very bad.'

'Oh, no, I should love to dine in Hall. I want to see exactly how you live. I told you. I want to see everything . . .'

'It's not so interesting,' said Cassandra, suddenly defensive.

Dinner in Hall was more of an ordeal than Julia had expected. They sat side by side at High Table, peering out over the rows of girls below them. Cassandra was enveloped in the folds of a black gown, over the already considerable folds of her black dress; like a bundle of old stuff, Julia thought, with her wrists and neck protruding from it, pale, stick-like, freckled, slightly shiny. Julia thought she herself would have been more at home amongst the undergraduates than amongst these women in jersey dresses, wine, grey, emerald, buckled belts riding over high bellies or dropping on shrunken hips. The younger ones wore twin-sets over tweed skirts. Someone said Grace in a cracked, female voice, and they all sat down. Conversation was made difficult by the general wawling squeal which bounded about in the body of the Hall, so that for a moment or two she watched her sister's jewelled hand carrying spoonfuls of soup regularly to her mouth, and kept silence. She turned to her neighbour – a plump, frightened-looking creature, with hair reminiscent of the White Queen's, to whom Cassandra had made no attempt to introduce her, and told her with enthusiasm, in a piercing near-shout, how much she regretted not having taken a degree. The confidence was met by a murmured and disjointed acquiescence; Julia understood from it that it was natural to desire college life but that since she had not come there she was probably not fitted to do so. She could hardly hear, and was not disposed to argue: she retreated into anonymous observation.

The main course was dried lamb chops, dried mashed potatoes, and drying tinned spaghetti in tomato sauce. Cassandra, leaning across to address someone, entangled her dangling crucifix in the spaghetti. It had to be wiped clean. Julia was rigid with embarrassment; obsessed by an image of the bloody loops of paste over the rigid, jewelled arms of the cross, she saw her sister ludicrous, even grotesque, and could not meet her eye. She thought she remembered, disproportionately, absurd facts of this kind; they made her books. They distracted one's attention, she thought, from the essence – although it was surely from such titbits of facts that one's attitude to other people was built up? She watched, hungrily, a pair of trembling blue-veined hands, clumsy, fragile, crumble the corner of a crust. Well, what was, she wondered, this essence she was missing? She looked from face to face along the table. Sexless, timid, judging, anxious, drawn-up faces, what did they want? Had they ever been like the screaming, sprawling girls below them? Were they, like Cassandra, in retreat into another world where things happened more perfectly and more intensely? Across the table two women had prolonged a conversation about brands and durability of sewing-machines throughout the meal. Did they want knowledge or power, were they hungry for the academic praise that had singled them out in youth? She collected their expressions with a speculative curiosity she would have said was akin to love. She looked at Cassandra and saw that she was being observed.

'I think we'll have coffee in my room,' said Cassandra.

They had not yet been in Cassandra's rooms. Whilst Cassandra made coffee, Julia wandered up and down, restlessly, touching everything, fingering figures over the hearth, rearranging pens on the desk, reading bits of essays, spinning globes with a finger-nail.

'Sit down, won't you?' said Cassandra.

Julia ran a hand along the top of the television. 'I see you've got Morgan here.'

'Yes,' said Cassandra. She set out cups and sugar. 'Black or white?'

'Black. What's all this?'

'A critical edition of the *Morte d'Arthur*. For students. Nearly completed.' She drew up a footstool, gathered herself into the crimson chair, pushed a cigarette into an ivory holder, poured coffee, and reiterated, 'Sit down, won't you?'

Julia took her coffee, and sat on a stool, opposite her sister. A clock ticked.

'Where did you get the lovely little figures, Cass? Tell me about your day – how do you spend your time? Do you enjoy teaching – do you like students? Do you hold with all this about the Grail story being really a fertility myth? Do you think . . .'

Cassandra told her, dry and informative. About the tutorial system, Cassandra's summers in Ravenna, the relationship between the Fisher King, the blind Norse God, Hothur, who slew Baldur his brother, because fate so willed it, and the blind soldier Longinus whose spear pierced Christ's side, released blood which restored his sight, and passed into the Grail legend with Joseph of Arimathea's cup. They both had a sense that they were restoring, through talking about these things, the good parts of the old relationship in an innocent way.

'It's like – it really *is* like – being in the room you have seen just a corner of in a mirror,' Julia said. 'I've thought so much about all this, I'm glad it's real, I'm glad I'm here.'

Cassandra looked at her sharply from inside the wings of her chair. What she would have said to this was lost, since there was a knock on the door and a girl came in with half an essay and an apology. Julia stood up, and slid into Cassandra's bedroom. Behind her she heard the beginning of a halting explanation.

She went round the bedroom with some thoroughness, fingering Cassandra's dressing-gown on the door, reading the titles of the books which covered the wall above the bed-head, surprised to find, shiny and virginal-looking, *The Silver Swan*, by Julia Corbett, and also *The Trivial Round*. She took these down and observed her own smile, apologetic and inviting, on the dust-jacket. 'Julia Corbett is an extraordinary woman who portrays with grim accuracy the trials of ordinary women.' Oh, Christ. She put them back. Had Cassandra read them? Or had someone sent them, and had Cassandra put them up there unread? She found several locked volumes of Cassandra's journal, neatly labelled simply with the year. So that went on. She turned back Cassandra's bedspread and observed a long-sleeved, navy, viyella nightdress and a lace bed-jacket under the pillow. She went through a pile of magazines on the bedside table. *Speculum*, *Review of Mediaeval English Studies*, *The Bibliographer*, *St Eusebius' Parish Magazine*, *Nature World*. This was a month old. On page 12 was an article: *The least-explored fauna in the world*. 'Simon Moffitt tells of new discoveries among the smaller reptilians in the Amazon basin. A new giant toad.'

So. Julia tapped the sad, slightly hairy face with a finger-nail and replaced the magazine where she had found it. So.

There was a palm-cross, slightly dusty, in a small silver vase on the same table and a letter from Gerald Rowell. This thanked Cassandra for her invitation, and agreed that his curate's views on the Church Triumphant, as expressed in his last sermon, might be said to be misleading. 'Like most young people, he's an enthusiast. Naturally, I have spoken to him about it.' The letter ended 'I was more glad than I can say to hear that all goes well with you, and that the terror is receding. I think it might reassure you if I tell you both that I know the terror is real and horrible, and that I genuinely believe you can bring yourself through it. You have a great deal of courage.'

Another, mysterious Cassandra. Julia thought a moment. On her way past the door she heard her sister's lecturing voice, accurate, mocking, repeating each accusation once, for emphasis, after the point had been taken. She looked at her face, alive and tremulous, in Cassandra's mirror, and allowed herself a moment of pure dislike. She knew where Cassandra had learned to wear people down in that way, to humiliate, to hurt.

She wandered back into the other room in time to take to herself an admiring glance from the departing student for her clothes, or her face, or both. Deep inside the chair Cassandra said, 'Would you care for a glass of brandy?' Julia looked sharply at her, trying to see under the bundle of clothes, under that harsh voice, through her own sense of failure and blunted love, the person who lived in these rooms alone. What was it like to be Cassandra? Like a spider, in a web, waiting. No, that was her own feeling about Cassandra. 'I'd love some brandy.'

Cassandra stood up and searched in a cupboard. 'I'm no good with girls. Too impatient. Not that they care, anyway.'

Julia thought, she is not attracted by them, as I suppose many of these women are. She is simply jealous of them. As with me.

Cassandra handed her a lady-like quantity of brandy in a liqueur glass.

'I enjoyed our talk, Cass. I'm so glad I came. I love seeing how you live, it's about time you were simply *real* as far as I'm concerned. Do you know what I mean?'

'Oh yes, I know.'

'We are going to be able to meet, and be pleased, and not think about each other, aren't we? Out of our different absorbing lives – the *real people*, meeting.'

'Yes,' said Cassandra, grinning.

'You're mocking me.'

'You are always too ready to think that.'

'I mean – we're just other people in the world, only we know each other well.'

'Oh yes, I agree.' Cassandra smiled. 'We are doing something perfectly normal, and we think ourselves clever.'

'Well it's about time we did see each other for what we are,' said Julia; they raised their glasses to each other with a queer courtesy, and drank.

When Julia had gone to bed in the guest-room, Cassandra went round her own room, twitching at curtains and chair covers. After some thought, she put Queen Morgan into a desk drawer. After some further thought, she plucked out the copy of *Nature World* and stuffed it into the bottom of a file labelled '*Sir Percivale: Variants*'.

On Saturday Julia insisted on an even more intensive course of sight-seeing than what Cassandra had already conscientiously planned. Together, in black patent knee-high boots and furred bottines they covered the wet streets, Bodleian, Ashmolean, Sheldonian, a string of college chapels and libraries. Julia asked intelligent questions about carvings and glass, and made confidences about Deborah – 'she's lucky to have you to complain to' – and Thor. 'The situation's got easier. He's got such a lot of visitors. Smelly old women he doesn't introduce. Indians in turbans. There's a sort of wild busyness about him. He doesn't seem to mind me so much – either way. I suppose that makes things easier.'

'I've no doubt he'll contain himself somehow,' said Cassandra. 'He seems determined to do so.'

Julia looked at her suspiciously and went back to her speculation: what was it like to be Cassandra? She was beginning to feel she could know this; as they came back up the High she felt that they had at last reached a point where the inevitable knowledge of long acquaintance could become an intelligent love. She studied the bony, rigid profile beside her and felt for a moment that she shared Cassandra's stern purposes, Cassandra's evasions, Cassandra's solitude.

Cassandra had to conduct an interview in the afternoon: Julia went through the curio shops in the High, looking for something for Deborah. At tea-time she returned to Cassandra's room, with a parcel.

'I bought you a present, Cass. It seems appropriate. I hope it's appropriate. It's very beautiful. I hope you don't think it's in bad taste. The moment I saw it I thought you ought to have it.'

Cassandra unplucked, slowly, Sellotape and two layers of bottle-green tissue paper. Julia's present was a snake, about two feet long, made of sulphur-yellowish glass. It was rigid from head to tail, although the surface was moulded to suggest a certain curving bumpiness; the head rested level with the body and the undersurface suggested to the hand the spread of slackened and easy muscles. The head was flat, and broad-snouted, with the suspicion of a horn above the nostril. It was beautifully coloured, with rhombs and coins of two dull greens and a dark gold all along its body, and a black line interweaving. Inside, flowing and turning under the green and gold, was a confused network of crimson lines, suggesting viscera, or a mapping of the nervous system. It had crimson, slightly convex eyes, which were the orifices of crimson funnels whose pointed ends met inside the skull. Between the flat lips, inside the delicately curving white teeth, lay a black thread of forked tongue, whose root was at the juncture of the eyes. Cassandra turned the cold glass in her hands.

'It's terribly realistic in a funny way,' Julia said. 'I mean, considering how artificial it is, it's realistic. And so very three-dimensional – I suppose because it's transparent.'

'A dimension of inwardness,' Cassandra said slowly. It was important to Julia that Cassandra should accept the gift, as it is important, after a reconciliation, that both parties should take, even share, a joke on the subject of the quarrel. This was between the two of them.

'You could look at it for a long time,' said Cassandra, 'and not come to the end of it. Thank you.'

She placed it carefully on top of the television. Julia noticed, then, that Morgan le Fay had been removed overnight.

They received the first dinner-guest, Father Rowell, side by side in front of the forbidding white marble hearth of the college's Havisham room – named after a benefactor, but associated by generations of irreverent students with dedicated and cobwebbed emotion. Julia wore a long, plain, flame-red fine woollen shift, with long sleeves, which she was glad of since the room was chilly. She had gathered a knot of her hair on top of her head and spiked it with a silver pin. Round her neck she wore a chain of flat, hammered links. The effect was one of organized barbarism. Cassandra had brought out her only evening dress, which appeared at all Gaudies; this was made of green and gold velvet, and had long, widening sleeves. She had strewn necklaces with more than usual profusion into the scooped-out neckline, and the knobs of her collar-bone protruded between fine chains of gold, parting them. Julia thought: we look like Goneril and Regan out of a bad modern production set in a cross between the Elizabethan and the Stone Ages. All we need is a white and Grecian Cordelia. She still felt great warmth and tenderness towards Cassandra, and was dismayed to see that her sister's dress was parting at the seams in the armpits. Cassandra was not a woman to whom one could point out these things. She herself was a woman only too easily embarrassed by them.

Father Rowell bent over Cassandra's hand and lifted it to his lips. 'Cassandra my dear. I trust all is well with you.'

Cassandra stiffened.

'May I introduce my sister, Mrs Julia Eskelund?'

'How do you do.' The priest put out a momentary, boneless hand. 'How do you do?'

His look met Julia's, flickered into focus, and slid away above her head. Julia thought, queer. She was one of those women who claim instantaneous recognition of homosexuality in men; 'something about the *eyes*' she would explain, wisely. Father Rowell's eyes were a very diluted blue, behind gold-rimmed spectacles. His face had the thick smoothness of wax, and so had his head, except for two tufts of very pale, gingery fluffy hair above his ears. He wore what Julia thought of as a long black skirt, under which his boots seemed large, and clumsy. Out of shyness perhaps, although it seemed more like deliberate rudeness, he did not speak to Julia, but turned one shoulder to her and said to Cassandra, 'I see you are not coming with us to Glastonbury this year?'

'Well –' said Cassandra, 'I have so much on my hands . . .'

'Too much work, perhaps,' said the priest.

Julia looked quickly from one to the other, collecting tones of voice. She had never heard anyone speak to Cassandra with that note of indulgent authority. Nor had she known Cassandra in that way shy, or placating. They moved on to some question concerning the curate's views on the Sarum and Roman chasubles, which Julia saw as low comedy; she felt immensely touched by a kind of gawky, ersatz domesticity that came over her sister. She is another middle-aged lady latching her feelings on to the necessarily available priest, she thought; she was unaware of Cassandra's momentary revulsion from her own consciousness of this.

The other guests arrived in a body. They were Professor Nathaniel Storrin, a mediaevalist, Martin Redman, a young Fellow of a college, his wife, Sylvia, who had been Cassandra's student five years ago, and Miss Vanessa Curtess, a Fellow of Cassandra's college and an expert on Huysmans. Professor Storrin greeted Cassandra impetuously, both arms outstretched. Cassandra, reaching for him, split her seams further, so that now a very large slice of pale flesh was visible. Storrin was a man who looked dignified and profound, with a long, aquiline, English face, silver hair and a tall stoop. Martin Redman was square and stocky; his wife followed at his heel: she was a round red-cheeked girl with a pudding-basin hair-cut and a short, emerald taffeta dress with a bow balanced on her bottom. Vanessa Curtess was a heavy, dark, shingled woman. She wore a dress of coffee-coloured lace whose square-cut neckline jutted forward like a boat's prow, revealing the line where the severe brassière cut across the swelling flesh of her bosom. When she was introduced to Julia she flushed, neck to brow. Julia was beginning to feel happy. She understood parties, even parties like this. In all the novels she had written parties had taken place.

A maid bobbed at them with a tray of glasses of medium dry sherry. Cassandra, Gerald Rowell and Storrin were engaged in an informed conversation about the Celtic Theory. Julia looked automatically across at Martin Redman, but Miss Curtess was telling him something about simple-minded insularity and looked angry. Sylvia Redman was at her elbow.

'You must be really Julia Corbett. I saw you on the television. It never occurred to me you were related to our Miss Corbett. You're so dissimilar . . .'

'No, I'm *really* Mrs Eskelund. I've got a husband and a great big daughter at home.'

'Yes, I know. I know that of course. I – I like your books. They – they deal with a real problem, one nobody thinks anything ought to be done about. That is – women, intelligent women, who are suddenly plunged into being at home all day. The – the real boredom. I – I love my babies – I've got two – very much. But some days I just sit down and cry out of a – a knowledge of waste. Waste. The indignity and waste of being a woman. I know. I'm much less interesting than I was as an undergraduate. And I can't say I don't mind.'

'I never was an undergraduate. But I'm sure you're right about waste. And boredom. Women get far too great a share of boredom. That's something the novel can explore. The novel makes it not boring.'

'The glory and the horror and the boredom,' said Sylvia Redman, predictably. Julia remembered Cassandra saying 'One should forgo one's need for a sense of glory.' Such a need leads one into odd habits, she thought, and smoothed the red dress over her hips.

'Life closes in, just when one imagines it will do the opposite,' said the intense girl. 'Now I keep telling myself I must keep up with things. Do some organized reading, or something. But – keeping up just simply for the sake of keeping up – seems so petty, somehow. Nothing more than not admitting defeat. And since the babies I get so tired. They don't tire me, it isn't that I work hard, but life's tiring. The effort of starting up again in the evenings. The awfulness, if one does start up, of them starting crying.'

'Yes, I do know.' Julia surveyed her absently. She thought, you tell everyone this, this is the only thought you think. You look to me as though you gave up without much struggle. And that green taffeta doesn't bear witness to any real acquaintance with the glory and the horror. If there was one thing you cared enough about, Julia thought, you'd start up again in the evenings fast enough. She grinned quickly to herself on this thought, looked up, and caught the priest's eye, cold and judging. Martin Redman seemed to be trying to shake off Miss Curtess; he joined Julia and Sylvia rather abruptly, trailing her behind him.

'All this prescriptive moral good health,' she was saying, 'is so limiting. We need a more passive freedom – to explore the intricacies of our real corruption, to know coldly what we are capable of –'

'I don't want that kind of nasty freedom, thank you,' said Martin. 'I happen to value decency. Scrupulousness. Good judgement.'

'Lawrence,' said Vanessa Curtess, 'was neither scrupulous nor a good judge.'

'Oh, my God,' said Martin. He moved sideways, opening the circle so that the group of mediaevalists was added to it.

'Darling,' said Sylvia, 'did you know that Miss Corbett's sister is really Julia Corbett, the novelist?'

Martin looked Julia over.

'I saw you on television,' he announced. 'Talking about your art. Hacking away at your husband's character. I wouldn't stand for that if I was him. I've not read any of your books. I just turned the telly on to see what that chap had to say about *musique concrète*, but all he did was put on a funny act like a monkey with a hurdy-gurdy. Don't you think that sort of programme hopelessly degrades art in any case? How can you take your work seriously and get mixed up in that sort of thing?'

'Oh, I don't think my work's good enough to take seriously in that sense,' Julia said slowly. 'Except, maybe, intermittently. Honest comfort for the masses, that's all it is, and fodder for the sociologist. But it is honest, and I'm not saying it's negligible – sociologists need a bit of imagination.'

She thought she might go on and defend the television, and decided against it; there she must forfeit his sympathy. He was very young and his rudeness, she thought, covered not only uncompromising morals but a will not to be impressed, which suggested he might be impressionable. She told him, half-mocking, that he clearly held an orthodox Lawrentian view about the subjection of women. As for herself, she had luckily found a way of life that could dovetail with normal female preoccupations without disrupting them. But this imposed limitations on her and he must allow for them. She claimed no more than the virtues of an accurate recorder; she did not write pretentious sub-literature. She spoke very seriously, with a kind of eager, wide-eyed honesty which at one level dispelled his fear of pretension or humbug and at another was direct sexual provocation. He expanded; he laid out his views on art and morals; honesty to the honest critic is always disarming. She could feel him enjoy a sense of coping with someone of her kind. 'At least you've got drive,' he said, with rough admiration.

Cassandra saw that Sylvia, one of the few students for whom she had felt affection, was looking distressed. She had suffered enough from

Martin's useful views on female subjection, Cassandra thought; it was too much that she should be further required to watch him admire Julia's ruthlessness.

'What became of your poetry, Sylvia?' she asked abruptly.

Sylvia flushed. 'Oh, nothing much. It wasn't very good, really. It was frightfully adolescent.'

Martin looked as though he concurred. Cassandra was irritated. Sylvia had been writing a good thesis on images of the Virgin before child-bearing overtook her, and had brought Cassandra one or two long, faintly Christian poems about Glastonbury, or Dame Julian of Norwich.

'They were very promising,' Cassandra persisted. 'Too many words, too much Dylan Thomas, but you'd have grown out of that. You had a real feeling for imagery.'

Sylvia hung her head and looked distressed.

'Charles Williams more than Dylan Thomas, I'd have said,' was Martin's contribution. Cassandra saw that she had made things worse and was humiliated. She moved clumsily towards the dining table. Martin and Julia turned to each other and shrugged briefly; Cassandra was exasperated by the lack of logic behind this alliance. She arranged the seating to separate them, which left Julia between Father Rowell and Professor Storrin, and Martin to continue his interrupted argument with Vanessa Curtess.

The dinner was the one the college offered for its student feasts. Grapefruit cocktails, roast chicken and sprouts, ice cream with chocolate sauce, a platter of cheeses: processed Camembert, Danish Blue, Edam. Julia turned her attention to Professor Storrin.

Storrin saw himself as a man of the world, and had decided already that, in this gathering at least, Julia was his foil. His reasons for being a mediaevalist were remote from Cassandra's. He liked the don's gentlemanly life, and had chosen mediaeval studies because they were largely untilled ground, where a clever man might rapidly make discoveries enough to establish himself. He did some solid and accurate linguistic work, wrote an elegant and emotive volume on the Dance of Death, and plunged into television, where he frequently put forward the views of the University on education, the nuclear bomb, premarital sexual intercourse, the degrading aspects of the current preoccupation with violence, child-rearing, and the ritual slitting of cows' throats. Julia found him familiar. She had met his kind in London and could handle him. For some time they spoke with graceful dignity of buildings Julia had seen, and of the real value of responsible, televised, summings-up of serious issues. But when they had all had several glasses of the college's good Riesling, and when Vanessa Curtess's voice was raised high about the differences between Lawrence's Dark Gods and Baudelaire's real knowledge of our separation from light, he leaned confidentially towards her, and, resting his long, ascetic hand gently on hers, he murmured personal criticisms of common acquaintances, and later, whilst they were waiting for coffee, even of those present. He told her, in a beautifully pitched undertone, a history of an uninformed High Table rudeness of Martin's which had been neatly twisted against its author. He gave her a gem of a lecture on the dangers of being a fat red woman and in love with *la vie Bohème* or Baudelaire. 'What virginal deprivations are there fed, Mrs Eskelund, what subconscious needs made respectable, what knowledge – precluded, one must suppose, by certain physical disadvantages – vicariously acquired and made, to quote Rimbaud out of context, *idéal* . . .' His clear eyes behind the grey lashes were delighted; everything was ridiculous. Julia, intensely happy, responded to the familiar movements of the familiar dance. When coffee came the general conversation died and Storrin and Julia took over completely, making a sidling circus parade of the physical, emotional, sexual and intellectual oddities of a number of public persons more or less known to them. Martin laughed robustly. Vanessa Curtess found the atmosphere both repulsive and interesting. Sylvia watched Martin, and studied Julia's deprecatory grin.

Cassandra was not happy. She was not the sort of woman who would have called out in Storrin the lively malice he now displayed. She had always, with a kind of innocence, expected of him a scholarly seriousness which he effortlessly produced. She found his work, and therefore himself, slightly pedestrian. Cassandra had always, like Charlotte Brontë incurably romantic, nourished a vision of herself, the epic written, arriving with all her integrity in the literary world to be belatedly *fêted* by the Thackeray of the day. She saw now that this world was not what she had thought and was for ever closed to her, and, worse, Julia's incursion into her own world revealed to her that that too had, and must always have had, dimensions she was incapable of apprehending. She looked at her brick-red colleague with Storrin's and Julia's eyes, and her stomach contracted with fear for herself. She remembered Simon's tea-party.

Julia, as if she read this thought, suddenly produced for the company an imitation of a forthcoming imitation of Simon Moffitt on a satirical television programme.

'We used to know him, didn't we, Cass?' she flung across at her, challenging, insistent on sharing. She pushed out her lower lip in a prettily ineffectual imitation of Simon's pout. 'We all have to suffer,' she droned. 'I have come out here at vast expense to expose myself to sleeping sickness, toothache, damp, sheat fish, piranhas, squeezing snakes and biting snakes, just to make sure I don't miss out on my share of it.'

Everyone laughed, even Sylvia. Cassandra fingered the velvet of her dress and forgot to offer second cups of coffee. The party, in consequence, broke up early.

Storrin said, 'Well you will have plenty of material for an authentic book about academic life, Mrs Eskelund.' Julia invited him to a drink in London to meet Ivan, whom she had not been able to avoid mentioning from time to time with an intonation of special knowledge and affection. She was momentarily chilled by Gerald Rowell's farewell.

'Good night, er, Father,' she said, brightly. He gave her a pale, preoccupied look and a command.

'Good night, Mrs Eskelund. I trust to see you tomorrow, after Sung Eucharist. Good night.'

When they had gone Julia turned to her sister.

'That was a splendid party,' she said warmly.

'I'm glad you thought so,' said Cassandra, the old, closed, blunt Cassandra, 'I must get to bed, if you'll excuse me.'

Julia, who had been prepared for an agreeable, slightly drunken, between-sisters, post-mortem, during which she trusted to efface any traces of a bad impression she might have made, felt cheated, and then hurt.

Cassandra did not breakfast on Sundays. Julia ate alone, and then went to ask whether she might go with her to church.

'I shouldn't have thought you would care to.'

'Oh, yes I do. I want to.'

'You must not suppose you will please me by coming.'

'Oh, no. It isn't that. But I do want to come, please. I brought a hat.'

She had indeed brought a kind of leather boater which she placed flat on her head when they set out together. Cassandra went fast and silently.

Julia felt bad, and wanted to cry. They had lost yesterday's ease, and were again suspicious. Julia was ready to take the blame; they had always so arranged it that she took the blame. But she was given no opening even for that.

Inside the church she was stiffly embarrassed whilst Cassandra bowed to the altar; she sat in the pew, staring round, whilst Cassandra bent her head. In front of them was a row of deaconesses; to the left a group of severe-looking undergraduates; the rest of the pews were sparsely scattered with old ladies, black felt hats, grey, feathered hats, swathed turbans, murmuring lips.

The service was more alien than she had expected, and large expanses of it were inaudible. She found Gerald Rowell, bustling to and fro in a stook of vestments, more than a little absurd; she winced when he intoned. A choir sang, shrill and sweet, the clear sound floating on a sea of cracked and lagging and troubled notes from the old ladies. Julia would have liked to be moved by the words, but could not. Her response to them resembled too much the easy-flowing sentiment she bestowed on Christmas card crinolines and candles. She tried to think what they meant to Cassandra. Form, certainty? She could remember Cassandra's chanting voice from their childhood. Cassandra had always been one for ritual, although it was herself, in her simplicity, who had worshipped the saintly Galahad. Cassandra had early recognized the dramatic value of the tormented Lancelot. She asked herself: what sins does Cassandra confess to?

Cassandra felt Julia's scrutiny like a sharp light on her thoughts and was superstitiously afraid to pray in case her prayer might be read. She looked up at the carving in the roof, curving, lacing, twisting, crossing, and slant across at a carved pew-end which sprouted, from a round wooden head, a feathery profusion of leaves, tumbling grapes, threading stems of vines. She tried to imagine how the church must appear under Julia's questioning gaze. The smell of incense, a little stale, a little sickly. The ruffled flock of old women come in for refuge from the cold. She was becoming one of them herself, despite the jewels in her hat and on her hands. Julia would judge it coldly, vestments, singing, clattering of bells, a tatty substitute for glory. We make these symbols from our own sense of glory? For a moment, not for the first time, Cassandra was fiercely hungry for the simplicities of the Meeting-house.

Afterwards, Cassandra was absorbed into the flock of deaconesses, and Julia found herself standing alone with Gerald Rowell just inside the churchyard gate. He had on a flat, rounded hat, rather like her own.

'Mrs Eskelund, good morning. When are you leaving us?'

'This afternoon. I've enjoyed my visit.'

He paused. 'And how do you find Cassandra?'

'Well,' said Julia. 'Isn't she?' She pulled at her rings.

'There was something I had hoped to say to you.' He paused again. 'I wonder.'

'You can't tell, until you've said it.'

'No. You were not very considerate, as far as Cassandra is concerned, yesterday evening. Forgive me.'

Julia stiffened.

'I know you are not particularly friendly. But I do not know who else . . .'

'We see very little of each other, that's all. I'm sure you know her better than I do.'

'She is not a woman who allows herself to be known. Or liked. I wish I knew, Mrs Eskelund, whether I were asking you for help, or warning you. In any case – yes – I think you should know. Cassandra is – not well. She has not been well for some time.'

'What do you mean?'

'I am not as well acquainted as I should doubtless be with psychiatry. I believe a psychiatrist would diagnose some form of – schizophrenia. Which covers many ills. Cassandra has' – he sought, overtly, for a proper delicacy of phraseology – 'only a very tenuous connection with reality. She is aware of this, which makes it, in some ways, worse. It is of course, partly, an occupational hazard. But her world is – remote enough from the usual cloistered abnormalities of college life.'

'She always had a powerful imagination,' said Julia, looking the priest directly in the eye.

'Precisely. I do believe she is in some danger. She is a courageous woman. And does not make things easy for herself.'

'What am I to do, Father?'

'Now I see you – I don't know. I had hoped you might – draw her back a little, as it were, into daily life. I don't know. Extend her possibilities? Although too much of the wrong sort of reality might endanger – a very delicate balance. Yes.'

'I do love her,' said Julia with simplicity. 'She's very suspicious. I think there's almost nothing I can do. But I do love her, and I'll do what I can. I do mean well.'

'It was perhaps impertinent to speak to you. I am sure – your sister – would consider it a betrayal of confidence. But I felt you should know.'

'Thank you,' said Julia gravely. She cast down her eyes. 'And you were right to tell me I behaved badly. I'm sorry.'

'It was impolite of me to mention it,' said the priest, and turned away to greet a parishioner.

Julia went to sleep almost immediately in the train and was woken, as it gathered speed, by the rattle of her teeth and the knock of her bones on the glass against which she rested her face. She sat upright with a struggle. She was given to thinking deeply in trains; the necessary loneliness and unrelatedness drove her to taking stock. She thought: I can't go on as I am. This was the thought with which she had come to Oxford; now she was more troubled, nothing was settled in her mind. Lately, at home, she had more and more obsessively related her fears to Cassandra – both her lack of self-confidence, and her feeling that the life she had was flimsy and meaningless. It all went back, it went back to the veiled subtleties of the Game. The train clattered on and her body shook.

She thought about her conversation with the priest, and about his letter to Cassandra. Cassandra had, had she, 'only a very tenuous connection with reality'? Well, what sort of 'glorious' reality did she inhabit? She remembered the copy of *Nature World*, and the photograph by which she had been, herself, not unpleasantly stirred, and thought she knew something. Oh, Cassandra.

I don't, she thought, use my imagination enough, and she uses hers too much. Like Wordsworth and Coleridge, one trying to 'give the charm of novelty to things of every day', whilst the other – Julia's memory struggled with a disquisition on the topic she had heard from Cassandra years ago – the other likes 'persons and characters supernatural, or at least romantic'. How did it go on? Something about transferring human interest from our 'inward nature' and 'a semblance of truth sufficient to procure for these shadows of imagination that willing suspension of disbelief for the moment . . .' – ah, yes – 'that constitutes poetic faith'. We are both too extreme. It's true what they say about me, I remain on a level of complaining about facts.

There's a theme for a novel, there, she thought: a novel about the dangers of imbalance between imagination and reality. 'A very tenuous connection . . .' I could do it, I think; it would mean coming to grips with the Game. It would be a way of coming to grips with what's frightened me, with what I could, but don't, understand. It would be a real novel, with a real idea behind it, not a complaint. It would be a way of coming to grips with Cassandra, but also of detaching us. It would be a way of seeing her as a separate individual. Knowledge, after all, was love. A lighting up of the other.

She remembered Storrin's voice. 'You will have plenty of material for an authentic book about academic life.' It couldn't be done of course. Cassandra would see it only as an attack. With all the dignity and imagination she was undoubtedly paranoiac. It would be interesting to explore that, in the novel, too. It was a pity it couldn't be done. Julia, who had been prepared to flinch from the memory of certain parts of her week-end, sat up suddenly and began deliberately to remember everything, relating one episode to another, one incident symbolically to the next. They were all lit and glittering parts of a pattern; one took possession and in the same movement detached oneself. Even the humiliations were precious. Such moments of imaginative vision were rare and valuable – knowledge, any knowledge at all, was beautiful, every accident of surface or emotion related, with no effort on her part beyond the simple will to see.

It would be a good novel, because it would not be about herself. It was a pity it couldn't be done.

Julia smiled.

CHAPTER ELEVEN

When Julia came into the hall of the flat, the telephone was ringing. She had heard it all the way up the stairs. She put down her suitcase and lifted the receiver. The voice began at once.

'Mr Eskelund. Mr Eskelund.' It was a shrill voice, on the edge of tears.

'This is Mrs Eskelund,' said Julia. She added: 'I'm sorry.'

'Well, is he there, then? Can you get him for me? Can you look, please, I've got to speak to him.'

'I'll look,' said Julia. 'I've just got in. I think he must be out.'

This was not answered. Julia rested the receiver on the shelf, and went into the flat. She could feel that no one was there. In the living-room was a pile of four large sacks, roped round with twine, and a baby's bath. In the bedroom the bed had not been made. Deborah's room had a notice fixed to the door with drawing-pins. 'Keep Out. At Work. This Means You.' Julia knocked and went in. She ruffled through a pile of papers on Deborah's desk, and turned over a Letts' Desk Diary; flicking the pages, she saw they were filled with close tiny writing. She stopped to read the first entry. 'I have decided to keep a diary to make myself think out what I really feel: I am not going to bother to record events for their own sake, daily happenings that are just as well forgotten. If I did that this diary might be interesting in 50 years, details for historians and novelists. As it is it will certainly appear banal in the extreme. But *I am doing it for myself*. Myself, now, and since I shan't re-read it I shan't bother if it's embarrassing.'

Good stuff, Julia thought, and remembered the telephone.

'Are you there? He doesn't seem to be here.'

'Where is he then? Can you get hold of him?'

'I don't know. I've just got in.'

'I need to speak to him. When will he come home?'

'I don't know.'

'Soon or late?'

'I –'

'It's *very* urgent.'

'Can I take a message?'

'No, no. I'll just ring later, that's best.'

'Or can I do anything to help?'

'I'll just ring later, thank you.'

'I'll tell him you called.'

'No, don't do that, I'll ring him later, that's best.'

'Can't you –' Julia began, but the caller had rung off. Julia, slightly unnerved, went back into the living-room and surveyed the alien sacks. The baby's bath was well worn, the plastic scratched and scored, the whole slightly grey. She kicked the sacks gently with one pointed foot. They yielded: cloth, of some kind.

She took off her coat and hat, feeling let down by her family's absence, and was heading for Deborah's room again when the front door bell rang. At the same time the telephone pealed again. Julia opened the door, beckoned vaguely to the man on the doorstep to come in and ran to the telephone.

'Hullo, Julia Eskelund speaking.'

'Is Mr Eskelund there?'

Julia could not tell whether this was the same voice.

'No. I don't know where he is.'

'Oh, God,' wildly. And then, more belligerently, 'I can't understand it.'

'Can I take a message?' Julia said, but the connection was broken.

Behind her a man in a duffel coat was carrying a pile of blankets across the hall, and a woman in tartan stockings and a young man with sparse curls and a dandruff-spattered olive-green sweater were carrying a cot, a potty, and part of a high chair into her living-room. She followed them nervously.

'Hullo,' she said, smiling. 'I'm Julia Eskelund.'

'Bill Terry,' said the man. He had a double chin and was moist with effort. He breathed heavily and volunteered no more. Julia turned to the others.

'Lorna Terry. And Douglas,' the woman said, brushing her hands together. 'Where do you want the cots, Mrs Eskelund?'

'I don't know . . . My husband . . . I don't know where my husband is . . .'

She could not bring herself to ask their business; they were sufficiently clearly something to do with Thor.

'I'll just get the mattresses,' said Bill. Julia began to push pieces of her own furniture ineffectively against the wall, to make room for what might still come. The thought crossed her mind that the flat had simply become a collecting depot for Oxfam. She did not, somehow, want to test this hypothesis by asking.

'Can I make you some coffee?' she said to Lorna Terry, who was screwing two sides of a cot together, just inside the kitchen door. The telephone rang.

'There's a woman keeps ringing up and frightening me,' she said to Lorna, confidingly. Lorna smiled briefly through the bars of the cot. The boy, Douglas, was for some reason undoing one of the sacking bales. This made her apprehensive. She went out to answer the telephone.

'Please,' she said, 'please, will you . . .'

'Ah, Ju. Ivan here.'

'*Darling*,' said Julia. 'Darling, I'm in such chaos.'

'As always, my beautiful. What is it this time?' Julia lowered her voice and cupped her hand over the phone. 'I don't exactly know.'

'What did you say?'

'Oh, forget it, I'll tell you later.'

'You do sound distraught. How did your exorcism go?'

'It wasn't an exorcism. It was a visit.'

'I adore you. You don't sound as though it's done you much good. Shall I come round?'

'Not at the moment. There's such chaos.'

'Can't I come and help?'

'Well, not exactly,' said Julia. 'Though of course I'd love you to help me with anything *at all*, darling, but this isn't exactly your cup of tea. It's something I expect I'll understand in a minute or two. It's a sort of *invasion*.'

Bill Terry humped a double mattress round the front door, rested it against the hall chest, and went in search of his wife, breathing even more heavily.

'I don't understand my life any more,' Julia said. 'It doesn't make sense. I need help. I do rely on you to sort me out, darling.'

During this speech, Thor came in through the front door and went across the hall.

'Well, can I come round and protect you?'

'No – love – no, not just now.'

'You do sound flapped.'

'I am, I am. I've got to see you.'

'And there was I thinking you'd come back a new woman. Come and have some supper and tell all.'

'I'd love to.'

'I'll ring you. Hey, Ju –'

'Yes?'

'Keep sane. Go and write it all down.'

Julia rang off. She followed her husband into the room; he was kneeling on the other side of Lorna Terry's cot, helping to screw it together. Douglas's sack was undone, and he was spreading clothing, all sexes and sizes, across the carpet in a bewildered but purposeful way.

'Well, I'm back,' said Julia.

'So I see.' He stood up, and came to embrace her.

'I've got a lot to tell you. I've done an age of thinking . . .'

'I shall be glad to hear it,' he said courteously.

The telephone rang again.

'Where's Debbie?' said Julia, and then, 'Thor, there's a fearful woman . . .'

'Excuse me, the telephone,' he said, and went out, closing the door behind him.

Julia thought she should help Douglas.

'What principle do you sort by?' she asked.

'Men's here, women's there, anything suitable for the babies in this corner, things you can't mend on that chair. Do you think you could put fly-buttons on this suit? It's a funny colour, but it's in good repair, apart from fly-buttons.'

'I'll see what I've got,' said Julia, associating herself firmly with the enterprise, whatever it was. Douglas smiled at her gratefully, and she felt better – accepted, occupied. Thor came back. He said, 'Will you have tea, Bill, Lorna?'

'I'll make tea,' Julia cried.

'That would be kind,' he said, gravely. Julia hung the suit, a grass-green and yellow tweed mixture, over a chair, and eased herself round the cot into the kitchen. Thor began to construct a second cot. He was humming to himself. He looked mild; Julia wondered why he had not told her what was happening.

As she laid out cups and saucers Julia studied the visitors with a quickened interest. Bill had rounded soft fingers; and words could be found for the ballooning smoothness of his intermediate chin; the skin had a kind of gloss and yet was not shiny; it was just taut enough to have a bloom, but not as the word bloom was normally understood. He was in need of buttons himself and had trails of thread caught unnoticed on the texture of his jacket and flannels. Julia put him down as a soft man; kind, a slow thinker. Lorna had false teeth, clearly; they had a glistening plastic completeness, no green, yellow, brown or chipped edges. This, Julia decided, was what gave her her air of artificiality – combined with the curls and red lipstick. Her clothes were all right, but typed her: grey pleated skirt, cable-stitch sweater, brogue shoes. Doubtless she wore, outdoors, a woollen cap with a tassel. Douglas had clammy hands and wrinkled socks. Julia decided that he either played a wind instrument in an amateur orchestra, or wrote bad poetry. It was in his face that he was a permanently hopeless intellectual. His curls at his temples were greasy. Julia decided that he had probably been imprisoned for his principles, and then that he might just have joined the ambulance unit. She poured out boiling water cheerfully and called to Thor, 'Darling, where's Debbie?'

'I don't know.'

Julia lifted the tea-tray and began to edge back round the cot. The door bell rang, very long, and Julia's tray tipped so that tea spouted out and swirled amongst the saucers.

'That will be the Bakers,' said Bill.

'I'll go,' said Douglas.

'No,' said Thor. 'I will.'

'Who . . . ?' said Julia. 'Milk, sugar?' she said to Lorna who did not answer.

Thor came back. He was followed by a tall man in a soft, grey woolly pork-pie hat and donkey jacket, a woman in a long blue felt coat with torn buttonholes, and two small children. Julia remembered nothing about children, but both of these were still at the short fat age and one had trailing scallops of wet nappy below her skirt. The woman carried a baby. The man was clearly largely Negro, with a kind of drained, dark yellow face; his wife was white, and the children had dark curls, large brown eyes, and, under dirt and stickiness, skin of a delicate gold like Easter eggs boiled with onion skin. They stared flatly at Julia, who stared back. The smaller child put its thumb in its mouth and rubbed its nose reflectively with a forefinger.

'Sit down,' said Thor. 'There is tea, for all.'

'May I take your coats?' said Julia. Thor looked up at her with a sharp curiosity. What *does* he expect of me, Julia asked herself. The Bakers, in the doorway shifted from uneasy foot to uneasy foot.

'This is Fred Baker,' said Thor. 'And Edna. And here are Trevor and Rosie, and the baby is Dawn.' He's learned them efficiently, Julia thought, who knew her husband to be bad at names. Thor said to Mrs Baker, 'We aren't so far ahead as we'd hoped, but I think you'll find we have everything we need. We've got bedding – and a few clothes.'

'We brought our own things,' said Mrs Baker, flatly. 'Out in the hall, they are.' She looked at Douglas's work. 'We've got clothes,' she said. She sat down on the edge of a chair and motioned to the children to stand nearer. Mr Baker took off his hat and held it submissively in front of him. His eyes were yellowed and bloodshot. It seemed to Julia now, likely that Thor meant to house these people; she wondered how long. They had had African and Indian students on the living-room couch for the week, or the night, and two pale Hungarian youths immediately after the Revolution, hungry crosses between gangsters and students of the kind England seemed not to produce. She looked again at her husband, and then asked brightly of the room at large:

'Well, what's the next move?'

Thor looked up at her and wrinkled his face – surprised, displeased? – and kept silence. Lorna Terry said warmly:

'How much space have you got? This is *very* kind of you, Mrs Eskelund. *Really* generous . . .'

'Very kind, I'm sure,' said the colourless voice of Edna Baker behind her. Fred Baker, who had not sat down, coughed.

Thor, not looking at Julia, said, 'I thought Mr and Mrs Baker could have the spare room. With the baby. And we can clear out my study for Trevor and Rosie. We can share the living-room and kitchen.'

Julia winced momentarily, then gathered herself.

'Excellent,' she said. 'We'll start on the study.' Mrs Baker said, defensively, 'It's only until Fred's got a job and we've got a place.'

Julia spun round. 'Of course,' she said. 'Of course. Now, *please* think yourselves welcome. We'll have everything fixed in a jiffy. And I'll show you the kitchen. And the children can have a bath . . .'

Thor looked at her, and smiled briefly. The telephone rang again and he went out into the hall. Julia motioned to Lorna Terry to take the other end of the cot, and they began to carry it through into the study. Thor came back again, pale, and strained-looking.

'I find I have to go out,' he said.

Julia looked at him through the gathering and smiled, warmly, generously.

'Don't worry,' she said. 'I'll manage. I'll arrange everything, by the time you get back everything'll be quite tidy.'

Thor looked at her heavily. Julia thought: he would find it easier if I'd been furious. Or hysterical. And then; well, I won't be. She went on smiling. Thor put on his coat.

Next week, Julia had supper with Ivan in his flat. They sat, youthfully cross-legged, one on each side of the hearth, eating avocado pears with teaspoons. Between them was a large bowl of savoury rice on an electric hot-plate. Ivan's flat was black and white leather, tiling, stainless steel, purple glass lights. His wife, Merle, who was an actress, was working. Ivan himself was a small, round, dimpled man, with a wispy skullcap of rather Chinese black hair, and slightly sloping eyes. He had a surprisingly deep voice.

'So what happened then, my angel?'

'So then I took charge, in a rather awful way, and we put up beds – the boy, Trevor, had the spare bed, and they had the mattress, and –'

'Spare me the domestic catalogue. I see it exercised your mind.'

'So then I *bathed* the children, darling, one of them peed in the bath. Then we all had supper – I cooked it – and then the older Terrys started giving clothes to the Bakers, and that Douglas and I did the washing-up, and he told me all. I liked Douglas,' said Julia, reflectively, meaning that Douglas had liked her. Ivan's soft lashes flickered and he grinned.

'What was *all*?'

'Well, they're London's homeless poor, and he's been in prison three times – once for breaking and entering, twice for malicious wounding, and the kids are bed-wetters and they don't want the family split. I don't know where Thor got them from – he's got on the committees of more and more of these Samaritan agencies – but anyway he apparently brought them to Meeting, and then stood up and talked for forty-five minutes about how we avoided the sufferings of others and paid out our cash so as not to have our lives invaded and how everyone had been romantically stirred by the Hungarian Revolution and had housed refugees, but no one thought to house those in need now, and that we had a duty to involve our lives in others' sufferings and most Friends, he guessed, had no moral right to the amount of space they occupied. If he'd been anyone else, he'd have been eldered after fifteen minutes. As it was, I guess from what I got out of Douglas by encouraging him with bits of jokes and things, that he thoroughly annoyed all the worthy Friends and hurt the Bakers' pride by talking about the bed-wetting, etcetera, in *front* of them.' She paused, reflectively. 'You know, the thing about Christ and St Francis and all those – even St Paul, whom I *hate*, Ivan, for his censoriousness – the thing was, they stirred people up, they appealed to their imaginations, they involved people in things. I know Thor; I've heard him speak. He thinks he can overcome people with flat facts and moral imperatives. He mumbles, too, and looks embarrassed. So that they feel a bit guilty, and a bit repelled by him, but not co-operative. So the upshot was, nobody offered, so Thor said he'd house them. But Friends feel guilty enough to be bombarding us with all their unwanted clothes, and blankets, and saucepans, and homebaked cakes and useful pieces of chintz. And we have to bundle it all up and take it round to Oxfam in vans, except what Mrs Baker thinks she might like for when they *do* get a place of their own. So I said, do make yourselves at home, and they have, for which I suppose I ought to be grateful. Only the bloody telephone never stops ringing now – I think it's not only *one* woman, it's about four, and so – so – *determined*. I think Thor's decided he's got to *live* his charity. And he's bad at it, and it involves us all.'

Ivan began to laugh.

'No, don't laugh. It's not funny. It's such a little flat, that's why I liked it. *They* think it's little, too, they keep telling me. The bathroom's full of drying-out sheets and nappies. Thor says I ought not to have scrubbed the children's heads, it takes away their dignity.'

Ivan laughed again. He laughed with his mouth closed, and twirled one foot, gracefully, in a black suède shoe and a purple sock.

'It's a judgement, Ju. He wants to drive you out. He wants to leave no room for you.'

'No, it's not that. I've thought of that. I'd know if it was that, I'm not *that* imperceptive. No, he really *is* involved in doing good. He's right in a way. If you start from first principles there *is* a sense in which we've no right to a flat, when people are being segregated into single-sex dormitories.'

'A rather remote, obscure sense, love, when you think of the complexity of modern justice.'

'He says justice should be simpler. I admire him.'

'And they? These people?'

'Well – he runs them. He says they *must* get a job. He's always on about their dignity and self-respect. And they take that, but not the way he means it. They treat him as a master. They lie to him. About – oh – minor things, breakages, telephone calls. He knows they do, he doesn't exactly mind. He's a bit clumsy – he respects them at the wrong times and then tightens up when he ought to be a bit blind.'

'Which *you* don't?'

'Oh, they love me. They don't like him, but they love me. Mrs Baker follows me from room to room like a large floppy dog peering through all her hair and telling me her life. I know a lot about her life. She's had two dead children and Mr Baker beats her. She used to work in a hotel stripping beds – you wouldn't *believe* what she saw. He was on the lift, a bit, and got sacked and took her with him. Everything she's done, she apologizes to me for. In a defiant sort of way. *Everything*. "I'm sorry to say –" she begins each sentence, and "if you don't mind" she ends it. And she has to *talk*. If I sit down to write she appears with some question about how to work the automatic potato peeler – she's broken that – and how to hang lace curtains the Terrys brought to stop the neighbours looking in at the bedroom. I *abominate* lace curtains. And – and she regularly uses my loofah and leaves black hairs twisted in it and god knows what else of my things when they're all in the bathroom.'

'Eat your rice, Ju, it'll go cold.'

'She makes things nice for me with little plastic mats –'

'*Darling*.'

'Oh, I listen, I listen, I'm not made that I can say go away. I say "it must have been dreadful". She hates everyone so for what she thinks they've "done" to her. And she expects nothing different, ever.'

'Well, you can write a domestic novel to end all domestic novels, amongst the suds and nappies.'

'That's what Debbie said. Debbie's furious. She locks herself in her room and won't come out except for meals unless he's in. She said to me' – Julia laughed nervously, because this had hurt – 'she said, "Well at least you've got some real difficulties to write a real book about, for a change." '

'A cute child. I don't like your daughter.' Julia, who was accustomed so to present Deborah that no one could like her was perversely hurt. And Ivan had not contradicted the judgement on the novels.

'She's just an awkward age. I wish she'd got a boy-friend.'

'Wouldn't let *you* have knowledge of it if she had, my beautiful.' Ivan showed all his small teeth in a white grin and began to scoop rice into his mouth with chopsticks. 'So all you can do is take voluminous notes on the tribulations of Mrs Baker.'

'*No*,' Julia wailed. 'I can't do it. Because her life was *really* awful, and I'd make her into a kind of wistful-comic charlady. Thor'd be furious with me and he'd be quite right.'

'Never mind. It can't last. Something ghastly's bound to happen, and then, my sweet, it will all be over.'

Julia persisted. 'I just can't settle to any work, I feel all uprooted, everything I do seems meaningless. I can't even – talk to Thor in bed – or anywhere – because They are always drifting by and I remember Mrs B. Seeing Everything, in her hotel.

'And I meant to try and write a *real* book – a complicated book – not about myself – and I haven't got time or space to concentrate.'

Ivan laughed. 'You all come to that. It's a mistake. You're a perfectly normal, fairly simple-minded, not unduly intelligent woman, and you write clever, circumscribed, pin-pricking little books, and you have this itch to be a prophetess, or a great sufferer. I've been waiting to say for a long time – come off it, Julia.'

'I'm sorry you see it that way.'

'You're silly. You're perfectly nice as you are.' Ivan rolled boyishly over on the hearth-rug and gripped her ankle, grinding the bones. Julia allowed this. Ivan caressed her leg for a few moments in silence. Julia sat, her legs together, straight out in front of her. Ivan ran his hand up her legs, under her skirt, and caressed her thigh. Julia said, not commenting on his activities, 'I don't suppose old Baker will ever get a job. Thor drives him off looking for them, in vans. But there's so much he won't do because of this dignity. Thor's so keen on . . .'

'Shut up,' said Ivan. He sat up abruptly and pushed Julia over on to her back, where she lay, staring rather pathetically at him.

'And don't look at me has it come to this, because this is where it's always been coming and you know it. You are the most provocative woman I've ever met. At a second meeting you offer no less than everything. And I want you horribly. So be honest, my love, enjoy yourself.'

'Don't mock,' said Julia. Her mind was tick-tacking over various uncomfortable calculations. She drew her legs fractionally closer together.

'I'm not mocking. I'm perfectly serious. I'm even laying myself open to appearing as the selfish lover in one of your books. Love could go no further, Julia,' he said, shifting closer and peering down at her with jetty eyes, 'I can't find any other way to speak to you. Don't be put off.' He put out his finger, with a real or assumed timidity, and drew it across her lips. Julia was touched by this; she was always ready to be touched.

'Anyway, where's Merle? This sort of thing is so *messy*, Ivan. It spoils things.'

'You've no guts.'

'Yes I have. But I *am* a sort of prude. I like friendship, not passion. Now, my sister has a positively Byronic hunger for passion and doesn't get much chance to practise. But it's not my line.'

'And for that momentary malice you deserve no quarter. Defend yourself, my darling.'

Julia was no good at self-defence when it came to a direct attack, and opened her legs pliably enough when they were pushed. She was not easy to stir, and had been, ever since Simon's first attempt to kiss her, neurotically afraid of being watched; she was unable, although she knew it to be impolite, to resist twisting her head from side to side to see whether the room had suddenly become inhabited. Afterwards, she felt hot and sticky, and, as Ivan handed back to her those of her clothes he had removed, a sense of temporary respite. It meant, at least, that she was able to lean peaceably against Ivan's small male warmth on the sofa, since she didn't need to fear provoking someone who had already been provoked.

'You're not really cross?' he said.

'Oh, no. No.'

There was a silence.

'Did you know that your friend Simon Moffitt was in difficulties? Lost his cameraman to a crocodile, or something. They've got a stock of films but then that's going to be the end of them for the time being, apparently.'

Julia thought of Simon, and the strained delicacy of his love-making and felt wistful. She should have been more abandoned. She thought of his knobby face, and his nervousness, and his meddling.

'Poor Si.'

'What was he like?'

'I hardly remember. I don't know if I ever knew, I loved him.'

'Good for him,' said Ivan. Merle came in, bundled in a white raincoat, smiling.

'You two look comfortable,' she said.

'I'll make us all some coffee,' said Ivan, kissing Julia and standing up. He said to his wife, 'We were talking about Simon Moffitt. Julia's got this *thing* about Moffitt. A real girlhood passion. One can just see *why*, can't one?'

'Not very salubrious,' said Merle. 'I mean, the sort of thing he does, the sort of place he does it in. It gives me the creeps, honestly, darling.'

Next day Julia left the flat early in the morning, carrying a brief-case and several note-books. She walked several times round Russell Square, past the gaudy tea-kiosk, past the fountains, granite griddle-cakes with single tubes of water suspended thinly above them. In the night she had slid one hand over Thor's huge rib-cage in tentative invitation; he had not responded. Outside, a child was coughing and she could hear Mrs Baker padding across the carpet. With her privacy she was losing her sense of identity. Thor excluded her and Ivan's grab, neatly defining her as a sexual object, diminished and humiliated her. He had said she was provocative; so she was, she needed to prove she was there to be seen; but the proof always, contradictorily, drove her to further uncertain agony of guilt and self-distaste.

She found it, rather grimly, good to be alone. There ought to be more things *possible* to me, she told herself. I think too much about limitations, I've lost my sense of possibility. Not marriage, nor childbirth, was responsible; the roots of the failure were older and deeper. She grappled with this idea of possibility and limitations. Modern novels – her own, amongst others – concerned themselves too exclusively with limitations. They enjoyed glumly setting them out. A novel ought, ideally, to balance in a perpetual juggling trick the sense of real limitation against a real awareness of human possibility. Cassandra, now, was aware of the grandeurs of possibility but had refused to explore her limitations, realistically, at all. It was all in the air. Cassandra *was* the solitary self. But if one could see – in the reality that restricted one – the nevertheless shining and extensive possibility . . . Not sum up, or give in, too soon, above all . . . There was a sense in which Cassandra's pursuit of a sense of glory was right and proper, if only it were at all related to the real world.

Julia had rarely had so many consecutive abstract thoughts. They were exhilarating – releasing her from Thor, from Ivan, from the Bakers. I could have called that novel, she thought, *A Sense of Glory*. It could have been about the way Cass sees Simon – intensely meaningful, unreal. The telly does have that effect, anyway. I know that from my own feelings when I see Simon on it. He seems substantial, important, as I was never sure he was, in the flesh. An idol, with a whole, ungrasped, different reality depending from him. A world with another world contained in it.

Now, I could write this novel about a woman with a dream world that – extends her possibilities. And she introduces a real man into this world, and understands – really understands – *one aspect* of him, this way. Julia tripped over someone's tricycle, smiled, apologized, hurried wildly on. And the dream world, which is beautiful, is quite shattered when she meets him again after a long time.

I've got to have a television idol, it's such a good image for this sense of glory. I couldn't use a naturalist.

She thought of Father Rowell, and Cassandra's deference towards him, and then of Simon's first television appearance and the priest who had preached the subsequent programme. I could make this man a television clergyman. Not a jolly one. Sententious – like Si – not simply chummy. Even God-like, until you knew him. He'd be clever, but not that clever. He wouldn't understand her, of course, he'd subtly fail her . . . He'd be, for her, absolute limitation and infinite possibility.

No, this is mine, she thought, and headed out of the square and down Southampton Row. She reached the public library in Theobald's Road in a state of tense euphoria, and took a lift to the Reference Library. There, seated in reasonable anonymity in a crowd of Afro-Asian students, she started on what was to be the most rapid and least altered piece of work in her life. It almost, eventually, wrote itself; she had much less work to do on it than on her more apparently artless and confessionally chatty pieces. She spent the next few weeks solidly working, closed away in the library in every spare moment.

CHAPTER TWELVE

Cassandra's Journal. April.

Tyranny of objects. There is a point beyond which the apparent antagonism of certain chairs, or paper-weights, if dwelt on, ceases to be ludicrous. As though they might crush or crowd out. This may also be true of human beings. I find myself assuming hostility in, for instance, Miss Barton, because of the configuration of her upper lip – somewhat swollen – taken in conjunction with the dark hairs at her mouth corners. Now, it is not these physical facts which menace, clearly – they must be simply a focus for my resentment of hostility that I assume is in her. There is, of course, real hostility. Yesterday she found it necessary to suggest that I had been too severe in refusing a reference to Gillian Sachur. A foolish girl. I had thought my decision out with care. She has a right to her view. But she expressed it with hostility, and concentrated her grim look on my hands in an obsessive way I could not like.

I must nevertheless keep in mind a distinction between Miss Barton, and chairs, or paper-weights.

It could be argued that I resent the simple idea of reality conveyed in the solid presence of chair and paper-weight. I am particularly disturbed by glass objects – increasingly, since that serpent has been in my possession – because they contain, being transparent, the suggestion that they are not simply solid.

> A man that looks on glass
> On it may stay his eye
> Or if he pleases through it pass
> And then the heaven espy.

Here is the paradox of all vision. But let it be remembered that these objects have weight, as well as transparency. Not only surface, and heaven beyond the surface, but ponderous weight. I do not express this clearly. There are degrees of reality to be apprehended in all objects, at any given time, and degrees of capacity, in ourselves, to apprehend them.

'All objects, *as objects*, are essentially fixed and dead.' It is this fixed, dead weight that makes them hostile.

Forms of glass. The pane of glass, for instance, through which I see the garden from inside my room. Last night, looking out from a lighted room, I saw the moon. The pane of glass reflected the yellow glitter of the lamplight; it was thus seen to be solid. But when I stood between the lamp and the glass, the dark circle of the shadow of my head contained the pale silver of moon. Here is an image of vision – a chain of alternating light, reflected light, and darkness. One sees, through a darkness which is a shadow of oneself – a reflection of one's absence – this pale light, which is itself, after all, visible almost always only in darkness, a partial reflection – off another dead, dull, solid surface – of the sun's vital unseen light. One creates an emptiness, a darkness, in which to see it, by interposing one's own solidity between the bright lamplight and the apparently solid glass surface which reflects it. And thus negates all solidity. It is all in the head, in my head.

Another form of glass. Mirrors, of course, are not transparent; they are, on the contrary, an assurance of solidity. There is an absolute difference between the recessive caverns of corridors of mirror reflected in mirror, with my face repeated idiotically on the perpetuated thresholds, and the receding open space my shadow, as it were, illuminates through plain glass. I do not need, or like, the reassurance of mirrors; they do not reflect the hollow in the skull; they close off ways. Mirrors are partial truths, like certain putative works of art. Like almost all works of art.

The television screen is a form of mirror. Mirror of our desires, of our ways of seeing.

J., last night, spoke on the screen about the relationship between art and life. I do not consider her an authority on the subject. The screen emphasizes the bones of her skull; over-emphasizes; she appears more clear-cut, less soft, less fleshy and speaks more decisively, although with little gestures of appeal to the invisible audience. A mirror-image of myself – a certain nod we have in common is emphasized, also certain tricks of speech, which have persisted and are more easily remarked in magnification.

'Why do you write, Miss Corbett?' they asked her. 'What drives you?' She replied, after some encouragement, as I understood her, with much smiling, that she did not write either to 'express herself', or to persuade her readers of any social or moral truth, or 'to put forward a view of life'. She wrote, she said, compulsively, 'in order to understand events, in her own life, or others'. 'Would you say that your novels were autobiographical, Miss Corbett?' they asked her. 'They have been. The book on which I am working at present is not autobiographical.' I suppose this may be the usual response. They asked if it helped her to control her life; she replied that it did not. They continued: 'And when you have finished a book do you feel triumph – satisfaction – or disappointment?' None of these, apparently. J., facing the camera squarely, honest eyes blazing, 'No, no, something much more neutral. A sense of release. And renewed vigour. I feel ready to start all over again on something else.'

I thought of Deborah, and her complaint that she is disposed of. She has cause.

With J.'s television appearances I have a sense of diminishing reflection. With his, on the other hand, I have the illusion of a world infinitely extended through dissolving glass, the Looking Glass. This must be untruth, and dangerous. Somewhere, in an unseen jungle, across an ocean and a continent, a real man, Simon, whom I love, is at this moment paddling through real water, or grubbing in real dirt, or losing real red blood from hands scraped, or cut, or sucked by flies. Here, now, I walk through unreal creepers, I study unreal dirt and water.

What I see on the screen is an image, but an image, not only of myself, but of a real man. And some of my thoughts about him are not fantasy, but knowledge. What he says, what he shows, I am occasionally, by careful attention, able to know and predict. I can accurately describe plants he must see that the screen does not show and I do not see. More than that, I know to a certain extent what he is afraid of – how well I know it I shall never tell – and what he thinks. Love is attention, though that is only a part of the truth. Between fantasy and reality are infinite degrees, and I bring myself, occasionally, to the illusion (or more) that we do share an experience or a thought. If, by denying my own solidity, I could see him as he is? Even so, the glass barrier is solid; screen, window or looking-glass. If it were not solid? No. Solidity is fact, is fact, it cannot be translated into pure threat.

Between fantasy and reality are the dreams. Things we touch, involuntarily, in dreams; things we possess there; untrodden paths we tread. This changes us. This changes also our relation to the dead weight of objects. Occasionally – I do not speculate how – what I have dreamed, and written down, he has afterwards said. I have dreamed other things he has not said. He spoke, tonight, about a moulting snake; I had heard it before, I knew it. He connected this release, as in my dream, with vision.

First he showed the animal lying torpid; then the splitting of the skin; then the animal leaving the skin – like oiled silk, like a length of live water. He was left with the stiff, semi-transparent husk, on which the scales seem harsher and larger. He said, 'If we had to depend on markings alone it would be impossible to distinguish snakes by their exuviae.'

During the period immediately before the shedding of the skin the colour of the snake changes; there is no gleam; he showed this, and pointed out that the black areas on this particular snake were a 'dead blue' and the creamy undersurface and olive rounds were as though covered with an opaque, milky skin. He showed the eyes, covered with a hardened slightly flaking film. They were expressionless, simple surface, reflecting nothing. He said it was not true that snakes were completely blind when moulting. The eyes are covered with a raised lens, which is also shed. 'Normally,' he said, 'snakes have very fine vision. This is a stumbling block to those who believe they lost their limbs, eyelids and ear openings as a result of burrowing, since most burrowing animals have their vision greatly impaired. Moreover this snake is a climber, and sees acutely.'

He related this torpor and partial blindness to the connection of the snake's moulting with myths of renewal and rebirth. 'Before any new life, or achievement, or insight,' he said, 'I have found there is a necessarily dull and stupid period.' I hate these simple analogies; he would have made a good florid preacher and his snake an admittedly excellent *exemplum* – but the preaching specification destroyed the resonance of the complex image. Our life *is*, but not in that tone of voice, an image for something greater than its simple facts.

He watched the animal move away in silence. It is as though each coil were separately impelled from behind, and the whole body, contracting and driving, a series of interconnected, fluid, uncertainly purposeful, tentatively directed movements after the searching head. I watched him feel and fold the discarded skin. I know what he felt. We die in pieces and patches, and dry up and are renewed – for a time only. He said, 'This wet, glistening sheen won't last long, of course, the skin dulls and hardens.' There is a new contusion just below his left ear, or at least, so I think: it is possible, but unlikely, that he did not present his left profile last time.

All facts, all facts, all solid facts and objects of our life are always themselves and more than themselves. And so I pursue, professionally, self-indulgently, any metaphor to the death, fanatical or truth-revealing, who knows which. I am driven to confess, the Church seems to me (to its discredit) to diminish him and his serpents, and the threads of thought I had believed securely fastened to feel along seem suddenly loose, floating wild and unattached. I connect and connect, meaninglessly, J.'s 'sense of release', his rebirth platitude, the hostility of the objects round me, and my need for release from them. Is this a game, or an action? Is that a real question?

I live in two worlds. One is hard, inimical, brutal, threatening, the tyranny of objects where all things are objects and thus tyrannical. The other is infinite: heaven, through the pane of glass, the Looking Glass world. One dreams of a release into that world of pure vision and knows that what would be gained would be madness; a single world, and intolerable.

Simon's embrace (if not impossible) is a function in this world of what has happened, what is misunderstood, other embraces. In that world, a release.

All I know is that at all costs the pane of glass between the worlds must not be broken. It serves, maybe, the function of the lens over the snake's eye. It seems, ideally, that the two worlds should run into each other; but practically, one knows this would be destructive. I must remain isolated.

Enclosed by light in a glass cage, outside a glass box containing light.

An image for myself? An animal formed probably by burrowing, without ears, limbs, or eyelids, deaf, unable to gesture, with acute, unvaried vision?

Cassandra. Not Cassandra Austen, sisterly supporter of the expressive Jane. Cassandra who was Apollo's priestess, and – since she refused intercourse with the Lord of the Muses, and was thus no artist – incapable of communication. Unrelated to the world of objects around her. (Apollo, besides being Lord of the Muses, was God of Light and thus doubly rejected for some impossible chastity.) Cassandra, like myself, like myself, a specialist in useless knowledge.

The Lady of Shalott, also. The web, the mirror, the knight with the sun on him, reflected in the mirror and woven into the web. I am half sick of shadows. A poem a great deal more intelligent than we commonly give it credit for. Tennyson has here both indulged, and provided a commentary on, his own mediaevalist romanticism. Cf. *The Palace of Art*. Solitude concerned with reflections.

Is it possible that one should recognize, and deliberately entertain, the harbingers of insanity? I have taught Swift, and maintained that he could not be described as insane since his thought-structure was so coherent. An over-simplification.

Since Julia's visit Cassandra had made several changes in her way of life. Work on the edition of Malory had scarcely progressed. Cassandra had not been at meetings of the intercollegiate Augustinian Group, which, with Father Rowell, she had frequently attended. She had purchased, on separate occasions, a sou'wester, brushes, pens and inks, oil pastels, various pads of paper and several canvases. So, whilst Julia, closed in the library, wrote, Cassandra engaged battle with the objects which oppressed her.

She painted some things indoors; fireplaces, banisters, one or two sketches of pupils' heads or legs. But she spent larger and larger stretches of time on wet benches in the Botanical Gardens, drawing tangles of soaked grass wound round tree roots, covering sheet after sheet of paper with patterns of broken twigs and mud and leaves. She discovered the hot-houses and made a series of studies of flowers and creepers, always from very close. These drawings were both violent and contained – a profusion of natural untidiness, meticulously reproduced, held together only by the edges of the paper and an occasional hint at a pattern in the faint emphasis of a line here or there. These pictures piled up in her rooms, thickets, jungles, patterns of chair-legs. She bought a pair of corduroy trousers, finally, and a yellow-gold oilskin cape. In these clothes, carrying her painting materials in a canvas satchel, she went on longer and longer treks into the countryside. Reports arose slowly, characterized by Oxford's indulgent and embroidering curiosity, of meetings with her in lanes or on bridges, of the red hair sprouting under the sou'wester, of the hasty arm laid over the painting, of the silent, furious, distant stare.

CHAPTER THIRTEEN

'Why do you go on coming to bed with me, Ju?'

'I suppose I must like it,' Julia said, unable to produce any more positive affirmative. She ran a toe down his leg and turned over on her stomach. It was late May. Merle was in Birmingham, doing a television. Julia was in Ivan's bed. It was four in the afternoon.

'Well, you don't seem to like it much.'

'Don't I?' Julia had thought she was doing rather well at disguising this fact. Ivan kicked her.

'What you really like is stroking me afterwards, like some sort of pet animal.'

'Do you mind that?'

He hesitated. 'Not particularly, no. But I wouldn't say it was a good thing for you.' Julia thought with a sudden access of rage that all she did enjoy was the after-calm, and now this was being shredded, too. Ivan persisted. 'You only let me make love to you in the first place because you were scared stiff if you stopped me I wouldn't like you any more. Didn't you? And now you're scared stiff I'll stop liking you because you let me go on. Aren't you?' Julia felt the extreme irritation one always feels when someone proves to be more percipient than one has decided they shall be. She said, 'Well, both of those are fairly normal male reactions.' She thought. 'And so is moralizing about it, before and after. You want me to be more enthusiastic about it than I am without your having to be any more enthusiastic than you are. Admit it. Well, I won't.'

Ivan sat up. 'I just want you to enjoy yourself a bit.'

'Well, I do, in my own way.' Julia dropped her face into the pillow and sighed.

'What women like you need to learn is that men are human beings. I suppose I ought to have known from your books that you were that sort. You're an awful stereotyper, Ju. Not that I don't have all those "male reactions" you spend your time cataloguing. Not that we aren't both – not that most people aren't – predictable stereotypes most of the time. I know what I am. Incurably promiscuous and emotionally lazy. But all the same, you know, I'm not stupid. And I do care for you. And I do feel some compunction – about using you, about possibly getting you in a mess, and so on.'

'I'm sick of people being *intelligent* about sex all the time. I like you, but I'm a bit sick of sex too. Culturally, that is, not you, sweetie. As for this compunction, I wouldn't boast about it. It's just another form of persecution, getting an ascendancy. Don't you think, really?'

Ivan grimaced. 'So according to you, it's simply my male pride that's hurt because you won't let go? Why are you always so bloody polite in bed?'

'Perhaps I'm not, always.'

Ivan moved his hand under the bed-clothes, and slapped her. 'I think you are. The guiding light of your life is this need to be liked. You don't want to give.'

'Well, if I don't, that's convenient for you if you look at it coolly. I don't think you've any right to go probing and analysing. All that does no good. Shall I stop coming to bed with you?'

'You would, wouldn't you? Tomorrow, with no regrets?'

'Of course.' Julia laughed, and rolled out of the bed in one neat movement. 'Except that then you might stop liking me. I'd be sorry for that.'

They both laughed. Julia began to put on her clothes. 'I do *like* you, darling,' Ivan said, and they both laughed again. Julia felt relieved.

'How's the book?'

Julia sat down in her underclothes on a circular chair with a shaggy pelt of white fur.

'I've finished it. I've never in my life written anything so fast. It's a sort of inexorable interior monologue. Mixed with bits of rather crisp and completely objective exterior description. For the shock value of the contrast. I think it works. I've never done anything remotely like it. Only I – I tried to – tug it away – from *her* – and I think perhaps I've not tugged it far enough. The truth is so much more compelling, you know. But I think it probably ought not to be published. Perhaps it's enough to have done it.'

'Is it good?'

Julia gathered herself into a childish ball on the chair, and grinned at him over her naked knees with the excitement which, he reflected, she had signally failed to show during their recent love-making.

'How do I know? Does one ever? It's probably just mediocre-shading-into-good-in-chapters. But it feels good. It feels bloody good. *Finished*, you know, darling, right outside myself, something I can look at objectively. I've never really had that feeling before.

'And – and the funny thing – I feel it's detached me from her, and at the same time – I've made such a real effort with her – so I feel I love her. I can grow on my own now, and I do, I do really love her. We could be friends, we could meet, we could share . . . Sometimes I think if she did read it she'd see it was written with love. Because it is. Real love. I know that, in myself.'

'On your own terms,' said Ivan. 'You mean, "I have written a wicked book and feel as spotless as a lamb." '

Julia blenched only momentarily. 'Who said that?'

'Melville. About *Moby Dick*. A considerable and impersonal work of literature. All the same, Ju, publish and be damned. I don't think you can be scrupulous. A writer can't, with his good stuff. That overrides any other consideration. Pack it off to the publisher.'

Julia bowed her head, blushing and smiling.

'I already have.'

This stopped Ivan for a good moment which he occupied in putting on underpants, dark grey shirt, and pale grey socks. He then turned to Julia and said, 'Well, I'd better stop telling you what to do hadn't I? Since you know? So tell me what happens at the end? How did you resolve your one-sided equation? One-sided, that is, because you've left out the persecuting female novelist. What's the sum of your wisdom?'

'Well, the end's a bit lame, I think. I just make her retreat further and further from any real human contact into this weird imaginary relationship with the TV clergyman. The unctuous epiloguer. I make her more or less deliberately destroy what contacts she's got.'

'I do hate this novelist's habit of saying calmly "I make" him or her do this or that. However. What do you "make" her do then?'

'No, love, I make him. He comes back. I make him go on one of these Missions the Church is always having, to Oxford, and they meet. And he sort of remembers her, and the pathetic thing is he likes her, he really likes her, but what the hell can she say to him with all those – those *forests* of imagination between them? She lets him go, she won't put out a hand. But of course she can't go on imagining, either. She sees him off on a train. I leave the end open. It's a bit like Ibsen's life-lie, you know: does his real presence free her to live in the world without him or does the loss of her illusion kill her? I leave her on the platform, watching,'

Julia said grandly, excited, 'all her limitations and all her possibilities steaming off down the line together.'

'Splendid stuff.' Ivan's voice had a note of hysteria. 'Do you believe in the prophetic function of literature?'

'No,' said Julia. 'You once accused me of thinking of myself as a prophet. But I don't. That's Cassandra. *Cassandra*. I only have hindsight.'

'Hm,' said Ivan. 'There's a lot of things I could say, but I won't. Get your clothes on, and let me take you home. I must admit to a mild curiosity about how much of all this about "all her limitations and all her possibilities" is your sister and how much is you. Were you so polite in bed with Moffitt?'

Julia did not answer this. After a moment she said, 'Emily in my novel is a composite portrait, like any. And of course Cassandra and me – it's a composite creature, in a way, a sort of binary fission.' She walked over and kissed him. 'I wouldn't have said I was *all* that polite, not really.' She said, into his shoulder, 'Ivan, do you really suppose she's never, I thought nowadays there was nobody left like that.'

'A literary convention,' said Ivan, with his white grin.

The liner came into Southampton on a grey day, at dawn. Simon Moffitt stood on the deck and watched the wash behind it, and marbled furrow and white, curding crest, falling in on itself, crossing, diminishing, as the tugs manoeuvred the heavy, helpless body this way and that. Then on the surface of the water a disturbance spread choppily, a kind of lolloping, eddying mess, no shape. Simon smiled; a momentary, mild smile.

He was leaning on his elbows on the rail. As the ship rode and turned he saw at last the long line of sheds, the dark metal. The sky was heavy and thick; there was a light, blown spray, water in the air quite unlike the continual dropping damp in the jungle. From a port-hole below him someone threw the body of a fish; stiffly arced it went up, the tail quivering slightly, and all the gulls came down raucously screaming with abrupt bursts of broken noise. One glided flat, close to the water, turned, snapped, rose with the tail hanging from its wicked beak, so bright a yellow and dabbed with scarlet, gulped, shook itself, and screamed again. Simon leaned out and observed this incident with passive attention.

After a moment he shook himself too, and turned his eyes down. He was not precisely not thinking: he was slowly reciting to himself what he could remember of *In Memoriam*, which was little enough, although he had been caused to learn large passages of the poem in childhood as an exercise, presumably, in religious resignation. It was not in these terms that he was thinking of it now; for the moment, simply, the vague grey sadness of it was appropriate to this homecoming. He did not like England. 'On the bald streets breaks the blank day,' he said in his mind. He was sorry that the solitude of this journey, outside time and place, was to come to an end, and in this chilly dampness. As the hooters blew, and the chains rattled, he went down again to supervise the unloading and packing of his snakes, his toads, his insects, his plants. He had a shuffling, meditative walk, his feet turning slightly out. He wore a whitish riding mac and an American, waterproof pork-pie hat, both of which sat uneasily on him.

On the quay a reporter took photographs of the canvas bags of snakes, the long crates and occupied cages; he also took several shots of Simon's sad, hunched figure in his raincoat, his face lugubrious and shadowed by a widespread but not luxuriant beard. He asked several questions, which Simon answered courteously, his gaze fixed on the ground or the sky, his hands twisting. Next day, the photograph appeared in the daily column of an evening paper.

'Yesterday Simon Moffitt, English snake-collector, familiar to thousands of viewers of TV's *Armchair Explorers* series, returned at dawn to his homeland with a marvellous bag of reptiles and insects, poisonous and harmless, savage and appealing, to enrich the zoos and his own pocket. He has been out of this country solidly for the past ten years, living in tents, often in very primitive and dangerous conditions. He believes that a continuous relationship between naturalist and the flora or fauna of any region is of inexpressible value, though he admits to having been forced to shift camp on occasion by fire or flood. I asked him if he went out there for kicks, or if he got real pleasure out of being uncomfortable. "Luckily you never realize what you've let yourself in for until afterwards," he said. He does feel a hunger for places where the earth isn't covered up by building and machinery. "I know it's not rational to feel things are more real out there but that's what I do feel." Many people share this feeling, even though they only indulge it by watching Simon Moffitt's thrilling programmes.

'Simon Moffitt has no immediate plans for another expedition. "I must write up results, house my creatures, and think." Tall, black-bearded, romantic Simon Moffitt is unmarried and says that as far as he knows he will stay that way. How many of his "fans" could really bring themselves to share his hermit life in the hot swamps with the crocodiles?'

Julia read this report over breakfast a day later. It was not from a paper she read, and had been cut out and sent to her in an envelope. Ivan, who had sent it, had decorated newsprint and picture with little drawings of curled snakes with bearded human heads in thickets of grass, an Adam and Eve recognizably himself and Julia with huge figleaves, and a border like those on illuminated manuscripts of rioting tropical foliage in fine red, green and black ball-point lines. Julia studied Simon's face so closely that she could only see the newsprint dots; he might have been anyone; Ivan had looped a crimson snake round his neck and had a green one clambering up his body and two small black ones peering from the brim of his hat.

Deborah looked over her shoulder and cried, 'Look what someone's sent Julia.' Thor looked up from his correspondence. Out of the kitchen Edna Baker shuffled in a hideous nightdress, followed by Trevor and Rosie. To reach the spare room, in which they ate as well as slept, they had to cross and recross the Eskelunds' living-room. Deborah read out: 'Tall, black-bearded romantic Simon Moffitt . . .'

'Let me see that,' said Thor. Julia gave it to him. The baby screamed across the flat. There was a smell of stale nappies. Mrs Baker had nervously washed them twice a day when she first came, but this was no longer the case, and Julia was too much afraid of being looked at angrily to ask for improvement.

'Who sent you this?' said Thor, in that absurd, overdramatic voice in which real passion often expresses itself. Julia looked up at him plaintively. Mrs Baker stopped, and turned back to watch, milk splashing from her waving jug into Julia's carpet.

'Ivan sent it,' Julia said. 'It was Ivan.'

'Why did he sent it?'

'Well, why not?' said Deborah.

'And you be quiet,' said Thor to his daughter. Julia grasped, suddenly, the precise cause of his displeasure. He was angry that she had told Ivan enough to put him into a position to send such a drawing. His own tolerance of her emotional vagaries was his pride; this was what he was for; that she should chatter so liberally outside was too much. She cried out of sympathy, 'I'm sorry, I'm sorry.'

'Yes, you are always sorry,' he said, 'when you have caused trouble. But not for what you have done.'

'Don't,' Julia cried, 'don't lecture me like a child. I'm not. I'm a responsible woman.'

'That is not how you behave.'

Julia stood up and found herself screaming. 'And in front of all these bloody dirty people you've dragged into the flat to persecute me. *Your* motives are above reproach, of course. Charity excuses anything. You should stop judging, or you'll get judged, you'll get judged.' He said nothing. Julia thought, as her own face crumpled into tears, that he looked ill: he had the taut, staring look he had had when she first knew him, and his lips were sore with a dark line cracking the surface. She looked at him helplessly and furiously, turned and ran and slammed herself into the bedroom. Mrs Baker dropped the milk jug and sniffed; the children howled. Thor went and put his arm clumsily and heavily about Mrs Baker's shoulder. Mr Baker lurched aggressively out of the spare room where the baby was now frantically and breathily screaming. Deborah gathered up the offending newscutting and carried it into her room.

The cutting reached Cassandra two days later. She found it on her way out to Holy Communion; she opened the envelope clumsily with black, kid-gloved fingers, and it fluttered to the floor. There was a letter with it.

'My dear Aunt Cassandra, Julia's television man sent her this. For some reason it has caused an almighty row at home. None of us speak, now. Except the baby, that screams.

'I thought you were really the best person to have this, though what I think may not be of much account. *I* would rather *you* had it. I hope you remain well; you never answered my last. I rather rely on getting letters from you. Now we have got a houseful of slum-dwellers my correspondence is all I can call my own; pitiable state of affairs. I do feel you and I ought to be more informed about things – we ought to make it more our business what's going on than we do. Perhaps I ought not to write to you. Unlike Julia, I am not able to write out how awful things are, but please believe they are awful. I do need to be believed, I think something awful's brewing. People neither tell one things nor hide them from one, this is a terrible strain, if you know what I mean?

'This amounts to a hysterical letter, Aunt C. – before you get too angry consider that I haven't written you any such, yet, and have much cause. Do you know what I feel like? Something crawling in the undergrowth, hearing things crashing and fighting overhead, that daren't move in case they put their feet on it but of course they may, *anyway*, put their feet on it. Consider the child, all the books say. Write and tell me I've got to stand on my own, I'll believe it if *you* say it. My dear aunt, your loving niece, Deborah.'

Cassandra studied the cutting intently: Simon's shadowed face, Ivan's serpentine decorations, raincoat, figleaves. She folded it, brooding, and put it into her handbag. The letter she tore up and dropped into the waste-paper basket. She went on to church.

She was glad to sit down. She had felt unwell for some weeks, and was liable to misjudge distances, to kneel too far from pew to hassock, to trip against steps that had appeared to be some distance away. The inimical aspect of her surroundings had increased to hallucination. She had, in church, a real sense that the building was falling open like a flower, and then closing, one half over the other, driving pews together, impelling pillars athwart each other. Or, in Hall, the mock mediaeval crossbeams of the roof edged slowly down, compressing the girls' din to a single intolerable shriek. She had added to the rising pile of studies of flora several very precise studies of foreshortened roof-tracery, bosses and joists. These had a new harshness of line.

She peered distractedly at the pew-end, drew off her gloves, and addressed herself to God. In Meeting, in her youth, God had seemed something approached through clinging grey floss, a kind of insulation which thickened as she raised her thoughts painfully, until these thoughts were finally blunted against a ceiling of compressed asbestos. Her attempts had most often ended in a defeated return to indulge in her live mediaeval action. In the Church, the same effort was not imperative; God had been present enough in a harmony between sounds and words and objects created by others outside herself. It was as though the Church gave to God that secondary, more intense life that literature had given to her own aimless emotion in youth; neither decorative nor hopeless. But lately this harmony had not held her. She had returned increasingly to private wrestling with the asbestos. Colour and sound had faded. 'We receive but what we give,' she said crossly to God through floating lumps of flock, uncertain whether it was herself or Him she was accusing. This private struggle had always been waiting for her; she felt too unwell to take it on.

When Father Rowell held up wine and wafer Cassandra, with the old ladies, came unevenly out of her stall and made for the altar. When she was in motion vision did its worst. She saw flakes of asbestos clustering like dead butterflies on the heads of the columns, which sagged, as though melting, like giant candles encrusted with simmering grey. She put up her hands to ward things off her face, things which hung festooned from the rood loft and collected in the air as though the air had burned and solidified into floating ash. Something hummed and sang.

'Miss Corbett!' said Father Rowell.

Cassandra heeled over and hit her head against a pew foot.

'Hysterical women dons,' said one undergraduate to another.

Cassandra came round, hearing a liquid gasp in her own throat, and found herself on Gerald Rowell's sofa, peering at her own black-laced feet. She saw his pale eyes behind his fine golden spectacles, and moved her head so that the light danced on the surface of the lenses. He waited for her to speak.

'I'm sorry, Father. That was vulgar.'

'Never mind that. Have you any idea why, Cassandra?'

'I am very tired,' said Cassandra, conventionally. He held out a cup of water; Cassandra sat up and sipped.

'You have trusted me in the past.'

'Yes,' said Cassandra vaguely. She could make nothing of his expression.

'You have no right to exhaust yourself. None of us has a right to destroy himself. You know what I am trying to say.'

'Yes.' Cassandra was barely listening. 'I am suffering a kind of metaphysical distress. Probably insignificant. I don't think it would be of much use to talk about it.'

'You cannot be sure of that.' He waited.

'Everything I touch – everything I touch – turns to ashes.' She smiled, privately, over the thought that he could not know how literally this was so. 'After all, in this world, everything must turn to ashes,' she said, in a tone abnormally matter-of-fact, a parody of his own preaching manner. 'We must accept these trials.'

'You make it impossible to speak to you.'

'Speech alters almost nothing. We talk too much. We should keep quiet and concentrate on survival.' She looked wildly past him, into the room beyond, and then stiffened again, smiling slightly. As though, even there, something lay in wait. She watched whatever it was, and Father Rowell watched her.

'God has not put us, Cassandra, in any normal sense at a level where survival is of paramount importance. You and I are born civilized, self-conscious, intelligent, physically fortunate. We are required to live in the world. We are required to speak to each other. We are placed where we have abundant spare energy, which it is our *duty* to expend in love. Love for other people. Love for God.'

'The glass,' said Cassandra, swaying her head and peering at his spectacles and his eyes behind them, 'and what is through the glass. I know, that is what we say.'

'That is what is true.'

'Yes, yes,' she said impatiently, 'but there are other truths.'

She stood up abruptly and gathered up gloves and handbag. 'As I said, it was a little vulgar. You will acquit me of making a habit of it. But let us not make it worse by speaking as if it were significant.'

'What other truths?' said Father Rowell.

Cassandra walked steadily to the door.

'Let me at least call you a cab.'

'No, no. I can walk.'

'If you . . . If you should have anything to say, if you should change your mind, I am here.'

'I know,' said Cassandra. 'I know.'

In her room she took out the cutting again, and studied it. She supposed that it made little real difference to her that Simon was again in England and she had not known. But she had spent time imagining him in the jungle when he was not there; and this sapped her sense of her own presence a little further.

She had recently bought an easel; now, she set to work on another painting. She sketched in the broad outline of a man in a raincoat under a tree. Then, carefully, as though all her other work had been preliminary studies for this, she began to spread behind him an intricate network of twisting foliage with tiny, formalized, haphazard creatures from the dreams clutching with claw and feeler to tendrils, to fronds, to broad, spatulate leaves. She painted a square inch at a time, peering closely at it. The tree rose like a pillar in front of the deepening backcloth. Above it, in great flakes of paint, Cassandra laid a grey, thick sky that furred the branches and impinged heavily on the whole scene.

CHAPTER FOURTEEN

'Yes, you know, but I –'

'It *is* an art form. Look what they said about the cinema. No, look, television's the new art *medium*. All the other forms have got worked out – *worked out* – too bloody self-conscious. The artists seem to be playing with the forms. Fiddling about with the *form* all the time.'

'You can't –'

'Now, the thing about television as an art medium – the real thing it's got, or ought to have got, over *all the other art forms* is this *immediacy*. Great flexibility and variety, granted, but also this *immediacy*. It could stimulate all sorts of new discoveries. Why not? I mean, this cliché about bringing art into people's homes, it's a truth. Do you realize just what power an *art medium* that's a casual part of almost everyone's life has got? I mean, it's *in there*, it's in people's lives. They get their thoughts from it. It's a fearful responsibility.'

'I hadn't seen it that –'

'No, listen. This programme. *The Lively Arts*. It's an attempt to relate the work of artists at all points – with this immediacy – to the way people live. Now art – art is a function of man's self-consciousness. Art's what he makes of the fact that he's *aware* of his life. Not like an animal. Or aware of more abstract things, like colour and sound. Now look, now look, television's man's self-consciousness now. I mean, how many people see life in terms of what the medium shows them? Many many more than ever saw it in terms of a Shakespeare play or a Tolstoy novel or even Charlie Chaplin. Now, what this programme's for is to make them conscious of what we're offering them. I'm not a dilettante don dishing out culture. I'm not committed – I don't want to tell them how to better themselves socially. I'm not interested in the sort of art that needs a lifetime's training to appreciate. I just want to increase the ordinary man's awareness. Of himself. Of the artist's awareness of him. Of things around him. I want to *interweave* the artist's sense of significance with people's lives. Does that make sense?'

'I –'

'And television opens up to art – to this consciousness – all sorts of things that weren't available or were getting excluded. Like your stuff.'

'Yes. I shouldn't have thought my work was of absorbing interest – or importance – to them.'

'Your ratings don't tell that tale. No, honestly, you show them wonders.'

'What I'm trying to say is, I'm not an artist.'

'I don't see that.'

'You don't listen. If – if there's an artist concerned, it was my friend, Antony Miller. Who is dead. He – he made the films. But I don't – I suspect your terminology. I can't put my finger on it, but I –'

'Well, we've got you.' Ivan waved an expansive hand. 'Even if we can't have him. Hamlet without Shakespeare. You did agree to appear.'

'Oh yes,' Simon turned away, leaned over the ice-bucket, and dropped, with tongs, two ice-cubes splat into his drink. It was almost an angry movement. Ivan watched him. He felt for some reason wrathful. On first meeting Simon he had felt, seeing in the flesh the patient face, loose and composed, curiously drawn to him. After a moment's uneasy silence, apparently weighted with significance, he had been impelled to talk, and to talk at length, without mockery, about what he believed in. For two minutes or so he had thought he was addressing an enthralled listener. Now, there seemed to be no one there. Silently, somehow, Simon had cheated him. He retreated into the professional thought that whatever he was in the jungle, on this programme Simon Moffitt was going to be an inadequate and embarrassing performer. Then, as the professional thought ran into the private thought, he decided that Julia could not, now, find this irritable person attractive. Ivan was satisfied with his own body and cared for it. Julia could not like this pitted skin, this nervous Adam's apple, these loose lips. Where Simon had shaved his beard a hot rash had spread disastrously, making his face a strange patchwork of walnut and rose. He caught Simon's eye.

'A lot of surface interest,' he said, waving a hand towards the face.

'What?'

'Surface interest. For the camera.'

'Oh,' said Simon simply, taking a large and apparently painful gulp of gin. He prolonged the uneasy silence that followed until the arrival of the other members of the *Lively Arts* team.

These were a poet, a musician, and a sculptor. They were all young, and struggling to become established. The musician, a pale blond youth called Percy Mottram, was doing best: he was both composer and violinist. He was unpopular with the other artists and popular with the public for the same reasons: he was very beautiful, with a diffident, appealing face, and contributed to discussion a personal, down-to-earth, no-nonsense touch, as though he spoke for the man in the street. The other artists considered this mischievous. Ben McIntyre, the sculptor, had once said that if Percy occasionally wrote like an angel he invariably talked with the vulgarity and banality of most librettos. Ben was vociferous and expected. He had a bushy red beard and a navy polo-necked sweater, and smelled slightly. There had been a good programme on his work, which was obsessed by a kind of wire puzzle trickery of bent, or mobile rods imprisoning an anguished, semi-human figure for whom escape was possible through a combination of padlocks, clues of thread, pressed levers. Except that the figure was welded to the base, or broken on the bars, or hung in chains amongst what looked like a forest of violent television aerials. These works had appeared more impressive under the camera's moving eye than they did standing alone on plinth or rostrum. The poet, Gordon Bottome, taught in a technical college, was the chairman of the meetings, and able to speak fluently through all gaps and uncertainties. He was metrically sound, Left-wing in sympathies, saw literature as the regenerating force of civilization, in so far as he had any faith that civilization could be regenerated, and wrote, largely, ironic meditations on strangers glimpsed on buses or in railway buffets and careful meditations on what poetry might be for, or might do to you. He irritated Ivan, and had been put on to the programme by Ivan's superiors to curb what was, in this context, Ivan's fanatical belief in his own powers, and to restrain Ivan from attempting to be over-ambitious or over-complicated. Ivan told him that he was an educationalist first, not an artist, and he retorted that if this was the case he was not ashamed of it. He was fond, also, of laying down the law about what the audience 'could take' of a given subject. What the audience could take was usually minimal.

To these persons Ivan introduced Simon Moffitt, who swallowed nervously and choked. He explained that they were first to watch several of Simon's films, and then would hold a 'completely random' discussion of his work; from the recording of this a more formal discussion could be plotted and laid out for the programme. Simon, his eyes half-closed, looked into his glass. Ivan tried to assess the effect of Simon on the team – he wished Simon would do or say something to sustain that pitch of fanatical faith in his importance which was necessary if they were to work well together. During his explanation Julia, who was, as usual, late, made an entrance.

She had come to hate arriving at *Lively Arts* meetings. Since she was the only woman on the team she had at first been an object for its attention, and had later become the object of a kind of clubbish exclusion which she felt another woman would have been able to avoid. On this occasion she was flustered by having, unwisely, provoked an altercation just before leaving by asking Mrs Baker to wash the overflowing bucketful of fouled nappies in the bathroom. Mrs Baker felt more secure, Julia had decided, now she saw herself as a weapon in a domestic civil war, rather than an object of charity. So she had made some play with the difference between her own grimy overall and Julia's fine woollen shift, low-necked, pale apricot, drawn up girlishly with a string under the breasts. Julia felt bad. She had made her stand just before coming out so that she would not have to stay in the flat and feel bad. But having come out, she felt distracted and disproportionately menaced.

She saw Simon before he saw her: beyond Ben, a drooping, horribly significant figure. Her stomach turned, and for a moment she thought of simply going away. Ivan at her elbow said, 'Come and meet our guest personality, Ju.'

Simon looked up, his eyes folded behind his cheek-bones. He said, 'Why, Julia,' and then, surprisingly, came half-way across the room and kissed her. Julia, who would have found this gesture normal in any of the other men present, clung to him, trembling.

'Simon and Julia were childhood friends,' said Ivan with his Chinese grin.

'This is your life,' said Percy. Ben, Percy, and Gordon grinned too.

'Simon.' Julia let him go and gathered herself. 'I've watched every one of your programmes all the way through. It gives one a funny one-way feeling of being in touch. But you've really been gone for ever. I honestly never dreamed you'd ever come back. Are you all right?'

He nodded, screwed up his face, peered at her intently, and said rather vaguely, 'Yes, of course. And how are you? How is Cassandra?'

'She's well,' said Julia carefully. Simon said nothing. Julia made an effort to elaborate. 'She's not very much changed. Not very much. She's a don, you know, in Oxford. One doesn't change as much as one thinks one is going to,' she offered.

'No. But I suppose you're both –' he looked round the room, took a gulp of gin, considered his own feet, waved his hand, 'I suppose you're both a bit more normal now.' He laughed. Ivan laughed loudly. Percy and Ben and Gordon laughed. Julia said with aplomb, 'Well, a little bit more normal.' But her cheeks, like his, were burning. It was an odd thing to have said.

Ivan poured gin and said, 'It depends what you mean by normal, Simon. From what I know of them, they're both monsters.' He laughed again. Simon's gaze rested on him and returned to Julia. Julia was suddenly possessed by the fear that Ivan intended to embark on a description of her book, and could think of nothing to say to stop this happening. She looked at Simon in despair; his flaming, chequered face, with its pimples, and the small, livid scars of countless bites even on the eyelids. I felt about him, she thought, oh yes, I did feel.

'How is the rest of your family?' Simon went on, doggedly. 'How is your father?'

'He died. In February.'

'I'm *sorry*,' cried Simon, in sudden, gawky, anguish. 'I'm *sorry*.' He twisted away from her and wrung his hands. 'I shouldn't have asked.'

'That doesn't matter. One can't go on and on being sensitive. I mean, one's got to talk, of course one has. One's got to get over things.'

'Do you think so?' said Simon, leaning towards her with sudden intensity. 'Do you find it easy? Do you find . . . do you find . . . tell me, Julia –'

'Time to talk about snakes,' Ivan said. 'You can talk about each other later.'

The team sat together on a set of Arne Jacobsen chairs which they had chosen from a furniture exhibition together, and watched through several of Simon's films. Julia was appalled and moved by these all over again, seeing them as a series of simple, perfected images, which she did not understand, and whose meaning she would rather not formulate. There was the husk of snakeskin, the dry, perfect mask of the animal which had rolled itself away sleekly elsewhere, the dead, butterfly-sucked pig, the anaconda coiled in a black pool under a milky froth of water-blossoms, its patterned skin blending with lights and shadows, the small constrictor which swallowed a white rat whilst Simon expatiated on its throat muscles and the scaly, pale tail twitched, protesting, out of the mouth corner. Once or twice she looked at Simon, who stared, apparently fascinated, at himself, blinking nervously and fiddling inexpertly with a cigarette.

Afterwards Ivan said, 'Now, I want a tape of a good general discussion on these films, with all of you throwing out any ideas at all you may have, and we'll see what we can make of them. I've been talking to Simon here about this, but I thought I'd go over the ground a bit just to give you a line on where to get started.

'Now we've had a lot of stuff on this programme about what sort of areas of human experience can be treated in different media. We've had Philip Larkin saying he used to think you could write a poem about anything and now he thinks there are specifically *poetic subjects*, and all that lark. Now the telly's an almost virgin and unexploited *art medium* and we've said nothing about it – bar that vile and acrimonious discussion of what differences there might be between television-drama and live drama. Now, I think the really worked out documentary is something unique in our time. I think it's more important than it may appear to be, for reasons I'll give you. But the first thing I want to say is, there are documentaries and documentaries. Some are just higgledy-piggledy thrusting of indiscriminate information at a voracious public. Some are something else. I find Simon Moffitt's programmes deeply moving – deeply moving – as I find a work of art. I don't know if the rest of you feel that.

'Now, the first thought I want to put in your heads is: we've got over-compartmentalized in the way we approach life. We see some things as art, some as science, some as information and so on. One of the bad things about this is the way the arts have got so *refined*. Abstract paintings, symbolist poems, *musique concrète*, novels full of symbols not people, we all know what I mean. Now, I'd have said one thing that characterizes our culture is a hunger for *facts*. A tremendous need to understand, to map out, to believe in the solid world we live in. Art doesn't give it as it used to. Indeed, it tries to fight facts – self-destroying mechanical sculptures, Pop Art making cigarette machines look absurd, or hallucinatory, that sort of thing. Now, look, now, look, people can't take this. They're reading more and more biography, popularized science, psychological case histories, travel literature, if you look at what they like on the telly – educated and uneducated, they all go for *Z Cars* – it's something that reproduces a reality they recognize. Now, once the artist – oh, think of the Flemish painters, think of the Victorian novelists – used to delight in reproducing the details of the world he lived in. But not any more. What documentary art we've got is a bit flat and uninspired. But what about our real documentaries? The film's the only art medium now where things've not got self-conscious to the point of self-parody or almost private meditation. Perhaps we artists ought to spend more time in the company of people concerned at first hand with facts. Or perhaps we aren't the real artists any more. Perhaps people like Simon Moffitt are. So I want us to analyse what we get out of these films.'

Julia looked at Simon, who, with shaking hands, lit one cigarette from the butt of the last.

Gordon Bottome said, 'I take your point, Ivan, about our lives having become over-compartmentalized. I should say, regretfully, that this is necessary. We can't hope in a lifetime to begin to come to grips with a large part of the areas of knowledge or the ways of life we know are available. But we should perhaps make a conscious effort to be less exclusive. In the seventeenth century any sort of treatise could be literature, could be art. Think of *The Compleat Angler*. Or, a medical compendium, *The Anatomy of Melancholy*. Or, a wrong-headed scientific venture, Sir Thomas Browne's *Garden of Cyrus*. Or Bacon. I can't imagine any modern arts department looking at the current equivalent of those, however well written. Not that most of them are, regrettably, well written. Our culture has indeed become divided. Our language is a blunted instrument.'

He looked around the group. Percy said, 'Yes.' No one seemed anxious to develop his point. After a moment he said, 'We might do better if we saw art as a technique, not a mystique. In the seventeenth century, if you said "He wants art" you didn't mean "He hasn't got a special vision of special meaning in life." You meant, "He lacks the power to make what he says coherent and meaningful and pleasing." If we went back to that, we might even be able to take in – some of us – scientific and technological subjects we now shy away from as if they smelled.'

Ivan said, 'What do you think, Simon?'

'Me? I – I can't say I think much about presentation. No, I can't say I do.'

There was a silence.

Ben said, 'I want to take issue with you, Ivan. I don't like your point about art having got so refined. You sound all regretful about it, as though it did it on purpose, and could be stopped if you lectured it a bit.

I don't like Gordon's view of art as a technique not a mystique, either. Technique's only useful as a means to presenting a vision of life. Art's a vision. It's got to be, or it's nothing, get that? And in our time art's almost *pure vision*, we try to see things as they *are*, *essentially*, not as they first appear to be. Now, you're way off the mark with all this about hunger for facts. We've got far too many facts in our life. They crush us. Pop Art and self-destroying machines are a guerrilla warfare on the part of the spirit against these deadly soul-destroying facts, get that? You can't get away from it, Ivan, modern man sees himself as essentially a *victim* of his environment – wherever you turn, you find thinking people writing desperately that they know their lives are like hallucinations, they know this is not all the truth, but –'

'Ben, that proves my –'

'Shut up a minute. Art gives expression to this vision. That's what it's for. Now, as far as a documentary goes, I'm going to produce the old bromide. The photograph destroyed once and for all the need for naturalistic art. Just as I suspect sociology and telly documentary are destroying the naturalistic novel,' he glared at Julia, 'the realistic play, the war epic, taking the meaning out. We don't need to reproduce any more,' he glanced at Simon, 'every wart, every pimple. The time for that's gone by. No, look, what *an artist* could make of Moffitt's stuff – by bringing his own individual vision to bear on it – would be something like this.'

There was always a large easel for Ben's 'visual' demonstrations of his points. Ben sketched now, hastily, lucidly, a formalized pattern of teeth, across a swelling curve, crossed by a limper curve recognizably derived from the rat-tail. He drew also a pattern of flecked white coils with an escaping black coil, geometric, but recognizably the moulting snake, and then a multiplicity of black and white formalized snakes facing each other in a geometric dance across the paper. 'That's the feeling it gives me. One thing inside another, positive and negative, engulfing and escaping, darkness and light. That intensifies –' He sat down.

'Simon?' said Ivan.

'I – I hadn't seen it that way. I – no – I hadn't seen it that way.'

'Does it mean anything to you?'

'Not – not much. Not – that is –'

Ben was drawing a pattern of pot-hooks. Percy said, 'I'd rather look at the original films. There's more there.'

Gordon said, 'I'd have said what Ben did to those snakes was only an extreme version of what Simon was doing in any case. "Art", in my sense. Selection, perspective, emphasis, explication. Take, for instance, that magnified shot of the eyes, before and after the casting of the skin. That was making some sort of a point. Or take the almost miraculous shot of the – the new snake – *through* the skin of – of the old. Simon was telling us something he thought, there, and using – ah – artistic methods.'

'Yes, and, you know,' Percy burst in excitedly, 'don't you think it's all being *vaguer* than what Ben did, as well as more immediate, increases, as it were, the significance . . .'

'It depends what real significance there is. I mean,' this was Gordon, 'we've got to stop talking about how Simon conveys "meaning" and talk about *what* he means. If anything. Why should he think it important to show us snakes? Or we think it important to watch them? Ben clearly does?'

Simon made his first contribution. 'Those snakes are real snakes,' he said. 'You watch a snake eating. You watch *it eating*. First, you watch that.'

'OK,' said Ben. 'So you watch it.'

'Well, you might just be curious about how it does it. Why not? You might just want to know.'

'Well, that affects you,' Percy said.

'It might not. Why should it? Why should it be anything to do with you? It's filling its own stomach. We don't know what it feels like. It's simply there. I – I wanted simply to – learn, to measure.'

'Simon –' said Julia urgently.

'Scientific knowledge –' said Simon, 'the thing in itself –'

Percy burst into speech. 'No, honestly, you can't get away with that. I mean, with all this rubbish about the pathetic fallacy. Snakes are absolutely *weighed down* with meanings for the average man – you kept referring to them quite naturally on your programmes – death and rebirth, evil and healing, water and light, oh, you know, and sex, look at your Freud.'

'Everything and nothing,' said Ivan.

'What I like about your films as opposed to Ben's drawings is that the thing itself is there. It's more than the sum of the meanings. That's what I mean by vagueness. Now, why shouldn't the thing itself *really* "mean" something? Since it has had these mythical meanings through the ages, why do we suppose science is the only truthful way of approaching it?

All this impersonal measuring and weighing and annotating. You don't talk like that on the air, you know, or people wouldn't listen the way they do. You don't *talk* as though the snakes were irreparably not part of – of our world. As though measuring was our *only* relationship with them. It seems to me just as much a pathetic fallacy to pretend we can have an impersonal and neutral relationship with – Nature – that it's *entirely* alien – as to pretend it simply reflects our passing moods. We're part of it.'

'You are confounding science, art, and religion,' said Simon.

'Why not?' said Percy.

'Oh, Jesus, Jesus,' said Ben, leaning back in his chair.

'Why for Christ's sake can't someone say something useful?' said Ivan.

Julia said, 'To return to what Gordon was saying. And Simon being an artist and showing us his view of snakes. Isn't it important that we see so much of him? And hear him talk? We see across his personality. We can't just take him out of the picture. We ought, indeed, to find out why he's in it. What do you think, Simon, what would you say drives you to – this work?'

Simon looked hunted. 'I like snakes. I – I suppose I'm a naturalist because I – I wanted something neutral to do. Something' – he blushed – 'where curiosity was simply curiosity.'

'And innocent?'

'Yes,' said Simon quickly.

'You don't think,' said Percy, 'that you went in for snakes out of any subconscious preoccupation with evil, do you?'

'Or sex?' said Ben, nastily.

'Julia tells me,' said Ivan, 'you used to want to go into the Church.'

'You can make anything of me,' said Simon, 'as you can make anything of snakes. But I don't like it. I didn't come here to be psycho-analysed. I came here to discuss my work. *My* work,' he said. 'Results, tables of figures, so on . . .'

He was crimson.

'I don't know,' said Ivan, 'if anyone realizes how *very* little of what's been said is any use at all. Banal or high-flown, and Simon might just as well not have been there for all the use you've made of him. You might *try* to speak up, Simon, if you wouldn't mind – we really can't afford diffidence, you are our guest personality, we've *got* to hear more of you. Now, let's start again. And let's keep it simple and concrete, will you?'

Julia, before the final recording of the series of simple and concrete questions and answers they had worked out felt blind, panicky stage-fright, of a kind she had almost grown out of. What was left of what they had said was largely Ben's drawings, Percy's musing on the myths underlying the snakes – Simon had been induced to expatiate, scientifically, on one or two of these – and her own questions about the effect of Simon's personality on his choice of occupation. Ivan had extracted from Simon a series of grudging statements about these. It was less a discussion than a slightly hostile interview, by now.

Julia's dressing-room was hot, full of mirrors and boxed light. Sweating, she retouched lipstick and mascara in one of the mirrors. Ivan came in and closed the door behind him. He put his arms round her.

'Let go. Get off. You'll mess me.'

He let her go. 'So I saw your meeting.'

'I hope you were edified.'

'Oh, by you, yes. You must have been a lovely schoolgirl. Gordon says *he's* a mistake. Says we won't get much life out of him.'

'Gordon can talk.'

'Gordon will talk, don't worry. What will you do now?'

'Go and talk about his art. That he says isn't art. I wish you'd leave me alone.'

'Now, now.' He said, crossly, 'I wish anyone had seen my point about the *immediacy* of television. About its being a perpetual self-consciousness.'

'Well, it's not a very nice one most of the time.'

Julia was always startled to find that people like Ivan took seriously programmes like *The Lively Arts*, since this accorded so badly with the rest of their personalities, and with most of the programmes put out by the television in general, and indeed with *The Lively Arts* itself. She felt momentarily guilty at not having lived up to expectations that Ivan, in some part of his mind, clearly had.

Ivan said, 'Well, anyway, he kissed you.'

Julia, who had thought this herself, did not want to discuss the point.

Until the programme began Julia had had the hope that it might, like so many things which seem likely not to be endurable, prove pleasant or even exhilarating after all. It did not. She was sitting very close to Simon and this made her nervous. Simon himself was very nervous, sweating heavily and answering questions monosyllabically, or with an attempt at unconcern that appeared sullen and almost offensive. The team, in consequence, by now simply a group of people accidentally engaged in that kind of interview which most closely resembles an industrial personality questionnaire, with traps for the unwary, the unsuitable, the unstable and the over-clever, developed a hostile and bullying tone. This provoked in Simon no fireworks, simply a further ungracious withdrawal.

After two minutes of this Julia became seriously afraid that she was going to faint. She looked wildly about her. They sat on a dais in front of a set that looked like a comfortable room, with one of Ben's cages balanced on a table like a pale mushroom. Beyond was the desolate dustiness of the studio, and the lit glass box where people checked the communications. Overhead was a woven ceiling of springy wire netting from which dangled, on innumerable coils of looping wire, clumps of microphones and lights. Technicians in blue jeans slid in and out of the equipment, manoeuvring cameras, lugging wire, signalling at each other across Julia.

Lights flared on and off; hot light poured down on her. Near the door, his face dark in shadow, Ivan lounged. Julia, sick and dizzy, had to be reminded when it was her turn to speak, and then forgot her question and its meaning. She addressed Simon absently, and pushed her hand again and again across her brow, in a peculiarly irritating gesture. Gordon felt it his place to intervene. Ivan had said once, in bed, 'The nerve-racking thing is that any mistake you make is seen by millions of viewers. Any *faux pas*, any vulgarity.'

She concentrated simply on sitting it through, not fainting. It is vulgar of Ivan, she thought, to trap me and my emotions in all this wire and light.

In hospitality, after the programme, Ivan became rather drunk. He told Julia several times that 'the bloody programme just didn't get off the bloody ground, it just didn't get off'. Julia reflected that undue intimacy within professional relationships had its advantages. 'As for you, I thought you were going to puke or something, you looked awful.'

'You shouldn't play the impresario with my private life,' said Julia. 'You can't have it all ways.'

Ivan took hold of the front of her dress. His knuckles brushed her skin. 'I've got to have some creative work.'

'Well, not me.'

'I like you talking. Talk some more. About *your* creative work. Where the finished product is indistinguishable from the process. Undigested gobbets of bleeding, disgusting domestic suffering.' He looked at her. 'Or perhaps not *all*. I don't see what right you've got to complain about me–'

'Look –' Julia said.

Simon appeared sober and flaming, in the face, behind Ivan.

'Is there any reason why I shouldn't go?'

'None whatever,' said Ivan.

'Will you come, Julia?'

'*Do* go,' said Ivan, quickly. Julia took Simon's arm.

'Yes,' she said. 'Please. Yes.'

They took a taxi. 'Where shall I tell him to go?' said Simon. 'Where do you live?'

Julia said, 'I don't want to go home.'

Simon pondered this. He was leaning back into his own corner of the taxi, away from her, almost invisible.

'Where do you want to go?'

'Can we go somewhere and talk?'

'Where would we go? I've not been in London since – since –'

'Where are you staying?'

'In a hotel somewhere. We can't go there.' He waited patiently.

'We could go to a pub. Or a coffee-place. Or just walk.'

'Walk where?'

'Oh, up and down the Embankment.'

Simon told the driver to take them to the Westminster pier. When the taxi started he said, 'I won't appear on any more of those shows. They make one feel savaged. Food for thought.'

'I know. It is rather awful.'

'It's a horrible job. They've always got to be thinking up something to have thoughts about. Points of view. Attitudes. Networks of words. The theology of television. That man said he wanted me to talk about my work. I don't want to talk about art. I'm a herpetologist.'

'I agree.'

'Honestly, all this tying up of loose ends seems so dishonest.'

'Oh, I do agree. My creative work is so much better if I don't think about it.'

'I haven't, of course, read your books,' said Simon's neutral voice, with a finality that suggested somehow that he never would. With these small hardnesses he had held her once. When he said nothing else, she told him, 'The reason I didn't offer to take you home is that my flat is full of dependants so you can't hear yourself talk.'

'How much family have you?'

'A husband and a daughter. She's fifteen. And a lot of people brought in off the streets. I married a sort of saint.'

'Like your father.'

'A bit like. Not altogether.'

The memory of Simon's wistful affection for her father brought back other memories. To suppress these she began to give him an account of the Bakers' misdeeds, deliberately laying herself out to entertain. Simon laughed once or twice and crossed and uncrossed his legs.

They got out of the taxi on the Embankment. Simon, paying the driver, dropped a handful of half-crowns and florins which rang on the pavement and glittered in the gutter. They both bent down and their heads knocked lightly together; she put out a hand and steadied herself against his shoulder. This contact affected her; she was aware of the bulk of Simon's body under the raincoat and was momentarily silly with a need to touch him. She wanted to slide both hands inside the coat and put her arms round him. They stood up, having retrieved the coins, and began to walk along the Embankment. Simon's walk was no more co-ordinated than it had been; he swayed like a poplar tree and occasionally twisted his legs almost round each other. They walked separate, fairly distant from each other, but collided frequently owing to Simon's Coleridgean motion. Every time they collided Julia suppressed a cry of anguish.

In this way they came to the *Discovery*. Simon leaned over the wall and stared at the ship. Julia stood beside him and watched an end of rope trail in the water and a red light, slung from the vessel, glitter on a floating patch of oil. She did not know what Simon was thinking.

'What are you thinking, Simon?'

'I was thinking that it's strange how people find things comic that aren't, not really.'

'You mean the Bakers –'

'I wasn't thinking of them. I was thinking of your friend.'

'Ivan?'

'Yes.'

'What did he think was comic, Simon?'

'The piranhas.'

'Piranhas?'

'Fish. Flesh-eating fish.' He held up his hands, cupped round the imaginary shape of one. 'So big.'

Julia shuddered. 'It's the sort of thing he would find funny.' Simon said nothing.

'I've read about how they can strip a man to a bare skeleton in ten minutes. Or did I get that from your talks?'

'I've seen that.' He looked at her, and away, quickly.

'Simon!'

'He found that funny.'

'Well, you know, it's the sort of gruesome thing he'd feel obliged to feel was funny. I mean, because it's so awful and *typical*. I really knew a chap once who had an uncle who was eaten by cannibals. A vegetarian uncle. It got to be a family joke.'

'I see.'

There was a long silence.

'I'm so glad to see you, Si. You can't know. You know, I've never got out of the habit of saving up things to tell you – all sorts of little things. I really do feel that relationships develop even if one can't do anything about them, just with the passage of time. But that's quite likely an illusion. I thought if I ever did see you you might be a complete stranger. But you aren't.'

'It's been a long time,' said Simon, in a muffled voice.

'Did you ever think of me, Si? Since you left? Ever?'

He hesitated. 'Oh, yes. Often.' He smiled. 'I don't know many people to think about. I think I was told you were married. I thought I might write and wish you well.'

'You never did.'

'No.'

Julia touched his arm, briefly. 'I wish you had. Would it seem silly to ask – after all these years – meeting like strangers – why you – why you just suddenly went off?'

She tried to catch his eye in the dark and could see only the rough cheek surface and its craters. 'Or have you forgotten?'

'No, no, I haven't forgotten. I – nothing seemed to be getting anywhere, I suppose. It just wasn't getting anywhere. I thought you knew that.'

This could not be described as a satisfactory answer.

'But I loved you, it was a terrible shock.'

'I thought it was the other way round,' he said, shifting slightly. 'Anyway, I'm sorry.'

'Oh, no –'

There was another silence.

'I'm glad you're happy, Julia. I thought you ought to have been. You had such a capacity for living – for attacking life. You are happy, aren't you?' He asked this with a kind of eagerness.

'Yes,' said Julia. 'On the whole, very happy.' She didn't know whether she was or not, but it was clear that Simon wanted her to be.

'I thought so.' He looked out at the water again, his lips moving.

'Oh, I *am* glad to see you.'

He said, into the water. 'You used always to be in two minds about seeing me. Always. You know you were.'

'But not now. Now I'm just glad.'

'Good.' He was silent again.

Julia felt that something was being achieved; that at last she was talking, with a possibility of further talk, to the real man. In some very simple way she was no longer in two minds about seeing him; he was no longer, as she remembered he had been, faintly repulsive or faintly menacing. She was visited again by the desire to touch him, simply to touch; she looked at his dark face and hunched shoulders with love and the surface of her body prickled. This is one of the few times, she thought, when my thoughts, and my body, and all my attention, have been in the same place.

'That comedian –' said Simon.

'Yes?'

'He took hold of your dress. I didn't like that.'

Julia did not know how to take this. It might well have been an expression of a kind of jealousy, but sounded much more like one of Simon's occasional blundering efforts at moral guidance. His expression was one of prudish distaste. She said, 'It's just his way.'

'Probably.'

'Shall we walk on a bit?' said Julia, to distract him. He seemed to wake up. 'No,' he said. 'No, I'll take you home, now.'

CHAPTER FIFTEEN

During the next three days Julia thought of nothing but Simon. She went over their inconclusive conversation several times. She was obsessed by the memory of the moment when they had collided, and by the idea that she needed to touch him. She had never before wanted to touch him in this way without any accompanying reluctance: she put it to herself that to touch Simon would 'make everything real'. She had two detailed and warmly erotic dreams about him – again, this had not happened before – and woke to a sense of loss. She felt that to meet him, to talk to him again, would be a completion of a part of her life and a beginning of a new part, a new revelation. She thought she had sensed this feeling in him, too. But he had hailed a taxi, brought her home, let her out on the doorstep, and, before she had turned round to ask for an address, to suggest a further meeting, had driven away.

Over the last months, after the death of her father, and particularly since the end of *A Sense of Glory*, she had felt that she had achieved a new sense of identity to act from. She had always been tempted to remain a child – well, she was ready now to grow up. Her teeth were cut, she was innocent and responsible. Touching Simon – from herself – was somehow to prove this.

After further thought she attributed her new sense of Simon's possible private reality to the complete absence – during that meeting – of any sense that she was being watched by Cassandra. She had always felt that her actions were being 'produced' by Cassandra's fear, Cassandra's expectations, Cassandra's idea of Simon. But this meeting had felt like her own. She was ready to have things of her own, now. Once the thought of Cassandra's watching had occurred at all some of the sense of innocence slid away; but this, Julia told herself, was because she did not see Simon and had nothing to bite on. She spent time imagining his hotel room, imagining unexpected meetings, adding explanatory sentences to the Embankment conversation. She avoided Ivan.

On the fourth day she woke to the sound of the telephone ringing. When it had rung for some time she struggled out of bed; Thor seemed to be nowhere, and the thing must be answered. When she arrived in the hall, Thor was already lifting the receiver.

'Yes,' he said. 'No, on the contrary, I do of course, very well.' He listened. 'I'm sure she would. Oh yes, certainly, by all means. And *I* look forward to meeting you. Yes, indeed.' He rang off.

'That was Simon Moffitt,' he said. 'He wonders if you would like to go to the zoo.'

'To the zoo?'

'He is coming round for you.'

'I wanted to speak to him. Why didn't you let me speak to him?'

'He didn't ask,' said Thor. 'He said he looked forward to meeting me.'

Julia looked, perturbed, at the telephone.

'I should get dressed,' said Thor, 'if I were you.'

Simon was wearing a sports-coat which flapped widely and unfashionably from the waist, and a huge pair of *veldtschoen*. He was carrying his raincoat, a canvas holdall, a brief-case, an umbrella, and a long canvas bag, tied and labelled, that bulged from itself once or twice. He put this casually on a chair, against which he tried to stack the other things; whilst he did this, Thor came out of the living-room, the Bakers collected in the living-room, and Deborah came out of her bedroom in pyjamas, dressing-gown, and thin, bare feet.

'Ah, Mr Moffitt, I presume.' Julia could not tell whether this was an accidental locution or a deliberate joke. Simon straightened himself, and put out a hand.

'Julia and I are old friends.'

'I know. I know.'

'I've got to go to the zoo, so I . . .' He stopped, and looked at Deborah.

'My daughter, Deborah,' said Julia.

Simon considered her. 'She looks like Cassandra. But I suppose everyone tells you that.'

'Even Aunt Cassandra admits it.'

'I suppose you're too old to be taken to the zoo.' Deborah smiled.

'Would you like to come to the zoo?'

'Oh, no, I don't think so. Not today, thank you. I don't often go.'

'A pity,' said Simon. 'Some other time.'

'Oh, yes, some other time, I'd love to.'

Simon wrung his hands, and then, without warning, knelt to retie a shoelace.

'Get your coat, Julia,' said Thor. He said to Simon, 'Maybe you could come back this evening to eat with us? I am anxious to know about conditions in South America at first hand. We have been in correspondence with the health education institutes there. I have a lot of questions for you, if you've not had enough questions.'

'I'd love to come,' said Simon, his face hidden. 'This is very kind. I shall certainly come.'

The bag on the chair changed position slightly. Thor gathered up Simon's effects and handed them to him, one by one. The brief-case he gave to Julia.

'Have a good day,' he said. 'Deborah and I will see about supper, don't bother.'

Simon took a taxi to Regent's Park; then he walked Julia across to the zoo buildings. Julia was carrying, now, both brief-case and umbrella; in this way she felt she had a hold on him. He offered no explanation for the invitation, nor for his three-day silence; once or twice he stopped and looked at her, with an expression predominantly anxious, but when he did speak, it was from a distance, as though to a business associate, or maybe a niece whom he was obliged to entertain.

'I've got – I've got – a certain amount of – of business. I do hope you don't mind a certain amount of – hanging around. Of hanging around.'

'Of course not.'

'Oh, good. I thought, then we could – eat something. Or something.'

'I didn't know if you *really* meant the zoo,' said Julia, at random. It had seemed so much like a rendezvous from a *Woman's Own* love story.

'Don't you like the zoo?'

'Of course I do – but –'

'I – I have to be here quite a lot. I don't like it much. But it seemed a good place – a good place to meet. In the circumstances.'

They went in. Julia took Simon's raincoat and restored his brief-case. She discovered rapidly that there was, indeed, a certain amount of hanging around involved; she followed Simon from office to office, watching him hand over typewritten sheets and little phials and boxes which he produced from the holdall, examine photographs and reports, and last, in the Reptile House, hand over the canvas bag. She sat in corridors or stood in doorways; no one paid her any attention, except that in one office she was given a cup of long-brewed tea and a chocolate jammy bun wrapped in silver paper. Simon himself hardly looked at her. She began to feel very female, an attendant servant-cum-girl-friend, his woman. This pleased her, finally, rather than insulting her. It disposed of the hysterical apprehension she had been feeling over being faced with his physical presence and finding it unreal, like a too long anticipated childhood treat. Simon, to the people in these offices, was real enough – solid, necessary, to be negotiated with. She was real to them in terms of him and it had always been so much the other way about. He kept signing things, and he, too, drank tea and ate a jammy bun.

Finally they were alone in the Reptile House. He looked down at her.

'Well, that's that, for today. A quick look round?'

'If you want.' He knew, and must be choosing to ignore, her dislike of reptiles.

The place had an unearthly glow, and was hot, damp, concrete and dark. Inside their little glass boxes of brilliance the snakes lay, heaped haphazardly together, almost all motionless. One narrow, stone-coloured, dark-eyed creature looped itself round the plastic foliage provided for it, and flickered its nervous tongue at the glass walls. It seemed aimless, poured along the leaves, leaned out and froze into a brittle twig; it gave no sign of further movement. Simon walked past it, heavily in his *veldtschoen*; Julia tapped two steps behind him. Around them, children squalled.

'I shipped them this anaconda,' Simon said. Together in the dark, they leaned on the rail and stared into the box. 'I had a battle with her in a tree. She just fell on me, suddenly – not what I'd bargained for her doing – we ended up wrestling. I had to be rescued. I came off lucky – a lot of bruises and a gnawed hand. She was slow and sulky – didn't eat for nine months after she was shipped. They tell me she eats well, now.'

'She looks rather scruffy,' Julia said. This was an understatement. The anaconda was lapped about herself in one corner of her box, one great coil draped into her shallow concrete pool. The water in the pool was dirty, and looked as though someone had shredded tobacco into it. All along the snake's back fragments of skin were raked up; the whole thing was fraying into transparent pieces and peeling away like old wallpaper. The head rested on the centre of the coils, the blunt, patient snout immobile. The eyes, which Julia had imagined would be black, stood out of the head and looked like opals – pinkish, with fine lines crazing the surface. For a long time the creature did not move, and Julia was almost mesmerized by the very slow rise and fall of the walls of the breathing trunk. Then, with no apparent disturbance of the extremities, the snake made a lazy attempt to hoist the fallen coil on to the ledge she lay on. The curve of the coil contracted, rose slightly, and began very slowly to slither back again. Behind the anaconda was a dark backcloth, perfunctorily painted with greenish fronds and dark roots. The olive-green underskin of the snake, and the black and creamy rings, gave the same impression of ageing oil-paint.

'Moulting. They seem largely incapable of shedding a whole skin in captivity.'

'Poor thing. She looks so appallingly tatty. Do you mind for her? Do you ever wish they weren't in here?'

'I don't know. Yes, I think. She doesn't look comfortable. As far as one can ever tell. There are all sorts of parasites that flourish only in captivity, too. And rots.' He looked gloomy.

'Si – can you get to know a snake? Can you *love* a snake?'

'Oh, up to a point. I have kept snakes one could play with. In a very limited sense of the word. Long acquaintance does give one a – a quickness – one knows much more quickly when they're hungry or angry or simply in need of exercise.'

'And that makes you love them?'

'Well, in a way. Partly it has the opposite effect. When I was young and kept adders – I knew them less, and loved them more.' He laughed. 'You put a bit of yourself into them.'

'Like cats. A friend of mine had this cat that she thought had an enormous amount of character, and then she got a baby. And the cat suddenly became just cat again and didn't have any feelings to be considered. I thought she *did* it to the cat – preparing herself to be able to have it put down, you know, without needing to feel she was destroying anything more than an animal.'

'Yes,' said Simon. He considered his anaconda. 'I suppose anyone who works with animal life ends up like doctors – very much more aware in a factual way of what creatures do, how they react – but much more mistrustful of any feeling of knowledge that comes from identifying with them. Or maybe that knowledge just becomes unbearable. Doctors, of course, can't afford to – to identify. But it's funny going into something out of – well, love – and ending up with simple curiosity. Worse for doctors. Good, for me.'

'Is *that* what you feel about love? That it's – it's impossible – because it's either subjective or unbearable? Is that what you're saying? *Must* it be? Is *that* what you feel?'

Simon looked impatient. 'You could say curiosity was the beginning of love. And most of us would do best to stop there since we aren't capable of anything better.'

'But don't you feel it's impossible to stop there?'

'How can anyone really bear another person?' Simon said. 'I don't know.' He shifted from one foot to another. Julia caught her breath.

'But don't you ever want to? Don't you feel urged to?'

'You and Cassandra,' he said abruptly, 'you were always collecting my feelings.'

'Out of curiosity. Only out of curiosity, Si.'

'I don't think so.'

He looked almost angry, and Julia was shaken by the sudden reference to Cassandra. She was silent; the snake in her prison sagged farther into the pool, under the steady glare of the light. Julia felt oppressed.

'She's so exposed,' she said. 'She's so horribly exposed. Oh, it must be awful to be so lit up and always watched.'

'I don't imagine that aspect of it bothers her. I should think she might really miss the freedom to move.'

'Well, I think it's horrid.'

'You know, I really am moved, by the thought of prehistoric reptiles,' Simon surprisingly said. 'The first developed life, you know – well, that we would recognize – crawling out of the primeval slime. At first they were small, and hopped and skipped, and then they grew. They lived so long because, like these, if conditions were wrong they could just give up irrelevant things like eating and moving. Pythons and boas have vestigial limbs and pelvic bones, you know. Imagine the antediluvian world, full of slow, deliberate creatures who just gave up when there was nothing to be done –'

Julia touched his arm. 'Can we go out of here? I can't bear any more of this dark and heat and lying around . . .'

'Did you know there's a tribe that believes that in the night the anaconda turns itself into a boat with white sails? Now, why *that*?'

'Yes, I know. You said. I saw you say it.'

He looked at her, brooding. 'It's a miracle – what we make, in our minds, of what we see, to fulfil what needs. What needs.'

'We ought not?'

'We do.'

Julia, whose desire to touch Simon had ebbed whilst they were watching the anaconda, was suddenly again overwhelmed by it. She shifted her brief-case and umbrella to the hand that already clutched her own leather bucket bag. Then she put her own hand over his, where it lay on the rail in front of the glass box.

'Simon –'

'Perhaps an ice-cream,' he said, vaguely.

In the next tank a dirty brown boa constrictor had just eaten: it lay extended, the various unconnected swellings in its body like toys in a Christmas pillow-case. It breathed faster than the anaconda; the distension of its belly dwarfed its head and tail.

'Eating and sleeping. Eating and sleeping. You made them look so very significant on those films. But here –'

'Here,' said Simon, 'the possibilities are a bit limited. Would you like an ice-cream?'

Simon made for a dark corner of the cafeteria, settled Julia at a table and returned with silver bowls containing pink and white oblong slabs of ice. Julia was depressed; the place smelled of disinfectant and damp, there were floating sweet papers, cigarette stubs and ash all over the table. And there was only a certain amount of aesthetic pleasure to be derived from the sight of Simon in these incongruous surroundings. He, alternately, took teaspoonsful of ice, grimaced and swallowed, and broke matchsticks into neat lengths, which he then scattered in the ashtrays. Julia watched him scrape up a bit of ice from the cuff of his jacket with the spoon. He had always been a messy eater.

The air was heavy, Julia considered, with unspoken importances.

'Simon,' she said, deciding on direct attack, 'why did you bring me here?'

He blinked. 'I thought it would be nice for us to see each other, again. I thought you might like it.'

'Why?'

'Well, don't you?' he asked, nervously.

'Of course. Of course I do.'

'I'm glad. I – it's nice when people haven't become complete strangers. When one's glad to see old friends. For me, that is, because I don't know many people. Different for you, you have a very full life.'

'You don't seem a stranger at all. I can't tell you how glad I am that we're so glad to see each other. It makes a difference to the whole of my life in between.'

'Well, hardly that,' he began. He started to clean out a nail with one of the matchsticks and looked quickly up at her and down again. Julia wondered how she had come so wildly to desire someone so disordered. He was waiting.

'As though we can – finish something. As though – something continued all these years,' she said.

'Do you know how many years?'

'Yes, I know. And now – I'm ready for you.' Julia wrinkled her brow. She could not be polite, she must plunge in or nothing, and he was waiting. 'I do love you,' she said, with a wildly light touch. 'I've always loved you, you know, in a way, whatever that means.'

'Well, hardly that,' he said again.

'I do want us to be able to talk to each other.'

'Yes –' He hesitated. 'Yes. But don't make too much of me.' His face took on a look of analystic helpfulness. 'I'm not that interesting. You and Cassandra had this gift for making things interesting. I always felt – both of you – were trying to make something of me. There wasn't enough of me to stand up to it.' He looked at her almost shyly. 'You won't start again? I mean, you don't need to. You've got so much.' His voice was almost hopeful. Julia rallied. Whatever he was saying, he had clearly given her some thought. Moreover, a man will not embark on an abstract discussion of love, in a reptile house or elsewhere, with a woman with whom he feels no pull of intimacy.

'All I'm saying is, meeting you again makes all my life more solid. More real. I was awfully put out by your going off. Shaken. You don't mind me saying this?'

'No, no –'

'You can't understand. Since – since Daddy died – I – I've been finding out just how much of me isn't involved in any way in the life I have. I've kept going over and over –'

Simon pouched his face into an agonized frown.

'Julia! I'm sorry. I'm sorry. Look, you can't let a shock make too much difference to you. It does have that effect, but you can't afford to let it, that's one of the things I do know. One of the few things.' He put his hand over hers, gently. 'I'm glad you've done so well. I'm glad you're happy. It means a lot to me that you should be happy. You ought to be.'

He was being kind. This was how he had always been; he would provoke what was apparently a moment of real contact, he would do nothing decisive to avoid it, and then he would slide away into priest-like kindness. He tightened his hand on hers.

'Don't be kind. You're not in a position to. You're part of my life, you've changed me.'

'Oh, yes. And you me.' He stared at the tea-urns. 'But don't make too much of it. Your imagination always frightened me.'

He too was speaking with abstract clarity out of past thoughts, rather than this present encounter. Julia could not reconcile the handclasp with what he was saying.

'But, Si, what do you want?'

'Nothing,' he said. 'But it's nice for us to see each other.'

'Is it?'

He gave her hand a final pressure and released it. 'Well, I think so.' He glanced at her, nervous, questioning, almost grinning. Julia's guts contracted. She thought: the truth is, he doesn't know what he feels. And then, if that is so, he can be made to feel. She did not formulate to herself precisely what she wanted of him, but she was suddenly energetic, with a sense of bright possibility.

'Well,' she said gaily, 'shall we look at some more animals?'

CHAPTER SIXTEEN

'So what will you do now, Simon?' said Deborah. 'Will you just go off again?' The baby squalled. In the kitchen Julia was attempting to cook veal in marsala on half a gas-stove. Thor was out. It was three weeks since Julia had gone to the zoo with Simon. On the other half of the gas-stove Mrs Baker was deep-frying fritters of corned beef; the kitchen was full of pungent smoke off the fat. Through this Julia could detect the insidious and now constantly pervasive sweet rotten smell of the nappies. She supposed she would have to speak to the Bakers about the nappies again. The presence of the Bakers filled her with the kind of female, housewifely rage which she mocked, sympathetically, in the heroines of her novels.

She wished Deborah would not call Simon Simon. She supposed it was the penalty she had to pay for never having been called Mummy, but she could not like it. Nor did she like Simon's pleasantly avuncular personality: the long travellers' tales he produced so effortlessly for Deborah, the way he settled into her chairs.

'Not for a bit,' said Simon. 'I'll stay put for a bit. I'm committed to various lectures in this country – zoos, zoological societies, things like that. And in Europe too – flying visits. And the doctors want to watch me for a while. A bit of intestinal trouble. Only what you might expect.'

He doesn't bother to tell *me* about himself like that, Julia thought, shaking frozen peas out of a packet into a copper pan. Mrs Baker, who had temporarily quelled the baby, shuffled through the living-room.

'Good evening, Mrs Baker.'

'Thank you, Mr Moffitt.'

Julia was wedged against the walls of her kitchen by the wide hips of Mrs Baker.

'I'm *awfully* sorry, Mrs Eskelund. If I'd known you wanted to cook just this minute I'd have waited *of course*, but you do *usually* eat a bit later, when he comes in, and I'm always particular to keep out of the way at those times –'

'Please don't worry. There's plenty of room for both of us.'

'It's a question of veg,' said Mrs Baker. She shook her chip pan aggressively and embarked on a further apology.

'Deborah!' cried Julia, shrilly. 'You might do a bit more than just sit there! You could get some knives and forks and things.'

Her voice sounded in her ears, middle-aged and irritable. In the flat Simon, because he was unmarried and a wanderer, seemed to belong to a younger generation than herself, simply because she was a wife and Deborah's mother. Nothing in me has changed, she thought furiously. But he enjoys this. And Deborah enjoys it. She likes to feel he's sorry for her.

'Oh, hell,' she said, curtailing Mrs Baker's continuing apology. Mrs Baker shifted her hips fractionally, offended into silence again: both of them wielded fish slices, grimly.

She spent a lot of time trying to understand Simon's behaviour. He had stayed and talked, tardy, affable and nervous, the evening after their visit to the zoo: then he had disappeared for another three days. Since then, from time to time, he had come back to the flat – once indeed, he had come back three times in one day – and had hung around, there were no other words for it, simply waiting to be invited to lunch or supper. He had not asked her out alone again, and made, as far as she could judge, no attempt to be alone with her, or to return to the ambiguous intimacy of their first two meetings. On the other hand he looked at her, when they did find themselves alone together, with what she could only describe as an expectant expression, and followed her from room to room, watching her silently and falling over the furniture or the crawling children. 'Alone' by now, in Julia's vocabulary, included the presence of the Bakers. Perhaps that was what was wrong. She herself was unbearably aware still of his presence; she had to turn her eyes away from him when she handed him coffee, she could feel his stare pricking the back of her neck and her spine when she bent over the stove. As though at any moment he would lay his hand on her and the waiting would be finished: but he did not. She was still avoiding Ivan; and Thor seemed to be avoiding her, or exhausted.

When Simon came to the flat he talked, at length, to both Thor and Deborah.

He had embarked on a long argument with Thor about the nature and value of modern civilization, which they took up and nagged at all over again each time they met. This argument irritated Julia profoundly, although she had no ideas of her own to contribute to it, and felt the claustrophobia of any woman trapped in an impersonal male exchange; she thought she knew that they were not even talking about the same thing and would thus never, however much they reiterated their own points of view, get anywhere. Thor used words like escapist, judiciously and frequently; Simon talked about homogeneity and mechanical monotony; Julia, bobbing choppily on all sorts of cross-currents of thought, began to admire herself more and more for the realism with which she refused to commit herself to an attitude, for the penetration with which she remarked that they were, both of them, constructing theologies to support patterns of behaviour to which they were both driven by parts of their temperament remote enough from logical justification. But after a time she was irked by a similarity between them which she had not previously remarked; they were seeking each other's company because they were both, in a sense, religious extremists, they wanted a way of life that would justify this world in terms of another. Simon was negative, that was all; all he was *certain* of was eating and sleeping; but he was, for this reason, a suitable testing ground for Thor's practical moral views about the organization of these basic activities. She thought, sometimes, that they were both, although she admired them, curiously lacking intelligence; Ivan, for all his silliness, was more clever.

But Thor was out, a lot of the time, and Simon talked more to Deborah. Julia suspected that Deborah was telling him at length those grievances against herself which she didn't like to admit her own consciousness of, much of the time; his evasive character made him in many ways the ideal confidant, and he listened with an awkwardly benign expression. Only he seemed to be doing a lot of the talking himself – this Julia liked even less – and today, coming in from a lunch with her publisher, she had found Simon and Deborah solemnly side by side on the sofa discussing, she was sure of it, Cassandra, the phenomenon of Cassandra. She was worried about Cassandra, and a little worried about Simon himself; her publisher's comments on the way she had, according to him, courageously 'let go', 'explored in depth', with these two characters in *A Sense of Glory* had troubled her; she had realized for the first time just how much she was depending on neither of the originals reading the book.

She put veal and peas together into the oven to warm and brought out the avocado cocktails; she still found herself cooking carefully 'for' Simon, who seemed to pay no attention to what was put in front of him. Deborah had laid a pile of cutlery haphazardly on the coffee table – they ate on their knees – and was sitting down again.

'Oh, it's all quite a business, it takes a long time,' said Simon to Deborah.

'Well, go on, tell.'

'I don't think,' said Julia, 'we'll wait for Thor, we never know when he's coming these days.'

'I thought he was in the relief centre,' said Simon. 'Perhaps we ought to wait.'

'He might not come at all,' said Deborah. 'He's been known not to. He's doing too much. Do go on, Simon.'

Mrs Baker, carrying a plate piled high with smoke-smelling fritters, passed, puffing and muttering, behind Simon's chair.

'They examine the contents of my gut, that's the essence of it,' said Simon. 'There are various parasites and things I might have picked up.'

'How do they do *that*?' said Deborah.

Julia, since she seemed to be the only one interested in the meal, took a spoonful of avocado. It's creaminess consoled her: she did not want to hear about Simon's gut.

The front door banged.

'That's him!' said Simon. He seemed pleased.

Thor took a long time to come in, and then stood, just inside the doorway, sagging slightly, his winged, staring look accentuated. He brought with him cold air and a tension of some kind. Julia gathered herself.

'You nearly missed dinner.'

'You look exhausted,' said Simon, clinically.

'I must change my trousers.'

'Have your dinner first, won't you?'

'Someone's been sick on them.' Julia took a quick look and saw that somebody, fairly recently, had indeed been sick on them, across both knees and down the left leg. More dirt, more smells, Julia thought as he crossed into the bedroom; lately he had been coming home smelling of all sorts of things; stale beer, rough pipe tobacco, disinfectant and on several occasions the really foul decaying animal odour she associated with rotting upholstery. She dipped her spoon into the avocado again and took several mouthfuls; so, absently, did Simon. Mrs Baker crossed and recrossed with Julia's Finnish peasant tureen full of disintegrating cauliflower.

Thor came out of the bedroom in a pair of jeans and his cream-coloured heavy sweater. He sat down on the spare bed and pushed his hands over his head, kneading his scalp.

'Who was sick, Daddy?'

'Have some avocado.'

'In a moment, Julia. In a moment.' He said. 'I miscalculated. I think it was only to be expected, but I –'

'Was it one of your suicides?' asked Deborah, knowledgeably.

Thor nodded. His fingers worked. 'It was the fourth attempt. I miscalculated. Three – the others – they were no good, they were never meant to be any good, they were only for the attention's sake. And it wasn't as though . . . that is . . . she would ring me up, and threaten, oh, innumerable times things that never happened. At first I always went, to listen. Later, well, one grows to feel one is doing more harm than good – setting up a habit, that is, she depends on an interest captured by threats – I felt – that was – no good to anyone. No good. No good depending on me. One feels one should listen and care, or not listen at all. That's a luxury, too, feeling that . . .'

'Is she dead?' said Simon.

'No, no. Not yet, at least. I used emetics. She has a chance.'

'You did your best,' said Simon.

'Not a good best.' He looked stricken; Deborah poured him a glass of tonic water.

'*Why* did she, Daddy?'

'This time,' he said, slowly, cradling his head in his hands, 'she left a long letter – a long letter – saying it was because I would not come.' He shuddered. 'A sickening letter,' he said, surprisingly, in his toneless voice, 'a most unpleasant letter. But she had certainly taken enough to kill herself. The letter, that is, was not simply a – an appeal. It was to make me sorry.'

'They always are,' said Simon.

'Well, I am sorry.' He screwed up his smooth face, and said, to Simon, 'These are the sicknesses of this – civilization – you won't have. She must have been nearly fifty, sold lace collars, she said – always dressed, when I saw her, like a – like a whore.' He gestured grimly at Julia. 'Emerald eyelids like croquet-hoops,' he said, 'and a wet scarlet mouth. Scarlet nails, jagged at the tops. Very tight black dresses, shoes with spikes, varicose veins, smelled sweet and rich and stuffy. Lived in a bedsitter with an electric ring. No relations. Had some anatomical defect she couldn't bring herself to tell me of, but she knew she wasn't "normal". I couldn't get her to the doctor. She only told me this *after* the last bid. She'd known she wasn't "normal" since she was ten. "I've lived with it all these years," she said to me. "Lived with what?" I said. "Oh, I couldn't say," she said, "only I'm not quite normal," and she laid her hands – on my knees. You see?'

'I see,' said Simon, comfortably. 'There was little you could do.'

Julia was faintly excited by Thor's description; like most men, he had never been able to tell her in any detail what anyone looked like, yet here was an appearance that had impressed him to the point of simile.

'It would be good to think that,' said Thor, 'if I could think it. If I could think it. But I have seen too many people tell themselves that. You, for instance.' He looked at Julia. 'Or you. Or you. You ought to know about all the misery – all the loneliness . . . the *real* suffering . . .' He looked at the three of them with flat hostility. 'Any of you – any or even all of you – could go out and relieve some of this, even one night a week.'

Julia felt this as the sort of practical truth that could not in fact be a truth because it seemed so simple and obvious, and clearly did not work in the world.

'I'd be no good at it,' she said. 'That's the trouble.' She thought a moment. 'Most of us'd be no good at it. And the professionals seem to be such weird people.'

'The maimed helping the maimed,' said Thor. 'I've thought that often over the last few months. But as for you – with all your friendship and imagination – if you'd been where I've been . . .'

'I wouldn't have them any more. The friendship and imagination. They feed on comfort.'

'This woman,' said Thor, 'is comfortable enough.' He dropped his head completely into his hands. 'I shall never – I shall never – I shall never *like* all this bored and empty brooding on imagined slights and fantastic illnesses.'

'*You* want,' said Julia, almost angry, 'to be able to watch sores disappear after shots in the arm, or blindness lift, or starved limbs round out, you can *see* that . . . And after *that*, what? What?'

The telephone rang.

'When you've cured it, what?' said Julia.

Her husband stood up without answering and seemed, for a moment, to steady himself on his legs. Then he went out into the hall.

'He ought to have been Albert Schweitzer,' said Julia, furiously, to Simon.

'I think so, yes.'

'But you're not going to tell me that's any answer, Si?'

'No. I didn't think you were looking for an answer.'

'Well, he is.'

'You don't have to make it difficult for him.'

'I've never met such a slippery character as you are, Simon Moffitt,' said Julia. Thor re-entered the room.

'Well,' he said. 'She is dead.'

Simon said, 'Have a drink, that's best.'

Julia imagined, for a flickering moment, the dead woman on a hospital bed, jagged red nails and drooping red mouth, crumpled fifty-year-old flesh. Everybody I know keeps seeing dead people; I always just miss them. 'You can't afford to mind, darling. These things have got to happen. You did your best. You are too thin-skinned.'

'I really do think you should have a drink,' said Simon, with a kind of miserable anxiety. 'Honestly, I think you should.'

'No,' said Thor. 'Thank you.'

He turned his head from side to side, as though he was searching for air; Julia saw that his eyes were full of tears. If he were a child, she thought, I could slap him, and he would break.

'Why?' he said. 'Why?' He was speaking to Simon. 'Why must we behave as though only extremity gives meaning to our lives?'

'Because, often, only extremity does.'

'She was sure she – was someone – with those pills and that glass in her hand. Wasn't it so? And I would notice her. Why do you go out where you go?'

Simon did not answer.

Thor said, 'It's a bloody lie.'

Julia stood up and walked into the kitchen; she came back with her warmed casserole of veal, and peas, the potatoes, the warmed plates.

'At least, we might as well eat dinner,' she said. 'We've got to go on, we'll be better with food inside us.'

Thor stood up. He had a dazed frown, and no one quite knew in which direction he meant to move; then he crossed to Julia's dishes, and emptied them out on to the table. 'I won't have this, I won't have this,' he said; Julia could hear him grinding his teeth. He said, still with a choked reasonableness, to Simon, 'You see, I wanted to break her neck.'

He gave the standard lamp a violent blow with the side of his hand, and said through its rocking, 'All I thought was, I want to, I want to finish this whining once and for all . . .'

'I can see that,' said Simon carefully. Thor hooked his foot under the coffee table and overturned it. 'It was pointless, you see,' he said, as though involved in a theological argument, 'pointless. Like all this.' He gave the table a violent kick, which drove it into the bed on which Julia and Deborah were sitting; the crashing and splintering sound of this drew out the Bakers, in whose lives violence was the only relief from monotony; silent, watchful, grinning involuntarily, they hovered in the doorway on one side of the flat.

'It's all right,' said Julia to them, 'go away, will you, please.'

'No, it is not all right,' said Thor. He was breathing heavily, but his voice was still cold; he bent, suddenly, gathered up Julia's smoky tumbler, hurled it at the window, listened to the small glass explosion, trembling slightly, and walked stiffly into the bedroom. Julia followed him; behind her, Simon and Deborah padded as far as the doorway; across the flat, the Bakers edged out of the living-room. Julia, at this stage, was still calm; she thought, since we have all got to settle down again after this, it seems a little unreal to have actually to live through it, and it goes on so. She said:

'Look, darling, you've got all this out of proportion, you've got it out of proportion, you can't go on like this.'

'What do you know about proportion?' said Thor. 'What do you know about anything?' Each of his careful sentences was followed by another abrupt, muscle-bound, violent movement: this time, he raised his leg and attempted with his foot to shatter Julia's dressing-table mirror; he did indeed catch it a glancing blow and for a moment was suspended in an absurd hop, his buttocks straining, his white flesh bulging between the tight cuff of his jeans and his socks. Julia gave a snort. He turned on Simon again and repeated, 'I wanted to break her neck. I knew how to start, I wanted to . . .' He turned round again, and with an outstretched arm swept away all Julia's silver-topped bottles, and little pots of cream, hairbrushes, tissues, false eyelashes curled in their plastic case, tweezers and hairpins, and, for Julia was untidy, little balls of coppery hair combed from the brush, round balls of cotton wool stained flesh and grey.

'What are you doing?' said Julia.

'I won't have it.' He began, trampling around amongst these objects, to tear out the drawers and pile them on the bed; Julia's clothes trailed between bed and dressing-table.

'Leave my things alone.'

'Your things. Your things. Bloody *things*. I want to get at my things,' he said, childishly. He said to Simon, 'You know, I should never have married.' He began to shake the wardrobe, which always stuck.

'No,' said Simon. 'Probably not.' He looked mournfully at the ground. 'But in our time it seems to be expected of us, by and large.'

Julia flew at her husband, who in the same moment burst open the rocking wardrobe.

'Will you shut up. What do you keep telling Simon things for? What the hell is the point of telling Simon about whether or not you ought to be married? Look, for God's sake, we shall *all* be sorry for this tomorrow. You ought to know better than to keep telling Simon.'

Thor tugged out a Gladstone bag, ripped open the bed, and pulled out his crumpled pyjamas, which he stuffed into the bag.

'You tell Simon enough,' he said, as though this were an answer. He piled in electric razor, bedroom slippers and hairbrush.

'What are you doing?'

'I'm going.'

'Don't be silly. Don't be such a fool, you can't go, that won't change anything.'

'I should have gone years ago.' He shook his foot free of one of Julia's nightdresses and ran into the bathroom. He came back, carrying his wet pack, thrust that into the bag, turned to Julia and said levelly, 'All I do is give you something to complain about. All I do. Well it's not good for you.' He struggled with the zip and then gathered up the bag and said, 'But that's not the point, and I know it. I want to break your neck, too, that's a fact, and I'm going, before I do.' He looked absurd, pompous and about sixteen years old. Julia thought, oh God, he will be so ashamed of having said that when he gets back, we shall all suffer for it for weeks. If I could cry, he might get more reasonable. She went up to him and put her arms round his neck; his shame and embarrassment had to be forestalled, somehow.

'Listen, darling, we can talk about this.'

He shook himself free and gathered up the bag. Then he filled his brief-case almost methodically, with papers which had been removed from his study, and clasped it shut. Then, followed by Deborah, Simon and Julia, now in that order, he hurried out into the hall.

'Just because you're overwrought, you don't have to humiliate me,' said Julia. Thor unhooked his overcoat and woollen scarf and put these on. It was then that Julia saw that he meant to go. Simon, for some reason, gathered up his own umbrella and brief-case and stood, dangling these. Deborah was standing very close to Simon.

'Well,' Thor said, opening the door. 'Well –' he nodded his pale head in their general direction, went out on to the landing, and closed the door behind him. For a few moments, they all stood, listening to his footsteps, running but unhurried, down the stairs.

Julia had a large audience for her reaction to her husband's departure. She turned and stared back at them all; Simon and Deborah; the draggled row of Bakers, black eyes and yellow faces, mute, patient, somehow greedy.

'Well,' she said, 'I'd better at least clear this mess up.' She spread a newspaper on the carpet and began to pick up shreds of veal, peas, slivers of broken glass.

'I hope it isn't along of us,' Mrs Baker offered.

'No, no. It's nothing.'

'I don't think it's nothing,' said Deborah.

Julia glanced at her with loathing.

'I think we'd better push off tomorrow,' Mr Baker said lugubriously.

'Don't be silly. It's nothing to do with you.'

Mrs Baker looked offended. Simon, incredibly, was struggling into his raincoat, in which he had entangled his umbrella.

'Simon!' said Julia. 'Please stay here. Please don't go.'

'I ought to be –'

'You *can't*, Si –'

'You have a good cry, that's right,' said Mrs Baker. 'It'll do you good.'

'Don't go yet, Simon,' said Deborah. Simon executed a complicated reverse loop with arms and raincoat, and stood, clutching to his breast a bundle of both objects. Julia threw a whole plate on to her newspaper, where it broke. Her fingers were slippery with gravy, and she had a narrow cut, from the glass, on one of them.

'I wish you'd go away,' she said, curtly, to the Bakers. 'We'll sort it all out tomorrow.'

Mrs Baker shepherded them all, with deliberation, into their own quarters; Simon sat down, nursing his equipment, on the edge of the couch. Deborah sat down next to him. Julia went and emptied the nappies out into the sink. Then she brought back the nappy bucket and began to pile her newspaper pickings into it. She did not look at Simon; she wanted him; for one wild moment she had seen the door closing behind her husband as a door closing her in with Simon.

'I wish,' she said, 'I could just get up and leave all this. Just go.'

'Simon,' said Deborah, 'will he come back?'

'I don't know. I don't know.'

'How will he be able to stay away? He believes in being normal. Having roots. He can't just go.'

'He wants to be good,' said Simon. 'But I think he may settle for doing good, now.' He twisted his umbrella. 'He's an immoderate man brought up in a tradition of moderation. So he was immoderate about that too. A naturally violent man, a fanatic, trying to be a reasonable pacifist.'

'He's a fool,' said Julia, 'and he doesn't know himself.'

'Which of us do?' said Simon. 'I never know how much it matters. Clearly, one ought to know oneself well enough – not to destroy oneself through making immoderate demands on oneself. One ought to know other people enough not to expect the impossible of them, either. And so it follows, one ought not to live by a theory of human nature that won't bear treading on, that caves in, under one's feet. But I think he's found that out, now. It only really applies to him. All the rest of us are probably too conscious of our limitations – we'd do better to expect more of ourselves, and know ourselves a little less thoroughly. As for him – if he goes out there now he'll go knowing he's a fanatic – and not bothering too about the element of self-aggrandizement in that – and knowing that small acts are something *in themselves*. Penicillin and milk, Deborah, facts, in themselves. I admire him.'

'Yes,' said Deborah. 'So do I.'

'If it weren't for you, Simon Moffitt,' Julia said, 'this would never have happened.'

Simon avoided her eye. 'I've had much less to do with it than you have.'

'You go about, offering helpful advice and comfort. Are you so sure your own house is in order?'

'All my life I've avoided having a house,' said Simon, 'for that reason.'

'Simon!' said Julia. She did not know what plea or confession should follow this: everything was out of proportion; she knew she should not be seeing Thor's departure in terms of Simon, but this was how it was.

But she was not seeing Simon clearly, either; she was too conscious of Deborah's watching eye.

'I've got to go,' he said. 'I'm afraid I've really got to go.'

Deborah held one shoulder of his raincoat for him. He looked dubiously at Julia.

'I'll come back,' he said, 'when I get back. I'm out of town for a few days. I don't know how long. But I'll come back.'

He wandered towards the door.

'You ought,' he said to Julia, 'to think out clearly what you really want.'

Julia was momentarily lightened by the murderous rage with which this remark filled her; she said, briskly, 'Well, if you must go, get on with it, for goodness' sake,' and strode into the kitchen. Here, from a need for martyrdom and activity, she began violently to wash the nappies. After a moment, Deborah joined her.

'If I were you I'd make Mrs Baker do those. This is a nice mess, isn't it? At least he didn't tell us to look after each other. Did he?'

CHAPTER SEVENTEEN

Cassandra watched the gardener turn on the tap. The hosepipe jerked as though it was alive, flung itself from side to side, and gushed water. The gardener closed it off, partially, and headed it into the pool; the whole glass-house was filled with a slow, bubbling, dropping sound. Steam hissed faintly. The gardener stumped along the grating that surrounded the pool, glancing only cursorily at Cassandra, to whose presence he was now used. Outside it was raining steadily; the beat of water on the glass roof mixed with the bubble of the hose. Cassandra covered a sheet of paper with a recurrent ribbed pattern in charcoal, clear and then blurred, the hosepipe still and in motion. On the rim of the concrete pool, beside her, lay a packet of cooling fish and chips and her canvas satchel.

In the pool a shoal of very small fishes moved, connected and purposeful, through the weeds, with hard little heads and tapered bodies. Cassandra was waiting for the big fish. When the gardener had gone she took out a cardboard pot of dried daphnia and sprinkled a little on the surface of the water. The little fish darted up and wheeled away, as, from somewhere amongst the tangled roots and liquid mud, the big fish rose, pink and bulbous. Cassandra watched it. It was the size of a man's fist and was pale and glistening. It had long, trailing, ragged fins and tail, sprouting from the rotund surfaces, and the dark coils of its entrails were visible through the walls of its belly. On the head its eyes stood out, straining, and the surface between them was cracked and crazed and patterned with little crevices and bloodshot streaks, irides-cent, discoloured, white, apricot, rose. It was extremely ugly and Cassandra knew every line of its body. It was clearly very old and made no unnecessary movements; slowly now, trailing its tattered appendages, it razed the undersurface of the water, sucking in with horny lips the specks of food, adding a series of dry little gulps to the other sounds in the place. Cassandra decided to paint it from underneath, distorting it carefully so that it was seen elongated, cramped to the surface, where its cracked head was reflected. It looked stonily at her; a thin black ribbon of excrement dangled from it. Cassandra upended herself beside the pool and laid her head sideways on the stone, staring in. Then she began to paint.

After a time the door opened and closed and steps clanged on the grating. Then the door ground again. Cassandra knew that someone else was inside; she could feel the faint sounds of clothing and breath. The fish goggled desperately under the surface of its world: Cassandra had to guard, these days, against feeling that the glass-house was hers and that no one had the right to intrude or disturb her fish. She tapped her teeth with her tongue and looked up with a momentary frown through the curtain of steam and feathery foliage. He was leaning on his umbrella, watching her; caught out, on hands and knees, sandy hair springing about her face, she stared back. She was completely and really uncertain whether she had called him up. Either way, she knew now what madness felt like. She remembered that she had not known whether her father was alive or dead. He was wearing a white mackintosh.

'Cassandra?' he said, dubiously. 'Cassandra!' His voice echoed against the glass. 'I – didn't know you were a nature student.' He began, with the same clanging steps, to come round the pool. Cassandra's painting slid into the water and skidded across the surface. The fish backed several feet, stirring troubled fins. Cassandra struggled to sit upright. 'Oh,' he said. 'Let me.' He stretched out his arm, coat, jacket and all, across the pool and made a lurching grab. He retrieved the painting and began to dab at it with a handkerchief.

'Am I doing damage? Am I making it worse?'

Cassandra, clumsy with shock, shifted herself and knocked the fish and chips into the water. The packet sank slowly; they watched it; the newspaper unfurled and a chip and a film of grease bobbed to the surface.

'Look what you've made me do,' Cassandra snapped, savage. He started slightly, and then began, patiently, to retrieve chips and flakes of sodden cod in handfuls. His sleeves dripped.

'I'm sure we ought not to disturb the balance. Or all the fish might die.' He righted himself, and considered her. 'Now, what are you doing here, painting hosepipes and fish? Julia said you were a don.'

'I am,' said Cassandra, strangled.

'Do you know, I've got water running right into my armpits? Trickling down my ribs. I don't suppose you want this fish and chips. Have they got a disposal bin in here?'

'I don't know.' Cassandra had begun to shiver; her mouth was dry;

she felt all the symptoms of panic fear. She had not called him up, but there was something wrong with him, something distorted, something not allowed for. 'Why . . . ?' she whispered, swallowing. 'Why . . . ?'

'Why am I here? I'm giving a paper. On toads. To a zoological group who kindly paid my expenses, and then there were some specimens. I've been helping with them here. I came up from Liverpool Street, I've got a room in the Mitre. It's all fixed. It's a good paper but of course I'm a bad talker.' He was not looking at her. Gathering herself to pay him attention she thought him, for him, garrulous. 'I was going to look you up, as a matter of fact, in your college, almost immediately. Deborah told me where to find you. There was something I wanted to . . . I've been hearing about you. I thought . . .' He looked at her, and waited for a response. Cassandra swallowed again. A cloud of little fishes had gathered round the remaining morsels of cod, sucking at them.

'Yes, I meant to ask you,' he said, still in the same bright, conversational tone. 'I knew a man who was eaten by fish. I saw it.'

'Piranhas?'

'Yes. I saw it.'

Cassandra looked down at the pool and then across at his face. There were, in the softness of real flesh, the scars, the pockmarks, the protuberances. He was assessing her in some way, and still smiling. Cassandra's imagination worked on the dead man and the fish: blood in water, flaps and shreds of flesh, eager toothed mouths. She saw, precisely, as though it was given from outside herself, stripped bones turning in water, drowned and floating reddish hair, torn tendons; the bones were not dry, but pearly and damp with life and streaked with red. She thought she saw what he saw; this was what, over the years, she had been training herself to do. No, she had not called him up, he was not her creature, but she shared what he saw.

'Yes,' she said. 'I see. I see.'

She saw also that he had reached some limit of his self-control; she felt, and then saw, his wrists dance on his knees.

'It's a bloody funny fate. Oh, horribly funny. Guts and cock and all, Cassandra, do you hear, every little bit except the hair and teeth, it's the sort of macabre joke I knew you'd appreciate . . .'

'Stop it,' said Cassandra. She could find only her old authoritative bark to speak to him in. 'I've got no sense of humour. None at all. I know what you are saying.'

He watched his hands tremble.

'I'm wet. I'm as wet as anything.'

'You will dry off.'

'Listen – I wanted to tell you – extremity was always your business . . . I want to explain, Cassandra. It's not as though I wasn't prepared. I – I thought I – could take anything like that, I'd allowed for it. Or why was I out there at all? Cassandra, Cassandra. I was taking it, I was over it. Only I didn't know. I – I'm alive, I was over it, I was over it,' he repeated. 'And now it's taken me over. Oh, can you see? Must I go through and through it? Like an expanding nightmare – literally, I mean – and who knows where it will end? *I am not out there any more*. But there's no – there's no – Cassandra?' He looked at her. 'Lately I really don't know whether I'm here or there. That's not a way of putting it, it's the truth. I thought you might –' He repeated. 'I didn't know,' as though he were offended as well as shocked.

Cassandra knew what he was saying. She said, 'Listen, I don't know much about this. But so few things happen to us that we have to undergo. Most of the time we're double, we can stand outside and see an event – hope, fear, anticipate, judge. And then something happens where – where we have no room for thought or imagining – where what happens is real and all that is real. We talk a lot about living fully, but the last thing we want to do is live anything through. We think that sort of single-minded grief is insanity, but it's only an acknowledgement of a factual truth. An intolerable truth.'

'You have thoughts about everything. Is that how you see it? We can't afford – but sometimes we have to –' He said, 'I thought you might know. You take everything so seriously.'

'Platitudes.'

He acknowledged this with a weary shake of the head. 'I'm tired,' he said plaintively. His mouth hung slightly open. 'It's the nightmares. I don't know why I have to live with it, I'm here, after all. Do you think I could come to where you live, Cassandra, I've got to dry off?'

Cassandra passed her tongue round her dry mouth, nodded, and gathered up her satchel. She thought he had not noticed her own fear.

She had not taken in her room as a whole for a long time. It seemed crowded; most of the chairs were stacked with paintings and the desk was piled across with drawings and manuscripts. She stood in the doorway and looked; Simon came past her, peeling off raincoat and jacket. He stood, dangling them; Cassandra approached nervously, took them, and carried them into the bedroom where she hung them over a towel stand. When she came back he had closed not only the door but the outer oak, so that they were locked in. He was propped in her crimson chair, head back, eyes closed; life seemed to run visibly out of his flesh, and he was shuddering. Cassandra laid on his chair-arm a lavender-coloured, lavender-scented maidenly guest-towel, one of a kind of trousseau provided by her mother many years ago and now never used. His teeth chattered.

'I'd better light the fire?' she said. He did not answer. Cassandra felt entirely at a loss; neither entertaining, nor caring for Simon had ever entered her thoughts and plans for him; her thoughts did not run that way. She felt gawky; she did not know what her acceptance of his confidence had committed her to; her own small, social terror increased. 'I could make you some coffee.'

He opened his eyes. 'Haven't you got a drink?'

'No, that is, yes, a bottle of brandy.'

She went down on her knees and, with a trembling hand, set a match to the gas-fire, which made a small explosion, followed by a high, blaring sound.

'I think I'd like some brandy. Can I?' Cassandra poured him a glass, taking time over it; he swallowed it in large mouthfuls, listening to the hiss and roar of the fire. She had always known that one day he would sit there, and had always known that he would never sit there. He held out his glass for more. When this, too, was drunk, he said, 'You live a sheltered life. At first sight.'

'At first sight, yes.'

'Padded in with paper. I'd imagined it all rather like this. I shan't ask if you're happy. The more I thought, the more there was only you I could – tell. You don't mind, do you? I know so few people, I – Can I have some more, is there any? Such small glasses. There was never any room, with you, for things not being at the worst. I – I didn't like that about you. But now, things look different. And you look different. I don't know why you should let me go on like this. Do you understand?'

Cassandra poured more brandy, and said, 'Yes, I understand.'

'You haven't changed. Or have you?'

'No, I don't change much.'

Simon was drinking brandy almost absently, as though gulping water. She was not sure that this was good for him; shock and terror she could recognize, and to these, in him, she responded; but she had no idea what effect brandy would have on these states. It was also surprisingly painful to be in a position to consider what was good for him; she trod on shifting sands.

'Simon,' she said, using his name, for the first time, awkwardly. 'Simon, do you think you ought –'

He looked at her with a kind of shy cunning.

'Yes, I do. I'm all right. I know what I'm doing, don't worry.' He did not look as though he knew anything of the sort. His face wavered.

'You are shocked,' said Cassandra. 'You should rest.'

'Yes. Yes, I should. You're right. Is there anywhere I could lie down?'

'Only the bed.'

'I think I've got to. Where is it?'

Cassandra led him into her bedroom. Simon supported himself on the bed-foot, and circumnavigated it. Then he sat down on the edge. Cassandra stood over him. At any moment, she thought, he might discover her real poverty and helplessness.

'I've really got to lie down, Cassandra, I'm sorry about this.' He unlaced his shoes, shivering, and took them off. 'You're sure you don't mind?'

'No. No.' She leaned across him, tugged out her nightdress from under the pillow, and pushed it under a cushion in a chair. Then she turned back the covers.

'Do you mind if I get right in?'

'You ought to keep warm,' said Cassandra. She looked away whilst he undressed further; he slipped, in shirt-tails, under the blankets, drew them up to his chin, and shut his eyes. Cassandra moved.

'No, don't go. Don't go. I shall start thinking again. I shall start going over, that is. Stay here. Sit down, why don't you? I'll feel better in a moment, I feel better already, lying down. Then we'll have a talk.'

Cassandra perched carefully on the very edge of her own bed, and considered the sprawling features on her pillow. They were not unfamiliar; she would have been hard put to it to describe the differences between what she saw and what she had imagined. She could hear, however, his stomach churning.

'I wish I was sure you didn't mind this intrusion. There's no reason why you should welcome me or want me, I do see. It was a bit melodramatic, but I thought I'd risk – I thought you'd let me talk. I know you wouldn't once, but we were so much younger.'

'It's good for you to talk.' Cassandra was producing all kinds of opinions she had not known she held. 'If you want to talk to me I – I'm grateful.'

'Really?' He put out his hand; Cassandra laid her own on it; his thumb travelled over her rings.

'I liked what you said about having to undergo things. It's funny how long it takes one to recognize these things – the things one can't get out of, the things that really happen to one.'

'Yes,' she said. 'It's surprising how rarely it happens, maybe. Most people can digest almost anything.'

'Oh, digest, yes. Even – even unpalatable truths. But what do you do – what do you do Cassandra – when something happens – that you're seriously afraid you might not – survive?'

Cassandra played with the metaphor; you reject it, or it poisons you, she thought.

'You can only keep still and concentrate on surviving. Better to let yourself know what's happened.'

'Do you think so?'

'In your case.'

'I thought I was past that point. I've been thinking out why I went out there. Why did I – why should a man like I was go out there?'

'Out of fear,' Cassandra offered.

'That's something you know about, don't you? You always did, it didn't make you easy company.'

'Explorers,' Cassandra pursued her point, 'are statistically unusually accident-prone. Some of us invite what we are afraid of.'

Simon flattened his hand against hers, interlaced their fingers, and gripped. He muttered something indistinguishable; then his voice came clearly.

'That religious phase we both went through. That was out of fear. Wasn't it? I lost that, I lost any faith. But I was afraid of – of meaninglessness. Shapelessness, formlessness. Things like my father's trench stories. The – the Amazon – I had a mystical feeling about it, it was the worst place. "I care for nothing, all must go," I've had that poem on the brain for weeks, for obvious reasons. So when I saw I believed in it after all – and when I saw I'd got to face it – I – I thought well, the only thing was to go and *live* with it. If – if one was afraid that life was only accidental survival – then one had better become familiar with the processes.'

'I know.'

'I thought you did. It worked in its way, you know, that's what I've got to make you understand. I – I was religious about that, too. I had little tasks. Used to live off grubs and fungus – you've no idea, Cassandra, how little food one can come to need. I – I tried to neutralize it in me. I mean, facts were facts. You survived because you expected them. Or went under if you expected wrong. I used to try it on. At first. Impossible treks. Sort of endurance tests. I only got little breaks, at one stage two broken fingers and a broken toe. Then a series of scalds. I kept pouring kettles down my front, I don't know why.'

Cassandra had known about the fingers; she nodded.

'It did get familiar. Oh, and neutral, almost nothing disgusts me now. I used not to be like that, I told you about my prissy childhood.'

'No.'

'It must have been Julia I told. Sorry. And fear – it changes. It becomes – perpetual and nagging. But less vast. Less urgent, too. I was happy enough. I never went over the edge into loving what's disgusting. Not like some medical missionaries. I've seen nuns touching running sores with a kind of sensual pleasure. In another day they'd have kissed them. To mortify the flesh. Well, I only wanted my flesh indifferent, not mortified. One told me once they'd made such strides with one really loathsome eating disease that soon there'd be no sufferers left. With a look of aimless regret. I said, oh well, something worse will probably crop up. It will, of course.'

'Why must it?'

'Balance of nature.'

'We seem to proliferate, despite the balance.'

'Oh, as far as nature as they used to understand it goes, humanity is the disease. Like a cancer. I see that's a useless thought. You'd say precious, wouldn't you? But it's a thought I have.'

'And the fish?' said Cassandra. 'Speaking of Nature?'

'Ah yes, the fish. Do you remember Merton saying that we must not get unduly attached to anything? Out of the subdued lusts of his own flesh, I've no doubt, though he had the sense to indulge the smaller ones. There's the root of it.'

Cassandra was silent. His fingers moved restlessly over hers. Then she said, 'Yes, but the fish?'

'You used to lecture me about fish. Order, intention, patterns in the nervous system, planets, natural selection, movements of shoals of fishes. Shoals of bloody fishes.'

'Simon, who was he?'

'I thought you knew. He made the films. His name was Antony Miller. Well, I say he made the films. He did some of the photography, and I did some. He put it all together. He did most of the talking.'

'It didn't seem like that.'

'No, it wouldn't, I see. I mean, he teased thoughts out of me. He was a fearful talker. Brought all sorts of things to life I was used to living with dumbly. I knew he was dangerous,' said Simon, 'and then I forgot.'

'What was he like?'

'I told you. A talker. Sort of man I take an instant dislike to. Imposed himself on me. I was living quite quietly on my own, just outside a village – I was mapping creeks. Painstaking and useless – they kept disappearing overnight. And the people from the Health Institute brought him up the river and just dumped him off in my village. He's a book-maker – a glorified reporter – he'd been digging dinosaurs in New Mexico with a mad American who had some crack-brained theory about why *they* all disappeared overnight as you might say – *Obsolete Monsters*, that book was called, I remember.' Simon settled more comfortably into the pillow. 'Live reptiles was the logical next step. Climbing the evolutionary ladder. Only he never got further than savage fish.' Simon gave a hysterical snort of laughter.

Cassandra kept silent; she could not find another question; her imagination reached for Antony Miller.

'He had a huge mouth. Always smiling. He was unsystematic. But curious, you know, genuinely curious. Followed me about with the camera, opening his mouth like a beak, and shouting, "And then? And then?" when you thought you'd summed up. Quite indiscriminate. Always roaring "Oh, look." Things you'd seen a thousand times before. But not the way he saw them, I suppose,' said Simon, gripping Cassandra's hand painfully. 'Everything was so real and important to him, he had so much spare power and spare attention. He was no fool, either, though it took me time to find that out. You thought he was a sort of fraud but after a bit you saw you could really rely on knowing where you were with him. I mean, if he liked you, he liked you, that was all there was to it.'

He seemed to have come to a stop. Cassandra watched him. He began, then, to talk, rather faster, turning his face away from her.

'At the time, I thought I was taking it. You know – Cassandra – I looked on in a sort of silly calm, telling myself, "I can take this."

I even felt a – a sort of triumph. And – you know – everything I'd learned – was a preparation, wasn't it? I knew – there was nothing to do – but take it. So I – didn't do anything. I don't think there was anything I could do. That is, if there had been, I'd have done it, in my experience that comes automatically, if there is anything one *can* do, doesn't it? Cassandra?'

'Yes.'

'And then – remembering took over. And the nightmares. And a silly game I used to play of seeing with his eyes that got to be not a game. I could see myself. From outside. Is that what they mean by beside yourself? And there were several of everything, like things going back, and back, in a mirror. And then hallucinations. I had to keep watching it happen again where I was. And other things. And now, God help me, I do think it might really go on for ever. At first I just knew it wouldn't. Cracked. You know how words grow more and more important. I know now why people say cracked. I feel cracked. Don't go away.'

'No, I won't.'

'Say something.'

'What was wrong, you know' – Cassandra thought aloud – 'with this preparation you talk about. What was wrong, was that you were preparing for your own death. Even inviting it. But not his.'

'Go on talking.'

'I can only think in abstractions. But they have their uses. Things one must undergo – I suppose one thinks of them in terms of one's own death. That, after all, one *must* undergo – one must come together, body and soul, imagination and senses, for one's dissolution. I fear that. I think you'd learned not to.'

She waited; he was silent.

'But this has to be undergone in the imagination. It's not like physical suffering, you can't endure or end it. You watch and know and remain inviolate. But not really inviolate. There is a real sense in which you are *both* the suffering creature under the glass and the watching eye over the microscope. You can't escape, but you are free to act in the rest of your life. And you are responsible. Real suffering would be easier: one would have a right to give up and suffer with dignity. That's what we crave – in love, or death. The completeness. We want the watching creature to be given over, we want – as much as we fear – pure feeling, complete feeling. I suppose it's a myth, this complete experience. But you and I suffer from it. We are extremists, in different ways, we will be destroyed or detached, but we will not meddle with half-knowledge, half-experiences, responsibility. No? I imagine we're a little old now to change. So we aren't,' she told him, studying the marks on his forehead, 'very resilient, when it comes to unavoidable blows.'

'Though good at avoiding blows?'

'That, yes.'

She thought, here she was, not only talking to Simon, but telling him what she had always wanted to tell him; she added, 'Though I, of course, avoid facts, whereas you avoid having to imagine. Or remember.'

'Not very well. You're a strange creature, you only choose to know certain things, but you do know those. Cassandra –' he sought for words, and then gave up. 'I'm pissed.'

'Yes,' said Cassandra, correctly interpreting a word she had not heard before. 'You are. You should rest, perhaps.'

He turned over again, lay on his back, opened his eyes, and looked directly at her. Involuntarily she closed her own. When she opened them he was still looking at her. He could not, she thought to encourage herself, be focusing more than hazily.

'Don't go away. Don't leave me. There's so much we haven't said, and better not, don't you think? We ought to have known each other better.'

'I don't know.'

'Oh, I think so. And differently.' He pulled her hand gently towards him. 'I never thought I'd have the courage . . . And I know well enough that isn't what you . . . not this way . . . But . . .'

Cassandra detached her hand.

'And we couldn't take it, could we? We couldn't have taken it? I've had enough of your brandy to break down a few. . . . But probably too much to . . .'

This last was lost on Cassandra, who was nevertheless more or less aware of what he was talking about. He was asking her, by indirections and negatives, for something she had often and improbably enough imagined him asking for more boldly. He was asking her out of a need for comfort? a feeling of duty? a sense, comparable to her own, of something old and unfinished? Cassandra had always despised Jane Eyre's prudery.

'You would be sensible to go to sleep,' she said.

'Yes I would. Of course I would. You won't go away? Nowadays, sometimes' – he turned his face away, huddling – 'I shout in my sleep. Let me apologize in advance.'

She sat there until she was sure he was asleep. He might have been asleep for some time when she decided – his hand twitched loosely, suddenly – that he must be. Then she stood up. She ran her hands down her body: man's shirt, corduroy trousers, bones: then, with an uncertain repetitive searching; over her face: bones, lips, prickle of lashes, softened wrinkling skin round the eyes. She went round the bed and looked at his face. He snored. She could see the wet inside of his mouth.

I wouldn't be too old, she told herself, if I didn't know so little. I can imagine ways it would be, I have imagined them. But there are so many practical things I'm too old to learn with any dignity. She remembered Julia's voice from childhood, righteous, complaining. 'Cassandra won't be part of anything she can't run all on her own.' As for him, she thought, mixing love with contempt as she had accustomed herself to doing, he'd be happy if I exacted it from him, he'd know where he was. He was always an emotional meddler. This is not something he's just thought of, but he'll be able to behave later as though it was. He will behave as though it had never happened. So better it does not happen. It would inevitably be too little and too much.

She collected the nightdress from under the cushion, folded it, and put it away in a drawer. Simon muttered wildly. Cassandra stopped, and ordered him, under her breath, 'Hush.' He was quiet. She went into the other room, leaving the door ajar, and sat down in the red chair. She looked round her room; here, across all the shining snail-trails of her thoughts about him he had left dark, invisible, real footprints. Indeed, indeed, she told herself, we are afraid of the moment when what we can imagine becomes inextricably involved in what is actual. What I could ceaselessly invent, because it was out of the realm of possibility, has become possible – limiting, actual, finally, after all, impossible. Nothing will be the same. When the prince kissed the princess, the forest of brambles shrivelled and vanished. Alternatively, when the lady looked out of the tower – seeing, simply, a lump of flesh and blood and a patch of sunshine – the mirror cracked and the web flew out.

We create each other. Through hard glass, one comes across the Red King, snoring and dreaming. Wake him, look him in the eyes, break his dream and you vanish. Apparently this dead man was the Red King;

Simon and the programmes were his. And thus myself? And Julia? Again, I pursue metaphors. Nothing is as we see it, as we imagine it. But we must go on seeing and imagining.

Cassandra put her head back and waited.

He slept seven hours; after this, Cassandra heard, without moving, the sounds in her bedroom which indicated that he was getting up, dressing. He came out into the room, still knotting his tie; she looked at him dumbly out of her chair; it was almost dark.

'Shall I put the light on?' he said.

'Yes.'

He found the switch. 'I must have slept and slept. Did I shout?'

'No.'

He looked at her quickly. 'You look tired. You look as though you haven't been very well.'

Cassandra nodded. She did not want to have to speak to him. He seemed lighter, now, as though he knew what he was doing. She was afraid, and rigid with it.

He went round the room, turning over paintings, and leafing through drawings. He uncovered the figure in the raincoat under the tree. He considered this.

'Me?'

'In a sense.'

'I see. I see. Well wrapped up, waiting for the sky to fall. Well, it fell, didn't it, you were right. So you've been thinking about me.'

'As you see.' Cassandra made a brief gesture in the direction of the television and the paintings. She compared herself to an old woman, locked in with a thief, stripped of her possessions and waiting for the *coup de grâce*. 'It needn't concern you.'

'Are you apologizing for having thought about me?'

'Clearly.'

'Oh dear. No, don't do that. Don't do that. I've thought about you, too. I've even dreamed about you.'

'Indeed,' said Cassandra. She did not ask what he had dreamed. Simon dislodged a pile of creeper studies and the cutting Deborah had sent fluttered to the floor. Simon studied it and laughed.

'Who did this?'

'A friend of Julia's, something to do with the television, I am told.'

'The one she sleeps with.'

'I don't know what she does.'

'Don't you? I suppose I don't, really. I'd have thought so, that's all, he meant me to think that when I met him.'

'I don't know him,' Cassandra said wearily. She had not, perhaps fortunately, seen Simon's brief appearance on *The Lively Arts*; his expression puzzled her. Simon replaced the cutting and sat down – he did not ask who had sent it to Cassandra.

'All these stacks of painting. Such industry. Is this recent?'

'Fairly.' She did not want to have to watch him think out her themes, her subjects; his look flayed her.

'Will you come out to dinner with me, Cassandra?' She hesitated. 'I need you to, I don't want to be alone just yet, I feel so much better for having told you. And you were so unsurprised. I was grateful for that, and you talked so solemnly.'

She looked round her room again, feeling trapped; how could he have seen what he had seen and not know what she had made of him? She would not take his kindness.

'I'm glad you've been thinking about me. No, really. Don't look so – so reticent. I've been in the habit – for years – of wondering what you would think of things. Antony, for instance. You wouldn't have liked Antony. You'd have thought he was dangerous, as I did.'

'Should I?'

'Do you want me to go? I will go. I don't want to annoy you.'

'You never used,' said Cassandra, 'to talk about yourself.'

'I don't remember you being particularly anxious to encourage me.' He looked at her, direct and earnest. 'You were so prickly and terrifying, among other things. Now, Julia –'

Fifteen years ago he had begun this sentence, today, having given up the thought of him, she would let him finish it.

'Julia was rather like him, I suppose. She liked you and let you be; you could talk about anything to Julia and she'd be so interested it would feel real. It's a gift. One I haven't got, and always – always fall for. You know?' He thought. 'She's changed, of course.'

'It was never the whole truth. About Julia.'

'I know. You two are more alike than you seem, straight away. I used to think there were people who *knew* how to live. You and I, we didn't did we? But she did. Silly, really – she was terrified of you, and she loved you. She talked about you. I started taking you seriously, then. I had to. I developed a tremendous curiosity about you. A bit late.'

'It's a curiosity I could have done without.'

'Of course, of course. An insult. But then – the uses you both made of me were insulting enough, too. Nobody likes to be a missile in a battle they didn't start. One can't afford to spend too much time being insulted.'

Cassandra bowed her head, silent and exhausted. That Simon should voluntarily stay in a room with her and tell her what he felt about their past had never occurred to her: still less would it have occurred that she could endure the listening. The romantic moment of recognition would not happen – although she had come closer to that than she could possibly have considered likely, and she had refused it. But what she had now, though not absolute, was more than that grey recognition of defeat, of pure limiting impossibility, that was the romantic recognition reversed. Simon, chatty, gossipy, nervous, kindly – which?, having made of her pictures – what? and of herself, too – what? was asking her out to dinner. And she had preached to him that the complete, the absolute feeling was not desirable. She did not know what he thought, and would not know. But she would take what was offered. Painfully, deliberately, still terrified, Cassandra, for the first time in her life, rose to an occasion.

'You didn't like things to mean too much. I loved you too much.'

'I wanted to be an ordinary man, not take on a destiny, that was all. You were a one for destiny.'

'You haven't behaved as though that was what you wanted.'

'No, I haven't. I expect you know all sorts of reasons for that.'

'I expect I do, yes,' Cassandra grinned, briefly.

'Well, don't judge me. That was a clever picture, but don't judge me.'

'I don't judge.' Cassandra thought. 'I don't judge you, at least.'

'You just think about me?'

'Yes.'

'Well, I don't mind that, if you don't. It makes me feel real, oddly, outside – what I was telling you about.'

Cassandra smiled to herself darkly over the irony that these wilder flights of her imagination should make Simon feel, not that she was mad, but that he was real. She looked at him; he was smiling too; when he caught her eye the smile broadened, and he gave her a nod, as though they had come to some agreement. She nodded back, donnish, business-like, and real warmth filled her.

'So you will come out to dinner?'

'Of course.'

'And we'll have a real good talk, and some more brandy. You look as though you could do with some yourself. We'll really talk it out. You don't mind me telling you things? You do listen. I've saved a lot up for you, it turns out.'

'I'm glad,' said Cassandra.

CHAPTER EIGHTEEN

Mrs Baker passed Julia in the hall and indicated the parcel. 'That come this morning,' she said flatly, and closed herself into her own quarters. She was for some reason not on speaking terms with Julia, and had not been since Thor's departure a month earlier. Indeed, nobody seemed to be on speaking terms with Julia.

Tucked under the string of the parcel were two letters from Thor. Julia had lost count of Thor's letters, which arrived at the rate of one, or sometimes two a day. They were long, theological, autobiographical, indecisive and peculiarly remote. He had, so far, neither come home nor, as far as Julia could find out, made any arrangements to go to the Congo. He was living in an hotel in South Kensington. Deborah had lunched with him in the Strand Corner House and reported that he seemed to be waiting.

'What do you want me to do?' Julia asked Deborah. Deborah said, 'I don't know that there's anything that you can do,' in her father's uninflected voice. *You* can do? You *can* do? You can *do*? Julia repeated to herself nervously. She had reached a stage where she examined herself hopefully for signs of incipient nervous breakdown. 'But I'm tough, that's my trouble,' she told herself aloud, opening the letters. 'Nasty, but tough.'

The first began, 'Dear Julia, it has seemed to me lately that our responsibilities properly seen, are infinitely extended, and since our capacities are limited we must of necessity fail and failure is of little importance. This affects you, Julia . . .'

The second began, 'It seems presumptuous to suppose that there is any order available for our immediate contemplation. Life is only meaningful in particular instances and in particular instances it appears random and horrible. In particular instances also salvation can be meaningful. Maybe not in general.'

Julia began to cry. Thor's letters often made her cry; she recovered herself enough to write careful little answers, covering several letters at a time, although she did not feel she understood either what they meant or why they were written. They seemed to her an accusation: she felt simply, and more and more exclusively, guilty. Everything was her fault. They all thought so. She was guilty of Thor's indecision. She was guilty of inattention to Deborah. Simon believed she was at fault. He was accusing her of not being happy, because he had wanted to find her happy. He also wanted Thor to be better off without her; she believed he was seeing Thor, and encouraging him to think this. When he came – erratic as always – his empty cheerfulness was an affront. So were his absences. His manner was pastoral: Simon, she was coming to see, had been prepared to love her because she was embedded in a family and thus *taboo*. Just as in the beginning she had been Cassandra's sister, and thus *taboo*. He wants one, once he's made sure he can't simply have one, she thought. She did not know whether she loved or hated him, but the desire persisted: she dreamed of having him naked in bed and biting him until he cried out. At times she saw her whole life as a problem of coming to grips with Simon.

Well, she thought, she was used to things being her fault. As a child, she had learned painfully that Cassandra believed her to be at fault simply in being alive. And at some level deeper than her surface attempts to attract love or prove herself she had accepted this judgement.

She began to open the parcel. Under a layer of shavings was newspaper and under the newspaper were books. Julia lifted one out and looked at it mournfully. *A Sense of Glory* by Julia Corbett. The cover was predominantly white. In the foreground a black nun-like figure, swathed in a cocoon of fine black lines, sat hunched in an attitude vaguely reminiscent of Rodin's Penseur. This figure was watching another figure, planted inactively in the middle distance as though levitating slightly and swathed in a much larger haze of yellow lines. The levitating figure wore a flat, wide-brimmed priest's hat. There were a few rather dangerous-looking spires in the background. Julia opened the book, grimaced at her own smiling face inside the dust-jacket, snapped it shut again and said, 'Oh Christ, oh Christ.'

Deborah came out of her room. Julia pushed the book back into the parcel and looked at her daughter over it.

'What's in there, Julia?'

'Books.'

'What books?'

'Never mind. Never mind.'

She thought: I shall have to go to Oxford. I'll have to go and explain, even if it does no good. I don't know how I ever thought I could risk her not noticing. I'll tell her it was done out of love – that the feelings about Simon are my own feelings. If I could only make her understand, if I could only make her understand that what *I* wanted was to understand . . . then? Then she might let go. She might forgive me and let go. The net was as tight and constricting as ever, and she herself had fastened it more securely. We think, Julia thought, that we are releasing ourselves by plotting what traps us, by laying it all out to look at it – but in fact all we do is show the trap up for real. Iron bars make a cage all right, and the more you look at them or reproduce them the more you know it's a real cage. Dimly, miserably, Julia became aware of what she thought was a truth. Whether or not there was a primal guilt, whether or not she was at fault in being alive, all her own efforts had been directed towards making the guilt real, weighty, binding. Because if it was real, then she was responsible. And if she was responsible she had a choice – her acts were her own. She could be detached from Cassandra. Alternatively, if she had committed a real crime, not conditioned by Cassandra's fantasy, it should be possible for Cassandra really to forgive her. That's what I always hope, she thought, that she'll forgive me. When I've done things, I run to her for forgiveness. Which she withholds. I ought not to care. I must go to Oxford and tell her how all this came about.

She heard Deborah talking.

'Simon said he'd drop in when he gets back today.'

'Gets back?'

'Gets back from Oxford. He's been in Oxford.'

Julia had nothing to say. She sat nursing her box of books. For the first time in her life her curiosity completely deserted her. She did not want to know, she wanted passionately not to know what Simon was doing in Oxford. She also wanted passionately never to see Simon again. She thought: I did it, he went there because I feared it, because I planned it, because I imagined it. What the book might now mean she did not want to have to think. After a moment the situation seemed vaguely familiar. She remembered Cassandra peering furiously at her out of the lilac when she had wanted Cassandra to know about Simon, and to forgive her. Cassandra had attempted to annihilate her by ignoring her. Well, she understood that, now.

And she could not, now, if Cassandra had possibly seen Simon, ask Cassandra to forgive her for the book in which she had imagined such a meeting. Who had stolen whose action?

She looked up from her books and met her daughter's inquisitive, hungry stare. Deborah grinned. Deborah was no doubt in a position to tell her what Deborah believed she wanted to know.

'Why don't you go to school?' she said. 'You're late.'

She went, when Deborah had gone, and stowed her parcel of books under the bed.

Much later in the afternoon she pulled it out again, and posted one copy to Ivan, with whom she was also, as far as she knew, not on speaking terms. Forgiveness was not part of Ivan's way of life.

Publication day began to look like an approaching execution; except that she had few illusions about her own powers of survival.

Cassandra and Simon had almost made a habit of walking together through the Botanical Gardens and down by the river. Cassandra told herself that to repeat an action three times hardly made it a habit; this was, nevertheless, what she felt it to be. Simon, she thought, meant her to understand that that was what it was; he announced his further visits to Oxford carefully by letter, so that she could expect him and prepare for him. He might have done this all those years ago, if she could have accepted it; it was what he would have wanted. She did not like to speculate about what might have been. But now she lived through her depopulated days and nights in a kind of tired ease that was vegetable, and slightly more than that.

When he came he talked to her as though she was what she had never been and had never hoped to become – an old friend. He was, Cassandra reflected, the kind of bachelor whose social life in general flowered late, became easier and less suspicious, as it became clearer that relationships of old friendship were now all that could ever be expected of him. Once this was accepted, much of the compulsion to be evasive could vanish: this was something she had had sufficient opportunity to observe within her academic walls. This on one level: on another he talked compulsively, from time to time, about Antony Miller: Cassandra listened neutrally, and felt a satisfaction when at last the tone of the stories shifted from metaphysical desperation, and from Simon's own dual sense of guilt and betrayal by events – as though those fish had been sent to try his spiritual resources and found them depleted by Antony Miller. He became in the end reminiscent, anecdotal, slightly sentimental; Cassandra smiled grimly and judged him out of danger.

He talked to her too of Julia and Thor, and even more of Deborah, whom he saw himself 'helping'; here, Cassandra could have detected another of his emotional meddlings, but she chose not to judge. She had almost certainly not done Deborah any good herself by not meddling. Simon's pastoral compulsion might, in that context, have its uses. Deborah was tougher than she herself. In the old days she would have attributed Simon's persistence in telling her about Julia to a largely conscious malice, a desire to stir things up; now she was sure that he thought he wanted simply to prove, both to himself and to her, that he lived on a neutral level, they were all together, people with equal weights in the world. Well, she would take that, too, and let the malice be what it would. She wanted so little, comparatively, of him now. She expected nothing.

And what she had was transfigured. Buses, pillar-boxes, telephones, staircases were there to be used. Food was there to be bought and eaten. She was balanced on her feet, she had weight, and was related to things. Distances were measurable and each distance was the proper distance. The air shone.

On the third visit they went back into the glass-house. Simon walked her twice round the pond and then stopped and scraped the gravel on the bench with a finger.

'Are you still painting?'

'No. No, I'm not. It seems to have worn itself out.'

'I thought it might. So have my nightmares. I've gone back to dreaming about my very early childhood for some reason. Why do you think you went in for that, then?'

'Recreation.'

He picked up the pun. 'You weren't satisfied with creation as you found it?'

'Which of us is? But I don't think I was trying to improve it. It was a matter of fending it off. Or maybe of relating myself to it. In the sense of making it manageable, in my own terms. It's a matter of weight. If one doesn't occupy one's space in the world, the world does have to be warded off – immobilized, reduced, kept down. Trimmed to size.'

'Yes, I see.' He did see. Cassandra closed her fist on a handful of prickling gravel. 'I suppose,' he went on, 'it isn't really odd that neither of us married. It's odder the people who do, when you think of it. Thor, for instance. He shouldn't ever have contemplated relating himself to the world in that way, should he? If ever there was a man whose good was single-minded violence . . . It was different for you and me.'

'There wasn't enough of us.'

'Precisely. But I suppose in general marriage is the best – the most usual, the most inescapable – way of making sure one does – as you put it – occupy one's space in the world. Harder to have the same doubts about one's own presence and reality?'

'Not having been married, I wouldn't know.'

'Julia says she feels unreal. But really she only feels limited. She's the sort of woman you'd have thought that was good for. As for me, what I clearly wanted, don't you think, was to annihilate myself? Make a space where I'd been into which the jungle would just move without any pattern, and I wouldn't be missed?'

'I think so.'

'And you?'

'That wasn't what I wanted. I wanted – I think – to make my own world. To contain all I could have or want – or at least to want nothing that wasn't mine, to let everything else go. I didn't want a jungle. No.' She indicated their surroundings. 'A carefully laid-out glass-house.' She grinned, and Simon laughed aloud. 'You can't do it.'

'No, but –' Simon thought, slowly. 'We aren't – we aren't, you and I, necessarily wicked? I've – I've often thought – you could make a good man, a really good man – out of me and Antony together. Or – or maybe you and Julia. The instinct to separate oneself isn't necessarily wicked, as long as you don't carry it to excess? The human animal is much the most aggressive, you know. Much the fiercest. Some of it got channelled into the buildings and society and machinery. We know what happened to the rest. I – I do believe in – exploring an essential solitude. K-keeping oneself to oneself, I've come to believe in that. It isn't simply a lunatic myth, Cassandra, that if one were really able to be alone, not out of lack, or need – *then* one might be able to – to cultivate one's garden – one's *own* garden – Look, and from the garden, we could see everything with, with real indifference, no one thing, no one person more than any other. A – an infinitely extended curiosity. A neutral love. A – an innocent vision where everything and everyone was indiscriminately and haphazardly beautiful? N-not being related might get rid of the aggression? One could just grow? I know what that feels like, I've felt it, once or twice.'

'And I,' said Cassandra, remembering how as a child, as it now seemed to her, she had told him about the beautiful network in which she saw the world hung as a fisherman's glass ball, and had thought that the seeing was a kind of growth. She said, '*Hortus conclusus.* Vegetable love, a green thought in a green shade. The innocent garden.' She waved at the creepers. 'Slow, non-aggressive growth. I don't think we can do it. It's possible to want it, possible to try to live towards it, not possible to have it. And anyway, why do we want it?' Her hands moved busily, sifting the grits, pushing them into a maze of little walls. 'You and I, because we both had more than our share of fear, too early. If an animal is, as you say, unusually aggressive, then the weaker specimens, the duds, will be unusually timid? We protect ourselves by burrowing. How can one learn vision by burrowing?'

'Simply fear? But why shouldn't fear produce virtue?'

'Oh, according to Hobbes, it does. All the virtues. But not' – Cassandra turned to look at him, and they watched each other warily – 'not innocence, Simon. Not that indiscriminate love you want. Not indifference. Fear produces pacifism, which I know about and mistrust, not innocence, which I don't. I don't believe in innocence, except as something we invented, to desire.'

'But you believe in original sin?'

'No. No. Not cosmologically. I believe in accident. In rents in the network.'

'I used to believe in that. But sometimes it seems haphazardly purposeful. It sounds to me as though you believe in Natural Selection, and you don't think you and I are the fittest. That's a bit gloomy.'

'Even plants contend that way. As far as the individual plant goes, they just respond to the sun. Or its absence. Vegetable love, as I said. But not in the aggregate, I gather.'

'You can avoid or control Natural Selection in a glass-house, true,' said Simon. He smiled. 'But out in the big world, well . . . "Natural selection, as we shall hereinafter see, is a power incessantly ready for action and is as immeasurably superior to man's feeble efforts as the works of Nature are to those of Art." '

'Who said that?'

'Charles Darwin. Before sin was, that is. Nature as the primal artist.'

'Nature,' said Cassandra, 'red in tooth and claw. *In Memoriam* was written before the *Origin of Species* was published.'

Simon grinned. 'Oh, well,' he said, 'we know where we are. We can't afford to care about that, can we? We must burrow, if burrow we must. Look, detachment can't bring innocence, but we can stop caring about what we can't help?'

'It is always foolish to care about what one can't help. But unfortunately we never know with any certainty what we can't help. And we are not usually capable of not caring.'

'What do you care about, then?'

Cassandra looked about the glass-house as though fearful it might be bombarded with stones. She said, 'Nothing much, at the moment. But I place no reliance on continuing in this way.'

Simon, comfortably, laughed.

CHAPTER NINETEEN

Cassandra went, on a Monday, as was her habit, into Blackwell's. She liked to spend time amongst the second-hand books, and on this occasion she had come to pay her account. It was thus she found herself behind Professor Storrin at the cash desk; his pale grey back was curved over in front of her towards the girl.

'Oh, yes,' he said, 'and could you order me – shall we say – a dozen copies, yes, a dozen copies, of that new novel by Julia Corbett. *A Sense of Glory*, yes, that's it, *A Sense of Glory*. Thank you so much.'

As he turned away his sleeve brushed Cassandra.

'Ah, Cassandra.' Momentarily his cheek touched hers. 'I have ordered your sister's book. The reviews suggest that it may be – it may be – interesting, I don't know if I'm right?' His grey face wrinkled at the eye corners. 'I thought I might present it to certain friends. Would you say that was wise?'

'I wouldn't know. I wasn't aware . . . Julia produces books so rapidly, I am never forewarned.'

Storrin took this in. 'You haven't seen it?'

'Not yet,' said Cassandra, taking a step to the accounts desk.

'Oh, I hope you will tell me what you think of it. I gather from the reviews that we all come out rather well, on the whole. Yes. And in any case, we all share, don't we, this deplorable vulgar desire for notoriety in any form? And a gossiping curiosity. Or perhaps you don't?'

'No. No, I don't.'

'It never does the academic fastnesses real harm to be shaken. I shall be most interested to know what you make of this book. I mustn't keep you, I mustn't keep you.' He extended a brittle hand. 'I saw you in the Mitre, with the television snake man, was it not?'

'An old friend,' said Cassandra.

'Indeed, indeed,' said Professor Storrin.

Julia's book had come out on a Thursday. On the Monday, when Cassandra went into Blackwell's, Thor returned to the flat, not to stay, but to pack and remove all his belongings. When Julia opened the door to him, unexpected, she thought he had come to reproach her for the book. But he treated her with courtesy, and was trembling with nervousness.

'I have decided,' he began, not meeting her eye, 'I shall go to the Congo, after all. I must be of some use.' He spoke with his usual lack of emphasis: she could not tell whether he was describing a moral imperative, an emotional urgency, or simply a dull conclusion that there, at least, what he did might make something, to some small degree, better.

'I can't stop you. I don't know how to start, and perhaps I ought not to try.'

He inclined his head. Deborah, behind them, gave a cry, and turned and ran into her bedroom. They heard the door lock. Both of them tried the door and called, without answer. It was Thor who suggested that they should leave Deborah until he had finished his packing. Julia acquiesced.

They packed together, largely in silence. Thor broke this once to announce that the Notting Hill Housing Trust had come up with something temporary and suitable for the Bakers; the Terrys would remove them, probably that evening, in their van. Julia said, in an echo of his own flat voice, 'You needn't have done that. I don't need the space.' He repeated his assurance that it would be done.

He could not take everything at once. They piled several bags and parcels in the hall.

'I shall have to come back. I hope you don't mind that.'

Julia looked at him, dazed by too many conflicting guilts, absolutely unwilling to face any discussion of any permanent arrangement. She would rather endure his going than have to discuss it; a state of mind she would normally have associated more easily with Cassandra.

'No, no. I want to see you. I want you to come back. As much as – whenever – you can.'

'As a visitor? You find it easier to be intimate with visitors, I have observed that.'

This was cruel; but she could not bring herself to open up a discussion of her failure in intimacy with him. Neither he nor Simon had any use for her real gifts in that direction, however initially attracted they were by them. She said, 'No, not as a visitor. I don't think we ought to try and talk about this, just yet.'

'We could be divorced. If you want to marry again, now, we can be divorced.'

'Thor. Oh, no,' said Julia quickly. She could not bear this finality. 'Oh, no.' It was only then that she realized he was thinking, not of Ivan, but of Simon.

She had heard nothing of Simon since the book came out, and rather suspected she would not. She felt, now, the impossibility of her attempt to know Simon, and realized that she must always, unconsciously, have felt this, since the book had always been there. Unpublished, it was true, the book had been simply another part of that structure of our thought about another person which we do not admit to, and therefore do not have to justify, or stand by. But once it was public, it was part of the relationship, it changed it, and indeed, made it impossible. She must, she had told herself often enough between Wednesday and Monday, always have known that, too: it had been one of those destructive moves we are only enabled to make by rigidly refusing to consider their nature, until too late. Although when the book was begun, this problem had been seen in terms, not of Simon, but of Cassandra. She had not known then, that there would be any continuing relationship with him to be threatened – though indeed, conversely, she would almost certainly never have embarked on one if it had not, as she now saw it, been doomed from the outset. She saw now that the description of, the nostalgia for, the long involvement in Cassandra's passions which came of writing the book had contributed to the violence of her own welcome for Simon, even whilst she believed she was free, at last, to see him new. She loved him, in so far as she did love him, as a child loves an imaginary hero, or a television idol. She did not know him; he did not let himself be known. He was never to be grasped and passion could be lavished on him forever without being tested out against real limitations, his or hers. Only he was not Sir Lancelot; she had conversed with real flesh and blood – only flesh and blood, as he had said of Cassandra so long ago, that gave the impression that it was irrevocably 'not quite all there'. Another kind of love, from another person might, of course, call out in him another reality; but that was only idle speculation. She had imagined him. And he had, as the book had foreshadowed it, gone to Oxford. So she had as it were, made solid for public consumption more than she could have known or bargained for. Simon she hoped never to see again, and told herself glumly that this was for the best. Cassandra she could not contemplate, although she knew she must.

The reviews had been both respectful and enthusiastic. She had expected of herself detachment and vulgarity enough to be, at least partially, elated by this. But she was simply horrified. She surfaced. 'Thor, I'm sure the best thing is not to talk, we're both bound to say things we don't mean.'

He accepted this, gathered up two heavy suitcases, and turned to her.

'You look tired, Julia.'

'It's this book.'

'I saw there was a book. I saw reviews.' Julia waited. He did not elaborate.

'It was the end of something, of a part of my life.'

'Do you think it can end? I do not know what you hope to achieve.'

'Thor – Thor, it wasn't a *wicked* book, was it?'

'Wicked?' he said, blinking. Julia looked up at him. He had stopped trembling and was looking over her shoulder towards Deborah's door. His hair was stubble-pale, his skin was tight over his skull, he was shining slightly with sweat and anxiety so that the planes of his face took on that angular glitter peculiar to perspex sculpture. A cross between an angel and a convict, Julia thought. She felt his presence almost as in the days of their first acquaintance, as that of an admirable stranger whose approval she desperately required.

'You know what I mean. Wicked.'

Initially he had been to her – taking these words as deeply and seriously as possible – moral support. He had been a judge, who believed, despite a concomitant belief in tolerance, in judgement. Because she had been able, because he loved her, to manipulate that judgement they had both been diminished. But, even diminished, he had been a court of appeal against Cassandra's automatic condemnation. He could still be. He was rock hard, at the centre, and he knew what wickedness was, and he believed in it. His leaving her was his judgement for the way she had distorted his actions; she was paying for that. Let him also now, she felt obscurely, judge her for what she had done to Cassandra, and impose penance: penance could free her. If he would do this, they had a remote chance of meeting again, honourably, as at first they should have met.

'Perhaps I shouldn't have written it?'

'I suppose you write what you have to write. If not that, it would have been something else, in the end. If I were you, Julia, I would not worry.'

'But Cassandra?'

'Cassandra is her own concern. I don't see that you are in a position to care about Cassandra.'

'It wasn't done *in order* to damage her, you must believe.'

'I don't know,' he said, dismissing the question. It came to Julia that he had hardened. At some stage in the past he had had enough of her problems; now he knew it. He was leaving her to herself. He would not come back.

'I really ought to try to speak to Deborah,' he said. He went and rattled Deborah's door, and called through it, for a moment or two. There was no answer.

'I would take her with me, if she wanted to come.' He came back to the door. 'Perhaps better not now, in a few years. Julia –'

'Yes?'

'Don't be hard on her. She will be all right. I don't want to leave her, it isn't easy, it is simply that I find I can't stay. But don't be hard on her.'

'I don't know why you think I should be hard on her. She looks after herself pretty well.'

'Yes. She does.' He began to leave. 'I shall have to come back again.'

'You said that. Any time.'

'We have to talk about money.'

'I don't want your money.'

'There is Deborah.'

They looked at each other, faintly puzzled, and then he left.

Cassandra came slowly back to the college. She was still, with some deliberation, largely inhabiting the indifferent happiness of the past few weeks. Her mind worked extremely slowly. She had been annoyed by a kind of glee she detected in Storrin. It was only after some time that she came to realize that what he had said implied that Julia had written a novel of which parts, at least, were set in Oxford. She had thought, irrationally, reverting to an earlier grievance, that his glee was something to do with the fact that she herself had not written a novel. She thought she had accepted, lately, that she could not and would not write a novel: thus her reaction to his glee was irrelevant, must be mastered. This brought her across the river. On the way into the college, making her further realization, she told herself that her reactions to Julia's prying had always been excessive; what Julia knew about Oxford could do little real damage, however embroidered.

She almost tripped over the step, in the entrance hall. On the table there was a very fat letter from Deborah. Cassandra's hand shook a little as she picked it up; hypersensitive in this one direction, she thought she sensed sympathy and fellow-feeling and in that moment knew and refused to know.

She pushed the letter, unopened, into her handbag and went, not into her room, but into the Senior Common Room. Miss Curtess was alone in there; she flushed and looked away when Cassandra came in; Cassandra did not notice this.

The window-seat, overlooking the college garden, was, as usual, piled, with papers; yesterday's Sunday papers, crumpled and spread, last week's intellectual weeklies. Cassandra sat down, opened and closed her handbag, looked furtively across the scattered chintz arm-chairs into Miss Curtess's equally furtive gaze, withdrawn immediately, and began to read.

> 'Julia Corbett has wrought a *tour de force* from apparently very unpromising material.'

> 'Julia Corbett has at last broken out of the suffocating domestic prison where she was strangled with her own waste fertility, to write a study of that sterile, in some sense permanently retarded emotion we call hopeless love, felt in intelligent if cranky, middle age. The book is set in a semi-monastic academic community whose absurdities are presented with vivid immediacy. Julia Corbett has a gift for the surface detail that implies a moral judgement; she can sum up a whole woman by describing the precise bad fit of an ill-chosen magenta taffeta dress, or the distressing juxtaposition of a dangling crucifix and tinned college spaghetti and tomato sauce. Her world, hovering on the edge of the grotesque but never engulfed in it, is, to an outsider at least, appallingly convincing.
>
> 'But this is not her main achievement. She has, against all the odds, succeeded triumphantly in calling up sympathy for her central character, Emily, the lady don, cherishing and repressing an imaginative life on the scale of Charlotte Brontë's passion for the Duke of Zamorna. Emily's Monsieur Héger is an unctuous, slightly silly television priest, one of the false, or at least inadequate prophets of

our time. She knew him in childhood and has studied him and given him imaginary life ever since. It is absurd; it is also genuinely pitiable. Naturally the man in the flesh, finally encountered, fails pitiably to measure up to the huge imagined expectations that have been built round him, the "sense of glory" he carries with him. Miss Corbett makes, *en passant*, some very intelligent comments on the adolescent religiosity of our modern devotion to the television idol. I have yet to meet a priest who fills her bill, but he is not inconceivable, and offers splendid opportunities for the exploration of the dubious roots of religious belief in emotionally starved women. We are left at the end with the question of whether the cold breath of reality on the glittering imaginative structure will prove absolutely destructive, or be the beginning of a more restricted, but more mature existence. Can Emily learn? The doubt is real, and that, too, is an achievement.

'Miss Corbett's weird heroine sees everything with a steady lunatic clarity.'

'There are a galaxy of minor Oxford characters, all equally obsessed by the unreal, the unattainable, and their obsessions reflect and illuminate each other. There is the suave don who wants to be a television idol himself, and produces deliberately, as the epiloguer does naturally, a false charm. A spinsterly, vulgar passion for the erotic works of the Earl of Rochester balances, and lights up, the antithetical purity of Emily's unreal world.'

'Miss Gee had nothing on Julia Corbett's Emily Burnett.'

Cassandra's mind fumbled defensively with irrelevances. 'Miss Corbett' bothered her: it was her name, the only name she had. And it was not, she thought, morally possible, let alone morally or aesthetically admirable, to 'sum up a whole woman' by describing the inadequacies of her clothing. She opened her handbag again, closed it on Deborah's fat letter, breathed deeply, and felt her guts thud and stiffen.

'You said nothing to warn us,' said Miss Curtess, in a thick, red voice, 'of what your sister was springing on us.'

'I could not have said anything. I didn't know.'

'I think it was ill-considered. There are moral obligations that come before self-expression.'

Cassandra stood up. 'I don't see it as a question of morals.'

'No, of course you don't. It seems to me unkindly meant, Cassandra. But beneath your notice.'

Cassandra could not, probably, have avoided recognizing the solidifying of the issue in the consciousness of those around her. Her feeling towards Miss Curtess was, however, rage, not gratitude. She could make no answer, and left the Common Room abruptly and silently: it was only on the stairs that she realized that her silence had effectively confirmed Vanessa Curtess's view of the situation. She went, heavily and slowly, into her own room, taking each breath carefully, incapable for the moment of thought.

Someone rang the doorbell, and, not content with that, rattled the letterbox and banged with fists and feet. Julia came out into the hall, stared at the door and made no move to open it.

'Julia!' through the letterbox.

'Go away.'

'I shall just go on ringing the bell.' The steady shrilling began. Julia opened the door.

Ivan came in, took off his coat, and settled into a chair. He extracted from his coat pocket a copy of *A Sense of Glory*.

'Well, how do you feel?'

'I don't know.'

'What does she say?'

'She wouldn't say anything. She may not have seen it, but if she has, she wouldn't say anything.'

'And Moffitt?'

'He doesn't read books.'

'Doesn't he?'

'He doesn't read my books, he said so.'

'Well, I asked him if he'd read this and he said no, but he'd go out and buy it.'

'I wish you'd keep out of my life.'

'You let me in. You invited me in.'

'To a tiny, not very important area of it.'

She decided not to tell him that Thor had left her. This and the other guilt were causing her, as far as she could judge, equally violent and differing pains.

Ivan grinned. 'It's not a bad book. Much more controlled and thoughtful than your usual stuff. I'd expected an outburst, I must admit. But this seems obsessive about the style and the structure. It even has that sort of lifelessness books have when they're overwrought. Overwrought in a literary sense, that is. That's rather a good pun, maybe the one causes the other, don't you think I'm clever, Ju? Do you think you'll write a good book, now?'

'I haven't the slightest idea. I honestly don't care. I –'

'Oh, but you will care. You can't help it. What's biting you, love?'

Julia looked at her hands and did not answer.

'Is it her? It beats me you can put off suffering so long if you're going to suffer. You just can't bear *facing* unpleasantness, can you, you never could? Listen, my darling, if your sister can't shake this off, that's her lookout, honestly. It isn't a *mean* book; it's not as though you'd screamed invective at her. And anyway I should think she deserved what she got. She must have been hell to grow up with. I get the feeling she's much more awful than you make her sound.'

'If she sounds awful at all you must have got the idea from me. It's so silly, I love her, I love her really. I just can't – couldn't – *live with* her.'

'The love,' Ivan said, in a soothing voice, 'comes out in the book. That's why it's so good, sweetie. Truly.'

'Oh, hell,' said Julia. This was not the judgement she needed. She began to cry. Ivan took her in his arms; it was not in his arms she wanted to be. Nevertheless she shifted her body against his, and stroked his face, sobbing wildly, whilst he kissed her on the eyes, and smoothed her hair.

In Cassandra's room a clock ticked loudly; outside, for some reason, Oxford bells were pealing. She had hardly, yet, begun to think it out. Almost anonymously her mind began the habitual motions: shrinking, rejection. She would not speak to Storrin again. Nor to Vanessa Curtess. It might be, it might well be, that Oxford itself was uninhabitable. There were, she supposed, other places.

Like certain reptiles she had learned to survive by leaving in Julia's hand the dead stump of the tail by which she had been grasped. One could even, she thought, sacrifice a more necessary limb, a hand, a foot, which would not grow again, and still survive. One could do this for ever, so long as one was not touched to the quick. Let Julia store and catalogue the limp relicts of what had been Cassandra. Successive skins, discarded hair and nails, the dead stuff of witchcraft, like the photograph, like the fiction. A thought, a story, a way of looking, a friend, a city. The image comforted her; she elaborated it; somewhere else, in the dark, she was coming to a decision.

What was necessary was to measure the extent of the damage and the extent of the requisite surgery. To tie up arteries – this image too, was capable of elaboration. Not to feel pain in an imaginary extremity . . .

Someone banged on the door. She did not answer. After a pause, nevertheless, Simon came in. Cassandra peered grimly at him between the crimson wings of her chair. He had not been in her mind; she had not got round to him. He was going to have to go, too. Indeed, she saw, now, he was going to have to go first. She tightened her mouth, drew back into the chair, said nothing.

'Cassandra –'

'Well?'

'Don't make it difficult for me? May I sit down?'

She indicated, with her jewelled hand, the window-seat. He perched there, awkwardly.

'Cassandra –'

She was reserving her strength. He took the book from his pocket and held it out; she made no move to accept it.

'I take it you have seen this.'

'No.'

'But you know?'

'Now, yes.'

'I think it's intolerable,' he burst out.

'It doesn't matter what we think,' she said, almost impatiently. One had no power to change what was accomplished; one's power lay simply in fitting one's life to one's new circumstances, in excising the affected parts. He was several steps behind her; he was less experienced.

'What I think about this ought to matter. It's aimed at me, as I see it. It concerns me.'

'Not much,' said Cassandra, coldly.

'Ah, Cassandra, don't. I was afraid you would be hurting yourself over this. Of course anyone would be hurt by it. Anyone. I was annoyed myself. And I know you. I know you. I came to say, don't . . .'

'Don't what? What are you afraid I may do?'

On this he swung his head, down and up again, stretched out his awkward arms in what could have been a gesture of despair or a broken-off embrace, twisted his sorrowful mouth and his scarred and fading face into an expression of extreme agony, levered himself to his feet and began to pace her room.

'I know you,' he said again. 'I know how proud you are. I – you don't mind me saying this? – I'm afraid you may just cut yourself off. From Julia. From me. I'd be sorry for that. And I don't think you can afford to. Forgive me if I'm wrong.'

'What do you suggest I do?'

He seemed discouraged by her tone, but went on. 'You've got to fight. You've got to stay in the open. Read this book. You weren't going to, were you? And then, if you feel angry, write and tell Julia so – give her a chance to reply, but attack her, face to face . . . I think she'd be glad of that. There's sympathy and understanding in this book, as well as . . .'

'I don't want sympathy. Or understanding.'

'No, of course you don't. That doesn't stop people extending them. Not only Julia. You can't brush yourself entirely clean of them.'

Cassandra smiled, thinly, evasively.

'Read it now,' Simon said urgently, 'and then come out to dinner. With me.'

'No,' she said, to this last. As he talked, her sense of the situation crystallized. It was worse, she saw, than she had thought.

'No?' He wrung his hands and turned on her. 'Do I count for nothing in all this? May I not feel? Do I have to be the rock against which you choose to dash yourself and have no choice? I think you ought to live in the world with Julia, you ought to be magnanimous in her direction, and I've said so, but I can't *make* you do anything, clearly. But, as for me . . . Listen to me, Cassandra, it cost me something to come here. That book – that book does make me feel a bit of a fool. Of course it does. But I don't think you and I can pay any attention to that, we can't afford to. Is it boorish of me to point out – since you don't seem to see it – that it makes some difference that I'm here? With you?'

Cassandra looked at him blankly.

'Oh, God,' he said, 'I want to help. I want to help. I don't want to be responsible for any more damage. Please –'

'You were never very good at helping. You had no gift for it. You are too much' – she produced, judiciously, their joint conclusion – 'an emotional meddler, Simon. You should let things be.'

She said, less guarded, not looking at him, 'Don't you see, above all, I can't take your pity?'

'I'm trying to say, it isn't pity. Or not only pity.' He was not used to fighting; the scrupulous, brave words had a note of defeat. 'And pity doesn't necessarily smear you, as you seem to think. It's meant something to me, to see you, these last few weeks. And to you, I think. Not much, maybe, but something. It was real. Wasn't it? It can still be real. This,' he tapped the book, 'this isn't real. This is a lie, at worst, and – and a piece of imagination at best. You can't destroy a reality with fiction. Can you? Oh, for God's sake, face up to it, Cassandra.'

Cassandra did not look at him: she said, 'It seems sufficiently clear – to me – that you can both destroy and create reality with fiction. Fictions – fictions are lies, yes, but we don't ever know the truth. We see the truth through the fictions – our own, other people's. There was a time when I thought the Church had redeemed fiction – that the Church's metaphors were truths – but lately that's seemed meaningless. Dangerous even, like any other fiction. We feed off it. Our fictions feed on us. "And to deform and kill the things whereon we feed." I don't know quite why Coleridge should have found the serpent's method of ingestion so peculiarly repellent . . . but it's a powerful metaphor . . .'

'I don't understand.'

'Julia does. I imagine that's the theme of her book. What Dr Johnson called "the hunger of the imagination that preys incessantly on life". She's saying, I assume, that I made too much of you. I lived off you. Well, that's true. So I'm peculiarly vulnerable to – to the imagination.' She smiled.

'Don't be melodramatic. You spin ideas, Cassandra, so you can't see for them. After all, here I am. Here I am.'

'Yes, but what can we have to say to each other? What can we ever say to each other now that won't be seen in terms of Julia's fiction? Our course is plotted for us in it, I understand.'

'Does that matter?'

'To me, yes. As you should know, I don't like,' Cassandra sighed, heavily, 'to be watched.'

'You ought to learn to stand it. It's a prerequisite of – what was your way of putting it – "occupying one's space in the world".'

'No one could say I had ever been good at that. It's too late to start.'

She had taken off all her rings, and made a little pile of them in her black lap. 'Leave me alone, Simon.' She looked at him with a mad, donnish, kindliness. 'It isn't your fault. Let it be.' She looked down at her naked hands. 'It's kindest to leave me alone,' she said, informatively.

'I don't particularly want to be kind. I want –'

'Go away, Simon.'

'You're mad.' She said nothing. 'I shall come back,' he said. 'Yes,' she said, with deliberate vagueness.

When he was gone Cassandra laid out the rings in a neat row on the desk-top, put her chains and cross with them, rearranged them so that the colour gradation followed that of the rainbow, drew the curtains, put on the light, climbed back into her chair and took up Julia's book. It took her three hours to read it.

Julia caught Deborah with a suitcase creeping out of the front door.

'Where do you think you're going?'

'I'm leaving. I've had enough. I want a life of my own.'

'Well, anyone who thinks they can have *that* is a fool. Are you going to your father?'

'No, as a matter of fact. Because (a) I don't want to live in the Congo. And because (b) he'd be better off without me.'

'Well then, where?'

'Oxford,' said Deborah.

'You're not!' said Julia. Deborah opened the door. Julia kicked it shut again and Deborah hit Julia, hard across the legs, with the suitcase. At this, Julia discovered that seeing red was a precise description of a physical condition. She wrenched away the suitcase and brought it down on Deborah's head. 'I say you're not! You can bloody well stay here!' Deborah twisted her hand in Julia's hair, slapped Julia's face, and made again for the door. Julia flew at her.

'Get your coat off! Get those things out of that case!'

'You don't want me. Let me go.' She ran back: Julia ran after her, into the silent flat. Deborah turned and screamed at her, 'You take everybody's life. I hate you, I hate you, I hate you.' She launched herself at her mother.

'I hate you, too,' said Julia, between blows. 'You are a censorious little bitch. You are only half-human. However, you've got to live with me.'

They were now fighting on their knees; Julia shook her hair out of her eyes, pinned Deborah down with one hand on the carpet, and said, 'It's a pity if we don't learn to live with people we hate. Cold hatred is *the worst thing*, let me tell you. I know I'm not one to talk. But you're an idiot to think of Cassandra. She may not hate you, but she doesn't like you. Does she? You need a bit of blood for Christ's sake. You are my daughter, I love you. I do love you. I can't let you go there.'

Deborah wriggled and bit and fought back; both weeping, they battered each other into a breathless and bleeding calm. Julia sat up, panting, and said to her daughter, 'I can't let you make a myth out of Cassandra. She's no good, not for you.'

'I know, really. OK, I know.' She looked at Julia gravely. 'You shouldn't have done that to her, though, Julia.'

Here was judgement.

'I know.'

'It's different for me. I mind, too, but your other books, they weren't really about *me*, they were about you, what you felt about me. But this was *about her*. It really was.'

'I thought that made it better, at the time.'

'You can't have really thought that. Not knowing her.' She paused. 'Do you think I've got to stay?'

'What else can you do? Listen, Deborah, make some allowances for me? Please? If I'd ever lived with people who made allowances – *real* ones – I'd not need to ask for so many.'

'I've made a lot.'

'Yes, well, it's you that gains from them. Let that console you.'

They looked at each other with a kind of animal affection.

'Julia, what will she do?'

'I don't know. I don't know.'

Cassandra, heading out of the doctor's surgery, was seen by Gerald Rowell, who called her name. She went away from him down the street so fast that he had to run, skirts flaring, to catch up with her.

'Cassandra!'

She turned into an off-licence.

'Cassandra!' He followed her in.

She leaned over the counter. 'I want a bottle of brandy, please. Rémy-Martin, if you have it. But anything will do.'

'Cassandra!' he said, more sharply.

She stowed the brandy in her knapsack, and faced him.

'How are you, Cassandra? I haven't seen you for some time.'

'Haven't you? Did you want to?'

'Have you time for a drink?'

'Later. Later. I may have. Not just now. Thank you.' She grinned. 'Had you anything particular to say?'

'I wanted your permission' – he was white, stammering slightly – 'to write a stiff letter to your sister.'

He watched her take this in. 'I don't mind what you do,' she said.

'Would it help?'

'It would upset her, I imagine. She's easily upset.'

'I meant, would it help you?'

'Please don't worry about me,' said Cassandra. 'I shall be silent. I thought you were troubled on your own account. Indirectly, I owe you an apology for that.' He was, indeed, she saw, possessed by a personal fury. 'You have, as it were, lent your flesh and bones to a more irresponsible spirit. I have seen the book: decidedly, yes, I owe you an apology. I should have foreseen this. But it will come to matter less, you know. You will survive. It was so far from the truth.'

'I should never have spoken to her,' said Gerald Rowell. Cassandra looked at him with a flicker of remote interest; he went on, too hastily, 'I wish you would come for that drink.' He attempted to lay a hand on her arm; she leaned out, suddenly, and tapped his spectacle-lens with her thumb-nail.

'I never noticed they were bi-focals. What happens, if you take them off?'

'Oh, everything runs into everything else, and the colours blur. I can't move without them, I have to sit still.'

'You should do it more often. Sit still and let everything run into everything else. We need a sense of being undifferentiated. Undifferentiated,' cried Cassandra. 'I keep chasing metaphors. Out of a desire for an impossible unity. Such effort, keeping everything separate all the time when under the sea, we are assured, no man is an island, we are all joined. You mustn't think too hardly of Julia for her artistic effort, Father, it's what we all do. We affirm that we can inhabit each other, body and soul, that's all.'

He tried to understand. 'We are all part of each other, in Christ, we are all made whole.'

'That wasn't quite what I meant. I think I had better go. Or what Julia meant. We overlap. I wish we didn't. We could tolerate it if we were separate or indistinguishable.'

'You alarm me.'

'Don't be alarmed.' She hoisted her knapsack over her shoulder. 'Think about it. I must go now, I have to be alone.'

'Cassandra!'

She let the door swing in his face and hurried away down the street. He saw her turn into the ironmongers. He thought a while, and then telephoned Miss Curtess, who promised to keep an eye on Cassandra, and was volubly indignant over Julia's book for long enough to exorcize his own anger and replace it with pure embarrassment.

CHAPTER TWENTY

Cassandra's Journal

So have I become a doll to stick pins in? Or a mirror on the wall to be asked what she, what either of us, means? At first I felt simply dirtied. My shoes, my nightdress, my pens, my papers, little dirty details of me lifted. Pinned out – oh yes, even my underwear – like a limp doll to be filled with puffs of her breath. What was missing filled in by her with dotted lines, pieces of new string to jerk the joints, or wood to replace limbs, as they do in museums, and never a footnote to say, this material is conjectural. This is an eclectic and conflated text.

Our normal intercourse is made up of this, all the time, I know. I know. We hide our knowledge of it. We could not live if we were made to see ourselves more than conjecturally as others see us. At best we translate their vision back into our own terms. But she does a little more than simply see me, and that little is intolerable.

When we were children, we were not quite separate. We shared a common vision, we created a common myth. And this, maybe, contained and resolved our difficulties. This is that primitive state that has been called innocence. We wove a web in childhood, a web of sunny air . . . But there is no innocent vision, we are not indistinguishable. We create each other, separate. It is not done with love. Or not with pure love. Nor with detachment. We are not simply specimens, under the bright light, in the glass case, in the zoo, in the museum. We are food for thought. The web is sticky. I trail dirty shreds of it.

I do not choose to stay to be pitied for that rag doll's passions. They are not mine. But they were fed and watered by me, too much of my energy went into their growth for me to be able to clear them away, or make myself a space to inhabit.

There is nowhere I shall not drag this grotesque shadow, our joint creature. I can choose, at least, to put out the light that throws it. I want no more reflections.

CHAPTER TWENTY-ONE

'Well, where do we start?'

'I still can't see why you wanted to come.'

'I wanted to help. If I could.'

'It might have been better to come on my own.'

'I don't know. It might have taken more out of you. Besides there seems to be an enormous amount simply to carry.'

'I'm not moving all that. Only the papers. The Oxfam people are coming to take what we don't. Only they've no use for the papers. The police went through all those. As you no doubt gathered. Mother doesn't want any of her things.'

'And you?'

'No.'

Simon took off his coat and hung it across the red chair. 'Well, where do we start?' he repeated. Julia wished, on the whole, that she had not brought him, although there was, absurdly, no one else she could have asked – no safe, ignorant stranger. And he had been genuinely helpful. He had hired and driven the car in which they would remove the papers. She had hoped he might provide protection against the college authorities, but he had left her to face these on her own. Her interview with the Principal had not been pleasant.

The papers had been stacked in the middle of the room. Academic files and boxes. Parcels of letters tied with string – Deborah's, her own, Gerald Rowell's. Cassandra seemed never to have thrown anything away. There was a shoe-box which proved to contain a rather haphazard collection of her own press cuttings. Notebooks full of remnants of narrative verse, blank, misty, decorated, concerning Morgan le Fay. The stack of paintings. Volumes of the journal. The last entry had been read out in court.

'When we were little,' Julia told Simon, 'I used to annoy her by taking all the books out of the book-case, piling them up in the middle of the floor, and sitting on them.'

'King of the castle.'

'She used to lock me out. When I stole the key she bought a bolt and screwed it on, herself.'

'So she'd had practice,' Simon said.

The deceased, the coroner had been told, had arranged matters with obsessive determination. There had been new bolts fitted to both outer and inner doors. A gap below the inner door had been stuffed with a gown, both doors had been sealed with cellulose draught-excluder and the window gummed up with wide strips of brown paper. The curtains were drawn and a bed of folded blankets arranged on the hearth near the fire. The deceased had swallowed a bottle of seconal and several glasses of brandy. She had also turned on the gas. There had been no note. The bolts and other precautions suggested, the psychiatrist had told the court, a degree at least of derangement; the deceased had been hysterically concerned to prove she was no gambler. It was, in these cases, just possible to assume that there was an obsessive attempt to 'play fair'; any rescuer who had broken down those doors would have been a real rescuer. We could not tell. It was this evidence, in conjunction with Father Rowell's, which had decided the verdict.

'While you were talking to that woman,' Simon said, 'I met some of the girls on the stairs. One of them said they actually saw her from the lawn, sticking the windows up – "like a great black bird beating against the glass" she poetically and inaccurately put it. Apparently, knowing her, they thought nothing of it. She said they all gathered at the foot of the stairs and watched them go up. The Principal, the chef in his white hat and apron, and the Senior Tutor. They broke the doors in. There's a Miss Curtess who's left in a state of nervous collapse because she suspected, and did nothing, except knock from time to time and get no answer. The girl thought I was the *News of the World*. She told me they're all shocked. She says they all feel guilty, and resent this. A proper little psychologist.'

'Don't we all?' Julia's voice was sharp.

'I don't know what you feel.'

'What you said, I feel,' said Julia. 'What she meant me to feel, but other things as well.'

Simon's look flickered towards her and away. He crossed the room, and stood by the hearth, on that piece of carpet Julia had not yet looked at.

'She always made the rules. She planned the story, and I fitted in, I carried it out. She made me what I am. She made perfectly normal behaviour into crimes – like borrowing books, like telling people things, like talking to you. She locked me out until I was crazy to get in. And then she saw to it I was guilty of real crimes, that what I'd done I couldn't change or undo. She made me – take things – and then left me in possession. She wanted it this way. Why should I be guilty?' She looked round the empty room, down at the books. 'Why should I take possession? I don't want her life. I never really did. Certainly not now.'

Simon said nothing.

'She meant to finish me off.'

'You see it simply as an act of vengeance?'

'I'd do better to.'

'You are still talking as though she were alive.' Julia hesitated, did not quite contemplate what he was saying.

'No, but *I* am still alive. I've got to live with it.'

'She said she couldn't bear being watched.'

He held, still in front of the fire, a stance uneasily reminiscent of the military 'at ease'. As though he was neutralizing the place, deliberately, Julia thought, wishing more strongly that she had not brought him. He had given evidence about his final visit to Cassandra. Julia had found this evidence intensely humiliating. Now, sensing instinctively that emotional self-indulgence was her best way to survive, she took him up, petulantly. Cassandra had died of preserving her dignity, had she not?

'I can't think what you had to come and talk to her about it for.'

'Somebody had to do something. I was there. I wanted to stop you destroying each other.' He produced a deprecating smile.

'Casting yourself on the swords? Well, you made it worse. I know her – I knew her. You made it seem *real* to her. Inescapable. And at the same time a drama. She liked drama. If you hadn't interfered, Si, she'd have slithered round it in her imagination, somehow, pretended it didn't exist. But you gave it body.'

'I meant to. With the best intentions. To make it real. It wasn't good for either of you to go on as you were.'

'Well,' cried Julia, on the edge of tears, 'what the hell had *you* to offer either of us to change anything?'

He did not meet her eye. 'Oh, I know, I know,' he said, rapidly, addressing his words to the pile of books. 'You're quite right. Yet Edmund was beloved. I seem doomed to entangle myself in others' self-destruction.'

Julia puzzled and then remembered. 'Oh, your father. Of course. I'm sorry, Si, it was nice of you to come and help, in the . . .'

He shifted from one foot to the other.

'I shouldn't rely on being able to be angry with her, Julia. Not for too long. You'll find that wears off.'

He gathered up several volumes of the journal.

'Are you going to read all this?'

'Yes. No. I don't know. I just don't know. I suppose I may in the end. Not for a bit. Curiosity'll get the better of me in the end, I suppose, it always does.'

Simon made no answer to this, except to walk to the door. Seeing him with those books in his arms Julia felt deeply shocked: as Cassandra, alive, might have felt at such sacrilege, at the sight of those two shifting her things. She had made a column of several rings on one finger; now, she fumbled to disperse them.

'Come on,' said Simon. 'Keep moving.' He made for the stairs.

In the end they had all the papers piled in the college entrance hall. Simon began to carry them out to the car; Julia went back up the stairs.

Alone in the room she saw why she had brought Simon. She was, she considered, unlike Cassandra, vulgarly insensitive to atmosphere. Her myths had not concerned themselves with hauntings. In the Tower or Holyrood House she was tormented simply by her own curiosity working on a superfluity of available information. She would attempt to embody the precise feelings of David Rizzio or Lady Jane Grey. Cassandra's room, without Cassandra's presence, was, if she chose, simply a college room; Cassandra's things were things, unconnected; their power to arouse desire or fear had been withdrawn. She wanted neither to inhabit nor to desecrate the place, only to let the objects as objects lie fixed and dead to wait for the charitable collectors to make use of them.

But this room was heavy with Cassandra, the air was thick with concentrated distress. The objects were live, potentially shocking. Julia made an effort of will not to imagine what it had felt like to be Cassandra, sustaining a furious intention through so much frenzied action: screwdriver, sticky paper, the organized cool interview with the doctor. She had not seen her sister; she had still not seen anyone dead. As she went into the bedroom she momentarily put up an arm to shield her face.

The bed had been stripped; nothing else was changed. On the chest of drawers, under the oval mirror, stood the clay Queen Morgan and the glass serpent. Objects out of a rite, Julia thought, who had last seen them perched on the television. Once, as a child of ten, she had surprised Cassandra before their mother's mirror, veiled in an old lace curtain, conducting between lighted candles an intense solitary dialogue. Discovered, she had shrieked with outrage. Julia understood that her sister had spent time in front of this mirror, encouraging herself. She felt hot, cold, slightly breathless. Very slowly, she approached her own face to the mirror and studied it – an ordinary face, frightened, lips parted like an actress's, strands of bright red hair straggling out from under a black silk scarf with vermilion roses. A melting, innocent face.

She said, softly, what she had intermittently been thinking since she arrived.

'Out flew the web, and floated wide
The mirror crack'd from side to side,
The curse is come upon me . . .'

Her own voice frightened her. She did not feel alone; she felt the terror with which she had woken in childhood from nightmares induced by Cassandra's too vigorous story-telling. She dared not look round for fear of what was behind her; she studied herself in order not to see that other gaunt, freckled, censorious, anxious face.

All her life Cassandra had been the mirror where she studied the effects of her actions. It was Cassandra's reactions that proved her existence; now, she had lost a space and a purpose. Cassandra had been to her, as she had been to Cassandra, both a live woman with whom she could deal and an irrational force, destructive, inimical, impersonal: She. Well, she was dead. She was dead, they were both dead? Any power, any existence Cassandra had, she, Julia, in the imagination, lent her.

'I can't afford it,' Julia said to her reflection. 'I've got to let go, there is no possession, I will be on my own.'

The soft face creased into the old, easy tears. 'I hate you,' Julia said to it, and stumbled across to the bed. When Simon came back he found her face downward on the bare ticking weeping wildly, for terror, for herself, for Cassandra, for loneliness, for the incompleteness of her solitude. He put a hand on her shoulder; Julia knew he had expected this.

'Come on Julia, let's get you out of here. I've got it all stowed away, we can go.'

They were well outside Oxford before either of them spoke. Julia let the tears run freely as she had always let everything run. Simon drove on in silence, a little too fast: now and then the hired car bucked in protest.

'Do you want to stop for a drink, Julia? Coffee, spirits?'

Julia mopped her warm, wet face. 'No, thank you.'

'What happened so suddenly?'

'The room frightened me.'

'She must have been so much afraid. She was so uncertain that she existed, anyway . . . And to give up that little certainty . . .'

'It was something she'd always partly wanted,' said Julia, deliberately.

'Do you think so?'

Julia glanced at his face to see what he might be thinking. If the girls in the college felt guilty, if her mother and the Principal, who could have done nothing, felt guilty, if the unpleasant, self-accusing letter she had had from Gerald Rowell told any truth, what must Simon be feeling? His face had a melancholy droop, a complacent sadness.

'There was nothing *you* could do, either, Si. She would die.'

'Nonsense. I could have cared more, I could have done more with what care I had. You frighten me, Julia. Listen – if there's one thing I know – never mind how – it's that one doesn't *at first*, recognize a real blow. You're trying to be too hard. Because you think she wanted to make a murderess of you you won't admit that you are – partly – a murderess. And other people are going to think so, too.'

'The book's best-selling, this week.'

Simon gave her a momentary look of pure dislike, which she accepted. 'I should have thought that proved my point.'

'It does. That's why I told you. Don't bother about me, Si, I shall survive.'

'Don't expect too much of yourself.'

'Nobody could accuse me of ever having expected too much of myself,' Julia said. 'I expect too little.' She thought of explaining that that would no longer be true and decided against it; she did not want to explain herself to Simon. Nor to anyone else; she wanted solitude; and this, too, was new.

She knew, or thought she did, what Simon feared. She knew at least what she most feared herself. It was possible that Cassandra's death – the vanishing of the real woman who wore absurd clothes, who could lock doors and be kindly on occasion, who could be elsewhere and known to be elsewhere – it was possible that this death had simply loosed that other who, unrestricted now, larger than life, narrower in purpose, dependent on Julia for breath and movement, would gnaw intolerably at her imagination in the future. By this she had been driven; but now she meant to work in freedom.

'I'm not refined enough not to survive,' she said, aloud, to Simon. Whatever the rights and wrongs of it she meant to live, now. She meant to be harder. She would not depend on other people's thoughts of her; she faced, coolly she thought, the prospect of being generally disliked for what she had done. She was no longer married. She would be better to Deborah; that was a positive guilt about which something could be done, and best by her. She would come to grips with things and write better books. But she would not come to grips with Cassandra; let what was finished be cast off. Nor would she come to grips with Simon; no beginnings were possible here, only labyrinthine recriminations. She was not curious about Simon, either; she was going to be curious about nothing that had to do, or had ever had to do, with Cassandra. She was going to excise Cassandra from her life; it was the only possible way. Before, her curiosity had been hysterical and indiscriminate, a grasping. Now, it would come from herself, but a detached, a judging, a discriminating self.

Simon was speaking.

'. . . advise a change of scene. Different sort of job, move house.'

'What are you going to do?'

'I thought I told you. I sail for Malaya next week. We are all driven – we repeat a certain chain of actions, with variations. We have conditioned responses. Mine is flight. Sea voyages. Jungles. Our area of choice is very limited.'

'But we have some choice?'

'Very little.' Simon turned a corner.

'You think I'm driven?'

'It's a view.'

'Well, we'll see.'

It is difficult to hold on to the certainty of a change in oneself – vague but certain – which has not been tested out against experience. Julia knew she was a new woman, but this woman had, as yet, no acts to her credit. She was like the tree in the quad, and her growth would be hard, stunted by others' need to see wrongly or not to see at all. It was no good talking, she had to start behaving differently, and this couldn't be done until they reached London. And then, Julia thought with realism, it couldn't be done at one blow, or in one movement. It was like slimming; one must not expect too much at once, nor give up or repine too much over occasional back-sliding. She would, for instance, continue to weep in Ivan's uncomprehending arms. But the will to change was there. Julia knew it was there. What was over was over.

Behind Julia and Simon, in the dark boot of the car, closed into crates, unread, unopened, Cassandra's private papers bumped and slid.

MORE ABOUT PENGUINS, PELICANS AND PUFFINS